Fierce Little Thing

"Responsibility, guilt, hypocrisy, the sins of the past, the innocence or lack thereof of the young, the lies we tell one another and ourselves, the easiest way to make a murder look like an accident, whether character is destiny—the book raises all of these issues and more. . . . Mostly, though, it's an examination of Saskia, weighed down and haunted as she is. She is a fascinating character, her strengths and flaws equally interesting. Her role as perpetual victim, forever reliving the horrors inflicted on her by others, might not be the whole story." —*The New York Times Book Review*

"Gripping." —*USA Today*

"*Fierce Little Thing* is written in beautiful prose, with a winding narrative of alternating timelines. The story is captivating, thoughtful, and tense, a great read for those who enjoy psychological thrillers and complex puzzles. Highly recommended." —*New York Journal of Books*

"An ambitious, mesmerizing coming-of-age story . . . Beverly-Whittemore crafts the tension so spectacularly. . . . This is a character-driven, slow-burn thriller, but it is creatively structured and just eerie enough to keep you glued to its pages. . . . She is tremendously skilled at evoking a sense of place and a sensation of horror. . . . Nail-biting, moody, and every bit as compelling as the cult leader at its center." —*Bookreporter*

"*Fierce Little Thing* devoured me whole. It is at once a propulsive, perfectly plotted thriller and an exquisitely written, marvelously dark coming-of-age story. Once I opened it, I couldn't stop turning the pages. Once I finished it, it continued to haunt my thoughts. A spectacular and consuming read."

—Cristina Alger, *New York Times* bestselling author of *Girls Like Us*

"A *Secret History*–esque tale of suspense about a group of childhood friends and the secret that haunts their adulthood. The book's got all the ingredients for the perfect summer read: short, breathless chapters; a sinister cult in the wilds of Maine; and beautiful, sharp prose."

—*The Millions* (Most Anticipated: The Great Second-Half 2021 Book Preview)

"A twisty, rewarding tale of friendship, secrets, and childhood trauma. Donna Tartt fans, take note."   —*Publishers Weekly*

"With its propulsive momentum and its lush world, *Fierce Little Thing* kept me up late at night and splintered into my dreams. I experienced this novel with my whole body—tasted its sourdough, smelled its hand-dug latrines, heard its crackling pine needles and whispered secrets—and felt charged and changed by its explorations of the ways our adult lives keep circling the wounds and betrayals of childhood—as well as its sharp, tender insistence on the ways darkness and beauty sit side by side."

—Leslie Jamison, *New York Times* bestselling author of *The Empathy Exams*

"Avoiding the expected storyline . . . Beverly-Whittemore crafts something else entirely as the sins of the past come home to roost. A compelling study of power, sociopathy, and the possibilities of survival."   —*Kirkus Reviews* (starred review)

"Exquisite narrative . . . Saskia is strongly reminiscent of Donna Tartt's Harriet (*The Little Friend*) and Shirley Jackson's Merricat (*We Have Always Lived in the Castle*). . . . Teenager Saskia will have strong appeal for YA readers."
—*Booklist*

"If what you're looking for is a smart, suspenseful escape, look no further. Miranda Beverly-Whittemore's *Fierce Little Thing* is a propulsive thriller full of rich detail and a story that won't quit."
—*The Observer* (Best New Summer 2021 Reads)

"Gorgeously written and brilliantly structured, *Fierce Little Thing* is a suspenseful, evocative coming-of-age tale about the unique worth of old friendships and the profound challenge of finding your true place in the world."
—Kimberly McCreight, *New York Times* bestselling author of *Reconstructing Amelia* and *A Good Marriage*

"*Fierce Little Thing* is Miranda Beverly-Whittemore at her finest. A moody, gripping, and profoundly haunting story of a young girl desperate for connection and salvation. Beverly-Whittemore renders a wild, treacherous world and invites us to stand perilously close to the edge."
—Taylor Jenkins Reid, *New York Times* bestselling author of *Daisy Jones & The Six* and *The Seven Husbands of Evelyn Hugo*

"A stubborn, elegant, terrifying study of human nature that manages to catch hold of the blur of human consciousness, the way reality shifts under us. If Donna Tartt and Shirley Jackson had a beautiful, terrifying baby, it would be Miranda Beverly-Whittemore."
—Rufi Thorpe, author of *The Knockout Queen*

Also by Miranda Beverly-Whittemore

June

Bittersweet

Set Me Free

The Effects of Light

FIERCE LITTLE THING

Miranda
Beverly-Whittemore

FLATIRON
BOOKS
NEW YORK

FIERCE LITTLE THING. Copyright © 2021 by Miranda Beverly-Whittemore. All rights reserved. Printed in the United States of America. For information, address Flatiron Books, 120 Broadway, New York, NY 10271.

www.flatironbooks.com

Designed by Donna Sinisgalli Noetzel

The Library of Congress has cataloged the hardcover edition as follows:

Names: Beverly-Whittemore, Miranda, author.
Title: Fierce little thing / Miranda Beverly-Whittemore.
Description: First edition. | New York, NY : Flatiron Books, 2021 |
Identifiers: LCCN 2021002109 | ISBN 9781250779427 (hardcover) |
    ISBN 9781250779434 (ebook)
Subjects: GSAFD: Suspense fiction.
Classification: LCC PS3602.E845 F54 2021 | DDC 813/.6—dc23
LC record available at https://lccn.loc.gov/2021002109

ISBN 978-1-250-77944-1 (trade paperback)

Our books may be purchased in bulk for promotional, educational, or business use. Please contact your local bookseller or the Macmillan Corporate and Premium Sales Department at 1-800-221-7945, extension 5442, or by email at MacmillanSpecialMarkets@macmillan.com.

First Flatiron Books Paperback Edition: 2022

10 9 8 7 6 5 4 3 2 1

For Caitlin, Christian, Emily, Ingrid,

Jenny, Jonah, Rea, Rollin, and Sasha—

who helped me imagine the children.

For Quentin and Kitsune—

who helped me imagine the mothers.

FIRST:

"I promised fifty times already," I said, looking down over the whole green world. "As soon as we get on the highway, I'll tell you the longest, weirdest story."

"With a mad doggy who rips off a kid's face, okay, Saski? A naughty kid. A bad kid like a bad guy." The wind tufted our hair, but offered no relief from the sun.

"I know, bud. A mad doggy and a bad kid."

"Pinky promise." You lifted your tiny finger in front of me. You wobbled on the banister, then dropped your hand to steady yourself. Below your feet lay four stories of air.

"You shouldn't sit up there."

"Daddy lets me."

"Last I checked, this is Grandmother's house."

You stuck out your tongue. You stayed put. Below us, Daddy stalked out the front door. He tossed our backpacks in the trunk and searched the lengthy drive for Grandmother's Mercedes.

"Whatcha looking at?" you said.

Daddy swiveled his head to scan the lawns. "Shh." I pulled you off the railing. I brought you back to the other side of the widow's walk, to the solid floorboards.

"Oww."

I put my finger to my lips. You quieted. Only four, and you

already knew too much. I crept back to the railing on all fours, pressing my face against the white balusters just as Daddy gave up his search. When he went back inside, Mother's voice hammered up the stairs to meet us: "—dare you speak to me that way?"

I crept to the door and closed it, quiet, like a fairy. When I turned back, your little finger was hovering right in front of me. "It's not a promise if you don't pinky promise."

"Yes, it is."

"It's kind of like, maybe a lie."

"It's not a lie."

"You could say no way, when we get on the highway. You could change your mind."

"I won't say no way. I already said, I'm going to tell the story. I said it a million times." But I had hoped that by the highway you'd be sleeping. I would make myself quiet. Mother would turn over her shoulder and her eyes would grow soft and she'd coo, "Look, William, how sweet," and Daddy would see us in the rear-view mirror, and put his hand on her knee. The argument would fly right out the window, at least until the city.

"Saski? Please?" You were addicted to stories, especially the ones you told me so that I could tell them back to you. You would keep whining until I agreed. So fine, I clasped the chubby caterpillar of your pinky with my own. Satisfied, you broke away. "Where's Topsy?"

Maybe the bunny had tumbled onto the roof that stretched below and away from us, on all four sides. But those long ears, that matted pelt, the sewed-on expression that seemed to change depending on your mood, were nowhere to be found. I bumped my head on the railing before spotting him back on the other side of the widow's walk, under your sweatshirt. I grabbed him out. I shoved him at you. "Open your stupid eyes." The sun was a dull throb. The city would be so much hotter. You stuck out your lower lip and fought back tears. I drew you close. I whispered apologies.

We were supposed to stay at Grandmother's another month. Do you remember? We called our visits to her home "Connecticut." What we meant was the green waft of cut grass, the digestive scent of Grandmother's horehound candies, the burst of Miriam's fresh lemonade. Grandmother and Daddy loathed each other, and Mother was willing to take either side, so the weekends, when he was up from the city, devolved into cruel, drunken affairs. But Monday through Thursday, when it was just you and me and Mother and Grandmother (and Miriam, although we were to "keep out of Miriam's hair," to which you replied, "But she doesn't really have much hair," which earned you twenty minutes in the mudroom), those sweet summer days were as close to bliss as we knew.

Weekdays began with breakfasts on the sunporch, where we wielded silver cups engraved with Mother's first name, from when she was a girl. The evenings began at four thirty, when we'd wake Mother and wash our faces and change into what Grandmother called "proper clothes" for cocktail hour on the flagstone patio: silvery martinis for the adults (except Miriam), and, for us, cordial glasses with chilled tomato juice and lemon moons. In between, the long days—the many rooms for hide-and-seek, the swimming pool on hot afternoons, the widow's walk for spying—shimmered our minds away from New York, so that by the time we returned to our "real life" at the end of August, the fug of hot dog cart water and the horns bleating up Park, and even, yes, Daddy in his wool suit, seemed to belong to a foreign land. By then, the only world we knew was Grandmother's grand, white, shuttered house, the lawns sprawling out to meet hedges and fields and woods, and the people the place turned us into: "orfangs" (your word) with British accents; or pirates lying in wait under the bay laurel hedge; or a superhero who could blast villains (you) and a bad guy who ate children in one gulp (me).

But Daddy and Grandmother and Mother had dipped their toes into the topic of the stock market at cocktail hour on a Saturday evening (which meant Miriam was with her family), which meant Daddy was bartending (he made doubles), which meant he started bragging while Mother heated up the casserole, and Grandmother's tongue was loosened enough to call him a greedy fool, which made Mother leave the casserole in the oven and lurch toward Grandmother to say all she had to do to find one of those was look in the fucking mirror. They moved into the parlor. We scavenged a dinner of fairy toast. I turned off the oven and made you tiptoe up the stairs. I tucked us into bed. You said I'd forgotten to brush your teeth. I told you we were punishing them with cavities. Do you remember how that made you giggle? Do you remember you conked out in three minutes flat? Eventually, Grandmother turned off her hearing aid and retired to her wing. By the time she left for church, Mother and Daddy had been fighting so long that what was left of the casserole was clumps of cheese and shards of ceramic littering the kitchen floor. But we never could have imagined Daddy would punish us, too, and make us leave a whole month early, and before Grandmother returned.

The sound of breaking glass carried up from a window below. The light was shafting through the Devil's Ramble—that glade of Japanese maples leading into the woods just beyond the southern lawn—with a quality Grandmother had described as "the gloaming," even though it was a July morning of full sun. I wanted to investigate, but we'd have to get through the adults.

"May I please have Topsy?" You had climbed up on to the railing again. Solemn. Teetering.

"I just gave him to you."

Your lower lip quivered. You pointed to the roof below us, where Topsy lay sprawled across a shingle, out of reach.

I sighed long and hard. You began to bawl. Now they'd find us for sure. "I'll get him, okay? But you have to shut up."

You nodded, snuffling in your next cry. I lay down. I reached out my arm. There was no way. I sat back up and rubbed my bicep, sore from being pinched between the wood. "I'll have to get a broom so I can reach."

You swiveled on the railing, and hopped back onto the decking. You crouched beside me. "Don't leave."

"What did you expect? Throwing him like that."

"I didn't mean to. I can get him myself."

"No, you can't."

"Don't be mad."

"I'll only be mad if you try to get him yourself. It's dangerous, okay?"

Was that wind through the tops of the trees, or Grandmother's tires? Eventually they'd find us up here. But what could I do? What could Grandmother, even if she came back in time to intercept us? I wanted to belong in an idea of Connecticut that didn't exist, for the moment at least. If only we could fly down to the Devil's Ramble, shot through with beautiful sun in a way that made me ache, and now a gentle breeze, which flurried the Japanese maples and the colorful rags tied to their branches. I'd thought for sure Miriam would have snipped the rags off by now; relics of a tie-dye activity Mother had organized. Of everyone in our family, even you, Mother was either the most fun or the least, depending. You'd told me once that Daddy was never fun, but if I scrunched my eyes shut, I could summon up the sound of his laughter, which I hadn't heard since you were born.

The magic light on the ramble switched off. A passing cloud? No. It was as though the place itself had had a bad thought. Even if we could slip down through the whole house, and across the lawn unnoticed, eventually we'd be found. Even if we weren't in trouble, we'd have to bear more glasses of whiskey thrown against the mantelpiece, and Mother sobbing in the pink bedroom. Better to return to macadam heat, hobbled pigeons, and the dusty penthouse Daddy called ours although it was still in Grandmother's name.

"You stay right here. Both feet on the deck."

"I want to come."

"Well, you can't. I'll be back once I find the broom, and I'll get Topsy for you, and we'll be happy, right?"

You didn't look convinced.

"Or I could leave him there forever."

"No!"

"Then you have to let me go."

It was your turn to sigh. "Saski, don't forget you pinky promised. When we get on the highway, you have to tell me that story." You rustled in your pocket for something vital, a blue scrap of construction paper, crudely scissored, covered in capital letters in random order. It was folded around a black feather, fringed at the end in brilliant gold. The feather fluttered on to my shoe. I bent to pick it up. I tickled your neck with the feather's gold tip. You smiled.

"I drawed this for you, Saski. It tells the mean doggy part of the story. I drawed the words so you can tell it the right way. You can't read it. You don't know the code. Don't worry, I'll teach you."

"I'll be back in a flash."

"Why's Superman always a good guy?"

I opened the door. "Don't climb on the banister."

"Can't good guys be bad guys, too?"

Inside the house, Mother let out a scream.

The feather must have sailed from my fingers as I slipped into the house, but I really can't recall. I've gone back again and again, too many times to count, but that part of the story is always just gone, like the feather itself, the first things lost in an endless list; although one might say that the story gained is something left in return.

1

*S*even A.M. The kitchen tumbles with light-tossed dust. Outside, the northern cardinal harangues, a bird so proud they named him twice: *Cardinalis cardinalis*. I sip my Ceylon tea. I check on the sourdough starter, better known as the Mother. She's ravenous on this June dazzler, and I sate her: one part starter, one part water, one and a half parts flour; mix to a tangy slop; shroud in linen by the window, below a fast-moving herd of cumulus clouds. Next, I marry last night's leaven with a pile of flour and a splash of water. And so the Mother and I begin again what we began yesterday and the day before, and all the days before that, since the very day sixteen years ago that I made Grandmother's grand, white, shuttered house my own: tomorrow's loaves.

The gate bell rings. Sludge covers my hands. I think to wash them, but the ring returns, relentless, insistent. This happens sometimes. City folks get lost. What a relief to discover an unfamiliar, dark SUV appearing now on the black-and-white screen just inside the front door. I'll just slap on a charming voice to send the lost soul on their merry way.

"You've made a wrong turn," I say into the box beside the door, pretending a slop of dough isn't slipping down my elbow. "What's your final destination? You'll need—"

"Saskia." The screen pixilates the man's face, but I'd know Xavier anywhere.

Topsy's all the way at the top of the stairs, hidden in my drawer. Already, my palms ache to rip him from his hiding spot. I'll bury my face in his scalp, so the smell of you can make me whole.

"Saskia, let me in." Xavier knows better than this. He knows to leave me alone—unless. Unless what's coming is worse than what I do.

2

You died.

Daddy went to prison.

Mother went to Mexico.

I didn't return to the apartment. The immense oak desk was moved out of the den, and a new queen-sized bed wrapped in thick plastic was delivered, and Miriam and her husband moved in. Grandmother made a big to-do, but it wasn't much of a change; poor Miriam had always been there when we awoke and she left after dark, and even on Sundays, the house remained fragrant with bleach and Murphy's Oil Soap. I was to call Miriam's mustached husband Mr. Jacobs. This I found hilarious because shouldn't Miriam be called Mrs. Jacobs then? But you were dead so there was no one to tell.

Mr. Jacobs was a retired police officer, but Grandmother told me he was to be known as her driver. A tutor from the university came to teach me math, joyless in a way I didn't know college students could be. I made sure never to tell him what Mr. Jacobs was retired from, but I didn't know why it was a secret. That special light in the Devil's Ramble didn't return. The rags you'd tied in its branches were gone.

One snowy midnight, Miriam and Mr. Jacobs were in the

kitchen, sneaking hot toddies. "The story does seem to be properly buried," she said, and he said, "I'm ready to sleep in my own bed, Miri," and she said, "But what if the press finds her? Poor little thing. I'm not sure I can have that on my conscience," and he said, "Miri, it's a tragedy to let tragedy define a child," even though we all knew Mr. Jacobs was only saying so because he wanted to sleep in his own bed. A week later, they went back to their bungalow across town. The next day, Grandmother announced I was returning to the city.

"But where?" I didn't mean to sound insolent. I meant, actually where, because you were dead and Daddy was in prison and Mother was in Mexico and the apartment was sold.

"It will be smoother," Grandmother said, as if that was an answer. A frown pinched her brow. "Someone your own age, guardians with more energy. Unless, of course, you want to go to boarding school." She finished her Lapsang souchang. Her hand shook as she crackled the bone china cup onto its saucer. "Frankly, you don't exactly come across as a rising Madeira girl." The dining room had always been my least favorite of her many rooms; no matter how sunny the day, gloom was always sealed in. She took my hand and clucked at the dirt behind my fingernails. "You must return to functioning society."

Xavier Pierce's family would take me. Our grandmothers had met as new mothers, and our mothers, in turn, had been at Bryn Mawr together, and Xavier and I had celebrated our joint third birthday at the Natural History Museum. I had a vague impression of what he looked like—luscious lips, a golden halo of curls. The last time I'd seen him, at a seventh birthday party for a horrible, farting boy named Walter, I'd found myself studying Xavier's mouth in the simple arts of talking, smiling, and frowning, amazed that a boy could be so beautiful and also so clearly be a boy. But I had no idea of his interests or character, for though we'd spent our primary school years in apartments only blocks apart, ours was a friendship born of the people before us, who hadn't even especially been friends.

Grandmother gave Miriam's sandwich platter another passing glance, then pushed it aside, untouched. I ignored the fist of my stomach. She informed me that I wasn't the only one who'd been through a big change; around the same time I'd come to live with her (yes, that's how she put it, as though we'd made a whimsical decision to move me in), Xavier's family had moved down to Chelsea. The fact that she would allow me to grow up below Seventy-second Street was the surest sign she was desperate to get rid of me.

"But why would they want me?"

"They're a family of means, if that's what you're asking."

"Are you paying them?"

"Don't be crude, Saskia." She rang the bell. Miriam collected the sandwiches.

That night, over breaded veal cutlets, she added, "The Pierces are the right sort of people. Jane travels quite a bit for her little boutique, so don't expect much mothering. But Philip assures me you'll receive plenty of care. He paints in a home studio, so you'll never be unsupervised. His work has become quite well regarded, you know. You're a very lucky girl. Granted, their lifestyle is more bohemian than you're used to, but frankly, Saskia, anything is better than you wandering these woods from dawn 'til dusk. Now, being a boy, Xavier won't expect you to be friends. Get the chance of that out of your mind right now. But you're certain to make some girlfriends. Someday." She set down her fork. She wiped her mouth with the linen napkin. "Let's remember our agreement." She waited for me to nod, then said, "Good girl."

Two days after I turned twelve, Mr. Jacobs dropped me at the Pierces' loft in Chelsea. The door to the building was propped open with an apple box. On the third floor, a film crew was shooting a man in a trench coat running across the open space. Three times they shot the scene. There were dozens of people on set, and lights and mics and makeup bags, cameras, clipboards, headsets. I stood still for the first time in days and realized my feet ached from all the miles I'd clocked on Grandmother's land since she'd informed me I was leaving. My sun-bleached hair still smelled of the Connecticut wind. I decided, just then, that I would have to leave the building and find somewhere else to stay; it wasn't fair to burden these relative strangers with all the reasons for my wandering. But before I could go, Xavier's scent presented him: musky BO, the mildew of air-dried jeans, Head & Shoulders, cafeteria French fries, a green apple Blow Pop, and Carmex. The room was bustling but all my attention stayed on the fleshy funk of Xavier's long body just behind mine, a body I realized, only then, I had known for nearly as long as I had been myself. So I wouldn't leave, not yet.

The loft, one floor up, had been Philip's studio since the seventies, back when he was a sculptor, but Grandmother was right, they'd lived uptown until Xavier turned ten, when the family decided on this "adventure," a word I was to see Jane say with a slant of disgust at the corner of her luscious mouth. She wasn't there that first day, though. She was in Ghana, buying fabric and goods to be marked up a thousand percent in her boutique.

The loft was a warren of rooms made from canvases, pallets, and plywood. The whole place was splattered: mustard on the ceiling, red on the windows, evergreen across a large swath of the unfinished floorboards in the great room. A single yellow toilet was housed in a dank closet next to the stairs, and the kitchen consisted of a fridge painted black and a hot plate for reheating takeout. But the views of the Empire State Building and the Twin Towers, and the city to the west and the east—framed by nearly three-hundred-sixty degrees of windows, interrupted only by the stairwell and Jane's toile curtains, and stacks of Philip's abstract paintings—made it clear that the Pierces were rich in more than just money, although, make no mistake, they also had plenty of that.

The fire door squealed across the concrete floor, announcing our arrival. A real-looking impressionist painting, featuring a herd of gloomy cows munching hay, hung just inside the door.

"Oh, it's dearest Saskia!" Philip cried from the center of the great room, as he lifted his attention from a canvas the length of a car. Royal blue streaked his beard. His kimono opened over a broad, hairy belly, gray Champion sweatpants, and volleyball knee pads. He smelled of sweat and turpentine and cigars. He took my duffle bag. He bisou'd my cheeks. "I'll make a room!" He meant he would make an actual room. It took two hours and a dozen abandoned canvases, each one a solid color: magenta, puce, violet. "Can you believe," he said, hammering them into a makeshift wall, "that I wasted so much time on these stupid color dances?"

Xavier created a bed from a stack of two-by-fours, a futon mattress, and an electric green afghan. He strung up fairy lights. He scaled a twenty-foot ladder to hammer red velvet fabric over the windows. "I've got homework," he said, when he was back on earth. I'd forgotten about school. No matter how many times Xavier brushed his forelock back, it settled over that right eye. I discovered that I wanted to land my breath on the pillow of his lips, which was called a kiss but didn't seem entirely like a kiss when I imagined it. I didn't want a thing to do with the rest of his body; mouth to mouth just seemed the most efficient way to suck him in.

He caught me looking. "Want a snack?"

I shook my head.

"We've got Mexican Coke. The kind with real sugar. Everybody likes that."

"Okay, thanks."

This drew a grin, revealing his wonky tooth, which only made him more beautiful. He reached out. He pinched my deltoid. "Liar." The lingering ache reminded me that to kiss him would be to lose him, and already I couldn't afford that.

Philip grunted. "We've been eating like bachelors, haven't we, boy?" He stuck a finger into my side. "She needs sustenance. The diner?" He wiped his brow, hammer still clutched in his fist, and swept back into the open loft, where the evening had grown golden. "Saskia, you can help me 'til he's done."

Out in the great room, Philip filled a bucket with paint the color of sunshine. He lined it up beside the canvas he'd been working on, a sea of blue—periwinkle, blueberry, azure. "Stand in the yellow." It was a relief to be told what to do, even if the paint was cold and slimy as I slipped my feet in. "Start here. Make your way to the other edge." I didn't want to ruin what he had made. But Philip held out a hand. I lifted my right foot out of the sludge. The color fell away, back into the slop. The evening glow lit a path across the canvas. I strolled across the blue, toward the windows. I left a trail of gold behind me. At the other side, there Philip was again, waiting with a towel.

3

Xavier will expect to bang on the door, so I leave it standing open. He parks in front of the house. His footsteps are crisp and determined across the white gravel, but he hovers on the doorstep. "Saskia?" In rushes the smell of clipped grass, the chirrup of the chipping sparrow, whose genus and species name, *Spizella passerina*, mimics its rapid-fire song. The outside steals every last tendril of the Mother's sour truth. "I tried to call!"

In the pink bedroom, my feet burrow between teetering stacks of Trollope and Dickens. I didn't make it to Topsy; too far. Had to barricade myself in Mother's bedroom. From here to the bed, and the window beyond, the floor is a city of books; highrises of words, sentences, and paragraphs. Downstairs, he hesitates. Good. If I can't get to pleasant, at least I might achieve unmurderous if he waits, penitent, for hours.

Then he speaks again, his voice delicate. "I'm not going in uninvited." I think he's talking to me, until I remember cell phones. "Absolutely not."

Could someone else be in that SUV, watching him? Could it be Billy? Wasn't I clear? No visitors, even if you're married to them.

"Sask?" He's off the phone. "Hello? Please, Saskia, I really need to talk."

A few breaths. Then another, softer voice issues forth from him;

the tone he takes when he needs something. "Billy. Thank you for calling back."

But if it's Billy now, who was on the phone before? Panic rears. Not today.

"I'm sorry," he says. "I'm so sorry. Can you just . . ." A sigh. "Baby, I told you. I'm doing this to protect you." I wait. "I do. I do want to be with you right now." But when Xavier's voice returns, it is full of steel. "This could destroy us. I have to fix it."

It's the grit in his voice. That's all it takes to know: the thing that I (or we, if there is a we anymore) have feared for more than half our lives has finally happened, or is about to, or might. I amble down the stairs while Xavier begs Billy not to hang up. He lifts his muddy eyes. He mumbles a goodbye. That damned forelock, always, ever flopping.

He carries his father's height but none of the old man's paunch. His skin gleams. It's mostly products and dermatology, but I can't help my envy. His mother lingers there, too, in the smear of his lips and careful waistline. He points to the threshold. "Is it okay?"

"I don't have Mexican Coke, I'm afraid."

I think he might pinch my arm, but he pulls me close. My bones creak against his chest. We pretend not to notice how he winces.

4

I was sipping jasmine tea at the kitchen counter when Jane returned home, her jet-black bob still immaculate after the international flight. Her suitcase rattled to the ground. Past midnight, her whispers tangled with the emergency vehicles wailing across town. "Philip, you don't make this kind of choice without talking to your wife."

"There was no way to reach you."

"You could have called the hotel." I wondered if her hairdo kept its shape on the pillow.

"I did. You weren't there."

"So you leave a fucking message."

And later: "What will you do when the press finds her, Philip?"

"Fuck the press."

"Okay, but what will you actually do? Flipping them off is not a plan. You need to have a plan."

And later: "Remember Xavier's third birthday, Philip? Right, I forget, that was the year you were buried in Nancy's glorious crotch. Well, there was a reason I stopped talking to them. I knew something like this would happen, yes, I did, I even told you so, but you never listen."

I reached my hand into the space between my mattress and the wall to find Topsy's most delicate part, right behind the ears, the part I only allowed myself to touch at night lest it grow rough too quickly. Every time I touched it, I knew I was one step closer to losing the last bit of you, but I couldn't stop, especially when I thought of being asked to leave. It had been so much easier to imagine going on my own.

But Jane let me stay. She draped her petite frame in both twin sets and saris, and the answer is yes, her hair always looked like that; she got it cut every five Tuesdays at a salon uptown. She didn't exactly like me, but when she took us to the Buster Keaton retrospective at Film Forum, I cackled in the same split second she did, then caught the glint of one tooth in the cinema glow and realized she was smiling. A week later, in the kitchen, she said, "You laugh like your mother, like you might burst into tears at any moment," and I tittered without wanting to, putting my hands over my lips as though I could catch Mother before she spilled out of me.

Philip was always laughing—hilariously, vibrantly, abundantly. He painted at the center of the loft; sometimes we'd keep him company. At night, he went places we were not welcome, but the booze didn't sour him, and Jane didn't seem to mind. I hung the painting we'd made together over my bed. He called it *The Good Path*. My footprints, smaller than they would ever be again, were always traipsing from the lower left corner up to the sky.

Xavier was as steady a presence as those footprints. Sometimes I'd cry out in the night and awaken the next morning to discover he'd come to read at the foot of my bed. He was loyal but quiet, like a mature Labrador retriever, although his body was all puppy; hands and feet enormous, limbs lanky and out of sync. He bumped his knees on everything and knocked over countless glasses of milk. We attended a new school downtown, a pseudo Reggio Emilia situation that Philip found, with six kids spread out over eight grades. We studied frogs for three months because neither Xavier nor I could think of anything better to suggest. "Well, at least the press hasn't found her," Jane said, over a takeout dinner of Cuban-Chinese. Philip shot her a look; he didn't know that I knew about the tabloids. Xavier had saved as many of the articles as he could, hiding them in the loft below, the one the landlord rented out for shoots. The story had quieted by then, but whenever a child died at the hands of their father, you could find a mention of Daddy on page A11 or 12.

We spent a year like that, a makeshift family: father, sister, brother, mother. Occasionally I'd come across one of Jane's dogeared home design magazines on the kitchen counter, belying her longing for ironed napkins and tufted couches. I couldn't understand how she'd allowed this lifestyle; it certainly wasn't her first choice.

"Philip said he'd jump off the brownstone if he had to spend another second with the snobs on the Upper East Side," Xavier explained. "So Jane said if he could support us, without using a cent of her 'snob money,' she'd move wherever he wanted. She didn't think he'd be able to do it, I guess." It was Philip's figurative painting project, *The Lewdnesses*—close-ups of lips, elbows, toes at angles which made them look like much less tame body parts—that had funded the move. Parisian collectors were buying the pieces for tens of thousands of dollars each.

"But he's bored now," Xavier said, his eyes darting around the loft.

"He seems happy."

"He keeps painting the same thing, over and over. He says they're a parlor trick now." Xavier was right, now that I looked around: all those body parts pretending to be something sexier than they were. "That one over your bed is the most different thing he's done in years."

One May Saturday, when Jane had gone to Japan, Philip took

us to the diner, for "our favorite," which was really his favorite—
Reubens and cheese fries and Mexican Coke—and announced we
were summering in Maine. We needed fresh air, which is what
children need when it's convenient for adults. Philip's reps were
breathing down his neck for new material, something just like *The
Lewdnesses* but also not at all like *The Lewdnesses*, which is what, he
expounded, gatekeepers require of artists in this hellfire we call
capitalism. Then he asked what we thought, because at least he was
the kind of parent discomfited by the fate-deciding part of his job.

"What about Mom?" Xavier said.

Philip let out a long, terrific fart.

"Dad. What about Mom?"

I looked out the window at Ninth Avenue. I thought about
that light on the Devil's Ramble. If I closed my eyes, I could
feel every morsel of the day I'd be having instead of this one—
standing at the lip of the ramble's auburn promise, backpack
heavy with cucumber sandwiches and a thermos of whole milk,
looking down at the spot where your hot hand met mine.

It was a seven-hour drive. Jane had extended her Asia trip. Xavier
was concerned. It seemed downright revolutionary that one could
grow tired of one's spouse and simply stay in another country, but
I kept that to myself. I ripped open the Salt & Vinegar Lay's and
passed them to the front seat. Xavier started crunching. The car
filled with the stench of Philip's cigarillo. I put my hands on the
back of their sturdy necks. This pleased them.

5

"**Y**ou really should reconnect the landline," Xavier says, "or at least get a cell phone." He has settled in front of the idle hearth. The grandfather clock grows loud as a sudden stillness hits the room, as though all the molecules in the surrounding world have made an agreement to pause. It's rare, anymore, for your last day to come back unbidden, but here it is, a freight train of memory: the ticking clock when I came down from the second floor, meaning to go to the broom closet; the sound of Mother wheezing from this very room in which we sit, her voice wet with tears or blood. Maybe he had punched her in the mouth. I crept closer from the foyer. Then Daddy was in front of me, filling the doorway with his broad chest, a solid Polyphemus like the one from his bedtime stories, down to the detail of one working eye; the other one purpling, punched shut.

Then, like a switch, what's happening now comes back: a mower, the northern cardinal, the chipping sparrow, an airplane beginning its descent. Xavier's eyes skim his father's painting, tracing my girlish footsteps toward heaven.

I perk up my face. "So? How's the beautiful husband?"

Xavier shifts his elegant gaze to the floor. His shoulders slump. They're ever so slight, these movements. No one else would notice. Then he musters up a smile like mine. "Billy's great."

"And your dad? And your mom?"

"Mom's fine. You know. Busy with her online shop. Don't you and Dad email? He's always dangling some tidbit about you."

I hear from Philip every few months. He's been living in one of the Pueblos Blancos of Andalusia for years now, but I can never get him to tell me what he actually does there. Drugs, definitely. He'll never answer when I ask if he's painting.

"I miss you," Xavier says. It's true; I am excellent when I'm excellent. But we both know I have not been excellent for some time.

6

Once we reached the thick, northern blue forests, Philip steered our caramel-colored Lincoln into a gas station. We were a few miles past a main thoroughfare of limestone stores shilling shovels and teacups. Across the street, an ivory church's steeple pierced the sky.

The gas station's sign read JIMBOB's. Ford 4x4s littered the parking lot. A menacing hook hung from a pole near the gas pumps, though I didn't yet know that it was built for moose carcasses. Two women crossed the parking lot. The younger one said something out of the corner of her mouth and the other laughed with her head tipped back, revealing eraser-pink gums. Here was the country like I'd never seen it in Connecticut. Gasoline stunk up the car.

Philip disappeared inside. I wondered why: we had plenty of snacks, there were only two stores in the country that sold his high-end cigarillos, and he hated asking for directions. He held the door for two men in work boots, arms strung with plastic bags. When the door closed behind him, bell ringing, the one in a Skoal hat sneered.

Xavier roused from his nap with a dazed swivel of the head. "The fuck are we?"

"Maine, I guess?"

"Jesus."

Philip reemerged with a piece of paper held high. The men had driven off, but they had taught me to see him anew: his long beard with the braid at its end; his graying hair pulled into a low ponytail; the Metallica T-shirt, taut over his round belly; the paint flecks smattering his skin; and, on his bottom half, his signature longyi wrap cloth, this one a deep prune. "You kids ready?"

The line of the shoulder belt had creased Xavier's cheek. The Lincoln growled back to life. Philip waved the paper like the golden ticket. "Right where they said it'd be!"

7

"Have you gotten anything in the mail?" Xavier asks. The Vermont Country Store catalog—I could wow him with my collection of long-sleeved cotton nightgowns. And bills—plenty of bills. But sure, fine, the mail is not what we might call my strong suit. Correspondence goes into the mudroom, unopened. I'd like to get some credit for my capacity on the internet—my own email account! An online subscription to the *New York Times*!—but he's scowling. "Simple white envelopes," he prompts, "that might not seem unusual until they pile up."

"It sounds like you have."

"I didn't pay much attention at first. Billy and I . . . we're public. Donations, boards." He hastens over the boast in a way that's practiced, as though it's the requisite defense to everyone wanting what he has. "I figured it was someone a little obsessed." If you look like Xavier, you take obsession for granted. "Or, you know, mentally ill." He casts his eyes away.

"What did the notes say?"

"Threatening things. Nothing that scared me"—white male privilege rears its head in the implication that a string of threatening letters sent to one's home wouldn't produce fear, even when you're married to a Black man—"but unpleasant enough that even

Billy wanted me to go to the police." His eyes dart back to my face. "Of course I didn't."

So he's still scared of me. "I don't know what this has to do with me."

"You really should have a working phone." His Adam's apple rises, then falls. "The others got the notes, too."

Here they are, then: the others. I knew they'd show.

"It didn't occur to me they were getting them until Cornelia called. She was at one of her kids' soccer games, hiding out in her minivan, absolutely hysterical. Started hyperventilating when she found out I'd gotten the same ones. She took the whole thing very personally. She said the last letter made her think whoever wrote the letters . . . knew."

Steady.

"So I called Issy. And I texted her. And I called her again. Finally got her through a Facebook DM though she claims she never checks social media. Anyway, I had an old number. She's not in Chicago anymore."

"Last I heard, she was in El Paso."

"El Paso was before Chicago." Xavier's the type who's smug about calendars and holiday cards. "I finally convinced her to reach out to her old roommate in Chicago, which was a whole thing because he'd moved to Virginia. Anyway, turns out it was the same for her. Six letters, all from Maine."

"And what does Billy think? He sounded upset on the phone."

Xavier raises an eyebrow but doesn't take the bait. "Ben got the letters, too. But of course Ben is almost as hard to reach as Issy. And you know better than anyone, he's . . . he called me a drama queen. Kept insisting it was some kind of prank. Until . . ." Xavier's gaze tips out the window, over my shoulder, like he's hoping the story can end a different way. "Until he called me back. He was upset. Honestly, more upset than I think I've ever heard him since . . ." Xavier leans forward, presses his hands together. "He's got his mom in an assisted-living facility up there, did you know that?"

Sarah's too young.

He sees me care. "Well, Sarah went missing. For a night. Someone sprung her out of the nursing home and she wasn't found until the next morning. Want to know where?" He hardly waits. "Wandering Bushrow Road. In her nightgown. When they found her, she said everything was going to be okay because he's back."

"Who? Who's back?"

"You know," he says. "You know."

8

*P*hilip's piece of paper held directions after all: *Turn right out of JimBob's. After fifty feet, turn right again onto the unmarked gravel road (Bushrow Road). Follow Bushrow up and over the hill. As the second hill rises, look for the broken fencing. Move the brush off the driveway. Find your way in.*

The paper was illustrated in the margins, with sketches of Bushrow Road wending its way through the trees, and the hill rising out of the valley. Windows finally unrolled, the world rushed to meet us. What we saw felt remarkably the same as it was drawn. Not just the landscape itself, but the essence of it: the dappling of sun upon the branches, the unforgiving bracken where road met land, the gravel dust kicked up by our tires. I couldn't imagine someone being able to tell that story with a simple pencil, nor taking the time to turn a list into a labor of love, but I had yet to meet Sarah.

The Lincoln climbed the second hill until we spotted broken fencing. We idled at a dramatic pitch. *Find your way in.* Philip clambered out. He kicked at the undergrowth. The bottom of his longyi snagged a branch. Deciduous and evergreen trees pressed their branches toward us. A mosquito whined in the open window. I let it latch onto my forearm, then flattened it into a red stitch.

Philip pulled at the bushes. He laughed. He cursed. We'd assumed a rocky coastline, maybe a funky motel, or a moody cabin set at the edge of a cliff. Xavier swiveled toward me, his breath a hot stink: "Whatever he's got planned, it's going to suck."

A knot of branches bigger than a man came away in Philip's hands. He raised his fists in triumph. Blood dripped down one arm. It took ten minutes to clear a dirt track. The Lincoln revved over the berm of gravel where the driveway met the road. Branches squealed along its side. Xavier leaned toward the windshield, but only the unsteady gravel track, under a cathedral of flourishing green, lay ahead. The woods on either side were dense and deep. The air was cool. I wished I'd asked questions.

"What the fuck kind of vacation is this?" Xavier said.

"A vacation of the soul, my boy."

When we reached the base of the driveway, a broad-shouldered woman pushed open the screen door of the log building directly before us. She took two steps out the door. Brown curly hair cascaded over her shoulders, vining down her arms and past her waist. She had ample breasts that quivered, unbound, under her mustard-colored T-shirt. She pitched back her head and yodeled. Her voice ricocheted down the valley.

The yodel called the people who made that place their home. I thought of Munchkinland. Mother loved the scene when Dorothy opens the door and the whole world becomes color, before she wants to get the hell out. The Munchkins creep out to look at the powerful girl who's killed the Wicked Witch of the East and these strangers, emerging from the woods and its log cabins, took the same cautious approach toward our car.

There were a couple dozen of them. Adults, mainly, wearing Goodwill T-shirts, except for one family who looked like they'd stepped right out of *Little House on the Prairie*: a small, tidy woman and a little girl of about six, both wearing long brown braids and starched white pinafores and old-fashioned ankle boots. The father wore black pants and suspenders and a wide-brimmed hat.

The tall woman who'd spotted us plucked a naked toddler from the path as she moved our way. The kid put his hand down the neck of her shirt to fiddle her nipple. Philip leaned out the window and said, "Okay if I park here?" but instead of answering, she began to sing in a determined alto: "Oh I once had a horse and his name was Bill." This melodic line gathered the others closer. They joined their voices to hers as they surrounded our car:

> When he ran he couldn't stand still
> He ran away
> One day
> And also I ran with him

It became a fast-paced song, the lyrics goofy. The people warmed to it, clapping along and laughing as they moved in a circle around us.

> Now in Frisco Bay there lives a whale
> She eats pork chops by the bale
> By the hogshead
> By the schooner
> By the hatbox and the pillbox

Xavier had a hand over his mouth. He glanced at his father, waiting for the practical joke to end, but if this was a joke, Philip was in on it. He raised his hands toward the roof of the Lincoln like a man in church. All the while the strangers whirled, a dizzying array of exuberant noise and shimmying bodies, a cloud of sweat and dust rising over us, the voices strong and lush, if not always on key.

She loves to laugh and when she smiles
You just see teeth for miles and miles
And tonsils
And spareribs
And things too fierce to mention

A slender man of about forty, with a long, dark ponytail, broke through the crowd. He approached us as a mayor would. I was set away from him, in the backseat, but his unblinking eyes found me at once. Philip got out of the car. He offered his hand and the other man pulled his eyes away from mine.

The song was louder with Philip's door open, verse after verse—"I once went up in a balloon so big, the people on earth they looked like a pig" . . . "Oh what would you do in a case like that, what would you do but stamp on your hat." The lyrics didn't make sense, but the people seemed euphoric to be singing them.

The mayor pulled Philip into a bear hug. They embraced as the people reached the end of their song, raising their hands and whooping. A troop of black birds lifted off the trees.

Over Philip's shoulder, the man's eyes, once again, found mine. He grinned, as though in simply seeing me, he had been paid a compliment. The others moved to greet Philip, shaking hands and patting his shoulder, as though he was a long-lost friend. The toddler shimmied down his mother and broke free. He ran to my open window. Xavier and I had an unspoken pact to stay in the car. But the child was too much like you to resist (those days, I found you in anything small—kittens, stones, acorns). The kid's eyes and hair were darker, but the important parts were the same. I found myself flexing the door handle and stepping out into the northern light with all those eyes watching.

"Hello." I crouched down.

The child offered a gummy smile. Without warning, he wrapped his hot hands around my shoulders. He smelled of piss and oat-meal and his mother's armpits. He sunk his teeth into the flesh of my upper arm. "Tomas!" his mother said. He darted into the woods. No one went after him.

"These are my children," Philip said to the tall man, and to everyone else. "My son, Xavier." Xavier got out of the car. He was scowling.

Together, the group said, "Hello, Xavier."

"And Saskia," said Philip.

"Hello, Saskia," they said in a single voice. Then, as though on some predetermined cue, the people broke apart, back to their labors—the old-fashioned family; the yodeling woman; everyone but the mayor.

"Welcome home," he said. His voice was melodic and precise, as though incapable of lying. "Welcome to Home."

"I still don't know your name," Philip replied. He sounded so timid.

"I'm Abraham." But Abraham wasn't looking at Philip any-more. He was watching me. Looking into me—I had never un-derstood that phrase until now. He came my way and rested his cool fingers on my wrist. "Why are you sad, Saskia?"

"I'm not sad." But I felt ashamed as soon as I said it.

His eyes, in description, were plain: brown with a speckle of gold. A beard smudged his jawline. His nose had been broken; a crooked hitch lay in its bridge. There was nothing pretty about him. There was nothing to explain the fact that since spotting him, my eyes had been hungry.

And then: a feather.

A feather from the sky, a black feather, fringed in gold, floating down. A feather just like the one you gave me on the day you left. Abraham plucked it up. He held it out to me and said, "Well, look at that."

I began to weep.

Xavier moved my way; it was the first time I'd cried since he'd become my brother. Abraham held up the hand that wasn't touching mine and stopped him. He spoke quietly, only to me. "It's all right to be sad here, Saskia. We will let you be sad. But you can also find joy. We ache for it so."

9

"Abraham's been dead more than twenty years," I tell Xavier.

"What if he isn't?"

"The body." I am laughing as I prove him wrong. "They found his body in the forest, in case you forgot that salient fact. He's dead, Xavier. Thank Goddess." I mean the invocation to be a joke, conjured up from our mutual woo-woo past, but I can't tell if he knows.

He reaches into his canvas bag and hands over six white envelopes, each addressed in a clean, unlooped black scrawl. The postmark is Maine. The stamps are American flags.

The one on top holds only two words: *Hello again.*

Xavier has sizzled through adulthood with that pornographic mouth and just-fucked hair. It's some boy is all it is, some boy who got the wrong idea, who happens to live in Maine. Probably a fan of Philip's. I myself was recognized on East Sixth Street once— "You're in that Philip Pierce painting! *Twins!*" Or maybe it's someone interested in defunct cults. (But the others? What about the others? Why send them the letters, too? There must be a reasonable explanation, one I haven't come to yet.)

The second note reads: *Did you miss me?*

But the third one catches. *I missed you so.*

"I love it so," Abraham would say of the land. "I need it so," when there was a job he wanted done right. "I thought it so," when quoting Gabby back to herself. "We ache for it so," on the day we arrived.

But then, people end sentences like that all the time. Don't they?

The fourth: *I need you, in fact.*

That settles it; it's not Abraham. He never needed us. We believed we needed him; that was the problem.

Xavier's eyes are on my hands. I struggle with the thin paper as I draw the fifth letter out: *It's time to come Home.* Poor Xavier, seeking doom. I speak to him as I would a scared child. "So someone knows you lived at Home. It's not a secret."

He waits for me to draw out the sixth letter. To unfold it. To say its words over the highboy and the lowboy, Grandmother's grandfather clock, the twin Hepplewhite chairs, the dust suspended in the morning sun. But I find I can't.

He lifts the envelope from my lap. He reads what's inside in his clear tenor: "All five of you. Or else."

10

Our first evening at Home, we ate asparagus frittatas, cabbage soup, homemade sourdough crackers, wet rounds of goat cheese, and blueberry wine, so sour I could only handle a swallow. We ate in the Main Lodge, the log building from which the tall woman had emerged. Soft light gilded the hair of the men and women gathered there. To the east, in the valley below, lay a quiet lake. Crickets hushed.

A massive fireplace, sporting andirons the size of Great Danes, was at one end of the long, open room, beside the humble screen door where the woman had spotted us. At the other end lay the kitchen, an ample collection of fridges and stoves and bags of onions and of potatoes, and, I'd soon discover, the occasional cured deer or moose leg, and an enormous farmhouse sink for washing dishes, where someone was always trapped like the Sisyphus of Daddy's stories.

Down the length of the lodge, from fireplace to kitchen, tables were arranged in two long lines with Homesteaders—for that's what they called themselves—hunched over their bowls like French peasants. Xavier and I got separated in the buffet line. By the time I found a spot at the middle of the dining room, Philip had settled in before the fireplace, at Abraham's right hand.

"You forget something in your car?" The man asking plonked

down beside me. I recognized him from our arrival: a carpet of dark hair escaped his holey T-shirt, down his arms and up his neck. "You keep looking that way."

"Trying to get my dad's attention." It was funny to call Philip that.

"My advice is let go of those labels. 'Dad,' 'Mommy,' it's all bullshit." He shoved in a bite of frittata, closing his eyes to savor the taste. "You guys are some VIPs for sure. Haven't eaten like this in months."

"You get plenty." The yodeler settled in across from us, her long, curly hair now cinched on top of her head. She was tall, even at the table, taller than he was. "You being nice?" She frowned at him playfully, then stretched out her hand. "I'm Teresa. Jim's wife." Her grip was firm; this close-up, her biceps were positively chiseled. The crook of her elbow held up the sleeping head of the toddler who'd bitten me. He suckled from her purple nipple, eyes rolled back in his head. "You've already met Tomas."

An enormous, taxidermied head of a moose hung from the old-growth beam above us. A furred cobweb dangled from the moose's nose. I was glad for that head; it offered a respite from the insistent gaze of Teresa's nipples, one of which was leaking a growing circle on her shirt.

"That's Grimm," Jim said, thumbing up toward the moose head.

"Did you shoot him?"

Jim's laugh startled me. "We're not those kinds of assholes."

"Oh, but Jim's definitely an asshole." Teresa's tone was affectionate. "Hey, I need soup." She switched the kid to the other side. Her long-necked nipple gaped.

"Saskia likes your tits, Teresa," Jim said.

"Fuck off." She winked at me before looking down over herself. "They are magnificent, though, right? Only good thing my mother gave me." She shook her empty bowl in Jim's direction. "More soup, dude. More soup for your breast-feeding wife."

"Sarah will bust my balls if I go for seconds."

I hadn't taken any soup. I picked up the brown, hand-thrown bowl. I moved away from them, down the line of tables and chairs, ariot with laughter and conversation. I joined the end of the buffet line again, feeling Grimm's glassy gaze on the back of my head, willing myself not to turn to see if Jim, or Teresa's breasts, were looking, too.

The room was the color of unfiltered maple syrup: beadboard walls; creaky floorboards; and those long, rickety tables. There were pencil and ink drawings pinned up along the walls, sketches of the natural world that bore the same hand as the drawings on the map we'd used to find our way in. Stained photographs, hung in fits and starts, told the story of the place: it had been a girls' camp once upon a time, when well-to-do families sent their white-frocked daughters north for wacky canoe races.

The small woman dressed in the starched pinafore oversaw the buffet line. Physically, she was Teresa's opposite: petite, contained. She was obviously the Sarah that Jim had referred to; the kitchen's queen. How she had carried that giant vat of soup from the stove all by herself was a wonder. She nodded to each person as they passed the aluminum pot, which stunk of cabbage.

Her little girl, in a calico dress and pressed pinafore, stood tucked in beside her. I was aware of the line moving on in front of me, but I couldn't bring myself to care, not when that child had a constellation of freckles over the bridge of her nose. A child can be the whole world. The girl tipped her long lashes, as though I'd said something terribly funny, then lifted her face and offered a toothy grin. She stepped forward. I thought she might hug me. But instead she flipped me the bird. Her middle fingernail held a half-moon of dirt.

I felt Sarah's gaze on us. The girl did, too—she hid her hand quickly, with a startled look my way. I felt a rise of panic. "Teresa needed more soup. You're Sarah, right? She said it would be okay to ask for more soup."

Sarah patted the little girl's head, whose eyes closed like a satisfied cat's. "Little Nora flip you off?" She shook her head but a smile hid there, too. "She's a beast."

Relief flushed my limbs; I'd been so sure Sarah was going to smack Nora that I hadn't even considered there was another way. My hands were shaking. Sarah took the bowl and sloshed a full serving into it. She waited until my hands stilled, then placed the pottery, newly warmed, back into them.

11

I'm scrambling away from Xavier before I know it, into the hallway, up the stairs. Halfway up, I realize I'm making the same quaking shriek that Mother did, when Daddy stepped toward me into the foyer. "Don't you touch her," she cried, wrapping her arms around him from behind. Blood garbled her words.

Into the first bedroom I go again, the pink bedroom, Mother's bedroom. I latch closed the door. Around me fall all those stupid books, an avalanche of words. It's only morning but I'm in for the night. Thank goodness I fed the Mother, though there will be no bread tomorrow.

Xavier bangs the door. He calls my name.

12

On the other end of the Main Lodge, the front door slammed shut. The tinny sound cut through the cacophony of voices and clattering spoons, the sneezes, Tomas's throaty cry as Teresa unlatched him, and the weight of Sarah's gaze. The room quieted as I turned to look.

An old woman had come in. Small, but not delicate like Sarah; she moved with a swagger I'd only seen in men. She might have been Grandmother's age, but she had a short crop of white hair, wore a fisherman's sweater with rolled up sleeves, and carried a faded L.L. Bean backpack. Even across the great room I knew she'd smell of wood smoke instead of talcum powder.

She held a handful of green; plants harvested from the forest floor. She strode to Abraham, who was deep in consultation with Philip, picked up his glass of water, and plonked the plant's dirty roots right in. Abraham held up the muddied glass, first to Philip in a toast, then to the old woman, and laughed.

A boy and girl had come in with her. They were the only other people there about our age. Their presence in the old woman's company seemed a point of interest for many of the Homesteaders. The girl was tall and ample and dressed like a lumberjack, and aside from the Black woman who'd been in the song circle and now sat at Abraham's other hand, the only person of color I'd seen at Home. She towered over the old woman, but she looked like she didn't mean to.

"So they were foraging," one of the women in line said to Sarah.

The boy had a round face and a nose pressed in like a bulldog. He was dressed old-fashioned to match Sarah and Nora—white starched shirt, black suspenders. He was small like his mother, and compact and strong like his father, who was watching from across the room. When Sarah gestured to the boy, the man went back to his soup. The boy loped our way. "Hey, Ma."

"Your father needed help today." Sarah filled a bowl for him.

"Can I have more?"

She pressed what was already there into his hands. "Ben, I'd like you to meet Saskia."

"Pleasure," he said, but he didn't even look at me.

"Saskia is from the city," Sarah said. "She has flaxen hair and long limbs. She is fiercer than she looks." It was odd the way she listed these characteristics, as though she was reading a poetic description out loud. Ben drew back, and though I would have described myself as tall and scrawny, with blond, scraggly hair, and a long face, I didn't think I was quite as bad as the nightmare he apparently saw before him.

"Why don't you sit together?" Sarah asked.

"I bet she's got a spot," he mumbled, before striding to the crowded table with his father. An old man with a long beard, sipping his soup like coffee, moved aside with a grimace. Ben teetered uncomfortably at the edge of the bench.

My cheeks burned. I turned back into the dining room. The soup stuttered in the bowl.

"'Tis a gift to be simple . . ." As I walked away, Sarah began to sing. "'Tis a gift to be free." The single soprano carried into the room, like a bird let out of a cage. "'Tis a gift to come 'round where we ought to be."

I gave Teresa her soup as she joined in—"And when we find ourselves in the place that is right"—and soon the whole room was singing along—"We will be in the valley of love and delight."

Their voices braided together. Sarah's notes were like bells. Teresa sang with more confidence for lyrics than for melody. Jim sang, too, but all the while he was watching, watching. Tomas dented a spoon upon the table, and Ben chewed as he mumbled the words, and Nora gobbled the last of the frittata. Abraham hummed along, closing his eyes at the top of the room. All the other's voices joined, too, all the others whose names I was yet to know: the old man with the beard; Ben's serious father; the girl who had come in with Ben. Even Philip joined in, even Xavier, who met my gaze with an ironic lift of his eyebrows.

I did not sing; I did not know the words. At the other end of the room, the old woman stood at the mantelpiece, her mouth clamped shut. She knew the words, I could tell, but she did not care to sing them.

13

Xavier's need is a train of language.

"Saskia.

"Abraham can't hurt you.

"It probably isn't even him.

"Please.

"There's some reasonable explanation.

"You don't need to be afraid of him."

As if that's why I'm hiding.

14

At dawn the next day, Xavier and I awoke on the floor of the Main Lodge to the old man who'd moved aside for Ben standing above us. His Calvinist beard hung bluish in the dawn. He waved the piece of paper that had borne us to Home. "Take it back."

Xavier propped himself on his elbows. "It's not even morning."

The old man dropped the map onto Xavier's chest. Philip wasn't beside us anymore, if he'd come to bed in the first place. My back ached.

From the kitchen came the gentle clack of a mixing spoon against a bowl. A humid, herbal sweetness clouded the room. Sarah's back was turned to us, but I knew she'd been listening.

15

Xavier's fists, relentless, rattle the door in its frame.

The therapists say to open one's toolbox when something is broken.

So, five things I can see: the tops of *Acer rubrum*, the red maple; *Betula lenta*, the black birch; *Fagus grandifolia*, the American beech; *Acer saccharum*, the sugar maple; and *Carya glabra*, the pignut hickory.

Four things I can hear: *Cardinalis cardinalis* boasting; *Spizella passerina* trilling; *Poecile atricapillus*, the black-capped chickadee, whistling its two tones; and *Tamiasciurus hudsonicus*, the red squirrel, chastising us all.

Three things I can touch: coverlet, eyelids, heart.

Two things I can smell: man, breath.

One thing I can taste: terror.

The sun hasn't moved that far when Xavier gives up. His feet pad down the stairs. The door clicks shut behind him. The house exhales.

16

O_{ver} a bowl of porridge sprinkled with plump blueberries, the grizzled man—whose name, Amos, came out in a low growl— explained that Home was shrouded from the Thinged World, but could be reached by those who quested for it. If someone who knew of Home thought you were ready to experience the life it offered, they would tell you where to find this map, hidden from the wind and rain in the depths of JimBob's, and you'd have to muster faith until you found the road in.

"Is that how you got here?" Xavier asked. "Stealing a map from a convenience store?" I thought Amos might be Abraham's father; he was tall like him, and lean—although his cheeks were almost hollow—but it didn't seem polite to ask.

"Put the directions back," Amos said, pulling out a hunting knife, "so the next journeyman may find us."

"Why does it have to be us?"

I put my hand on Xavier's arm. That knife looked sharp.

Out of his other pocket, Amos drew a piece of driftwood, with the face of an owl carved into one end. He began to whittle. "Your father has been seen." Splinters scattered over the table.

"But it's like three miles away."

Amos stabbed the knife into the table. "I warned Abraham about children."

On Bushrow Road, dust kicked up from my Keds. Birds chirped from the dense forest on both sides. There were probably frogs and squirrels and ferns and mushrooms in there, too, but I didn't know anything about them, didn't know their names or habits. We walked in silence, sun winking through the tops of the impossibly tall trees. I wish I'd brought a water bottle. The hard-boiled egg Sarah had slipped into my pocket thudded with every step.

"It's a cult," Xavier said, at the bottom of the hill.

"They're just a bunch of weirdos."

Xavier lengthened his stride until he was ahead of me. He thought I liked Home. But "like" wasn't a word I'd use to describe the gratitude called up in me when Sarah hadn't smacked her child. The closest I'd felt to that unnamed feeling had been with Xavier, back on the day I'd decided not to put my lips on his: a bruised hunger that even kissing wouldn't satiate.

Only the day before, JimBob's had seemed a haven, filled with the trappings of the known world: orange chips, waxy chocolate, frigid lockers of soda. But by the time we went in, past a lady in a down vest ringing up a customer, the idea of a convenience store already seemed foreign. We returned the paper to its proper hiding spot, below a stack of cooking oil. This was stealing's opposite: giving something we hadn't even known we had to give. Xavier plopped a pack of Big Red onto the empty counter. The cashier glared. Probably we smelled like cabbage.

17

Now that Xavier's gone, the Mother will require extra feeds and a hum or two. She'll be sludgy, shy, but I'll coax her back with flour and the tiger maple spoon. I'll put her in the window, spill her in sunlight. But not yet, not yet. On the inside of my door, Mother's brass hook and eye clasp each other. The bed calls. The books kick away, leaves on an autumnal stroll. Head finally on the pillow, I listen for the motor. Xavier will be back again, surely, but I've won this round.

It's just some cute boy playing games with him.

Any minute now, the motor.

But then, instead, the front door moans open. And there are voices. Voices? Surely not. It's just Xavier on the phone. I rise to my elbows.

The stairs cry out. His step is louder. Perhaps he's carrying something heavy. But no. There, between his steps lies another set, hiding.

He's brought someone in.

18

We deserved a dip in the lake after bald noon on the gravel road. I would wear the turquoise bikini Jane got me at the Barney's warehouse sale. But once back at the Main Lodge, we discovered that our suitcases—which we'd put beside the fireplace—were nowhere to be found.

"Did someone move our stuff?" Xavier asked Teresa, who was hunched over a basket of receipts. Her curly hair blanketed her broad back as she added, subtracted, multiplied with a worn pencil on the back of an envelope. She smelled of goat manure and sandalwood. She waved us toward the kitchen. "Have to get these numbers crunched before Jim heads to town."

In the kitchen, onions sizzled in a cast iron skillet the size of a tire. Leftover soup bubbled, the tang of curry on the air. A dozen sourdough loaves cooled on the counter. The sight of them made my stomach rumble for the first time that day. Sarah washed dishes before the open window; pinned up on either side of it were sketches of the forest and the lake, of birds darting from branches, of porcupines, of moose. The drawings—all made on the backs of envelopes—quivered in the breeze.

"Do you know where our bags are?" I asked.

Tomas was crouched outside, below the window, digging with a stick. A clod of dirt sailed through the air. He went back to digging. Another brown chunk emerged from the bushes, hitting the boy's arm with a thwack, which he ignored. But when a third hunk sailed from the undergrowth to smack Tomas's cheek, the little boy sprang up like a wild dog. Nora, braids unkempt, pinafore filthy, emerged from the bushes, roared, and took off down the hill, Tomas at her tail. Sarah's small hands worked a wet rag along the inside of a mixing bowl.

"My suitcase is red," I said.

Sarah's metal bowl rattled into the sink. She turned toward me. She offered a smile, which made her face a different country. Her blue eyes held mine much longer than was comfortable. This look gave me over to something strange and powerful that slowly, surely, filled me with a giddy understanding: what I was asking about—the suitcase, the swimsuit—didn't matter. Here she was, here they all were, with work in their hands. It wasn't that it was selfish to be thinking of swimming while the rest of them worked; but why would I want to do anything but join in? Sarah watched me understand. She pulled my gaze, with hers, back toward the outside: a bumblebee lobbing from tuft to tuft of purple clover; a woodpecker rattling a dead tree; a motorboat growling a fine line across the lake. There were cabins below us, and people I had yet to meet, and land I did not know.

I pulled Xavier outside. Back in the sun, in front of the Main Lodge, he said, "So, where's our stuff?"

I shrugged.

"You didn't find out? But you said to follow you!" His face was pink now, his forelock dangling with sweat. His mouth was dusted

Cheetos orange in each corner. I gave him the hard-boiled egg. He bashed it against his forehead. Brown shell rained over the dirt. You were like this when you got hungry, too.

I explained that I had come to understand that the suitcases, and what was inside of them, didn't really matter. "You don't think underpants are important?" he said. I didn't know how to explain that we weren't on the subject of underpants anymore.

But Xavier was. He gestured over his shoulder at the Main Lodge. "One of those psychos stole our stuff."

"Maybe we're getting a cabin," I said. "Maybe someone moved our things for us." I couldn't say to Xavier that what I wanted, more than anything, now that I'd noticed this world the way Sarah did, was to feel Abraham seeing me the way he had when I'd arrived; that I wanted this much more than any of the things I'd brought from the outside world.

Before us, at the base of the driveway—where Philip's Lincoln was parked beside a trusty old pickup—stood the camp's flagpole, flapping with a red piece of frayed cloth. Fifty yards behind us lay the stinking latrine. I laughed as Xavier glared. I laughed because the latrine was disgusting and yet I'd come back willingly, even knowing it was my only place to shit. To our left lay a handful of cabins. It was hard to imagine calling one of those squat brown squares home, but maybe I'd get to. Xavier made his way up the steps of the closest one, shielding his eyes to peer in the window.

"What are you doing?"

"Looking for our stuff."

"That's someone's home." Mother's sharpness spilled out of me. All those walks to and from the park, when you'd dash ahead and let yourself through some stranger's gate and dally on their limestone stoop. She always called out to slow down; she couldn't keep up in her high heels. In the half block before we caught up, she'd laugh and call you naughty, but by the time we spotted you again, all you got was the threat of Daddy.

Xavier and I followed a yellow butterfly down a path to our right. It dipped under tree cover, toward a faint chorus of song.

19

"Please open the door, Saskia." Xavier's voice coaxes from the hallway.

There's another breath out there, filling my home with its stink. How dare he? He's made my world so small now, so indescribably small—just this bed. Just this room. Just these books. No sourdough even; Mother's door now another line I cannot cross.

20

Downhill sat a rusty camper that had been repurposed into a chicken coop. Beside it lay a meadow enclosed in wire where a few dozen birds paced jerkily, like dinosaurs. Nora and Tomas tore around the camper and up the hill toward us, the toddler clutching something in his arms. It was wrapped in a piece of familiar turquoise cloth.

"You little fucker!" the girl screamed.

Xavier put his hand out to stop Tomas. The toddler dodged him and darted away up the path, but not before Xavier had pulled my bikini top away. I caught a glimpse of what was wrapped inside. I knew that white fur as well as I knew myself, but it was impossible; I'd left Topsy back in Chelsea, telling myself it would be good to try out life without you tethered so close. Except here he was.

Topsy's floppy, felted pelt was revealed in Xavier's palm. Xavier yelped and grimaced, holding the bunny away from his body as though he was real and dead. Nora jumped for him. I scrabbled forward, making a desperate sound, taking him back.

"Finders keepers," Nora cried, grabbing Topsy's arm.

"Let go!" I must have screamed this. I must have looked terrifying, my mouth fomenting wrath and grief. Xavier and Nora shrunk back. My face buried itself in Topsy; head filling with the dusty smell of him, which was the smell of you.

"What's all this?" Abraham was there, too, then. It was impossible to know where he had come from. Nora darted toward me, coming for Topsy, but he held her off. He leaned toward me, requiring my gaze. "This is special to you?"

"It's a Thing!" said Nora. "She's Thinging!"

"Enough."

Nora folded her hands behind her.

"This was your brother's?" Abraham said.

Of course he knew about you.

"All right," he said, "all right." He placed his hand upon my head, warming me there. "Sometimes, when a hole has been torn inside of us, a Thing can fill that hole."

Nora stepped forward boldly. "But you said that if we Thing—"

"Am I the authority?" Abraham said. "Any more than you or Saskia or anyone else living on this land? Saskia teaches us something today." He put his hand out, asking permission. With anyone else I would have refused, but I let the bunny leave my hands.

Abraham handled him gently, as if he was a real, orphaned animal. He scratched behind Topsy's ears. He stroked his nose. He smiled. "This belongs to Saskia," he told Nora.

"But no one can own—"

"There are exceptions to every rule. This bunny is hers, because this bunny was Will's"—my mouth grew dry—"and that means no one may take it from her. Do you understand?"

Nora scowled, but she nodded. Xavier, I noticed, was nodding, too, looking more than a little alarmed.

Abraham lifted the bunny up to his own face then, and whispered something into Topsy's long, dangly ear. Then, slowly, carefully, he turned the bunny back to me. Somewhere downhill, a chorus of Homesteaders was singing.

It was then that Abraham began to glow.

I know. I know he wasn't really glowing. But he seemed to be.

That's what I want to explain. It was not the first time I'd seen a glow like this; I recognized it because it was a trick I'd seen you perform. You'd cackle at a fart joke, or stand on one leg after begging me to watch, or hang upside down from the monkey bars—and you'd suddenly light up from within. It wasn't a magic trick made only by you. I knew it came, at least a little, from inside me, too; the bliss of your you-ness and my me-ness meeting in the air together, in a place of delight that some people call Love.

But how could I love Abraham? I didn't even know him. I couldn't have been brainwashed; I'd only just arrived. I was unsure and scared and truly, I'd been hoping, as much as Xavier had, for a fancy hotel with white porches overlooking the sea—and yet, I can't deny it, Abraham glowed.

21

On the other side of the bedroom door, Xavier clears his voice. Good. He's nervous. "Hey, I brought someone. I know, I know, you hate visitors, but I think you won't mind."

"Saskia?" The voice is strong and familiar. "Can we talk, love?"

I want to cry that it's too much, that I can't, I can't, but the tears have come to choke me.

22

It was silly to have made such a big deal out of a stuffed animal. The thought of Abraham's attention made me grin even as Nora darted up the path to the Main Lodge, and Abraham strode past the chicken coop to the goat enclosure, where Jim shoveled manure. Xavier moved down the path. I slipped the bunny into the waistband of my jeans, pulling my T-shirt over him. Probably Philip had packed him for me, thinking he was doing right. Or maybe Jane still offered surprises.

Down the path, the singing was loud. "I'll sing you seven, oh."

"Green grow the rushes, oh! What is your seven, oh?"

Now that we were close, we could make out the particulars of who was singing and when. "Seven for the seven stars in the sky," was warbled by a man's voice, alone.

"Six for the six proud walkers, five for the symbols at your door, four for the changing seasons"—but that single tenor was then joined by a group of voices sailing together up to the summer sky—"three, three, the sacred tree." The song hovered, for a moment, at a contented rest in its middle. Then, together, the voices flowed back toward the end of the chorus: "Two, two, the lily-white boys, clothèd all in green, oh, one is one and all in love and evermore shall be so."

The original voice began again, with the same descending melody, all by himself: "I'll sing you eight, oh," and once again, the rest met him in the air, "Green grow the rushes, oh! What is your eight, oh?"

Xavier and I came upon a greenhouse with a large garden set along its length. It was the gardeners who made up the chorus, led by old Amos, his singing voice surprisingly vigorous. They were busy on their knees, hands deep in the earth. Singing seemed to focus their agricultural tasks, none of which my city mind could name.

Ben was there, too, crouched on his hands and knees beside one of the men with whom Xavier had dined the night before. Ben was working on a hose that ran up to a barrel. I pretended not to notice him, but I couldn't shake Sarah's odd description of me, nor how cold he'd been at its mention. I blushed, knowing I'd have to face what he thought of me all over again. His lips mumbled along to the lyrics—"Three, three, the sacred tree"—just as they had at dinner, as though the music was medicine he might as well just take.

I had thought him ugly the night before, with his big head and pug nose. He had recoiled from me, so why did that make me want to go to him now? Sure enough, he frowned when he noticed me. But he came forward, and I flushed with a tentative hope until I saw he was coming for Xavier. "Can you help?"

"We're looking for our suitcases," I said.

"I'm no good at gardening," Xavier said.

Ben scratched his forehead, leaving a slice of dirt behind. "You're from the city, so pardon me for asking, but how do you know?"

I thought for sure that Xavier would hate him, too, now, but he leaned forward, ever so slightly.

"What about finding Philip?" I said. But Xavier was already stepping away. A few of the gardeners lifted their eyes as he left me. He was punishing me for not caring about our bags, and for being weird about Topsy, and for priding under Abraham's attention. I went back to the trail without him.

Down the incline, nearer the water, there were nine more cabins. The smell of fresh sawdust lifted on the wind. On one of the roofs, two men in overalls hammered shingles. One of them was dressed old-fashioned: Sarah's husband, Ben and Nora's father. Ephraim, I think I'd heard him called. Ephraim drove in those nails with determination. I thought to ask if he'd seen Philip, but there was something in the unflinching power of his arms that meant "do not disturb."

White pines scraped the sky. The ground was slippery with their discarded, golden needles. Some of the cabins had porches with rotten floorboards, but the front window of one offered a surprise—a tightly made bed beside a bouquet of wildflowers.

Wind ruffled the leaves and trees and ground cover relentlessly. I saw, now, that there was as much movement as in the city, only here it wasn't cabs and bikes and buses; this was a living thrum in a language I didn't yet speak. Birds with yellow bellies darted from branch to branch, worrying the bark, their euphoria in the breeze contagious. Could they smell life in the air? Did birds even smell? Or did they have some other, special bird sense that meant they could commune with light and wind?

I made my way toward the sloshing lake. Some days, it would be still as glass, and others the wind-tossed waves would bring to mind the ocean, but that day, the first day, the lake moved constantly and yet showed no roughness.

A chipmunk darted before me, lobbing off into the woods at my right. I caught a movement behind one of the pine trunks. Whoever was there was quick. I stood still. I thought of you: Topsy in my waistband, your name on Abraham's tongue, and the feather, that feather just like yours, that he had plucked from the air. I waited, leaning left and right to find the culprit—really, what I wanted was to find you, even though it was impossible—but nothing was revealed. I pulled myself along. I made my way the last few steps to the lakefront. I stood on a small, rocky peninsula, water lapping on three sides.

The lake was bigger than I'd imagined, stretching beyond the bounds of what I could see. On the opposite shore, at least a quarter mile away, lay a smattering of cabins, with white porches and long docks. Endless evergreens stood guard. In the center of the lake was an island topped in green bushes, close enough for a strong swimmer to reach on their own. I wondered what I'd look like from out there.

Home's shoreline was much the same as what I saw on the other side: trees and the small cabins I'd passed dusting the waterfront. A pair of ducks paddled in and out of a cove to my right. Back to my left, a gray, weathered dock stuck into the water. Abraham was standing on it. I shrunk back into the shadow of the trees. The Black woman I'd noticed the day before stepped forward along the shore. She had close-cropped hair. Her arms gestured as she spoke. She leaned toward him, offering a private word, although there was no one else near. Abraham closed his eyes, taking in whatever she had said. He opened his mouth to speak. She held up a hand to silence him, but that only made his need spill more freely toward her.

"You know how to play Spit?" The voice, a girl's, came from behind me. I almost fell into the drink.

It was the girl I'd seen at dinner. Our eyes stood at the same height, but that was the only trait we shared. Her Afro was an exuberant corona; her breasts large and high; her legs pouring out from spectacular blue jean cutoffs. She was substance and I was air.

"The card game?"

Apparently my half nod was satisfactory. "How old are you?" she said.

"Thirteen."

"Me too." She pointed back toward the dock, where Abraham and the woman were still locked in conversation. "That's my mother, Gabby. She's in charge."

"I thought Abraham was in charge."

"Abraham's in charge of spiritual matters. Gabby decides where we shit and who sleeps where. More important. They're probably talking about you."

Gabby reminded me of a marble; fast and efficient. It was hard to imagine her kissing Abraham, but only people who kissed each other—or had kissed each other once upon a time—spoke as intimately as they were. They reached some kind of agreement. Gabby turned and walked back into the woods. Abraham trailed after her.

"I'm Issy." The girl had waited for me to turn back around. Her smile was a disco ball.

"I'm looking for our suitcases."

"I think Nora destroyed them. Nora the Destroya." From up the hill came the clang of a bell. Issy made her way to the path, then turned. "But I'll help you look after lunch, if you play Spit. Come on."

23

*K*nocking. Knocking. Another whisper, one that rises to full voice when she declares: "We don't know what she's doing in there."

"Give her a chance to come out."

"Xavier, we tried it your way." The knocking becomes banging, wallop wallop, and the door shudders, again again, and then there's a splintering racket and Mother's trusty brass latch flings across the floor in a tinny cry and the door stands open, and Issy stands where the door once was.

24

*I*ssy cleared her plate before I managed one bite. I didn't like hummus; she gladly took my share. So it went with the curried cabbage, and the sautéed onions and dandelion greens. Across the room, at the table of gardeners, Ben and Xavier were locked in conversation.

Issy hadn't been born at Home, but it was the only home she could remember. The story went that Gabby—whom Issy called by name—was holding Issy on her lap on the T, "without a friend in the universe or a penny to her life," when Abraham walked up and handed her a roast beef sandwich. "She didn't know if he was one of those white hippies with a Jesus complex. She refused to eat the sandwich in case it was spread with roofies, but then he sat down next to her and asked about her dreams—not the dreams you have at night, but her dreams for me, and for our life together—and she says it just hit her in the heart, you know? No one had asked her what she wanted in so fucking long and she aspired to so much"—Issy pointed to the glistening pile of coleslaw on my plate—"you going to eat that?" I shook my head. She swallowed it in a few bites, then tore a second piece off the boule at the center of the table and ripped it in half, handing the larger piece to me.

The bread was still warm. My mouth watered. The smell was

yeasty and sour, but as I put it to my lips, I thought of Daddy on the edge of your bed, telling us of Persephone and the six pomegranate seeds she ate in the land of the dead, which trapped her there for half the year. Home had shown me glimmers of the same kind of enchantment, and I wondered with amusement, as I bit, if this bread held the same trickery. But I soon forgot; the first morsel landed on my tongue and filled my nostrils with the alchemy of a newly baked loaf. You loved bread with a slab of butter so thick that it made your lips greasy, and now I knew why; I couldn't get the bread in fast enough. I hadn't gobbled down anything in so long—but here, now, with Topsy hidden at my side, it was impossible not to. My stomach rumbled. I took another bite. I couldn't remember the last time I'd loved being filled up.

"So good, right?" Issy said. "Sarah makes it. She's, like, the queen of bread. She'll teach you, if you want."

"Really?"

Issy cackled at my full-mouthed enthusiasm. "The ladies are going to love you. Bread with Sarah. Foraging with Marta."

"Marta—is that the old lady you came in with last night? The one who put the plant in Abraham's glass?"

"Don't call her old to her face—she'll kill you." Issy was joking, but she lowered her voice as she said this.

"Where is she?"

"Oh, she's not a Homesteader. She just comes by, you know?"

I didn't, but I didn't know how long I'd have Issy's attention, and I had to know about Abraham. "On the T, when you were little—is that when your mom and Abraham got together?"

"Yeah, that's when Gabby and Abraham started making plans. They're peas in a pod. He's an heir. You know what that is?"

"Like, he inherited something?"

"Exactly. His father died so he got his money and was looking to invest it in something that stood against every single thing that old devil stood for, and he and Gabby were talking a lot about intentionality, you know? And, of course, Unthinging, and one day she said, 'Hey, Abraham, how about you put your money where your mouth is?' and he found this place for cheap, with the buildings and the pots and pans and canoes and everything, and he just plunked down cash money and bought it."

Jim wandered up to Sarah and asked for more food. Teresa waved from the far end of the Main Lodge to let Sarah know it was meant for her, but Sarah eyed Jim before nodding. When she turned into the kitchen, he stuck out his tongue at the back of her head.

Issy prattled on. "First it was just Gabby and me and Abraham. I barely remember it. But Gabby says this place was a wreck. The lodge was packed with garbage and spiders and broken furniture. But also, you know, they found a lot to work with—one person's trash is another's treasure—and little by little they figured out how to repair first one cabin, then another. And they learned to grow things. Well, Gabby did. Then Amos showed up. He's old and grumpy but he's a real horticulturalist with a degree and—"

"Isn't he Abraham's dad?"

Issy cracked up. "I told you, Abraham's dad is dead as a doornail." She pressed on. "Ephraim is the carpenter, but don't bug him while he's working. Sarah runs the kitchen and she loves help, so watch out coming in here unless you don't have something better to do. Jim and Teresa are in charge of the goats and the chickens, but she also helps with all the stuff the men do, and honestly, Jim's kind of useless. I mean, he's good if you have a job you can give him, but he isn't exactly a self-starter. Gabby oversees all the other stuff, like repairing chimneys and digging latrines. She got tips from the guy at the survivalist shop in New Hampshire, although I hope to Goddess she never screwed him. He smells like fish guts and—"

"So Abraham's like your stepdad?"

She looked at me like I had three heads. "I don't have a father."

"But he and Gabby . . . ?"

Issy giggled. "Gabby is Unthinged from the patriarchy. And Abraham doesn't engage in physical validation as a pathway to happiness. He says sexual attachment is the basest form of human need, even if it's sometimes unavoidable."

I didn't know if I should feel relieved. I definitely felt confused. "So that's what the Homesteaders believe? No"—I lowered my voice, even though this was the kind of place you didn't have to— "sex?"

"Home is where we discover our Unthinged selves." Issy slowed down, as if she was talking to a little kid. "I'm not a sexual being yet, even though I've started menstruating. When I'm grown, maybe sexuality will be a Thing for me, or maybe it'll just be a form of Unthinged self-expression. Whether I should engage in it or not will depend on whether it Unthings me."

Jim's laugh cut through the noise. Amos was whittling again. Nora ran a pile of dirty dishes into the kitchen. The room was hotter and louder by the second, rattling with the clatter of humans, and Issy was throwing around terms I didn't understand. "Gabby and Abraham and I woke Home up. Then word spread across the Thinged World. These people heard its call. Just like Philip heard its call. More people started showing up, like you showed up, sometimes in families, sometimes alone. We're all learning, every day, to be Unthinged."

"But what does that mean—being Unthinged?"

"Well, it means feeding ourselves, which is a lot of work. Planting, watering, weeding, picking, milking, shit-shoveling, egg-hunting, food prep, cooking, washing up."

"So, then, why doesn't Sarah want Marta teaching you to

forage? Isn't that that the whole point of foraging—feeding your-self?"

Issy lifted her eyebrows, impressed I'd picked up on this detail. She screwed up her mouth as she tried to explain it. "It's like, Sarah thinks we should use our hands. All the time. Fold the dough. Cut the carrots. Stir the soup. And that's good. It gets the job done. It Unthings us, the act of that work. But Marta says we should use our minds. She told me once that when a girl is clever, she must use her brain like a muscle or she'll go crazy. I'm not smart like that, though."

"You're smart, Issy."

"Not the way Marta means. I get the names of plants all mixed up. Honestly, it's pretty boring going out with her. I mean, you should definitely try it. You've been to school and stuff. You prob-ably already speak Greek and Latin." Issy gazed out the window. "It's like . . . it's like, Sarah's teaching us how to live here forever, with this kitchen and the same beans, until we're old. And"—here she whispered, as if this was something dangerous—"Marta wants us to go back into the world."

25

"I had to make sure you weren't hurting yourself." Issy is blurry from the humiliating wash of tears. "Can I come in?"

I wish I could say yes. I wish I could say anything.

She lifts one foot over the threshold.

"I don't think you should do that," Xavier mutters.

"Will you please go do something useful? Elsewhere?"

Xavier's hand swipes back that hair. But he listens. His footsteps trail down the stairs. The light dazzles my old friend as she becomes just for me.

26

Abraham and Gabby and Philip came into the Main Lodge (Abraham, unavoidable as the sun; Gabby, sharp and careful; Philip with an unfamiliar expression that kept him far away). Sarah thunked down her wooden spoon; Nora shot out of the kitchen and onto Ephraim's lap; Ephraim fed his daughter a bite of cole-slaw; Teresa turned away from a debate with Jim; Jim rubbed Teresa's shoulders while Tomas stuck his hand down her shirt; Issy sat up under her mother's eye; Xavier watched his father; and Ben watched Xavier watching, and then turned to watch, too.

"Good people!" Abraham called.

The Homesteaders spoke as one: "We listen."

"You've met the newcomers." Abraham gestured first to Philip (there was definitely something different about Philip; when I tried to catch his eye, he pretended not to notice). Next, Abraham's long arm swept to Xavier, who raised his hand in a shy wave. Then he found me. I could hardly bear those soft brown eyes, the twitch of his smile.

"Philip is a painter. He learned of us from our ambassadors in New York, where he was living at the time"—what a funny turn of phrase, as though yesterday was the distant past—"and he read my manifesto and they told him of this place, and I guess he liked the sound of what we're up to!"

The Homesteaders clapped.

"We talk of Unthinging." There were nods of assent. "We talk a lot about Unthinging." Laughter. "Unthing. Unthing. Unthing. Unthing Yourself! We do our best to practice this. Sometimes we succeed. And we've learned"—now Abraham turned to Gabby, who was still at his other elbow—"that sometimes Unthinging can look a lot like Thinging." Gabby nodded once, authoritatively. "We want to get off the grid. We all know that's the only way we will Unthing ourselves of the trappings of the Thinged World. But to unburden ourselves will require machines that harness sun power and wind power. This great task of making our own oasis requires equipment, and unfortunately, equipment costs money."

"Equipment"—Gabby chimed in with a steady voice—"is a Thing. Acquiring it requires us to make tough decisions. It means considering choosing Things in the short run for the sake of being Unthinged in the long run. Is eventual Unthinging worth Thinging?" She gave Abraham a significant glance. He grinned like a child who'd been caught with his hand in the cookie jar. "We disagree on this point." She turned back to the group. "But we are only two voices. We need to know what you believe."

"Philip here"—Abraham clapped Xavier's father on the back—"has offered us a good deal of money. He believes that we must Unthing ourselves. He likes the sound of getting off the grid. This giving is an act of Unthinging for his sake, too. We can help him with this Unthinging. But. This money Philip offers is tainted—by oil and by blood, by the military industrial complex. By patriarchy, and rape, and misogyny. By genocide. By racism. By the destruction of our planet. Using this money is not something we'll do lightly. But Gabby and I believe it is something we must consider."

"No," Amos said. The old man was whittling again, the owl almost finished. He didn't look up. "We won't take that money."

"Speak for yourself," Jim said.

"There is no self," Amos grumbled.

"Exactly. We decide things together."

Amos's eyes found Philip. "We won't take that money."

Jim's hairy hand slapped the table. "That's bullshit." He turned to the rest of the room. "The old man doesn't say what we do. No one does. Not even fucking Abraham."

Ephraim stood. "Abraham isn't finished." Jim's eyes shot to the ground. Amos went back to his owl.

Abraham nodded to Ephraim, who sat. "Think about this. Talk about this. Question it, as Gabby and I are. Help Philip here under-stand why we can't accept his generous offer without considering the consequences"—Abraham's mouth curled into a wry smile—"because he thinks I'm being a stubborn ass."

A roar of laughter swept the room, followed by a round of clap-ping. Issy leaned forward, and whispered, "You've been keeping secrets."

I was nauseous. Why was New York no longer our home? Why hadn't Philip told us of his plan to bring us here? Had Philip really decided to give money to these strangers? Did Jane know about this? What was the reason for the giddiness I felt when Abraham looked at me?

Issy rose to clear her plate. I grabbed her, pressing into the flesh of her forearm. "What is Unthinging?" My voice surprised me with its force.

A look of pity crossed her face. The huddle of her breath was steady as she lowered herself to me. "Your suitcase—the one Nora took, with your special things—your favorite sweatshirt, your jour-nal, whatever? None of it matters. Think about it. You're born without a single Thing but your own body. But the world you grew up in—what we call the Thinged World—taught you to believe you need Things, because the system that operates it—capitalism—can only sustain itself as long as you buy more, get more. We're all going to die, though. None of us is taking a Thing with us. And Things are going to kill us, at the rate we're going. Here at Home we Unthing before our mortal endings. It's the only way we'll save the planet, but that's not the only reason. Abraham says when we leave the lie of accumulation back out in the Thinged World, we get to live as we were meant to. Free."

Issy thumbed a fat tear off my cheek. She assumed that I was crying because Unthinging frightened me. But really, it was a relief to hear someone say what I'd understood since the very moment you left.

27

*T*he house sighs around Isobel. We love her solid truth: the tizzy of her hair as she moves into the room, the thump of her feet, the impressive ridge of her breasts (she's discovered what Grandmother would call a brassiere), her plum-shaped cheekbones, and her wide, open palms, which she uses to coax the books back into their stacks, like wayward lambs. Xavier would simply get them straightened but Issy glances at their spines.

Or maybe she's noticing how Thinged I've become. I feel the gentle tug of shame. I'm no better than a scrub jay—genus, *Aphelocoma*—caching junk. But Issy laughs and says, "You read a lot of romance novels."

"There are classics, too."

She sits at the bottom of the bed. "So, what's all this nonsense?" She doesn't mean the books. The woman before me resembles the Issy I once knew—eyelashes curling up, lips like pillows—but of course she's different. Seventeen years have passed since that evening in the East Village, when she asked how I was doing and I told her I was happy as a clam—which wasn't a lie, because who can say if clams are ever happy? Her ample smile lurks in the shadows of her older face, but as she studies me, it stays shy.

28

What a virtue I found it, to be moving toward the lightness of Unthinging. My body had started down that path on its own, but I'd been waiting for philosophy to justify it. Home, with its scarlet dawns and stockpiling chipmunks, with its soaring hawks and pine needles pitter-pattering down like rain, was constantly shedding its former self in place of the present and future; the perfect expression of Abraham's beliefs. No wonder I wanted him to see me: he noticed everything that mattered. Over morning congee, dressed with goat's milk and maple syrup, he reminded us that we know how to Unthing the moment we are born: that to breathe, that to bleed, that to shit is to Unthing. The struggle comes after, as we are taught to accumulate.

"The trick," he said, his stare long—sometimes it seemed as though he didn't need to blink—"is to get back in touch with your instincts and shut out what the Thinged World teaches. And lest you think I am above this same hard work, let me say it out loud—I, too, am weak." He caught Gabby's eye across the long lodge. She nodded, as though accepting an apology. "Every day, we go back to the beginning. Every day, we try again. With every step my feet take across the earth, I repeat: 'Unthing Yourself.' In this simple action, with every step, I start to make it so.

"But let me ask you this: when is a Thing not a Thing?"

There was a murmur of confusion.

"Perhaps it's better to ask: when is a Thing not only a Thing? When does it not being only a Thing mean it sails above our rules of Thinging and Unthinging?" He lifted his hand toward me. Everyone looked. "Show them."

I undid the bunny from inside my waistband, where I'd been tucking him every morning since he'd been rescued from Nora. I held Topsy up in a flush of embarrassment—Ben was frowning at the edge of my vision—but then I found Abraham again. His gaze steadied me. The bunny's head listed to the right.

"All this time, I've believed in two categories: Things and not. But see that little bunny there? That little bunny is not a Thing. It is not a bit of cloth and stuffing, or not just a bit of cloth and stuffing. It is Love. It is where Saskia's brother William's love resides." I held my chin up. Philip was watching, tears brimming in his eyes. But I couldn't tell if he'd packed Topsy.

"I've been definitive in the lines I draw. We want to Unthing ourselves, and it is right to do so. But certain Things may be more important than others. Perhaps it is right to do away with the Things that are not filled with Love, and keep the Things that are. Out loud, in front of everyone, I want to thank Saskia for teaching us that."

Whispers filled the room. Ben's arms were crossed and he was looking out the window. Why did he hate me?

Abraham laughed at the effect of his speech. "I didn't say everyone go to Kmart! Sarah's sourdough starter—is that a Thing?" At the edge of the kitchen, Sarah blushed. Ephraim lifted his head as if he might have to defend her.

"That's food," Amos said. He was whittling a fox now. "Doesn't count."

"Your rake, Amos? Ephraim's hammer."

"Tools."

"Philip's paintings?"

Philip held up his hands, in a gesture of count me out.

"Philip's money?"

Amos looked up, and so did Jim, and Gabby and Ephraim both moved to the edge of their seats. Abraham put up his hands to stop them before they started. "Philip's money, if used by us, will bring more Love into this world, there's no doubt in my mind. It will allow us to share what we know with the Thinged World. But that money is a Thing borne of many terrible Things—many more terrible Things than that bunny right there in Saskia's hands—and yet what that money could afford us to give back out into the world . . . ? That feels like Love to me."

"I've got weeding," said Amos, before Jim could open his mouth. Breakfast had lingered. So we scattered to our work.

29

I see myself through Issy's eyes: a cowering pile.

"Are you mute?"

No. But I tell her with a shaken head.

"Then what the hell's wrong?"

"It's Xavier's fault." I sound like a whiny teenager.

"I thought you and Xavier were besties." Do I detect a note of envy?

"He says Abraham is back."

"And you don't like that?"

"Do you like that?"

"Do I like that he said it? Or do I like that he thinks Abraham is back?" Her graceful neck swivels to the window. "If I'm being honest, I never thought Abraham was dead to begin with."

"But his body in the—"

"With Gabby, I knew she was dead. I couldn't hear her anymore." Her hand moves to her heart. Her eyes come back to find me. "Didn't you know, with your brother?"

Mother and Daddy, wrestling in that tight spot between the parlor and the foyer, the way she had him around the neck, the way he growled as he tried to throw her off, and how, in that moment, I realized I didn't have to stand there and wait for whatever was going to happen to happen to me.

Issy pats her chest. "If you listen, you'll hear Abraham still inside you, telling you what to believe. He's alive, Saskia. There's no way we got off that easy."

30

*S*omething private swelled as the summer grew from June into July, something I couldn't mention, even to Issy. It had begun the moment Abraham plucked that feather up on the day we arrived. I was a rational girl; I knew it was absolutely appalling to believe that it was you who'd offered up that feather from the beyond, telling me in your otherworldly way that Home was my true home, that on this land, I would be safe—but it was hard not to entertain the thought. Then had come the bit with Topsy, someone slipping him into my bag when all along I thought I'd left him in New York, and Abraham's permission to Thing him as my own, and Abraham's glow.

I startled a cardinal; it flew so close that its wing brushed a kiss onto my cheek. How could it not be a kiss from you? The quiet of your pucker, the gamey smell of your scalp, the wind of your breath—all those tiny bits of you came to find me together in a single red-winged flash.

Issy and I canoed out to Blueberry Island and played six rounds of Spit with her bent, dirty cards. We filled a metal pail, the blueberries falling off the bush by the handful. Back on shore, something invisible bumped the pail's bottom, spilling the fruit across the ground. Tomas and Nora were upon it at once, giddy thieves.

Your giggle burbled through my ears on a gust of wind, but when I turned to catch you, you were gone.

On a warm night, symphonic with peepers, I sat out on the porch of the Main Lodge. The lakeside bonfire was roaring. There was laughter as Amos wove a Puritan tale of a punished whore and a penny-pinching gentleman. I had not taken a bite of bread, not yet—I wanted to savor the thought of it before I put it in my mouth. I set it down on the armrest of the Adirondack chair when Issy tried to tempt me into cards. I said I'd come soon, then watched the night swallow her. I picked up the bread. Cut into its crust was a surprise: the concise half-moon of your bite. The children were nowhere near—Nora was at the bonfire, and Tomas had been sound asleep in Teresa's arms for hours.

I was a reasonable girl, but the only reasonable explanation—unreasonable anywhere but the Unthinged World—was that you were making Home your home, too.

31

"So okay, what if Abraham is alive," I offer. "So what?" The hair on my arms and legs is at attention, but my voice is calm.

"Oh, I don't know, Saskia, maybe he could tell our families, and our bosses, and the police that we killed—"

"Shh." I'm upright now, my hands on her hot mouth. It's a reflex, like gagging on something putrid.

She waits for me to claim my hands. "You think if we don't talk about it, we can pretend it didn't happen?"

32

*S*arah kept the Mother in a paint bucket, covered with a piece of linen. She fed her every morning, and made a leaven every night, and early in the day, before the light lifted, she used the leaven to make bread. Sourdough consists of nothing but the Mother, salt, water, and flour, but it's also temperature and light and humidity. Sarah spoke the language of those ephemerals fluently, able to sense how warm the water should be on a given day, and whether less or more of it should be used than the day before, and how long, exactly, the rise would be. Everyone was game to devour the final product, but soon I discovered that having patience for the scale, and strong wrists, and not minding the Mother caking the hair on my forearms into a dry, wheaty crust, put me in rare company. Before long I was joining Sarah in the dawn kitchen, sticky with the scent of rising bread, which was how I discovered she was the one who did the drawings pinned around the room, of foxes and chickadees and rowboats. If I got there early enough, I'd find her alone with a cup of tea in that vast dark room, finishing up a sketch by the light of a candle. Once, I asked whether she'd seen that skunk in real life, and she stood and sputtered a question about the day's menu, and I knew I'd invaded something so private I wasn't even supposed to apologize.

We worked in silence, with swift attention. Teresa would drift

in around sunrise, to chop and dice and simmer. The Homesteaders would descend about an hour past that, which I liked to take
as my cue to leave. But before I skipped off, Sarah would press
a muffin or a hunk of sourdough into my hand, slathered with
golden honeycomb or a knob of beef tallow. These small offerings seemed like more than Mother had ever passed along, even
though she'd given me life itself.

I didn't mind the days starting early. Each one held a surprise:
a heart-shaped rock in my path; a harmony of birdsong playing
out the four beginning notes of the "ABCs." Now that I knew you
might be close, I was eager to collect evidence of your return.

That windy day, ferns roiled my ankles as I set down the hill. I
passed the chickens and goats, then the garden. It was still breakfast, but I'd already spent hours inside Sarah's tasks. I noticed
Ben coming up the path; something about the sun dappling the maple branches and the muffin in my pocket swelled me with hope.
I was thinking of Sarah's newest drawing, of a moose lifting one
foot as it looked across a clearing, how even in the sketch, the animal looked more real than poor, decapitated Grimm hanging on
the wall. Before Ben got too close, I said, "Your mom's a really
good artist."

He startled. He hadn't seen me. He stepped off the path to let
me pass. As I neared, I caught the fragrance of the goat's milk soap
he'd used to wash up, and the salt of his sweat persisting through,
and I couldn't help turn to meet his eye. His look of curiosity,
and pleasure, surprised me. A thread pulled so tautly between
us that I knew if could pluck it, it would make a beautiful sound.
But then he looked away. He turned uphill, the wall of his back
reminding me of his father—austerity, resolve.

I went on. It was nothing more than the rush of being seen, I
told myself. We'd just gotten swept up in the opportunity that the
whole Unthinged World, wind-tossed, seemed to be celebrating

on that new day. "Unthing Yourself," I chanted with every footstep, just like Abraham. The path took its familiar turn downhill. Then Marta, the old woman who was not a Homesteader, stepped out from the forest, a few dozen yards ahead of me. Her attention was turned away, back into the trees. I could go on as I had with Ben, could say something free and easy about foraging, but I ducked behind a birch instead.

Small and wiry, she wore the same L.L. Bean backpack as she had that first day, one of the frayed straps repaired with dental floss. She was speaking to someone behind her. Perhaps chiding was a better word; the timbre of her voice was quiet, but from the vehement wag of her finger, I could tell she wasn't holding back.

I leaned forward for a glimpse of whomever she was chastising, resting my cheek against the shiny silver bark. Her hand gestures were absolutes, slicing the air. From the woods behind her came Abraham. I'd never seen him lose his cool, not even on the dock with Gabby, but he was angry. They squared off, blocking the path. Even far away, I could see that Marta owned him; a woman nearly half his size and twice his age.

The wind drifted her voice my way—"have no right, blocking her chance to make this place what you've promised, just because"—then cut away. Who did she think she was, chastising him? And not even a Homesteader. Someone called out from the water—Ephraim, maybe. Abraham raised a hand in greeting, his whole being becoming sure in an instant.

I watched Marta watch him change. She shook her head. Her sweater glinted white as she picked her way into the wooded undergrowth without him.

His shoulders slumped. He ran his hand through his hair. He lifted his eyes to the sky and closed them again, and breathed out and then in. I darted onto the path a few yards back, then walked toward him with an impassive face.

He heard my footsteps. He turned uphill and gave me the same enthusiastic wave he'd offered Ephraim. "No breakfast for you?"

I held up the blueberry muffin Sarah had pulled from the oven before I ducked out the door. Close up, he smelled of turpentine, and unwashed armpits, and something deeper: sleep, or dirt. Not sex, but hidden in the way that sex is. Seeing him locked in an argument had churned something up. I felt that same urge to kiss him that I'd known with Xavier; to get as close to eating him as I could. I blushed when his warm hand came to rest on my shoulder.

"You're not sad anymore." I realized that he was right. I wasn't happy—I would never be happy—but I was certainly no longer sad, or at least no longer only sad. The ache for you had weaned into something else, now that you and I were both making Home ours. I felt for Topsy at my waistband and squeezed his pelt.

"I'm glad of this, but Saskia, we cannot find happiness while living someone else's life. That's Thinging." He stepped forward and touched me again, this time on both shoulders. "You are remarkable, Saskia. You are enough. The work in your hands should be remarkable. It should be enough."

"I help Sarah in the kitchen." This would please him, surely.

"That's as it should be." He put his hand over his heart. "But you must find your own path. Your own calling. I wish for it so."

He reached his right hand behind his back, into the open canvas bag hanging there. He pulled out a small axe—a hatchet. Its worn wooden handle was the length of one of your shins. He held it out between us—the wedge of the blade in his palm, the smoothed grip toward me; an invitation. The hatchet was the opposite of Topsy; heavy and built to work. I shivered my finger along the blade, dark and old, flinty in spots. It wasn't half as sharp as I thought.

33

"We killed someone." Issy leans toward me, her voice steady, as though we are discussing the weather. "We killed someone we loved. Does that make it worse? It feels that way. It shouldn't. It should be bad enough to have simply killed someone."

She cannot still her hands. "We were children. Does that make it better? There were five of us. Does that make it worse? Five people planned and carried out a murder, together, and no one thought to stop it. When we got away with it, we thought that was a good thing. But I think that's the worst part of all. And now someone knows."

She looks around at all of Mother's pink: the sashes on the curtains, the rosebuds on the chair. She says, "I know, with your history, with your father and all that—I know there must be part of you that hoped keeping things quiet, no trial, no press, just knowing what we did and having to live with it, was better for everyone involved. But I don't think it's better. I don't feel better. Do you?"

34

In the woods, alone, I looked for you, for surely you would become solid at some point; you wouldn't always only be kisses of wind or feathers in the air. I pretended I was out there to do useful things with the hatchet. I tried my hand at hacking down rotting trees, until one I felled narrowly missed knocking Ephraim off the roof of a cabin. I tried splitting firewood, but Amos chided me: "Use the maul, girl; a hatchet's not built for that."

Behind the Main Lodge, there were fewer cabins, which meant fewer people to distract from our reunion. I found your footprints there. They had to be yours; I recognized your extra-long second toe. A blond tuft of your hair fluffed from the side of a bird's nest, although I couldn't climb high enough to touch it. One deep dusk, Tomas had pointed to the stone wall that cut across the land and told me there was a secret friend who hid behind it and came out when the sky was "like this, dark and light together" to play hide-and-seek. You. I was sure of it: you, you, you.

There was a dead tree out there, too, or rather, a magnificent mountain of what had once been a tree, the top of which had fallen off and was now rotting into the forest floor. The remaining trunk had become a vertical toothpick of rotting wood. I'd taken to leaving you a bite of my crusts between two of its roots where they met the ground. That day, the most recent offering was just where I'd left it. There'd been not one hint of you, not even a rustle in my hair. I was a little angry, to tell the truth, because I was being so patient, and what I wanted was so simple. Why not just show yourself, if you were close?

The hatchet was heavy. I let it fall, out of frustration, to the ground. This was stupid—I could have cut off my own toes. I must have flung it with more vehemence than I realized, because it had flipped in just the right way as to stick into a root. And I thought—aha—I could learn to throw this thing. Abraham had said my work should be remarkable; some part of me believed, hoped, imagined that I would discover I was gifted at hatchet throwing on the first try. The tool would sail from my open hands, making its own wind as it flipped away from me, and sink its tooth into the hungry wood.

I stepped back twenty paces. Too far. I stepped forward five. That seemed doable. How hard could it be?

It took forty-five throws for the blade to even kiss the wood, and twenty-five more to get it to stick in place, at the bottom of the trunk.

"Persistence pays off."

I turned, startled, to discover Marta standing a few feet behind me. I'd heard no sign of her approach, not even over the leaf-layered forest floor. Her look of gloom irritated me, as though my triumph was something to mourn. I strode to the angled marriage of blade and wood, and pulled the hatchet out. "I saw you fighting with Abraham," I said.

"I don't like it when he acts imperial." She watched me for a minute, as though she was trying to find something out. "I'm Marta. And you're Saskia." She pointed to the dead tree. "And that's *Fagus grandifolia*, otherwise known as the American beech—from the Latin *fagus*, meaning beech, *grandis*, large, and *folium*, leaf. Shade-tolerant, and usually a sign that the forest is in the last stage of ecological succession. You'd say the tree is dead, right?"

"Yeah."

"You're slightly correct. This particular one is likely the victim of beech bark disease, which occurs when *Cryptococcus fagisuga*, commonly known as the beech scale insect, attacks the bark and creates a wound, which is then invaded by a fungus in the genus *Nectria*. But that's not the fun part."

"There's a fun part?"

She grinned, the sun coming out from behind a cloud. "As decay progresses, and the tree becomes a snag—that's the proper term when the crown has broken off—microorganisms move in. Fungi, insects, woodpeckers. Think of a snag as a hotel. As the tree 'dies,' really what it's doing is sustaining life, continuing the life of the forest all around it. In fact, as it goes from injury to humus, which, in the life of this beech was a relatively quick few years—some trees, maples, for example, can spend up to eighty years in decline—it sustains more life than it ever did when it was a single organism." A black-and-white bird flew overhead. Marta froze, so I did, too. The bird flitted onto the top of the snag and began to beat its beak against it. A hammering sound filled the woods. Marta whispered. "See? *Dryobates pubescens*, the downy woodpecker, picking up some grubs for lunch."

I wanted to pretend I didn't care about all those facts, and ignore that this strange little woman had somehow understood I'd been hungering after the names of things ever since Grandmother told me the Devil's Ramble wasn't filled with purple trees, but with Japanese maples. I looked down. There was a little hump in the pine needles at my feet. It was funny, that hump; there was nothing to explain why the needles would be domed there. I crouched over it. I moved the needles aside. A beetle scuttled out. An ant skittered across my thumb. Surely Marta knew their names, but I wouldn't ask. The undercurrent of Maine soil, damp and loamy, filled my nostrils, along with the darker, deeper dank of the rotting leaves. I could feel the woman's eyes on me as I dug into the earth.

Underneath the layers of earth lay a surprise. A dome of white, like something out of science fiction. But then I discovered that it was not an alien, not once I understood it. It was terrestrial: a mushroom.

Marta walked over. All her attention was on the mushroom now. Her face was cast in delight, her eyebrows pulled up, as though she was greeting a long-lost friend. A part of me wondered if, in naming what was around us, she had bewitched me into noticing something new. Like magic words.

Marta unzipped her backpack and pulled out a pocketknife. She flipped it open and held it out to me, as though I knew what to do next. I shook my head. It was much farther down to the ground than I thought; she reached her hand in under the leaves until it almost disappeared. She cut the stalk at the base and lifted the mushroom, so white it almost glowed, into the light.

"*Amanita bisporigera*," she said. The way she pronounced it sounded like a love poem. She used the knife as a pointer, listing off the parts of the plant as though I was familiar with the scientific terminology, which sounded vaguely pornographic: "annulus," a ring around the stalk; "volva," a cuplike shaft around its bottom.

"Should you eat it?" she asked, moving the mushroom toward my face. The first and only thing I knew about wild mushrooms was that you weren't supposed to eat them. She wiggled her eyebrows. She danced it back toward her own face. "Should I?"

It seemed as though she was really asking. She knew the name of the mushroom, didn't she? And its parts. She brought it to her lips.

I nodded.

She opened her mouth. Moved the mushroom closer. Then stopped the fruit a centimeter from her tongue. "One experiences a little tummy trouble. But the symptoms pass. By the time they get worse again, it's already too late. Your liver and kidneys are failing. You go into a coma. Then you die. All from this humble fungus, pushing her way up from the forest floor." She pulled the mushroom back out toward me, requiring my examination. "She has a more popular name: destroying angel. The amatoxins found in her and her sisters are responsible for almost all mushroom-related deaths." Yet she was looking at it like it was her friend. "I suppose I'd like a turn," she added.

I'd forgotten about the hatchet, but that's what she meant. She tossed the mushroom off into the forest, then held out that same hand. I gave her the tool, but I wondered how someone her age—not to mention size—could have any chance of making that hatchet stick. She ran her left hand, then her right, over the handle. She felt the head—first the blade, then the smack of it against her palm. I followed her back to the spot where I'd stood for my many attempts. She was so small beside me. She spread her legs apart. She lifted her right hand over her head and stepped with her left foot. The hatchet sailed through the air and made the sound I had wanted all along. The blade dangled from the trunk as though it had been embedded there for years.

Marta slung her backpack back over her shoulder and started to walk away.

"Wait."

She turned—not to look at me, but as though to say, fine, ask away. I had so many questions: how she knew so much about that mushroom and the trees and the birds, how someone so small and old could throw a hatchet like that, and why she'd snuck up on me,

and why she had fought with Abraham, and why she had said my
name so knowingly, and why she didn't live at Home. But none of
that came out.

Instead, she spoke. "Come visit me sometime." Then she
moved into the knot of the woods.

35

"If Abraham is alive, he can tell anyone"—Issy cuts herself off, then censors herself—"what we did." She looks at me with rare distaste. "Even if no one can prove it, even if we don't go to jail, it will change how every single person thinks of us. You obviously don't care, but I—"

"Since when do you care what people think of you?"

"Those of us with regular lives don't have a choice."

Issy's spent her adulthood bopping from California to Senegal to Mexico to Santa Fe, with only a hiking backpack and a pair of shoes to her name. She's neither a homeowner nor a taxpayer. She once walked twelve miles through an Alaskan snowstorm because she wasn't going to ride in the car of a man who yelled at an old woman about crossing the road. There's resolve in her voice, though. Something has changed.

"Don't you care if people find out you murdered someone?" she asks.

"You know I murdered someone. That's been pretty okay."

Issy sighs as though I am an impossible child.

"Anyway, why would Abraham tell anyone?" I know I'm grasping at straws. "He'd implicate himself."

"Who besides the five of us knows he made us do it? Really, Sask? Can you think of anyone?"

I'll never say, but I think of you. That word, "killed," let loose, has flayed me like a newly caught fish. Every time I think of it, I must, of course, remember you as well.

"Abraham's hands are clean," Issy says. "He made sure of that." Her eyes fill with tears, a cloudburst of grief, but she manages to keep them from spilling over. "You know what gets me the most? How I treated my own mother because of him. And she was the only sane one."

"But you had time with her," I say, trying to soothe her, "after Home. You found her, you made up for it. You had a whole life together."

"And then cancer ate her up. She said everyone gets a reckoning."

"You think Abraham is our reckoning?"

A screech pierces from the side yard, knifing up my spine. I find I'm already at the window, ready to discover something out of a medieval illustrated manuscript on the grounds. For now, it's sound alone, but its shadow cuts across the yard.

36

"Well, how much do you think he's giving away?" I slapped at a mosquito, from the family *Culicidae* (I'd looked up the name in one of the encyclopedias moldering in the Main Lodge). I was lying on the top bunk above Xavier. Most everyone was at the bonfire but we were whispering anyway; Philip's donation to the Homesteaders was a volatile topic, despite Abraham's insistence that it was something we should openly discuss. "Forty thousand dollars? Four thousand?"

"How am I supposed to know?" Xavier grumbled. "He told me it's his own damn business."

"Or do you think Ben was right?" Even saying that name made me nauseous. Since that day on the path, when our eyes met, he had avoided me more than ever. He made sure to get Xavier to himself, but if Xavier noticed, he didn't care. I steeled my voice. "Four hundred thousand dollars just seems like way too high for Philip to give away to virtual strangers." This was the figure Ben had told Xavier he'd overheard his parents discussing in the middle of the night. Like most of the women, Sarah thought Home should accept the money but Ephraim was undecided.

"Why do you care so much?" Xavier said.

I knew my voice sounded giddy and that this annoyed Xavier, and really, I was trying to temper it. But the Unthinged World was unlike any place I'd ever known; so full of possibility. Since that day with Marta in the woods, I wanted to know the name of every single thing that grew and breathed there, wanted to eat its fruits and bathe in its waters, and I didn't mind a bit that Philip's money would bind us closer. The closer we got to making Home our home, the closer I got to you.

But not everyone loved how readily we'd been welcomed. I'd passed the garden just the day before, and only after I'd gone by, remembered I'd forgotten to tell Issy where I was going. So I turned back, just in time to hear Amos tell Gabby that if money didn't have any sway in the Unthinged World, Philip and Xavier and I would still be sleeping in front of the Main Lodge's fireplace. At the sight of me, Gabby frowned, and Amos went back to weeding.

Our tidy cabin was in the collection of buildings Ephraim was fixing up, close to the lake. We were not supposed to call it "ours"—that was Thinging—but when the word accidentally tumbled off our tongues, no one but Amos seemed to care. From the open windows one could hear the slosh of the water down along the dock, and the cry of the djembe and the strains of a guitar carried down from the bonfire. We were lucky that the metal screens were intact; the mosquitos were ravenous.

"It's just so strange that Philip would give his money away like that," I said. "Don't you wonder why?" The knock of Xavier's elbow on the wall shivered by my ear.

The cabin had been subdivided with knotty sheets of plywood, giving the illusion of privacy. The small front area held a dusty armchair and a firewood box and a stone hearth that coughed up smoke. Philip slept in the back, on a mattress on the floor, with a bold family of mice for roommates. Xavier and I were in the middle "room," just a little bigger than the built-in bunk bed. Our belongings covered what little floor space we had, since being rescued from near the latrine. (Nora had been made to peel three hundred potatoes on the day Amos found the ransacked suitcases. But I couldn't help thinking there'd been an additional, private punishment, exacted behind closed doors. I recognized the weight of Ephraim's fist upon the breakfast table, and the wide-eyed skittering with which Nora backed away from it. When I told Xavier, he said good, she deserved a good wallop for stealing our luggage—a phrase for which I hated him.)

T-shirts and underpants and jeans we would have called dirty in our other life, we now wore day after day, since discovering that laundry involved hauling water from the lake, plunging our hands again and again into the cold bucket, and rasping goat's milk soap over the sodden fabric along the washboard—all while our knuckles turned raw. It was better to just rinse out your underpants when they started to smell.

Despite the laundry and latrine situation, I was glad to stay. But I couldn't help wonder what was in it for Philip. "Why do you think he likes it here so much?" In New York, his consumption was Dionysian: of butter and vodka, cheese fries and chocolate, pasta and cake, and plenty of illicit substances I wasn't allowed to see. Home was crawling with teetotalers, and what little there was to eat was green, fermented, and whole grained. Yet he rhapsodized about the purple dawn and the slate hue of the cloud cover. He'd driven to Portland for a roll of canvas and taken to painting small panels of color to replicate sky or water or earth.

"What does your mom say?" Xavier walked down to Jim-Bob's every Saturday for a phone call with Jane, but Ben had told Issy that for the past two weeks, Jane hadn't been there when Xavier called. Of course, he hadn't mentioned anything to me. He moaned from the bottom bunk.

"Dinner was kind of . . . wet tonight, huh?" I said. Xavier was not a fan of lentils. "Issy says you should keep a secret stash of junk food. That's what she'd do if she had the taste for it. She doesn't even know what Doritos taste like."

"Issy's a freak."

Fury streaked through me. "Ben's a freak."

Xavier's feet slapped the floor. Then his head was right there in the darkness beside mine. "Despite the fashion choices, which are not his, Ben is cool. He knows how to skin a rabbit."

I would never say out loud how cold Ben was, and cruel. I would never suffer the indignity of describing how he sat wherever I wasn't and frowned whenever I tried to make Issy laugh. He was using Xavier, turning him against me, and Xavier didn't even care. I would never say how disgusted I was by my desire to be liked by someone whose feet stunk terribly whenever he kicked his stupid boots off, or how humiliatingly nice it had been when he looked at me as he moved aside on the path. Instead I said, "I take that back. Ben's an asshole."

Xavier pulled on a sweatshirt. The stench of mildew hung in the room long after he went into the night.

37

*I*t's a child.

Black curly hair, bare feet, red T-shirt, a high shriek of laughter as it circles. Can I really smell it, all the way up here? Scalp, cheek, neck.

There's Issy, at my elbow. "Fuck naptime, I guess."

Maybe Xavier emailed a picture. It seemed so far away. All their lives do: the broken hearts; the mortgages; the jobs. What happens outside the gates is easy to ignore. So it was with this child: I believed I'd never lay eyes on it, so I allowed myself to forget. The child is the reason Issy cares what people think. Rather, Issy cares what the child thinks. She'll do whatever it takes to keep what we did a secret, so that the child never has to know.

Someone chases it into the light. Not Xavier; a woman. She darts quickly, threatening a tickle. The way she moves is familiar, and though she never wore her hair so short, I'd know her anywhere: the cinch of that waist. "You brought Cornelia?"

"Oh sweetie, it is all hands on deck time." Issy's eyes are on the kid. "He's pretty cute, huh?" The truth is, I'd already eat my own heart if his safety required it. Then Issy's smile blooms, broad and beautiful. She knew I could not resist; that's why she brought him along.

38

*T*hree days later, Abraham announced he would take Philip's money.

Two days after that, Philip announced we were going back to New York.

It didn't make sense, not now that he'd gotten what he wanted. I appealed to Xavier to talk to him. "Well, I do really miss my mom," Xavier said, choosing the side that wasn't mine. I wanted to scream that with Jane skipping his phone calls, he should understand, better than anyone, that we were better off at Home, safe from the disappointments of the Thinged World. Then I realized I was thinking like Mother, so bit my tongue, actually bit it, and it bled.

"I have to stay," I said as Philip pulled longyi after longyi off the clothesline. I couldn't tell him how close you were, that to leave you would be dying another death.

I followed him inside. "They're taking your money. Isn't that what you wanted?" It was hot in the cabin—our cabin—after weeks of August sun. "And you're painting such beautiful things here." I didn't want to weep, but perhaps that's what would do it. "Please, Philip, we can't leave now. Why now? When this finally feels like home?"

He was about to cry; I could see it in the quiver at the corner of his lip. But he went into his room and didn't look back. "I'm sorry, Saskia." He kicked closed the door.

Amos whittled an eagle beside the flagpole while I helped Philip pack the Lincoln. Issy watched from the step of the Main Lodge, her knuckles gripping the deck of cards. When our bags were in, she followed me onto the porch at the side of the lodge. The land and water unfurled away from us, a sunbaked promise of work and song and bread and birds. Nora and Tomas dashed by. Issy dealt.

Spit: five stacks in front of both players, and two piles—which start out empty—in the middle. Both players yell "spit," and, using only their right hands and the stacks in front of them, build up the piles in between them either up or down in numerical order. When one of the players runs out of cards, they slap the smaller pile. Then the whole thing starts again, until one of the players runs out of cards.

For the millionth time, Issy beat me, but she didn't even smile.

I took the hatchet from under the porch, where I'd hidden it. It was a wonder Nora hadn't sniffed it out yet. I thought, I'm Unthinging myself. Maybe Abraham would see this Unthinging and command Philip to let me stay. Issy took the hatchet without a thank-you, and rubber-banded the cards, and went down the slope.

I stood in the stillness of the morning. I closed my eyes. I heard footsteps, slow over the pine needles. Abraham, I thought, coming to say goodbye. I let him stand there, let him see my bravery.

"You're really leaving?"

My eyes startled open. Ben. I tried to make my voice sound breezy as I stepped off the porch. "You finally got rid of me."

"I didn't mean it like that."

"I'm out of your hair."

"Hey." He got closer. "I'm sorry, hey, don't cry."

"I'm not crying." I brushed past him.

"Can I explain?"

Why did boys and men want to explain their meanness; wasn't their meanness enough? I found solace in the car, filled with all the things we had learned not to care about. I hugged the glass jar filled with the Mother that Sarah insisted I bring along.

We got to the city at sunset. The Thinged World was a decayed landscape of grays and browns: buildings, water, sky. How had I never noticed? Humid air hung over the garbage heap of human waste. Philip tapped the steering wheel to "Take the A Train." Xavier was asleep, his gorgeous mouth hanging open as though he didn't mind anything flying in.

39

*I*ssy opens my window. "Hey down there!" My body shrinks back and the world rushes in: the flow of *Acer rubrum*'s leaves; *Poecile atricapillus* playing the same two notes; and below that, the drone of a far-off mower.

"Mama!" I can't see, but I know the boy's hands are reaching up. "Mama, Mama!"

"Is Saskia all right?" Cornelia's voice carries judgment.

"Still breathing."

"Mama!"

"Come in," Issy calls.

40

One step into the loft and we knew something was amiss. Jane's Daubigny, that muddy composition of clouds and cows, was gone from its spot opposite the door.

"Mom?"

We found Jane's cosmetics cabinet bare, as well as the shelves where she kept her jewel-toned cashmere sweaters. Xavier jogged toward the curtained area where she slept. Philip's hand, gripping for the doorknob, was all I needed to understand why he'd brought us back—he had known she was leaving. He had hoped we would get here first. Between throaty sobs, he explained: Jane had fallen in love. She'd told him she wanted a separation in the spring, but he'd begged her to think things through—"for your sake, my darlings, for both of your sakes"—and that was why he had swept us off to Maine: "So she would miss us."

"You thought abandoning her would convince her to stay?" Xavier Frisbee'd his *Star Wars* plate at his father's head. Philip ducked. The melamine clattered but refused to shatter. "Tell us where she is."

I fixed my face so it looked as though Jane mattered to me. Really, my insides were howling anew for the loss of Home, which was the loss of you, the only place you'd shown yourself since leaving. If Philip had brought us to Home only to get away, there was hardly any reason to take us back.

Jane was living with her boyfriend on the Upper West Side. This boyfriend was younger than Philip. He worked in imports, which was how he and Jane had met, on a trip to Egypt. Philip glanced up at Xavier, a look of terror crossing his face as a helicopter hummed over the building, rattling the windows: "She's pregnant, my darlings. She's going to have his child."

41

"Would you like to meet my son?" Issy asks.

I need peace. I need quiet. I am a solitary creature. I want I hope I need for there to be no children. Children ruin things. I want to stay in this pink bedroom with Issy forever, both of us undistracted.

But then, of course, with every aching bit of me: yes.

42

"You talk to our boy today?" Philip asked.

I had, in fact, locked eyes with Xavier across the cafeteria, just before he laughed at a boy sticking a French fry up his nose. It seemed worse to tell Philip this detail than to swallow it with the instant oatmeal he offered. Somehow, in our absence, Jane had gotten Xavier and me admitted to the kind of school she approved of—uniforms, textbooks, lacrosse. Philip wouldn't let me unenroll; he was desperate to look good in her eyes. It wasn't a bad school; we were actually doing math. But Xavier wasn't talking to me so I had no friends. Of course Philip didn't know this, nor did he know that a photographer had started following me home, or that half the girls ignored me because of Daddy and the other half were obsessed with me because of Daddy, and that the boys called me "Spooky Saskia" (a relatively innocuous nickname, as these things go) and made ghostly sounds whenever I passed (which was, admittedly, better than having my bra snapped), and although I knew this was thanks to something Xavier must have told them about Daddy or about you, I had no idea what that something was, because the day after we returned to New York, Xavier had moved out.

"He's just visiting her," Philip mumbled for the millionth time. "It's not forever." But we both knew that although Xavier had only taken a backpack with him, Jane's apartment with her boyfriend on Central Park West was Xavier's home now.

Philip ate and drank and smoked more than he had before Home. He tore up the longyis for painting rags. Women slept over, many of them far too pretty. I got into bed every afternoon as soon as I finished my homework, grateful for the escape of sleep, and for the touch of Topsy in the spot between my bed and the wall. I fed the Mother as Sarah had taught me, but the glop grew thin and started to stink of acetone. I plopped her into the garbage and gagged.

And you? You were gone—or rather, I was. I'd always thought it was worse to be left behind, but being the one who did the leaving certainly gave that experience a run for its money. You'd obviously stayed right where you finally felt at home, at Home. I tried not to think of you wandering those woods, leaving signs I wouldn't find; even the gentle spot behind Topsy's ears couldn't soothe that.

The urge to suck in Abraham—far away as he was—gaped raw in my mind, those few times, that is, that I allowed myself to fully imagine putting my face up to his eyes, cheekbones, nose, jaw, lips. It was better to imagine nothing. I devoured *Jane Eyre*. I limped through *Wuthering Heights*. I watched a lot of *Star Trek*. I was sure to be as boring as possible whenever the photographer followed me back to the loft, and although a few shots of me ended up in the papers, they didn't make the boys meaner or the girls any more interested. I considered getting a job babysitting before I remembered all the reasons I shouldn't.

Did I think of getting on a bus to Portland? Did I consider hitchhiking along the scrubby back roads, past shuttered cottages and windswept lakes, toward the edge of the small town where JimBob's sat, a fortress of road salt and potato chips? Yes, as other children fantasize a Disneyland vacation. But I had only a vague memory of the town nearest to Home and was afraid that if I looked at a map of Maine I would discover that there was no road leading up the mountain from JimBob's, that Home and Abraham and Issy and the whole Unthinged World was something my terrible mind had drawn from thin air. And though I was livid at Philip for giving me the taste of new life only to rip it away, some part of me knew that if I ran away, his search for me would be halfhearted. I wouldn't survive his abandonment.

Meanwhile, he waxed poetic about Home to his girlfriends as though our time there had been a quaint vacation. He extolled Unthinging even as he invested in a new Harley. He started referring to Jane as "My Wife the Gaping Cunt" (for they were, apparently, still married). What I mean to say is he did his best.

"You haven't painted since the summer," I said one cool Saturday evening when I caught Philip with his hands in his pockets, staring north toward the Empire State Building. I did not say, "Let's go back." Instead, I said, "I might visit Grandmother," which was not what I expected to say. I tried my best to never think of Grandmother, but now that I'd announced the visit, it was the only logical next step. Grandmother had been distant, surely. But if Mother was her blood, then so was I, and Grandmother loved nothing so much as blood, except, perhaps, for money.

43

Without Issy, it might have been weeks before I made it downstairs again.

Perhaps I'm being dramatic. A descent to the first floor would be unpleasant, but I'd manage. I'd have to; otherwise, the last of the Mother would die.

On the stairs, an orange square of sunlight lights my hand, the same color that filtered into the Devil's Ramble when I slipped into it at last. That blessed glow had come back in the time it took me to make it from the house, into the purple leaves. I didn't look back. I grasped at a trunk to catch my breath. I moved into the lurking forest.

Issy's arm is firm under my touch, and I have, for the moment, the sensation that she is carrying me, that I owe her a great debt of gratitude—until I remember that her and Xavier's and Cornelia's arrival is the reason I am undone.

44

*T*he metal gate swept open. I'd taken the Metro-North from the city and then a taxi from the station. As I pulled up Grandmother's long drive, I thought myself quite sophisticated for asking the driver to idle under the porte cochere.

Miriam let me in. "You want a biscuit?" She meant a cookie. The house smelled of floor wax and mothballs and Grandmother's horehound candy. Your lack, inside those walls, felt like a physical weight, one that pressed so hard on my shoulders that I thought, for a moment, I might faint.

We heard Grandmother at the top of the stairs. Miriam hurried me from the foyer into the parlor, and had me sit in the wingback chair. No cookie appeared. Grandmother took her time. When she finally entered, her hand flew from her brass-handled cane to her chest. "Is no one feeding you?"

"Oh, Jane's a great cook." I hadn't had a vegetable in months. I approached Grandmother's brittle frame. Talcum powder was doing its best to mask the fresh urine, but I decided to notice, instead, how much taller I was now. She settled on the velvet settee. She motioned that I join her.

"I trust everything is all right," she said, "at the Pierces?"

"Naturally."

She nodded. "You belong with young folk." She lifted the bell. Miriam appeared in the swinging door.

"Send that taxi away." So she was letting me stay. "I'll have Lapsang souchong." The door swung shut. Her lips pursed. "Your mother isn't here anymore."

"I thought she was in Mexico."

"Well, she came back."

The room started to swim with that same pressing heaviness. "Where is she now?"

Grandmother leaned forward, her pupils tight dots. The tick-tock of the grandfather clock filled the room as I watched all the possibilities quiver through her face—where Mother might be, and what she might tell me about where she was.

"I need to see her," I said. It was the wrong move.

Grandmother broke my gaze. "You may have three thousand a month, in addition to the school fees. I should have insisted, but the Pierces wouldn't hear it."

"Where did you find Topsy?" As long as we were changing the subject. "That day, when you found me, you had him in your hand."

It was Grandmother who'd discovered me in the forest behind the Devil's Ramble. Her arms were scratched up and she was barefoot, but she was still wearing her church clothes. She reached out her hand. Topsy was in it. When we climbed back onto the lawn through the Japanese maples, the driveway was a swirl of blue and red lights. The night was moving in, but it was light enough to see Mother squatting in the middle of the driveway, shoulders hunched. One of the police officers standing over her looked up, and saw me there beside Grandmother, and said something into his radio.

Then Grandmother said, "Your brother died today, Saskia. You understand? He did not survive. Your father is, of course, responsible. Your mother is understandably upset." She spoke in a rapid, steady voice, as though she was a reporter who'd happened upon a late-breaking story. But what she said next, she said quietly. "We will go inside and the police will have questions. You will tell them what your father did. Then we will be done with it. We miss William, we will always miss him, and we will be tempted to go over and over what happened here. But the only way to put this behind us is to give the police what they want, the truth, and be done."

Mother looked up then, at her own mother and daughter, standing together at the edge of the Devil's Ramble. She was broken, I could see, but she'd looked that way before. I could fix her. I had tried. I took a step. But even across that wide lawn, I saw her flinch. Her hands tightened across her knees. She began to sob. The officer crouched over her. Grandmother picked up her shoes. I thought I might try to get closer, but Grandmother steered me to give a wide berth. Mother stayed in the driveway until the middle of the night, when Mr. Jacobs arrived to carry her into the pink bedroom, and she stayed in the pink bedroom until the day we awoke to discover she'd gone to Mexico.

Now, Miriam returned to the sun-filled parlor with a rattling tray, and I knew my chance to hear where Grandmother had found Topsy—was he holding him? was he on the roof?—if there'd ever been one, had passed. Grandmother admired the tea set with its forget-me-not pattern, and ignored the plate of little cakes flowered with yellow frosting.

"My portfolio, Miriam, from the desk."

Miriam walked the length of the room to the secretary, then presented a fountain pen and Grandmother's leather checkbook. All the while, steam snaked from the neck of the teapot. Once the door closed again, Grandmother folded the thin piece of paper into my hand. "This is for the year. With a little added on, for taxis home from school. We must keep our business private, Saskia."

I knew, then, that she had seen the photographs of me walking to the loft. I tried to make my face look like hers, with no trace of sentiment. But then I thought of you on her lap, how bravely you'd pat her cheeks, not knowing it wasn't proper. You were the only reason I knew her cheeks were soft.

"I could come and get the money every month."

Grandmother's mouth thinned.

"Or I could come live here again. I could help you, you know. Jane's always saying how helpful I am."

Grandmother folded her hands. "When I was a girl, my father died. Did you know that? My mother was too heartbroken to care for me. Perhaps you've heard this story? No? Well, she sent me to school."

"Did you like it there?"

"Did I like it? Does it matter? I discovered that what I wanted was no more important than what my mother needed. And that I was quite independent, quite strong. Put your mind to it, and you'll discover you've got more mettle than you know."

Perhaps it was that simple: deciding.

"Sometimes I wonder, what if we had sent you away?" She narrowed her eyes, then shook her head after a moment. "But I suppose we are who we are."

"I don't know what you mean."

She blinked at me, with her small, patrician eyes. "My dear, you know exactly what I mean." She raised the bell. "Miriam? Have Mr. Jacobs drive Saskia back to the city. Be sure to pack him dinner—it's a considerable round trip."

45

The downstairs air, rushing in from the parlor, is cool. I can't help but call it the parlor, even after all this time. Someone has opened a window, perhaps; a bumblebee—genus *Bombus*—zips by.

46

*P*hilip and I spent Christmas Eve snoozing through a Fellini retrospective, then walked home through a night drizzle we wished was snow. Cab tires thumped the manhole covers. The sidewalks glistened red and green. Jane always brought umbrellas.

"I haven't been painting," he said as we kicked off our wet shoes, "because I've been punishing myself." The windows shimmered with rain as we waited for him to tell me why. "It wasn't my money I gave to the Homesteaders; it was Jane's."

"But you're still married, right? So what's hers is yours."

"She said she'd met someone. I thought, look, we all mess around. Probably this guy is good at sex, and that's fine, a marriage doesn't have to be about sex, you know?" He'd forgotten me. His eyes welled up as rain lashed the windows. "I should have given her forgiveness. I should have begged her to stay, turned out my pockets to show the love I carried everywhere I went. But instead I told her I'd ruin her life. She'd be sorry, that kind of thing.

"She called my bluff," he said. "Told me that if I thought blackmailing her would make her stay, I was a fucking fool. It hadn't even occurred to me to call it blackmail, that's how stupid I was. I should have gotten on my knees and begged." Instead he took us away, to Maine, to Home. "It was a place I heard about from a few friends, you know, spiritual folks. I thought I could use some centering." He swiped his fingers over the top of his head. "And I heard they could use money. I thought—what's the thing Jane will fucking hate for me to do with her money? Most of all? What will she fucking hate?" His mouth twisted, then he met my eye. "The thing is, I really liked it there, kid. Not as much as you did, but I liked it." He tapped his chest. "But that pride"—he shook his head—"the fact that she just let me walk away. . . . Some part of me believed that if I gave away some of that precious inheritance she's taken for granted her whole fucking life, she'd drive right up to the Main Lodge and at least she'd stand out there and yell at me, you know? And it would be something. Something's better than nothing, I thought." He laughed bitterly.

"Gabby was all for taking the money, but Abraham. . . . There was so much analysis. Was it ethical? Was it sustainable? And all the time, I'm saying, 'Take it already,' because I was afraid I'd have second thoughts."

"And did you?" I asked, because now he was looking out the window again, smudged with the gray, cold night.

"Not until they accepted it. That's some irony, right? Gabby came to the cabin after you kids were asleep and said it was done. They already had the check, you know? I got in bed and lay up all night and thought what the fuck did I just do?"

"Did you ask for it back?"

"Of course. But Abraham"—he smiled now, quick and brutal—"he said he wouldn't dream of letting me Thing myself all over again." There, in his voice, a touch of dislike.

"I called Jane and confessed everything. I said I'd get the money back. But she was done with me. She'd been done for much longer than I realized. I drove us back down here thinking the sight of us"—of Xavier, he meant—"would convince her. But she was already gone. The baby, you know? I didn't count on a baby."

When I awoke to a milky Christmas dawn, propped against the kitchen counter was a massive, wet canvas in thirty shades of green—the colors of the lake on a windy morning, if you leaned over the Home dock and tried to make sense of the muck. Philip's hands, crisscrossed with verdant stripes, poured me a cup of blood-thick coffee.

I'd gotten him a pair of cashmere gloves for Christmas, which he must have assumed I'd shoplifted, since I hadn't told him about Grandmother's money in my private bank account. He tried them on, turning his hands over and over, and said he was working on a special present for me but Santa hadn't delivered it yet, and I flared with you you you—you, who loved Santa with a fierceness—and some magic, stupid, childish part of me thought for the briefest of split seconds that, in some impossible way, he had gotten you back. He knew. He did not speak of it. He sat with me until I fell asleep again. When I awoke, it was just us and grilled cheddar sandwiches and the smell of oil paint. Then he was painting on another canvas, coppers and oranges and golds, which he said would be Home's sunrise, if he could manage it.

Before I slept, I pulled open my curtains. The night rain cast *The Good Path,* usually golden from my painted footprints, in grim gray scale. It would be quiet at Home tonight; snow covering the roof of the Main Lodge and the Homesteaders inside it. They'd be singing "Silent Night" (proud Abraham; diligent Gabby; efficient Sarah; irreverent Teresa; hungry Jim; wild Tomas; naughty Nora; solemn Ephraim; terrible Ben; kind Issy—and you, out there, in the woods, wandering, waiting). Then it was my turn to weep.

Carefully through the dismal dining room and into the relief of the kitchen—and there they are, around my table. At the center lies what's left of this morning's loaf, hacked open.

"She lives!" Xavier's enthusiasm is too much.

Cornelia makes to stand. I wave; she flashes a smile— it's enough to get us both out of the hug. The child has black curls, fronded eyelashes, and rosebud lips. He launches from the chair. Issy releases me to enfold him. I try to remember Mother holding you. But even on the best of days, her tie to us was never orbital, never like this.

"Mama," whispers the boy. He turns his cheek to Issy's. He considers me. "Who this?"

"Ah." Issy buries her nose at his temple. "This is my friend Saskia." Her hand covers the real estate of his chest. "And this is my son, Sekou."

The Mother wafts off Sekou's lips. Blink blink go those dark eyes—his mother's eyes, his grandmother's. Then he's squirming down to the floor. Back to the table. Back to Cornelia. "We coloring, Mama!" Sekou grabs a crust and gnaws.

My Christmas gift from Philip didn't arrive until February. I walked into the loft after a long, lonely Friday to discover Issy at the kitchen counter, gulping a glass of milk.

A jubilant sound warbled from my throat. Issy whirled us through the loft, firm and loose in her particular way, smelling of BO and burlap and old wool. She unpacked the four loaves of sourdough Sarah had sent along, and flopped down on my bed, and asked about *The Good Path*, and ogled the white Christmas lights. She ran her hands over my red velvet curtains. She shuffled her cards.

"There's a new girl named Cornelia. Her parents got divorced. Her dad was fucking around and then he moved in with some whore in the Valley. Her mom changed her name to Butterfly from Valerie or something and drove all the way from California with a box of oranges in the trunk. She's perfect."

"Butterfly?" I asked hopefully.

"She's, like, a mall person." She pressed her nose against the glass overlooking the city. "I love it here. I've never been to New York City. It makes me feel small." Her breath made a cloud. She drew a face. "You ever been to a mall?"

"You'd hate the mall."

"Cornelia says I'd love it. There's a food court where you can get anything you want to eat."

"But the whole point of the mall is to buy things."

She was still at the window, caught in her game of breath and faces. I was on the edge of my bed keeping very, very still.

"Where's Xavier?" she asked.

"He moved in with Jane."

She turned. Her eyes were kinder then. I told her everything, including the bit about Jane's money. The story was messy in a way Issy understood. Eventually we were on the bed, limbs flung over each other as though we'd never spent a moment apart, her sour milk breath offering comfort: "To be honest, Butterfly's kind of, you know—like Jane." She lowered her voice, although the loft was empty save for us. "Slutty." Issy's whisper made my neck hairs stand up. "I overheard Gabby and Sarah talking after I fell asleep. Butterfly's been putting her mouth on Jim's penis."

That sight flashed in my mind: pink, quivering dollops of flesh rubbing each other. My stomach flipped. "What does Cornelia think?"

"I can't tell Cornelia."

"Poor Teresa."

"Teresa proposed a threesome. But Butterfly only likes dick."

"Poor Cornelia." Although this was the happiest I'd been since learning she existed.

Issy brought her face to mine, so close she grew one-eyed. Her lips were right there, too, and I knew, again, that longing to drink someone in. I thought to do it, to start it; how good it would feel to press forward against another body and borrow its solid parts— but the door to the loft squealed open along the concrete floor. Behind Philip's footsteps came another.

Issy sat up. "I shouldn't be gossiping."

"It's not gossip if it's true."

"Gossip is a Thing. Abraham said so." My heart seized at the mention of his name. She was off the bed, already digging through her backpack. "Can we go outside? Philip said you'd show me around." Around her neck she wound a hand-knit scarf: magenta and crimson and peacock blue. For just a moment, I wanted to see how the girls at school would hurt her.

"How old is Cornelia?"

"Younger than us. But she's got boobs. Ben follows her around like she's Morgan le Fay."

"He likes her?"

"She's very well put together."

"Girls? Saskia?" Philip had come into the loft. The main door squealed.

Issy lowered her voice. "You should be careful: jealousy is a Thing."

"I'm not jealous."

She went to the curtain. She pulled it aside. "And anyway, I thought you hated Ben."

49

Cornelia points to the desiccated bread. "I hope it's okay. He was desperate." Issy and I each nod, unsure which of us she's addressing.

"Beautiful picture," says Issy, looking over Sekou's shoulder. Brown scribbles. "Did he use the potty?"

"He said he didn't have to."

"Honey," Issy says, bending down to the boy, "do you have to use the potty?"

Sekou shakes his head.

Xavier watches me. "You're not mad anymore, are you?" I wonder if this trick works on Billy.

I lean over Sekou. "Can I draw, too?" A grin sweeps his face as he hands me an orange crayon and points to the edge of his drawing. They watch with relief when I brighten that corner. Maybe the drawing is beautiful.

Cornelia's watch chimes. She scrolls its tiny screen. My computer keeps me up on the world, but I lost the thread on tidbits like watches actually being phones and computers and an infinite collection of music and movies. Everything moves so fast.

"We have to get going," Cornelia says. "It's nearly four."

"You're going?" I say.

"You too, sweetie." Her voice drips syrup. "Didn't they tell you? We're driving up to Maine."

"To Home?" Surely even in this desperate state, we wouldn't wander those woods at midnight.

"We'll get to town tonight," Xavier says, his voice a taming thrum. "Tomorrow we'll figure out next steps."

"Where are we staying?"

Cornelia crosses her arms. "Some of us have families to get back to. I can't exactly treat this like a vacation, lovely as your grandmother's home is." It's my home, first of all, but the twins, oh yes, Cornelia's precious twins—Madison? Mackenzie? Rosencrantz? Guildenstern? Her matched set of little girls.

"Where," I repeat, "are we staying?"

Xavier's eyes skitter over the marble countertops but eventually come to meet mine. His voice is so small I can barely hear it: "Ben's."

"How does Ben feel about that?"

"Ben's feelings on the matter will change when we remind him what's at stake," says Cornelia.

"He has no idea we're coming?"

A guilty glance passes between Issy and Xavier.

"You don't think you'll actually convince him to go up to Home?"

"Why not?" Cornelia fiddles with a phantom necklace she must have forgotten to put on. "He has as much interest as we do in keeping this quiet. More—if you think about how getting exposed would ruin his life up there. It's personal for a local."

"It's personal for me."

"It's personal for all of us. Saskia, honestly—"

"Let's be easy on each other," says Issy.

Cornelia clamps her jaw shut. She puts a blank piece of paper in front of Sekou, though he seemed perfectly happy with the one he'd been working on. That's when we all hear the front door open, followed by the outside—smell, sound—spilling in. Who else did they bring? From their looks of surprise, no one is expected.

Sekou bounds into the dining room. We rush after him, Issy at the front. In the foyer, Sekou laughs and points and waves, but there's nothing to see out in the sunlight.

"Hello?" Xavier steps into the day. The hollow drone of a leaf blower, the endless frittering trill of *Spizella passerina*. He turns and shrugs. "I guess it blew open."

Sekou's eyes linger. I lean down to ask what he saw, but he scrambles into the parlor. Cornelia's wrist chimes again. She rushes to her phone in the kitchen. Xavier comes back in and latches the door, and asks Issy if she knows if Cornelia figured out the route. They talk interstates. I find Sekou in the parlor, standing under *The Good Path* where it hangs above the sofa. He peers up at the painting, his finger hanging from his mouth. I crouch beside him, slowly.

"Did you see someone out there?"

The boy dips a shoulder, then hits me with a coy smile. I know he understands. He breaks away, jumping to the sofa with a shimmy, glad to have an audience. I clap. He rolls his head onto the sofa cushions, digging his little hands between them. Then he titters and turns, and in his hands is Topsy.

Topsy lives in my drawer, wrapped in Grandmother's Hermès scarf, the one with the ponies on it, the one she let you wear when you were playing pirates. Is it possible I brought him down this morning without remembering? It would be strange not to remember, but all right, it's possible. Is it possible Sekou discovered him before I came downstairs, and squirreled him away? Well, anything is possible, despite the fact that I never heard him on the stairs—which is why it's also possible that it was you who opened the door, and you who hid Topsy just where Sekou would find him, so that I would find him, too, and know it was an invitation. If it is you, I think, as I smile at the little boy, petting Topsy's head, pretending it's perfectly normal to have found him where I found him—if it is you, then it's clear what I am meant to do.

All at once, I resign myself. With that resignation comes clarity. Why have I been keeping myself away when Home was where you came close? I give Sekou the kiss he deserves. I stand in my conviction. The adults are in the dining room, whispering about me.

"I'll get my things together," I say, as I breeze by. Into the kitchen I go, pulling the Mother from her spot. She fills two bowls: leaven for tomorrow; fed starter to keep alive. "I'll need a cooler," I say, knowing Issy has followed, "and that container of flour, and my wooden spoons."

Xavier hovers. "We should confirm you got the letters."

"The mudroom."

He goes.

Small feet patter toward me. Then comes the gentle tug of two small arms around my legs.

"Would you like to see?"

Sekou nods. I lift. I do my best not to press my nose into his curls. I take off the cloth. He gazes down. She bubbles from her slumber.

"Is that Sarah's sourdough starter?" asks Cornelia, but they know the answer.

50

*P*hilip set a bag from the bagel store onto the coffee table, filling the loft with the smell of garlic. From the couch, Gabby fixed me in her gaze. I should have guessed she'd come with Issy. Officially, I was glad to see her; her presence reignited the possibility of Home. But without the Homesteaders to distract her, I felt naked, shy, scrutinized.

Issy grabbed an everything bagel and plopped onto Gabby's lap as though it was the most hospitable place on earth. Only then did Gabby look away from me, wincing under the weight of her daughter's exuberance, taking a breath and making the choice to fold herself back into the girl she'd made, all while Issy prattled on about the loft and pigeons and the subway.

"Is there money for doughnuts?" Issy asked, closing her eyes as she bit. Poppy seeds rained over her lap. "Cornelia says they're good here." She glanced up at me, stuck back by my room. "Don't you want an adventure?"

"How are you, Saskia?" Gabby asked.

I couldn't tell someone so solid, so clear, how mixed up I was: the need for you, and for Home, and for Sarah's bread and the sound of the hammers, for Abraham's steadying regard, even for little Nora flipping me the bird. But I couldn't lie to Gabby, either.

"We miss you, Saskia."

"Really?"

"Why do you think we're here?"

Philip rustled in the bagel bag then, making a racket of paper and plastic. "Anyone want coffee? I was going to make coffee. You want coffee, Gabby?"

The woman shook her head, and brushed her fingers along her daughter's bare arm as Philip turned to his task. Issy closed her eyes like a baby, slipping her face against her mother's neck. "Sarah was saying just the other day that the bread doesn't taste as good without your hands having been on it. And Tomas asked for a story about you the other night. He laughed when Teresa told him about little Topsy—how you carry him around in your waistband. Oh, and Ben said to be sure to tell you hi."

"Ben?" Truth be told, I'd been hoping to hear that Abraham missed me, but this news bruised in a different way. Issy opened her eyes.

"In fact," Gabby said, "you have Ben to thank for putting this trip of ours together."

"Hey, wait a minute." Philip's voice boomed from the kitchen. "Who's paying for all this?"

Irritation passed over Gabby's face, but she tamed it. "Oh yes, Philip, you've been very generous. But this trip was Ben's idea."

I came forward into the room, drawn by the impossibility of it. She meant Ben—the Ben who'd hated me from the moment we met?

Gabby laughed at my expression. "Back in October, he told me he thought you must be missing us. He's been corresponding with Xavier, and Xavier told him he'd moved out and—"

"You knew about that?" Issy turned on her mother. "Why didn't you tell me?"

"I keep what's private private." Gabby patted her daughter to get her to stand up, a request to which Issy reluctantly agreed.

"Saskia thinks Ben hates her," Issy said.

"I suspect," Gabby said, after a moment, "that it's more complicated than that."

"Can we go on our adventure now?" Issy said. I was dizzy. I was filled with a feeling that reminded me of anger but was more hollow, and rang, uncomfortably, of hope. "Time for doughnuts!" Philip gave us money, Gabby folded back into herself, and we headed off into the day—Issy ready for the world, and me, stunned by the way it can surprise.

51

Xavier returns with a thin stack of envelopes. "You got seven letters."

Cornelia moves in on him. "What does the extra one say?"

He hands them to me with an apologetic glance her way. Opening someone else's mail is a federal crime, but I don't say a word. I pull a knife from the drawer.

Xavier has arranged them in order by postdate. The paper yawns open. The first six letters are exactly the same as the set he already showed me.

The first: *Hello again.*

The second: *Did you miss me?*

The third: *I missed you so.*

The fourth: *I need you, in fact.*

The fifth: *It's time to come Home.*

The sixth: *All five of you. Or else.*

But he's right. There is a seventh letter. The four other bodies in the room—even the boy's—lean in when I get to it. We are all holding our breath.

52

"I've told you a thousand different ways, I'm not here about more money." Gabby's voice woke me. It was their last night in New York. Under my watch, Issy had gaped at the high-rises of Times Square, moaned rapturously at the Veselka pierogis, and sprinted into the throttle of pigeons in Washington Square Park. I'd bought her a new deck of cards at a magic shop, which she refused to open, as though the cardboard box itself was a priceless artifact. Meanwhile, Philip and Gabby stayed in the loft and talked—about Jane's money, I assumed. Now Issy snored abundantly beside me.

"Why did he send you, then?"

"You invited us, Philip."

I extracted my foot from under Issy's, avoiding the creaky board as I crept toward the curtain. Philip's loft gave the illusion of spaciousness, but really it was a warren of art supplies and rescued furniture. It was into this chaos that I scuttled, rawly awake, all ears. The scent of General Tso's chicken lingered in the loft.

"This," Gabby went on, "is what I've been trying to get you to see: you and Abraham—both of you—need to stop this alpha male bullshit. You want the same thing. Yes, you do. It's just because he's not on his knees in front of you, begging, that you can't see it."

"He wants more money," Philip said.

"Abraham doesn't even understand how money works, much to my eternal frustration. No, Philip, he wants to protect her." She dropped a newspaper onto the table, and I recognized it—a picture of me walking home, from the beginning of the school year. A flood of knowing filled my limbs: warmth, surprise. They were talking about me.

"Let us take her back." She was pleading now, the longing in her voice so striking, so surprising, that it threatened to make me cry. "You mentioned your concerns to Abraham. He listened. You cannot insist on keeping her here simply because you are lonely. The prophecy states—"

"I don't believe prophecies, Gabby."

There was a prophecy? About me?

"Then look at how miserable she is. That should be enough. You're welcome to come, too. Philip, you've always been welcome. But if you can't leave this life, send her with us. And not just to keep her out of the public eye. Abraham knows she's special. That's what he told me to say—I don't know the details, but when Abraham insists, I've found it best to listen. We'll keep her safe— Abraham, Marta, Sarah, and myself. What she has been through— she deserves stability."

What a horrible, wonderful thing, to discover that they wanted me because of who I was, and not in spite of it.

53

As with the first six envelopes, the edge of the knife finds the space between the flap and the body. The blade slits the paper open at the fold, sending linen fibers into the air, like juice spritzing from an orange peel. The slip of paper waiting inside is another edge. It stings a red line along my fingertip.

The seventh letter, which they press in close to decipher: *Convince the other four, Saskia. You've always been their leader.*

Cornelia blurts: "That's not true at all."

54

I thought Philip might say yes, all right, take her, but instead he stretched into a bear yawn and said he needed shut-eye. Gabby and Issy were leaving in the morning. I could reveal myself and tell her I was coming along. But I couldn't bring myself to do it, not if Philip didn't think it was the right choice, no matter how deeply I longed for Home in my bones. For a long time, I watched Gabby meditate beside her bed, an Unthinged World all to herself. I wished I could be like Issy, and dare to press myself against her.

55

"I'm hungry, Mama," Sekou whispers when Issy returns with my suitcase. We've been drawing at the kitchen table while the adults gust toward departure.

Issy lifts the boy into her arms. His skinny legs snake around her waist. "My ravenous tapeworm." She plants a line of kisses on his brow. "You want to use the potty?"

"Billy! Don't hang up!" Xavier's sharpness from the mudroom gifts me Issy's glance. He's in there to sort through unopened mail for "clues," but really it's just to have another dustup with Billy.

"Let's see about snacks, okay?" Issy says. Before I can stop her, she opens the nearest cabinet. It's bare. My face flames. She peeks into two more before she realizes. When she turns back, it's with brimming eyes.

"Bread," I say. Just enough bread to keep me going, which is not the whole truth, since occasionally I get a brief notion and have vegetables delivered from the grocery store. My hands find the sky, channeling culty bullshit. "The Mother provides."

"I have Goldfish waiting in the car," she whispers into the little boy's ear. "And we can do McDonald's. But before that, we need to use the potty." He lets out a cry at the mention. She calls out, "Are we going or what?"

56

One rainy March afternoon, I arrived home to discover a teary Xavier sitting at the kitchen counter. It occurred to me he hadn't been in school for a few days.

"Xavier's moving back in," Philip said.

Xavier shrugged his father off and lifted his eyes to mine. I saw apology there, borne of finding one's self on the side of those who are not wanted.

"You're both wonderful," Philip said. "Wonderful, beautiful beings who deserve to be loved for exactly who you are."

Xavier looked like he might sob so Philip boomed, "I believe this calls for cheese fries." At the diner, their bellies stuffed, he put his hands on both our shoulders. "Finish out the school year, darlings. Finish out the school year and we'll go north."

57

*T*he outside doesn't scare me. It's being in the outside—but not the way they're thinking. What the outside might do to me is not my concern.

Grit under my soles. The sneeze of cut grass. Evening light in Renaissance flares. Vast sky. Whisper of *Acer palmatum*, the Japanese maples. Clouds that dance over the sun. The urgent chick-a-dee-dee-dee that earns *Poecile atricapillus* its common name. Hum of an airplane, hum of *Apis millifera*—the honeybee. Crunch of gravel off the step. Imagine the blast of noon. Imagine the veil of midnight.

They surround me. Breath on my shoulders, arms, neck. Eyes all over me. We move to the SUV, a movie star and her entourage. Sekou's hand rests in mine. It's hard to sort the view. Maybe my eyes are like a newborn's and the accumulation of stimuli is too much information. Or maybe that's vanity talking—maybe I'm just an old loser who's been afraid for too long.

They are waiting. Maybe they want it. Who could blame them? A scream, some ravaged weeping, the rending of garments, a spasm of the lungs. Me on my knees, declaring defeat. Why else would I have locked myself in there? Why else, if mine is not a terror that lives just under the surface of my skin, ready to burst into flames upon activation?

They do not understand; I am not afraid to be in the outside. They do not understand; I am afraid of *being* in the outside. I am afraid of what my being is capable of, now that I have entered the world again.

What keeps me going, despite the fear? Well, the fact of Topsy, left out for Sekou to find. The fact of the door to my home, flushed open with no explanation. The thought of you in the Home woods, wandering.

Fear is for tomorrow, or tomorrow's tomorrow. Fear is for the choice I will make when what I do unfurls. But for now I'll take a few steps, one foot in front of the other. Then I'll sit for a while as Xavier drives.

You know what I am. You know what I do. You know that I am right to be afraid.

58

"*I* am Love."

Abraham's voice was a just a man's voice, yes. But in the fog of the early morning as it rose off the lake, it was so much more than that: it was the single note to which every Homesteader attended. A bell had rung out when the night was still black. Then came a knock on the door. Philip and Xavier and I stumbled from our beds. Ephraim was on the porch. He held out his hand to Philip and the men shook their hellos—we'd arrived the night before, after most of the Homesteaders were already in bed. "No need to dress," Ephraim said, although he was in his white shirt and work pants. We followed the trail of Homesteaders down to the lake, where mist was rising, milky white, into the arrow of dawn.

Pants sodden to his knees, Abraham stood in the water before us, a dog beside him with short, bristled hair and a rib cage like a barrel. It turned to sniff the wind.

"You are Love."

Issy and I shared her quilt on the bank. Beside us, Tomas, more boy than toddler now, snuggled under the shelf of Teresa's breasts. On our other side, Sarah's hands lay still as she leaned against the oak of Ephraim's body. Ben and a squirmy Nora sat cross-legged at their feet.

There was a crunch of pine needles as two figures approached.

They'd loomed large in my mind in the months since Issy had mentioned them. Cornelia was even prettier than I imagined: petite, with a steady flow of brown hair. She settled in at Issy's other side with a whispered hello. Her mother, the infamous Butterfly, was tall and slender. She wore a blond coif and a sweater that nipped in at the waist and then out again at the bust and hips. She had what I'd heard described as "bedroom eyes," a phrase I'd never understood until I saw the languid way she lingered at the edge of the group, gaze fixed on Abraham, and how he seemed to straighten, ever so slightly, in recognition. She was nothing like Mother, but in her bearing lay the same wounded demand.

"We are Love."

I wasn't the only one looking at Butterfly. Jim's eyes moved across her body as a breeze buffeted the water. It made my stomach churn, the brazen way his gaze fondled her in front of all of us, his wife most of all. Jim wasn't allowed to look long; Teresa noticed the swivel of his head and jabbed him in the ribs. He coughed like a kid caught cheating on a test, and moved his body away from hers, but lesson learned; he didn't look at Butterfly again.

Then it was Philip's turn to flicker his eyes over that woman. I shouldn't have been surprised. I was even a little pleased for him, and for myself; maybe Butterfly could be the way back to Home. I checked to see if Xavier noticed, but he looked asleep.

"I am Love. You are Love." I longed for Abraham to look my way. There was a prophecy, after all. "We are Love. Sounds good, right?" He opened his eyes then. His laugh was contagious. Happiness flushed through me, in spite of my jealousies. I was alive again, after nine months in the underworld. You were out there, in the woods, waiting. A feather would fall, or your breath would whisper into my ear. It was only a matter of time before we found each other again. I wiggled my toes. I wiggled my fingers. I met Gabby's eye and Amos's eye and Sarah's eye and Philip's eye. We filled the air with laughter. Abraham was right; those sentences he had uttered about Love had sounded good. We were so lucky that Abraham would explain why they were false.

"These statements make us feel safe. I am Love. You are Love. We are Love. The idea of I and You and We. The idea of Love. But what if we Unthing ourselves? What if I and You and We are just Things?" The dog's tongue flourished over his nose.

"What if we said, there is no I. There is no You. There is no We." Abraham jerked his head to look at the sky, and suddenly his voice was yelling: "What if we said there is no Love?" Abraham's voice ricocheted across the lake. Tomas jerked awake with a cry. Teresa pulled out her breast to suckle him, and held out her hand to Jim, who removed his jacket and lay it over the drowsy boy. Sneaking another glance at Cornelia, I noticed a scuttle of movement far off in the woods. It took me a moment to decipher that it was Marta back there, picking silently through the trees away from us.

"What if?" Abraham's voice boomed. He was smiling now, as if we were all in on a beautiful joke. He waved his hand. "What if Love is a Thing, what if it isn't a Thing. What if I am, what if I am not. What if you are, what if you are not." He ran his head along the dog's head. "Rhetoric is only a path. We only have words to say what we feel. This, too, is a Thing—but don't get me started on that. I am talking about Love."

The mist was gone. Butterfly's arms found their way into the air. She was swaying as a sapling does in the wind. Even Tomas was eyeing her from Teresa's breast, and Jim's eyes flitted back, too, until he caught me looking and looked right back, his gaze a sticky, urgent need. We were all knit together, holding each other in place.

"I am talking about Love on this glorious morning as it blooms on earth, and what I want to say is that Love is the master. Love is not a Thing. Love is the answer. Love is the breath. Do not let yourself think of Love as a Thing. That is what I mean when I say Love is not a Thing. I mean Love should never be made small by turning it into a Thing. I mean you should never make yourself small by turning yourself into a Thing. I am Love. You are Love. We are Love."

Abraham stopped abruptly, looking left, then right, as though he'd remembered something silly. He stretched his arms wide. He fell backwards, into the water. The dog leapt into the lake, too, a splash of legs and torso, joining Abraham with a volley of barks. We shrieked. We clapped. Abraham waved to us.

We threw off our blankets. We, too, jumped in. The liquid shivered over our limbs. It drenched our hair. We were filled with water and Love and Abraham and I and You and We, Unthinged. Home.

59

*T*he world. Everything skipping past. Halfway down the drive-way we're already going too fast. Organs shift. Eyeballs ache. Red smudge of *Cardinalis cardinalis*. The crown of *Acer rubrum* blurring green in the gloaming. The Devil's Ramble, a purple goodbye.

The back seat, in the middle, safely buckled between Sekou's bulky car seat and Issy, seemed just the thing—but the SUV is too big. Wide leather chairs, cup holders, headrests, and legroom, three rows of humans and still plenty of space in the back for our bags and the Mother and all her accoutrements, and a baby ele-phant, if we happened to have one. The best seating arrangement we could muster is Xavier at the wheel; Cornelia, his navigator; me in the next aisle, beside Sekou; and in the back, Issy, who can put one hand on me and, with the other, make a plastic giraffe tap-dance atop the seat for her rear-facing son.

We brake. The gate. "What's the code?" Cornelia asks.

"There is no code." Xavier punches a red button. The gate swings open. All this time, I thought one had to enter a password to leave. He might pause at the last bit of my land, check me in the rearview mirror and ask if I'm ready. But Xavier's eyes are on the road.

Issy's fingers stay sure at the nape of my neck.

Xavier presses the accelerator. The SUV purrs to life. Then we are hurtling. The world flames toward darkness. We are out in it like we belong.

60

Nora passed around Sarah's zucchini sourdough muffins when we were done swimming. The sun was getting hot. Xavier finished his muffin in one bite. I gave him mine. He turned toward Ben. It might have been wiser to share with Issy, because in the meantime she had folded into Cornelia, who had a freckle-dusted nose and narrow wrists.

The dog stalked the promise of crumbs into our huddle. His head was the size of Tomas's torso. The swagger of his hips, the alert perking of his ears, the solid snap of his lips awoke any part of me still sleeping. He yawned, the band of his jaws elastic, pink tongue stretching back, revealing his teeth. Issy lifted a bite of muffin to her mouth. The dog gingered forward. Issy pulled the food away. He snarled. She shrank, a sight I'd never seen—Issy, scared.

But Cornelia wasn't. She snapped her fingers, pointing off, away. The dog eyed her, then slunk along toward Tomas, who squealed and lunged at the sight of him. Teresa swept the boy up just as the dog got close. She handed him off to Jim like a sack of potatoes. The boy kicked, but Jim held him firm as he and Ephraim discussed the day's repairs.

"Where'd the dog come from?" I asked.

"A meditation retreat," Cornelia said. "Someone important gave him to Abraham." I heard in her answer everything she knew and I didn't. Meanwhile, her mother was spinning in the light.

"Does he have a name?" The dog moved like Butterfly: wildness, power, the element of surprise.

"Nora calls him Fucking Dog." This was Ben. He was sitting close to me now, as if it was nothing to have plopped down into the pine needles beside someone he'd only ever disdained or ignored.

I laughed and hated myself for laughing. I couldn't look at him. I wouldn't. "What does everybody else call him? What do you call him, Iss?" But Issy was whispering something to Cornelia. "Is he dangerous?"

"Probably." For some reason, Ben was eager to answer. He wasn't any taller, and he was still wearing those ridiculous clothes, and I officially hated him. But I couldn't help thinking of what Gabby had said—how he'd urged her and Issy to come to New York. Why?

The dog had come back, and was licking Ben's face. Ben squirmed away, wiping at the slobber.

"You have to be in command," Cornelia said. She snapped a finger at the dog, who jumped off Ben.

"You don't think I'm in command?" His grin was easy.

The dog's tongue slickened up the side of Ben's cheek, from his chin to his forehead. Cornelia giggled. "Totally," she said. "Totally in command."

Cornelia pointed to the muffin Xavier had scored. "Thanks for sharing." Xavier divided the crumbling muffin into fourths. Nora wandered over, basket finally empty. Cornelia patted her own lap and the girl found a spot there, and Issy braided her hair. They all made it look easy: to eat, to laugh.

At the front of the congregation, Abraham held up his hands to silence us. "I forgot something." He smiled as everyone gave him back their attention. "I forgot to mention that today is a special day."

Since overhearing Gabby talk about the prophecy, I'd known, for certain, that Abraham found me special. But he hadn't given me any notice since we drove up—in fact, I'd only glimpsed him for a moment in the Main Lodge before bed, when he'd greeted Philip with a handshake. But now he would celebrate my return. I sat tall. I waited for him to claim me.

He held out his hand toward our group of children. I lifted my head.

He said, "Have any of you heard this girl sing?"

Sing? I opened my mouth to offer a playful protest—what would I sing if he made me?—but Nora was scrambling off Cornelia's lap, and then, already, Cornelia was standing. Abraham nodded in approval as his open hand turned into a summons. He meant her.

"I was passing the bathing lodge the other day. I was lost in thought, and then I realized I was humming, and then I realized I was humming along with someone who was already singing— singing a song I have sung a million times and never thought of as even remotely beautiful." A titter swept the group. "But from this singer's mouth, the song was just that—a revelation."

Cornelia was walking to him now, too, the dog sniffing and wagging beside her. "Go, Cornelia!" Issy shouted, clapping riotously.

Butterfly whooped. "That's my girl!"

Ben's gaze was positively rapturous as it followed Cornelia as she made her way to the front of the group. It took all I had not to channel my inner Nora and throw a clod of dirt.

Abraham placed one hand on Cornelia's shoulder. "Won't you do us the honor?" He used the same private voice he'd used with me, on my first day at Home, on the day he'd named my sadness.

Cornelia looked nothing like Butterfly—she was short, brunette, and small-breasted. But I saw, for just that moment, all the ways they were alike, as the girl's long lashes swept down over her cheeks. She knew to hold on to her modesty as the Homesteaders' applause rose from encouragement to fervent desire. Only then did she nod, once, as if to say, well, if I must.

"While you listen to this child sing, ask yourself, what is your hidden gift? What is the piece of you that you keep back, bridled, because you are afraid of how it might change your life? What would it mean to Unthing yourself of the idea that it will hurt you to let this part into the light? What would it give the rest of us to share it, freely?"

Cornelia closed her eyes. She lifted her face to the day. The melody unfurled from her delicate, pink mouth. The song was "A Horse Named Bill." Abraham was right: usually it was jolly and jiglike, reserved for giddy celebrations or campfire sing-alongs, but on Cornelia's tongue, it was the story of misfits who can't get things right, a mournful, melancholy tale.

Abraham gestured for her to keep going, and he made his way into the congregation as she rounded into the second verse. He crouched beside Jim, whispered something to him, and Jim said, out loud, "What, now? While she's singing?"

Abraham nodded.

Jim cleared his voice. "Um, I guess I'm good at carrying stuff?"

Abraham tipped his head back and forth as if to say "so-so job," then went to crouch beside Ephraim. Cornelia's voice remained steady.

Ephraim nodded at Abraham's prompting. "I could find more pleasure in my duties."

Abraham shot us all a comic look and said, "Maybe third time's the charm." He moved on to Butterfly. She was waiting for him.

She smiled as though they were alone, her nipples hard against her T-shirt, her hips moving just a bit, side to side. Truth be told, it was hard not to imagine him lying against her. Cornelia faltered in her song—she started in on the wrong verse, and had to circle back to get it right.

Abraham didn't have to prompt Butterfly to share her hidden gift. She lifted her voice to the sky. "I'm afraid of working hard. My husband made me believe I was only good for these"—she grabbed her breasts—"and these"—she grabbed her hips—"but why not these?" She lifted her hands into the air. "Why can't I find pleasure in the work these offer?"

Abraham did not touch her, but his eyes were everywhere. All of ours were, even Sarah's, especially Jim's, especially Philip's. Abraham turned, then, and moved toward us children. Dog yawned and stood as Abraham crouched before us. Cornelia was still singing, rounding to the end of the song.

"Xavier?" Abraham said.

Xavier's grin was crooked and glancing. I startled to see he felt as shy as I did in the face of Abraham's attention. Maybe there was a reason he'd come back, besides the rejection he'd suffered at his mother's hands.

"What is it?" Abraham said. "What is that specialness inside you that you could let fly free?"

Xavier shook his head and looked at his feet.

Abraham leaned forward. "Say it."

Xavier shrugged, but he was laughing, as if he did have a wonderful secret.

Abraham turned to the rest of the group. "Tell him, tell him we want to know him," and then everyone was clapping, whispering encouragement. Butterfly shouted, "Say your truth," and Amos nodded as he worked at his whittling, which was the most you got out of Amos. Xavier opened his mouth to speak, and the whole sound of us stopped to receive his words. Even Cornelia paused her singing.

"I'm . . ." Xavier glanced at Philip. Philip looked as though he might cry, too, a look of love and pride. Envy burst inside my chest. "Well, I'm . . . I think I might be . . . gay?"

The Homesteaders erupted. Dog jollied and jumped and barked. Ephraim turned away—the only Homesteader who didn't look thrilled. Abraham pulled Xavier to his feet, clapped him on the back, took his face in his hands, said, "Yes! Yes! You are you! You are wonderful you!" He pulled Xavier into his arms. Before Issy and Nora and Teresa piled on, Xavier's eyes met mine. So that was why Jane had kicked him out. It was selfish and childish, I knew, to care more about the fact that he hadn't told me than that he'd been through what he had, so I made myself smile.

Abraham clapped his hands toward Cornelia: "Finish! Finish!" The girl took up the final verse, sweet and soaring. The Homesteaders joined her for the final bars.

61

"*O*h, Xavier. What a heartbreak." Cornelia whispers her reply to some story Xavier just told, which I've missed because I fell asleep. Her voice is just one degree louder than the humming tires. The sky's that hazy orange of suburban nights and my forehead aches against the window. I missed the burgers and fries that left their stink behind. I close my eyes before Cornelia and Xavier notice me and shut up.

"Billy is beside himself," he says. "I've never seen him like this, Cor. He's been crying for six weeks straight. And abandoning him like this certainly isn't—"

"You're saving him."

"He's furious that I wouldn't tell him why I had to go."

"I didn't tell Eric."

"What did you say?"

"Something about Saskia and a nervous breakdown. Not entirely a lie. Oh, but the baby, Xav. You must be devastated."

"No, I . . ." He sounds shaken. "Cor, I think there's something wrong with me."

"There's nothing—"

"The whole time we were filling out the paperwork, and paying for everything—adoption is not cheap, you know—I kept telling myself, you don't want it now, but you are going to want it.

Months of waiting, all the while Billy's decorating the nursery and cooing over tiny socks and registering at Buy Way Too Much Shit for Your Baby Dot Com. The promise of it! We were going to make a family. But I wasn't excited or happy or any of the things you're supposed to be. Who wants to bring a child into this awful world, if you stop to think about it? No offense."

"None taken." Dutiful, but curt.

"When the adoption fell apart, Billy did, too. I understood how it destroyed him. I admired it, even. But Cor, I was fine. I felt nothing. No—even worse. I felt relieved."

Xavier was going to have a baby?

"Every couple has a rock," Cornelia says, after a moment. "You're the rock." The highway roars. Sekou and Issy's tidal breaths move the air as they sleep.

"I'm sorry, Cor. I didn't mean—"

"How do you think Saskia's doing?"

Xavier clears his throat. "I think she handled the news well."

"It's going to be a disaster, putting her in the same room as Ben."

"I meant the news about Abraham."

"The more I think about it, I'm positive it's just a practical joke. I don't know why I got so upset. It was shock, more than anything. But now I'm a hundred percent sure we're going to get up there and it's going to be, I don't know, a bunch of teenagers who heard there was a cult up there once, messing with us."

"Maybe." He thinks it's more serious than that. Well, of course he does. He's making us go north. "What do you think's the worst-case scenario?"

"Jail."

"Really?"

"You're eager to go to jail?"

Xavier sighs. "Iss and I were talking about it. I don't think they'd be able to prove anything, you know? I mean, what do I know, but they thought it was an accident, didn't even investigate it as a murder, and the sheriff's probably dead by now. It was so long ago. Even if someone went to, I don't know, the authorities or whatever, they'd have to come up with evidence, exhume the body, and—"

"I get it. But what's worse than jail?"

"Billy." His voice quavers. "I can't hide it from Billy. I mean, all this time, obviously I hid it, but only because it's never occurred to him to ask if I've murdered someone. But if he came up to me one day and said, 'Did you kill someone?' I don't think I could lie. If news of this got out . . . well, every single person in our lives would be asking. Wondering. Your daughters."

Cornelia visibly shudders, puts her hands over her ears. Does some breath work. Then: "Did you see your father's painting in the living room?" I catch the sneer there at her jaw, before she turns back toward the passenger window. The SUV swerves right, then left, jostling my forehead on the window. Something in the road.

"Philip and Saskia have a relationship independent from me," Xavier says, when we're zooming straight ahead again.

"Doesn't it annoy you—your father choosing her?"

"He abandoned both of us. She's just more forgiving."

"Isn't her real father alive?"

"That monster gave up his right to be a father the moment he murdered his child."

"You're right. Of course you're right." Then: "Are you still paying Philip's rent?"

"How's your mom, Cor?"

That shuts her up. For a minute. "That big old house gives me the creeps. So many rooms. All that old furniture. That's where"— she quiets her voice—"the murder happened, right?"

"Yes, that's where Will died."

"Just tragic." Of course she wants every detail. She'd be disappointed; Xavier doesn't know much more than what the papers printed: a father filled with rage on a beautiful Connecticut day. I made my pledge to Grandmother as we watched Mother weep in the drive. I've kept your last day locked inside me ever since.

"Don't you think the house is pretty, though?" Xavier says. He's good to me, that one. "It must be hard, to live alone inside the museum of your worst day. No, I really do, I feel terrible for her."

"You're a saint, Xavier."

He ignores this. "Real Chippendale, a lot of that stuff. Priceless."

"I thought her grandmother disowned her."

His gaze hits the rearview mirror, but I close my eyes before he catches me. "The old woman was a bitch, but she knew Saskia didn't get a fair shot."

"What about her mother? Where is she?"

Sekou wails with a bad dream. Issy rouses, hands over the seat before her eyes even open. The little boy thrashes at his restraints. He hits a high shriek, zero to sixty. I produce a very convincing, very disoriented yawn, if I do say so myself.

"It's okay," Cornelia singsongs from the front seat. "It's okay." But the boy is not to be consoled.

"Oh I once had a horse and his name was Bill"—Issy eases into the song right away, her voice still groggy—"When he ran he couldn't stand still. He ran away one day, and also I ran with him."

The effect is immediate. The boy's eyes open from the trap of the nightmare. His body stills. Issy strokes his hand. He starts to cry again, in the absence of the song.

"He ran so fast that he could not stop. He ran into a barber's shop, and fell exhaustionized with his eye teeth in the barber's left shoulder." She's singing quietly, but it fills the car.

"How about 'Itsy Bitsy Spider,'" says Cornelia, voice sugary with false cheer.

Issy sighs.

Cornelia begins her ditty, hand gestures and all.

Sekou screams: *"Horse Named Bill!"*

Issy gives a sad smile. "It's the only thing that works." I know, then, that she has tried many songs, and that the fact that her baby loves this one has been a difficult truth to bear. We take up the familiar melody together. Eventually even Cornelia warbles along.

62

When Cornelia was done singing, the Homesteaders made their way toward their morning labors.

Philip clasped a hand onto the back of Xavier's neck, and they strolled to the cabin together. Why hadn't Xavier told me he was gay? Why hadn't Philip? It made me feel cold inside. I wanted to know the right thing to say, but I supposed if he didn't want to talk to me about it, then the right thing was just not to say anything?

Ben asked his mother what we were having for dinner. She called to Nora to gather up the baskets. Ephraim pecked Sarah on the cheek and left for the toolshed, and Sarah, in turn, took Ben by the arm, while he grumbled that just because he asked about dinner didn't mean he wanted to make it.

Cornelia watched Ben go. Issy took her cards from her pocket, slipped her arm through Cornelia's, and whispered something into Cornelia's ear that made her blush and giggle. They headed out along the waterfront.

Teresa, already halfway up the path, told Jim to pick up Tomas. He obliged but trudged behind her slowly, until Teresa yelled back down, "Could you go any slower?" He returned the favor by setting Tomas, howling, into the dirt.

Nora skipped up the path past them, empty baskets dragging.

Tomas hopped to his feet as if nothing was wrong, and chased Nora under the cover of the trees.

Teresa watched Jim return to the shore, to Butterfly, then resumed her climb alone.

Butterfly waded into the lake again, skirt blackening. Abraham approached her. "Did Cornelia get that glorious voice from you?" The dog licked Butterfly's hand.

She laughed, glancing at Abraham over her shoulder. "Absolutely not."

It was hot now, the sun shimmering over the top of the lake all the way out to Blueberry Island. I couldn't tear my eyes off Butterfly. It was like I wanted to solve her, solve why I liked the way she looked at Philip, but not at Abraham. I wanted to understand why I could find Jim's interest in her pathetic, and yet still want to know everything about it, and how someone like Cornelia, tidy and discreet, could come out of someone like her.

"That Cornelia girl can sing." Jim appeared beside me. We watched Abraham and Butterfly, how their heads curved toward each other. I told myself I was looking because I needed Abraham: I'd sidle up as soon as he was done with Butterfly and say something wise. After Cornelia's performance, after how he'd seen Xavier, I needed to be noticed, too. Why hadn't he asked me about what made me special? Why didn't he want to know?

Jim chuckled at my silence. "Don't like her much, do you?"

"I like her."

"Abraham." That was Gabby, from ten yards down the shore. "I told you, we need to talk." Abraham drew away from Butterfly. In his absence, she lifted her eyes to Jim. Jim stepped toward her as though I wasn't even there.

"Saskia was just saying your girl sure can sing," he said.

"My mother was in the church choir. I used to sit in the front pew and think she sounded like an angel."

"Church?" Jim laughed. "It's hard to imagine you in church." The thunk of hammers started from the hillside.

Gabby was leaning toward Abraham, ticking off points on her fingers. I wandered between the two parties, to the dock. I busied myself with unwinding the kayak ropes. The dog found me fast. He sniffed my fingertips, then settled in beside me, panting and eager, less of a threat now that he knew I had no food. The water glugged, rattling the boats against their moorings. I made every effort not to look at Gabby and Abraham as they huddled, but I couldn't help overhear.

"Surely you agree we need to pay our mortgage." Gabby's voice was careful.

Abraham waved his hand. "Unthing yourself of this concern. I've told you, it's working out. Unthing yourself of the idea that you must take this burden on alone."

"It's not my burden," she said. "I've been asked to manage our money. You've got to let me do my job."

"That's just it," Abraham said, and there was ice in his voice, "you must Unthing yourself of the idea that you have any kind of job here." He pointed back to where he had embraced Xavier. "Our job, if you want to call it that, is to Unthing ourselves of what is expected of us, and expand our—"

"Okay." Gabby collected herself. "Abraham, I get it. What I am trying to tell you is that we have to pay the bank this month. If we want to stay on this land, we've got to pay our mortgage every single month. You asked me to help you, so I'm—"

"Jim?"

Jim's head lifted eagerly. He came right over.

"I need your help," Abraham said.

Jim lifted his eyebrows in surprise. "Yeah, sure."

"I need you to take over the banking."

"Really?"

"No," Gabby said, "not really."

"You don't think Jim will do a good job?"

"I'll do a good job," Jim said.

"Gabby has so much on her plate."

"Abraham, come on," Gabby said.

"She helps us so," Abraham said, "but it's time she Unthings herself of the idea that she must be the one holding the purse strings. Don't you agree, Jim?"

"I can absolutely help."

"Abraham," Gabby said.

"Walk with me."

Jim grinned. The dog scuttled to Abraham's heels. They moved on, away from Gabby.

Abraham stopped then, as if he'd just thought of something important. He turned and looked at me on the dock.

"Glad to be back, Saskia?" It was feeling the sun again, to have his eyes on only me. "Good. Good. Take up that hatchet. Issy's been keeping it safe."

I tried not to look disappointed that this was all he said, that then he climbed the hill without another look. Jim and the dog trailed behind. Gabby ran her hand over her skull and sighed, and quickened her steps to catch up. I watched them move up the hill, watched how Abraham kept ahead of her so that she found herself talking to his back, until their voices faded and all I could hear was the lap of the water, and the scolding of a chipmunk, and, far above me, a cardinal ringing out his competent song.

"Dog likes you." A voice from behind me.

I'd forgotten how small Marta was up close, her face wrinkled below the silver cap of her hair. I pretended not to be startled. "You call him Dog?"

"Better than what Nora wants to call him." She came closer. My hands stilled at their false task. How much had she overheard?

"I've decided to teach you," she announced, "about the plants. And the animals. I'm going to teach you about what lives on our land." Abraham would have said to Unthing ourselves from the notion that any of this was ours. But the day Marta had thrown the hatchet, I'd seen she understood something different about the natural world; that to name it was to know it, and to know it was to love it. I wanted to understand, too—the common names, and the scientific ones, the uses for whatever we discovered. Not only because I was interested, but because to speak the language of this place was another way to get close to you. You were out there somewhere, wandering, waiting; I had come upon bits and pieces of you, and haphazardly. This way, I could show you how serious I was. I'd pluck a flower and Marta would tell me it had your name folded within its own, or I'd find myself marveling at a field adorned with golden-tipped feathers.

"It's not all tromping around the countryside," she said. "There is plenty to memorize, and that requires discipline. Most folks here think the best thing for children is to keep their hands busy. But I see more for you than making bread."

"Abraham wants me to learn to use the hatchet."

"Bring the hatchet, then. Bring your friends, if you want—Isobel, Cornelia, Benjamin, Xavier."

I opened my mouth to protest—Cornelia and Ben were most certainly not my friends—but she cut me off. "Studying will be good for them. We'll keep your minds nimble, despite what these people want." I saw plainly, then, how someone who knew the scientific names of every living thing would chafe here. I wondered why she stayed.

63

No one can make anyone else eat, except Issy. Over the back-seat, she hands Sekou a leftover burger bun. He offers it up in his sweet, small palm, and next thing I know, I'm choking down a nibble. I manage to swallow, my stomach a fist. Sekou babbles a happy song, a toddlerized version of "A Horse Named Bill," with some "ABCs" tossed in.

We're on a curvy road now. The country. No oncoming traffic; perhaps, already, Maine. A sliver of moon.

"How are your girls?" I ask Cornelia. She'll be useful later.

"They're fantastic!" Cornelia unlocks her phone, fingers flying. She spins in her seat to hand over the device. "Margaux's in the ballet two program at the dance school! And McKinley's pitch-ing for her softball team!" Where are the gap-toothed smiles and knocked knees? Their breasts already press at their T-shirts. The arm of the pretty one is slung over the shoulder of the one who'll surely explore her sexuality. "They're both doing better than a 4.0 GPA and are in a chess club, though we're not going to hold on to that much longer because it's just not where their passions lie. Just wait, Issy. All these extracurriculars to get into college!"

Issy taps my shoulder for the phone. She whistles at the sight of them. "They're—what? Thirteen?"

Cornelia nods. "My St. Patrick's babies."

"They have serious boobs."

Cornelia coughs politely. "They both have crushes! But Eric is vehement—no dating until they're sixteen." She holds out her hand, an impatient waggle. Issy passes the phone to me but Sekou reaches for it. Now he's crying again, laden with want.

"Let him have it," says Cornelia. "I've got unlimited data."

"He doesn't watch TV."

"An hour of screen time isn't going to kill him, Iss. And I think we could all use a break from that horrible song." The boy settles after Cornelia calls up Elmo and the machine is back in his grubby little hands.

"Thirteen, huh?" I say. "That's how old we were when we met."

"I was twelve," Cornelia says. "Ben and I, always trailing a few months behind. Of course I was madly in love with you, Xavier."

"Who wasn't," says Issy.

"I wasn't," I say.

"Because you," Cornelia says, "were in love with Ben." We all remember her eyes were drinking him in, her nervous laugh when he looked at her, the twirling of her finger in her hair. But I'll save this retort for when it matters.

We steer through a small town. A corner pump, a general store, electric in the night—then gone. "Do you think Gabby and Abraham ever did it?" I ask.

Issy cackles. Sekou brightens at his mother's pleasure and drops the phone into his lap. He pulls a fistful of French fries from his drink cup. He shoves them into his gleeful mouth. You're there in the gesture. Then it's only him, peering again at the small screen, and he is enough.

"I have no idea who she had sex with," Issy says. "Not even my bio dad. Maybe I'm the product of a virgin birth."

"Gabby was too smart for sex," Cornelia says. "She didn't let it control her." In that comment hides Butterfly's shadow, but none of us are touching it with a ten-foot pole.

Instead I say, "I always wondered about Gabby and Abraham. He was so . . . charismatic. There has to have been some reason she put up with his bullshit."

"She believed in his cause," Cornelia says.

"But it was also that he was sexy. Come on, it's not going to hurt you to admit it. We all wanted to fuck him. I mean, of course we didn't fuck him, and we didn't even know that that's what was driving us. We were children. It was easy to have a crush on him, or whatever we want to call it. We were supposed to! That was how he got us to do what he wanted. He used it, that . . . thing he had, charisma, whatever, to get us to do what he said."

Their collective silence hangs over me like the funk of the fast food.

"Did Abraham ever . . . ?" Xavier says. "Saskia, he didn't ever try to . . . ?"

"No," I say, although now whatever I say they'll doubt. "No, of course not. Never."

Issy and Xavier's eyes meet in the mirror. She sits forward. "Because the whole thing with—"

"I don't want to talk about it."

"But if you—"

"She doesn't want to talk about it," Cornelia says, surprising us all as she defends me. Elmo's whine fills the car.

"Maybe Gabby was just at some higher level of consciousness than the rest of the human race," I finally say, to try to salvage the conversation.

"She probably would have been happier," Issy says, "if she'd have just done it every now and then. I don't know about you guys, but if I go awhile without sex, I turn into some kind of maniac, amputated from rational thought, sure I don't need it at all, when what I really need is to cum hard."

Cornelia covers her mouth in shock. I don't imagine Eric is giving it to her that often. Between that, and Xavier's domestic tragedy, and how I've spent the last decade and a half, there's a good chance Issy's done it a lot more recently than the rest of us. I'm about to say as much, when she fumbles toward an ugly truth. "Cor, how's your mom doing these days?" The train of thought: Gabby was not a slut. Butterfly, on the other hand . . .

"Oh, she's . . ." Cornelia says, "well, I suppose she's fine. She's um, she's still up in Canada. I mean, I think she is."

How cruel Cornelia was with Xavier, pressing him about my relationship with Philip. What goes around. "You're not in touch?"

"We are! Kind of. I just. You know. It's hard."

Xavier clears his throat. He turns his head Cornelia's way. "Is she still with Ephraim?" Good to get this out in the open before we're with Ben. Historically, he hasn't been a fan of discussing his father leaving his mother for Cornelia's.

Cornelia nods. Xavier pats her arm. "It's okay."

She shakes her head. "No." Grief swells her voice. "No, it's not okay. None of it was. I feel so awful that my mother was responsible for so much of what went wrong."

"Don't slut shame her," Issy says. "The end was coming long before Butterfly fucked Ephraim. I mean, sex is power or whatever, but your mom's magical pussy did not destroy Home."

Cornelia doubles over. She covers her face. Her shoulders start to shake. When I glance Issy's way, she mouths: "Oops."

Xavier touches Cornelia's shoulder. This gesture lifts her head. Unhinged laughter fills the car. She has not, as we've all assumed, been sobbing. In fact, she can barely breathe, she's laughing so hard. We chuckle as she cackles. She wipes tears from her eyes.

"Magical," Cornelia manages to gasp. "Her pussy was . . ." and we lose her again.

Eventually she stops laughing hard enough that she can put together a string of words. She dabs at her eyes. "You have no idea how good it feels to be able to talk about this. Do you know that Eric thinks my mom is just 'eccentric'? What the hell am I supposed to tell the girls?"

"Tell them Grandma likes cock," Issy says. "Sex positivity is all the rage."

You can practically hear Cornelia's eyes roll.

"I mean it! Butterfly didn't do anything those men didn't. Abraham shouldn't have been fucking anyone at Home, not to mention a newly divorced hottie under his spiritual care—no matter how sexy Saskia thinks he is."

"I don't think he's sexy, Iss."

"And Philip was married to Xavier's mom, and Jim to Teresa!" Technically, Jane had already left Philip by then—and had another man's baby—but if Xavier doesn't care to set the record straight, I'll hold my tongue. "Not to mention," Issy charges on, "Ephraim was also supposedly quite happily married to Sarah—Mr. Do unto Others—and even he couldn't keep his dick out of her! And still can't, apparently!"

"Okay," says Cornelia.

"Don't be hard on yourself, Cornelia," I say, as we pass a truck stop. "You don't owe anyone an explanation for your mother's choices."

She swivels in her seat. "Oh, sure. We'll all be like you, Saskia." Her voice is a blade. "Why take responsibility when we can just bake our daily bread and live on our big, beautiful estates and pretend we didn't murder—"

"Stop," Issy says. Cornelia stops. Xavier drives on.

64

Abraham took us out on the water. He paddled a kayak; we took two canoes. Never in a million years would I have said I thought him handsome; I considered my devotion far more complex. But it did not escape my notice that with his hair knotted on his head, I could see the muscles of his back move like machinery whenever his hands pulled the paddles. When he turned to see if we were coming, his eyes finally met mine, and a part of myself, at the root of me, shivered.

Issy and Cornelia pushed off without me, so I rode with the boys: Ben steering at the back of the canoe, Xavier paddling at the front, which left me, jobless, in the middle. The opposite shore, fixed in my mind, sprang into three dimensions as we moved toward it: trees, cabins, boats. We turned south. The familiar landmarks dissolved as we rejoined the Thinged World. New trees, new cabins, a smattering of islands, a pair of loons.

"You want a turn?" Ben asked. His newfound friendliness was so puzzling that I still couldn't tell whether he was being genuine. But when I looked back at him, risking tipping us, he offered up his paddle.

I shook my head. "We'll capsize."

He pointed at the girls ahead. "Let's beat them." Ben and Xavier paddled like anything and we pulled far ahead. Cornelia's shattered expression as she watched us sail by filled my heart with mean hope.

I thought of Odysseus and his exploits, which Daddy liked to regale us with at bedtime. He'd look at Mother over our heads whenever he spoke of Penelope, weaving patiently, fending off her many suitors—a threat veiled as a compliment. I thought of you pointing at a barge on the East River and asking how something so big could go so fast. I thought of how in paddling away from Home, I was leaving the search for you behind for the day, and hoped you didn't mind, and couldn't feel my mild wave of relief; it was exhausting to hold the whole possibility of you inside every minute.

We came to the end of the lake and then we kept going. Abraham led us through a secret passage only a little wider than the canoes. The channel was shallow and sandy, maybe twenty feet long, curving gently to the right. Abraham called it "the Dugway." It seemed we would run aground—Ben's words, spilling from just behind me—but we soared over the close bottom like an airplane above the earth. The view opened up again, at the lip of a whole new lake, like *Alice Through the Looking-Glass*.

65

*F*our spotlights spring on when we pull into the driveway. Next comes a volley of barks from the belly of the house. The dogs' voices knot together; it's hard to tell how many. Maybe I'm afraid, after all.

The house is made of big, round logs. It's two stories tall and wide-spread on the land. It clearly has a view, but anything outside of the lit circle we're caught in has been eaten by the night. Xavier cuts the engine. We sit there until the front door yawns open.

Ben.

Ben in a white T-shirt and plain boxers, shielding his eyes. He looks small from this distance, just a regular man on this earth. At his command, the animals charge from the house. Four dogs: square heads, rib cages like metal crates. Brindled and snarling, they snap against the car. The hot bodies smack the metal again and again. Sekou utters a manic cry.

Xavier unrolls his window, just enough to speak through. He holds up his hands. "We come in peace!"

Finally, Ben understands. "No," is all he says. He calls to the dogs. They leave us in an unexpected show of obedience, and disappear inside at his heels. Do we imagine the sound of the bolt locking the door, or does sound really carry that far across the Maine night?

Xavier undoes his seat belt.

"No," I say. "I'll go."

66

Abraham steered us to an untouched beach skirted by forest. The boys took turns bursting out of the surface of the new lake, fists of black gunk clutched high. Cornelia and Issy had a treading water contest. Ben swam close, his body swift and strong. When he surfaced, he grinned, then splashed me.

"You've got Cornelia to thank for this bounty," Abraham said, as we dug into a half peck of apples, two pounds of bacon, and boules of Sarah's sourdough. "She created a diversion." He unfolded a piece of wax paper, revealing a hunk of Teresa's goat cheese. "So innocent-looking, but I tell you, this girl's a criminal mastermind."

"Sarah said we could take it," Cornelia said.

Abraham stopped sawing and caught her eye. "Unthing yourself of the notion that you must be good all the time," he said. "I promise, you'll find yourself much happier." He was looking at her in the way I longed for, a beam of looking. He hardly blinked. He did not look away until she smiled shyly. Then he nodded and carried on with the knife.

My mouth watered as he spread the cheese onto each slice of bread, and topped it with slabs of bacon. This was one of Home's magic tricks: a new desire to devour my fair share. Afterward, belly full, I toppled back onto the warmth. Cornelia and Issy started up a game of Spit, and Xavier played the winner.

"Can you believe that when I first imagined Home, it didn't occur to me to think about children?" Abraham's voice surprised me. Maybe I'd been sleeping.

"I was there," Issy said, slapping the empty pile before Xavier had a chance. "You thought about me."

"I treated you like a small adult, Iss." Abraham unbound his hair and wrung it out like a fine linen cloth. Beads of water thumped the bed of sand. "I didn't understand that a child is a force unto herself. I was so focused on building what I'd imagined that I never looked up to notice that it was already being shaped by you."

Issy opened her mouth to disagree.

"Let me own my weakness," Abraham said. "Unthing yourself of the idea that I cannot make mistakes." He tossed her the remnants of his apple. She popped it in, core and all, then shuffled the deck again. Xavier flopped back into the sand.

"Anyone want to play?" Issy asked. She dealt herself a round of solitaire.

"I never considered," Abraham mused, weaving his fingers through the knots the water had tied in the ends of his hair, "how the community of children that is at the center of Home's daily life might and should change our mission. You're a vital force in shaping what we do. I've started to think of you as our North Star."

It was easy to feel left out when Cornelia and Issy whispered shoulder to shoulder, and Xavier preferred to tell his secret to the world before confiding in me, and he and Ben got to be boys together. But wasn't I here now, with all of them, with Abraham sharing his wisdom, on the lip of a sparkling lake with a full belly?

And Ben's private smile in the water, and the mystery of his newfound kindness.

"Xavier," Abraham said, and though Xavier stayed in the same prone position that looked like he was sleeping, his energy changed; every inch of him attended. "How do you feel after announcing who you are?"

"Okay, I guess?" Xavier propped himself onto one elbow, and his look asked what we thought. "I mean, everyone's being nice about it."

"Why wouldn't they?"

Xavier shrugged. "I don't know. I just." He shrugged again. "I didn't want to make it about myself or whatever."

Abraham was fixed on him now, just as he had been on Cornelia, and then on Issy. "We do our best to Unthing ourselves of our selves, but life is a subjective experience. Besides, it's a marvelous thing to discover who you want to fuck."

Xavier's laugh barked with shock. Cornelia covered her mouth. Issy guffawed. Ben dug his feet into the sand.

"Oh dear," Abraham said, "did I say a very bad word?"

Xavier shook his head, laughing. "No, go ahead."

"I embarrassed you," Abraham said. "Only I meant to celebrate. Only I meant to say that what your mother did was awful, Xavier. I hate that she turned you out just at the moment you were able to tell the truth about who you are."

"Yeah, no, it's okay," Xavier mumbled. "She didn't . . . it's not a big deal."

"You are safe here, with us. You are safe to be who you are."

Xavier nodded, but it was clear he was on the verge of crying. Abraham turned, abruptly, to Ben. "Your father has a problem with gayness, doesn't he?"

"No," Ben said. He scowled.

"It's right to disagree with him, and stand up for your friend."

"Ben's been cool," Xavier said. "He's been helping me a lot."

"I love that so," Abraham said. "I love that so, Benjamin." He placed his hand on Ben's arm. "I knew there would be a day when you would challenge your father's views, and stand up to his fists."

Ben's gaze was a line across the water.

"I know it makes you angry when I speak of your father this way. I, too, had a father whose views I disagreed with. I, too, lived and breathed in the wake of his expectations, and his anger. I want you to know that once I grew, once I forged my own path, our difference became easier to bear."

Ben nodded once, as if to say, please end this. Issy pointed out a pair of loons fishing, their black heads scanning left and right before they dove under.

"I'm glad to see your sadness leaving." At first I didn't know Abraham was addressing me. His voice grew intimate, as if it was just the two of us. "I wished for it to be so." He started a braid at the nape of his neck. "You are getting stronger, turning your sadness out. Do you feel it, how strong you are?" I should have brought the hatchet along; it would have pleased him to see me throw it. "I wanted to ask, Saskia"—and he leaned toward me with a furrowed brow—"who you consider to be the leader of this group."

The lake and wind seemed to hold themselves suspended. "The leader?"

Abraham finished his braid and let it hang, unbound. "Let's Un-thing ourselves from the idea that it is good or bad to be a leader. Of course there are benefits to leading. But it is also hard work. Sometimes it brings work that will break your heart. I believe that those who are born to lead know it all along. I myself knew it from the time I could talk. There has always been something in me that can't help but make big decisions."

Ben was still looking off across the water, only the loons weren't there anymore. My belly tightened.

"I could see," Abraham continued, "what should rise to the surface, and what was better to let sink. I could see what was worth bringing into the light. You know all about that, don't you, Saskia?"

My face was burning. I couldn't look at the others now. How would they punish me for the way he was setting me aside? But my insides were flipping and twisting, like a dog being offered a meaty bone.

"Cornelia sings like an angel," Abraham said. "Ben works hard. Issy lifts us with her spirit. Xavier . . ."

Xavier turned then, panic racing across his face.

"Xavier is loyal," I said.

Abraham nodded after a moment. "Xavier is loyal. And why," he said to me again, "do you think I gave you that sharp little axe?"

My hands buried themselves in the sand.

"An axe is built to destroy," he said.

Ben audibly groaned, then stood, and walked off along the shoreline, as if I had done something terrible he had known I was capable of all along. "Are you saying," Cornelia said, "that Saskia is built to destroy?"

"I am saying," Abraham said, leaning back into the sand with his hands behind his head, like a man on vacation, "that there is always the possibility of violence. Especially when living as we choose to, removed from the Thinged World. Removed from its strictures. The sheriff has his eyes on us. Did you know that? I ran into him in town the other day and he glad-handed me and told me to just plain call him Sal. Sounds friendly enough, doesn't it? Well, let me tell you about friendly. He'd love to come up to our land. He'd love to get to know you all, especially. The children. They always want to know the children. You know why? So they can take you. Sal could do that—did you know? He could take you, Saskia. You're here without a parent. He could snatch you up and put you in the system. He would call it protection."

67

I have to knock and knock and knock and knock. The night tightens, but at least it's not daytime; I'm not sure what would happen if I stood in the sun this long. Maybe I'd flake off, like sand in a windstorm. At least in the dark I can breathe. The others are watching, so I have to succeed.

The last time Ben or I knocked on the other's door, I was on the inside. I'd just settled into a Friday evening alone in my Park Slope apartment, planning for a movie night, maybe, a self-pedicure—during that steady phase in my early twenties, after Home, when I believed having a regular life was as simple as getting a paying job. Did he knock this desperately? Did he feel this much regret? Did he feel whatever one calls the premonition of regret, knowing that when the door opens, what will happen is inevitable—and terrible, and necessary? Not anything like a choice.

I feel his steps before I see him. The dogs are there, too, snarling, yipping, but he calls to them—"Hush now!" My hand shrinks back just as the door opens.

Here he is, then. The expanse of his face. His eyebrows, furrowed like a little boy's, then involuntarily eager when he sees it's me, though he tries to hide that. He smells of dried sweat and evaporating whiskey. He is puffy and middle-aged, but I notice him in there, under all of the changes. He snaps his fingers. I think, at first, that it's meant for me. But the dogs sit.

He's standing in his kitchen. He's put on sweatpants. He folds each hand over the bareness of the other arm; it's this tenderness that urges me to look him in the eye.

"I thought you were a shut-in now." He's got the same pug nose, the cowlick at the forehead, like a puppy licked him. "They kidnap you?"

"I came because I wanted to," I say, wondering if I'm right. "Because if Abraham is back, we have to stop him."

He rolls his eyes at the mention of that name. I change tack. "Can you let us in? Issy's kid is in the car."

Ben runs his hand over his face. Then there are footsteps. His eyes dart left, toward the rest of the house, still dark.

"Everything okay?" It's a girl, a very pretty girl, a very pretty young girl, with wavy raven-colored hair and ample breasts and a face shaped like a valentine. On second glance, she's a woman with a bit of girl left in her. She's wearing his flannel robe. She cinches it with a blush, but not before I glimpse the turquoise slip beneath it.

Ben's daughters are tall and blond and strapping. They inherited these traits from their mother, who is positively Viking; Shelley-Ann, his wife. Shelley-Ann looks nothing like this fresh young thing. Believe me, I know.

"I told you to stay upstairs," he says to the pretty young thing.

"I was worried."

"Go back." His finger points toward the belly of the house.

"I'm Saskia." I stretch out my hand. "One of Ben's oldest friends."

The girl smiles, broad and easy, reminding me of Issy the day we met. Her palm is soft. "Jenny." She peeks over my shoulder at the SUV.

Ben has his arms crossed, eyes to the ceiling.

"Jenny," I say, "we're super tired. We drove up from Connecticut. We've got a baby with us. Ben probably has a couch the baby can sleep on, right? The rest of us are fine with the floor. Could you help us? Please?" My eyes slip off of her and onto him. "We can talk in the morning, but for now, we just want to sleep."

Jenny looks to Ben, a pleading look to do right. So she knows him then. She knows he has it in him to turn us away.

Finally, he says, "I'll lock the dogs up."

68

"Certain fungi and plants have what is called a mycorrhizal relationship," Marta said over her shoulder as she clambered the long hill. Wind swirled the maples and sent leftover rain down onto our heads.

"You know the other day, out on the other lake?" I whispered to Issy, letting Marta keep her healthy lead. I'd being trying to figure how to broach this topic. Xavier would call me a show-off; Cornelia would analyze the situation within an inch of its life; and Ben—well, no; I definitely couldn't bring it up with Ben. The only problem was I could never get Issy alone. It was always Issy and Cornelia doing laundry together, or us three girls walking down to the campfire, or the five of us on the Main Lodge porch, playing a Spit tournament because there was nothing better to do. Then Marta showed up to take me foraging, and I asked to bring a friend.

Above us, on the path, the old woman commanded: "Repeat the difficult word."

"Mycorrhizal."

"Don't sound so glum! It's an evolutionary miracle."

A week had passed since that day on the lake with Abraham. I was supposed to be enjoying learning from Marta, but I couldn't shake the expression on Ben's face, or that groan, or the way he'd walked away when Abraham said I was built to destroy. Now he wouldn't even talk to me, as though he'd been dreading those words for longer than he'd known me.

I might have gotten up the guts to ask Abraham why he thought Ben had reacted that way—but Abraham had left the next day. His note, which I'd found before dawn, attached to the door of the Main Lodge with a paring knife, read: "Off to share our ways with the Thinged World. Back when I need to breathe again."

Marta forged uphill. "Hurry up, buttercups."

"My ankles are soaked," Issy grumbled. If she'd heard my question, it hadn't registered.

"I've got sourdough in my pocket."

"You can't bribe me out of wet socks." Issy placed her hand over her eye to shield it from the emerging sun, and whistled at the coming climb.

"Fungi are heterotropic," Marta said. "That means they can't make their own food; they have to take it from someone else. Well, guess who they take it from? Hmm?" She swiveled back with a tight frown. "Girls?"

I raised my hand. "Trees?"

"Smarter than you look."

"Did you notice," I whispered, once Marta had turned back around, "that Ben got . . . kind of, I don't know, mad or something when Abraham started talking about—"

"You are such a baby about Abraham. He'll be back soon. I told you already, he goes off sometimes—he has to spread our word in the Thinged World. We can't Thing to him. It's not right." She was never this grumpy with Cornelia.

We climbed past a rotting white birch stump (*Betula* something; Marta had said it too fast when we passed a stand), and a darting gray bird I thought was called a phoebe. I would have to just come out and say it. "Ben seemed really upset when Abraham said . . . when he said I was built to destroy."

I had thought Issy incapable of lying but I understood, in the way recognition surfaced on her face, then dove, that she was keeping a secret. I opened my mouth to insist she tell me everything right now but Marta had planted her walking stick into the land and was pointing out a red-tailed hawk—*Buteo jamaicensis*. We had no choice but to catch up and stand with her as it sailed over the ridge. "And what," she said, "do trees do that's so special?"

"Perform photosynthesis?"

"Confirmed, they produce their food in the form of carbohydrates through the process of photosynthesis." Marta looked up to the top of the hill, then back to us. "Do you understand? The fungi piggybacks on the root system of the plant. That's how it gets its food. It's symbiosis."

"From the Greek?"

Marta looked pleased. "Yes indeed, meaning 'living together.' You speak Greek, Saskia?"

"No. My father loves the Greeks." Issy looked up; she'd never heard me mention him. I took Marta by the arm and escorted her up to the ridgeline, asking the names of all the plants we passed. Elderberries were properly called *Sambucus canadensis*, which can be used as a cold remedy (when combined with mint leaves and yarrow blossoms). Then came yarrow, *Achillea millefolium*, which I made sure to pronounce the way Marta did, just loud enough so that Issy could hear.

From the lookout at the top, the lake had become an outline. In fact, we could count six lakes between us and the horizon. Mountains brushed the sky; distant houses, small as matchboxes, were sprinkled across the foothills. A fog shifted, cloaking and revealing the miniature world below. A wind cut over us, bringing up the wet lake funk that had become familiar. A motorboat puttered. I searched for a sign of you—or maybe you, yourself, standing far below in one of the meadows, flailing your arms like someone on a desert island—but of course it was only pine needles and cabins down there, and the lake, and the boats.

"Well, howdy." Butterfly had emerged from the forest at the top of the ridgeline. From behind her came a cross-looking Cornelia. But Cornelia's face lifted at the sight of Issy.

"Out for a walk?" Marta's voice bloomed with approval.

"My girl and I needed alone time."

Cornelia went to Issy. Butterfly wore a crown of cornflowers, and carried a second one on her wrist. I held out my hand. "Can I wear that?"

"Oh of course, sweetie." Butterfly placed it on my head. She lifted her eyes to the view. "Gosh, it's pretty up here."

"Be careful back in those woods." Marta did not approve of waxing poetic about the landscape; it was something to know, not admire.

"Plenty of bears, I'll bet."

"Two-hundred-foot cavern, cut right into the forest floor. A chasm, guess you might call it. You don't break your neck on the way down, you'll starve to death stuck down at the bottom. You'll scream, and no one'll hear you. Not many folks up here, looking for lost hikers." With that, Marta wandered away toward the edge of the ridge.

"You ever miss California?" I asked Butterfly, whose eyes had drawn wide. Cornelia's version of California was outdoor malls, endless sunshine, trees laden with free oranges. "Cornelia sure does."

"Really?"

I lowered my voice. "Don't tell her I told you, but she wants to go back."

"She said that?" I had her attention now.

"Well, it's where her dad lives."

Butterfly's mouth clamped down. It was the first time she didn't look beautiful.

"You know the other day Philip said he wanted to paint you."

"Really?"

"He said you've got rare cheekbones. You should tell him if you're interested." I let that sit, then added, "In having him paint you, I mean."

Her hand went to her cheek. "He's, like, famous, right?" Now that we were talking, she seemed more like a babysitter than a mom.

"So what makes the mycorrhizal relationship mutually beneficial?" Marta commanded our attention. She was met with blank looks by Cornelia and Butterfly, and explained the day's lesson, then circled her attention back to me. "Surely the tree is getting something out of the deal?"

"Well, fungi grow in the ground," I said. "And the tree has roots in the ground. So I'd guess that the fungi assist the roots somehow."

"You are correct, Saskia. I'm glad you've dispensed with pretending you don't know the answers." Marta wiggled one hand on top of the other. "When fungi form a mantle on the roots of a plant, not only do they get food from that plant, but they lend themselves to that plant. They extend that plant's root space, which means the plant gets more water and nutrients than it would on its own. You see? They're more than friends. They need each other to survive."

She unzipped her backpack and handed over well-wrinkled plastic bags and small knives. "We're looking for maitakes today. *Grifola frondosa*. Perhaps they'll be up here, nestled into the bases of their preferred mycorrhizal partners—oaks, most commonly, in these parts, *Quercus velutina*." She regarded each of us then carefully. "Now, what am I going to say about safety?"

"Don't eat anything," Issy said, "because it can kill you." Cornelia shrunk back in a satisfying tremble.

Marta went squarely into the woods. We wandered behind her, under the cover of the trees, keeping an eye out for that cavern she'd mentioned. For a time all we could hear was the padding of our own footsteps, and the high chirp of a bird Marta stopped to tell me was an osprey—*Pandion haliaetus*—cresting over the ridge. Sometimes we came together, in pairs or trios, sometimes we wandered alone.

Issy drew close. She pointed down. Marta was right—there, cut into the forest floor, was a secret mouth of rock, maybe ten feet across at its greatest width, so dark inside that it was impossible to see the bottom. She whispered, "Ben acts weird around you because of the prophecy." But when I opened my mouth to ask for more, her back was already a closed door.

69

*S*ekou shrieks, and there's a torrent of barks, and Issy's laugh. Leaf shadows filigree across the ceiling. A blast of sun.

I'm at Ben's.

The thought is a glimmer until it explodes into all that will surely go wrong and has already. For one, it's clearly past eight. At Grandmother's, I'd guess eight thirty, but everything flares new— *Acer saccharum*, the grand sugar maple just outside my window; the cirrus clouds above; the angle of the sun. I haven't slept past six in years. My gorge rises. Here comes the rush of what I know is just the blood in my ears, I know this, I know this, but it boils up like the lonely howl of the whole needy world pressing in against the too-bright pane at my head and I remember what I've done, how back at Grandmother's, first Xavier came, with news that Abraham is back, or he isn't, but whether it's him or not, someone knows someone knows—

But, no: you opened the front door. Sekou saw you, didn't he? He gave me that smile when I asked. And then: Topsy on the couch for him to find. How else could Topsy have gotten there? You wanted me to come along with Xavier and the rest.

So, then, deep breaths. Stop my rushing heart.

Five things I see: dusty gingham curtains; too-shiny paint on the ceiling; my worn sweatpants; my flimsy fingernails; my yellow split ends.

Four things I touch: the cotton of the quilt; my lips against each other; the cool of the window; my heart, thrumming in the cradle of my skin and bones.

Three things I hear: Sekou's bubbling giggles; the dogs barking; a red-breasted nuthatch—*Sitta canadensis*—tooting its insistence.

Two things I smell: bacon, mildew.

One thing I taste: the sourness of my tongue.

So, then, Home. Today, Home. I rise—and then, oh, the Mother.

The Mother makes it another thing I've only just remembered. There's so much more to keep track of in this great outside. Back down into the bed. She was fed upon arrival, her leaven made before we went our separate ways—me into the older daughter's childhood bedroom; Sekou and Issy into the younger one's; Cornelia and Xavier onto the couches in the great room downstairs—but don't get distracted, the Mother needs attention and day shine is burning and the others will think they can do it but they'll ruin her. Cornelia will mess with her. Cornelia will ruin her. So, up again. Steady my feet onto the ground.

The name Anna is embroidered on nearly everything in here—on Raggedy Ann's stained pinafore, and a creased handkerchief, and a bit of cross-stitch framed, lopsided, over the bed. A high school transcript, five years old, hangs on the corkboard over the desk; Little Anna is, apparently, not so little anymore.

There are country touches all over the second floor—a butter crock in a hallway tableau, calico pieced in hearts on the bathroom hand towels, and "Home Sweet Home" in an embroidery hoop hung over the stairs. How long ago did Shelley-Ann leave? What made her finally do it? Was it Jenny?

Stop. Just stop.

Playmobil figurines are piled at the bottom of the stairs. Sekou is their giant, sorting the people from the cars, the beds, the trees. Out Ben's log-trimmed windows, the view is spectacular, land falling away in three directions. I remember now when Ben bought Shelley-Ann this house, his steady breath during one of his phone calls, the mention of the blueness of a lake below, as though I would agree that if it was truly as blue as he said it was, of course he should marry her.

The boy lobs himself into me. There's no choice but to pull him into my arms. He's pantsless and proud. "I peed in the potty!" He presses close, sucking on the foot of a Playmobil ambulance driver, which I make a solid effort to admire. In the kitchen, Cornelia tells the rest of her story: "So then Eric is hanging from one arm, one foot on the ladder, and the girls and I . . ." and Jenny emerges in polyester slacks and chalky cosmetics.

"You sleep okay?" I ask.

Her curls, crispy with product, boing when she nods her head. "Want to play some more, buddy?" She puts her hand on Sekou's back. He buries his face in my neck. Good boy.

I carry Sekou toward the others. Ben must be tending to the dogs, but the rest of them are in the kitchen, Cornelia in running clothes, having already put in her exercise (of course). Their plates show a finished feast: waxy yolks, grapefruit rinds, bowls swiped clean of yogurt. They pretend to be fine with my nightgown and unbrushed hair. I want to yell that I never sleep this late—I am ever up with the dawn! Sekou's finger bores through the buttonhole at my neck and reminds me who I want to be.

I say, "Did everyone sleep well?"

I say, "Looks delicious."

I say, "We should probably get going."

"Oh, you're leaving?" Jenny's followed me in. "I hoped you'd stay for at least another night. I think you're all lovely."

Cornelia smiles. "Well, isn't that nice!" But you know what she means if you know her.

"Ben says you have business in town. The closest hotel is twenty-five miles. Can't I convince you to stay?"

I can't help myself. "I think Ben's the one who needs convincing."

Jenny's pink hands fret over themselves. "What is your business here, if you don't mind my asking?"

Xavier lifts an eyebrow.

Issy pulls Sekou from my arms: "Let's get some fresh underpants on you."

Cornelia scrapes the breakfast plates.

But I'm not afraid. "Have you heard of Home?"

Cornelia says my name.

"What home?"

"It's this place nearby, where—"

"The summer camp?" Jenny says. "Where you met Ben?"

"Sure. A summer camp." So that's why he picked her; too young to have heard the stories.

Ben's voice is harsh in the far doorway. "Jenny, I thought you'd left for work." The dogs swarm behind him like one enormous beast, but they stay behind the lintel as he moves toward her, steps heavy. "You don't want to be late."

She pops a smile. I want to tell her not to perform for a man who barks orders, but she smacks a kiss onto his lips, then swivels to Sekou, grousing on his mother's lap—he has no interest in fresh underpants, thank you very much. Jenny tells him she hopes they'll get to play again soon, and it stills him, and I like her a little better.

She gathers her purse and a Tupperware salad from the fridge. Sekou reaches his arms back up to me and Issy turns him over with a sigh. I bathe in the wash of the boy's puppy breath while Jenny's lips meet Ben's yet again. She grabs her keys. She waves. Ben whistles to the dogs and they rush out into the open day. I wonder if Jenny likes them against her legs. Ben's got his own van out there, with competent lettering on the side: *HVAC Services. Heating. Cooling. Heat Pumps. Plumbing.* He stands at the window, watching his animals move onto the land.

"How old," I say, "is that girl?"

He wheels around. He looks to Cornelia while pointing my direction with a shaking finger. "Tell me every single thing she said."

"That poor little thing wanted to know about Home," I say, before Cornelia sells me out.

"Don't talk about Home." Ben's hands curl into fists. "To me or Jenny or anyone else. Jesus Christ, are you fucking stupid?" The little guy slips off my hip and dashes back to the trove of toys. Issy goes after him, but not before she glowers at us. Ben is already yelling. "You know how hard I've worked to make sure no one around here thinks about that hellhole anymore, let alone associates me with it?"

Cornelia crosses her arms. "Well, of course people remember. It's seven point two miles away and it was only twenty-five years ago."

"The people who remember keep their mouths fucking shut."

"It's a cliché," I say, "a man your age with a girl like that."

Ben lifts one finger. "Do. Not. Talk. About. Jenny."

I don't let my gaze waver. I drain the fight out of him. He leans over the countertop, hands spread wide, then looks up at me again, and oh, those eyes. "Saskia, you of all people. You don't really think Abraham's alive . . . ?"

My heart flops as Ben says that name, as though his words have made things real. He frowns, briefly, in concern at my response.

I forgot. I forgot how well he sees me. I brush past the table, past him, straight to the Mother.

Xavier says, "Look, Ben, none of us want to go back up there."

Flour, spoons, water, thermometer. Let the grown-ups talk.

"The sixth letter said it has to be all five of us." Panic laces Cornelia's voice; on the drive up, she was so sure we didn't have a thing to worry about.

"I don't give a shit," Ben says.

Issy storms back into the room. "Ben, you should want, more than anything, to make sure Abraham isn't the one up there, sending us those letters. You think showing up will ruin you? If he makes good on his threat, that will be what ruins you. Let's drive up there. We can end this today."

But Ben grabs his keys. "In a day or two, when you realize it's someone messing with you, you'll go home. But this is my home. I have a life here. I'm not gambling everything for six creepy notes, just so you can drag me back into your bullshit."

"Our bullshit?" Xavier's enraged, a rarity. "I'm sorry, last I checked you were in that cabin, too. In fact, if I remember correctly, you were the one who held—"

"Let it rest! We're free. Why can't you people just let it fucking rest?" Ben is already out the door.

70

Marta and Issy and Cornelia and Butterfly and I gobbled omelets dripping farmer's market cheddar, served beside the gathered bounty of the last of the season's fiddleheads. Maitakes were nowhere to be found, but the tight fern spirals—the tips of *Matteuccia struthiopteris*, ostrich ferns—made up for it. They tasted obscenely of the color green. Grease slicked our lips. One bite and appetite was an old friend. Teeth and stomach and fork and butter and salt and cheese and egg and parsley and Ceylon tea and turbinado sugar and the tips of brand-new plants, unfurling on the beds of our tongues.

71

Maine teems by. *Acer saccharum*, *Cardinalis cardinalis*, house, flash of lake, hill, *Betula papyrifera*—but they pass so much faster than words can muster, a rapid jumble of a countryside we once knew. We bank right, and Cornelia's GPS tells us to join the road we are already on. I'd close my eyes but then every bit of me would be hurtling without remembering why.

"I don't recognize a thing," Xavier says.

"Take this road the other way," I say, "and you end up on Marta's favorite mountain."

In her front seat throne, Cornelia harrumphs. "It's a game to her," she mutters. "Everything is a game." Then anger overtakes her. She wheels around. "I don't care about Marta's favorite mountain or who Ben's screwing. I care about shutting up whoever's up at Home. And I'm not going to forget that you're the reason he isn't in this car when whoever's up there tells us to go fuck ourselves because he didn't come along."

"We're adults," says Issy. "Can we act like it?"

"I'm not," says Sekou. We all crack up, even Cornelia, who offers an apology for swearing. Issy tells her to fuck off, and we all pretend, for a moment, that we believe everything is going to be okay.

Tap tap. There's a tap tap on my arm—five of the boy's little toes lined up in a neat, sweet row. His foot is warm. I let my eyes close so I can feel only it. Then I'm less afraid of the hurtling. I don't tell them what I know, that Ben was never going to come along. Ben takes time. You have to let him feel. The sooner you encourage him to fume, storm, rage, the sooner he'll do what you want. Well, thank you very much, I got him there.

72

*T*hwack.

Butterfly sat with Philip as he painted, cross-legged, eyes closed in a shaft of morning light. He stroked azure paint onto a large canvas. The lake lapped. All around, wildness flourished: the clattering of the battling eastern chipmunks—*Tamias striatus*; the exuberance of the black-capped chickadees—*Poecile atricapillus*; and the occasional zipping of a ruby-throated hummingbird's wings—*Archilochus colubris*.

Thwack.

I was watching from the shadow of the lakeside woods—eastern hemlocks (*Tsuga canadensis*), whose new growth can be steeped to make a tea rich in vitamin C; eastern white pines (*Pinus strobus*), which can grow to be the tallest of any trees in the Northeast. Butterfly and Philip did not notice me in the thick of the trees as I perfected my hatchet throwing. Thwack, thwack, thwack. Really, I was missing my target, then stumbling over the rooty ground to dislodge the tool Abraham had said was built like me. It sometimes found its home in the trunk of a snag, but more often bounced off of the red needles on the forest floor.

Thwack.

Really, I was hiding from both Sarah—who had said that now that I was on my way to mastering sourdough, it was time to learn how to cook—and Marta—who had come to expect my company on foraging hikes, which were really oral exams on species, genuses, and taxonomies.

Thwack.

Really, I was annoyed, and also, pretending not to be annoyed—lest the dead read thoughts—because I had been back at Home for more than a month and you had not thrown any special signs my way. I would have taken anything as a sign by then: a crow's feather in my path, or a funny-colored pebble on the lakeshore. I'd left offerings: slices of sourdough, a hard-boiled egg. I wandered the woods, calling your name. But no birds sang out your syllables. No footprints were to be discovered in the red crunch of pine needles. If you were at Home, you were punishing me.

Thwack.

I was getting better at hitting the trees, but the blade never sunk into my target—in this case, a burl six feet up, twenty feet away. Marta had made it look easy, hopeful. Maybe that was my problem; hope felt like a distant country, growing more out of reach with each passing day. What did it mean to be built to destroy? I had no idea, yet I'd been abandoned to it. Issy refused to discuss the prophecy. Only this morning, she and Cornelia had sung "A Horse Named Bill" at the breakfast table and then skipped off to tend the chickens.

Thwack.

Meanwhile, Ben and Xavier were closer than ever. They ate dinner with the men and stayed out at the bonfires. Of course I wanted Xavier to have a friend; I even admired Ben for this acceptance in the face of his father's disapproval. But surely Xavier had noticed Ben give me the cold shoulder. I pictured Ben's face on that burl.

Thwack.

I'd thought for sure that after Abraham singled me out, he

would fold me closer. But he was still out in the Thinged World somewhere. He'd left me to this loneliness, and to Dog, who bathed my hand in slobber.

Thwack.

Out in the sun, Philip said something quiet. Butterfly opened her eyes. She was golden in the light, cheekbones high, hair sparkling. It had only taken that one mention of Philip's interest, up on the ridge, to bring them together, and now he was happy and she was happy. She probably didn't even remember she had me to thank. Abraham would come back from the Thinged World and see that she and Philip were together, and either he'd be sensible, forgetting he'd shown any interest; or he'd be angry and turn Butterfly out, Cornelia with her—which might not be the worst thing.

Thwack.

Each of Philip's canvases, which had begun to line our hallway, held a slice of Butterfly's body—the pelt of her armpit, a constellation of moles on her shoulder; her smallest toe—juxtaposed over a colored landscape (the mawkish green of the lake on a gray morning, or the sunlight streaming in over the tops of the pines). Unlike the body parts in *The Lewdnesses*, these bits of Butterfly weren't performing the trick of pretending to be something they were not; these were honest, hungry expressions, humming with desire. The day before, Xavier had kicked a hole in a larger-than-life frosting of Butterfly's eyelashes blocking our door, then staged the scene of the crime to look like a chair had toppled into it.

Thwack.

"Your stance needs help." Jim moved toward me from the far end of the property. He could have been watching Butterfly and Philip for hours.

Thwack. The hatchet caught its mark. "I think I'm doing pretty well."

Dog sprang up as Jim neared, lavishing the man's hairy hand in licks. Jim was kind with his scratches behind the ears. I felt for him the way you might for a child forced to share his favorite toy; he already had a wife, and a decent one at that. But he might answer questions. I turned my head to the side in the sympathetic way Mother would when courting one of Daddy's good moods. "How long have you lived here, Jim?"

"Let's see, we came in . . . eighty-seven? Eighty-eight? Got married here, on the land. Hand-fasted. Teresa gave birth in the Main Lodge. Sarah caught Tomas while I paced the porch."

"Must have been scary, having a baby way out here."

"Well, I didn't have to do the hard work." He was finally looking at me, and not Butterfly. "I said we should go to the hospital but Teresa says, 'Jim,' she says, 'women been doing it this way for thousands of years. You think some rich asshole in latex gloves is going to do a better job?'" A smile gathered him into the memory.

"I don't know much about the beginning of Home. Issy said there was some kind of prophecy . . . ?"

"You know about that?"

"Hard to keep a secret here." My heart pounded. But I risked losing him; talk of secrets had him glancing back to Butterfly. "She said it's why Ben doesn't like me."

"You got the hots for Ben?"

I shook my head, but my tongue had grown dry. "No, I don't like when people don't like me."

Jim leaned against the nearest pine. "Well, I wouldn't take it personal. He probably doesn't want anyone telling him who to marry."

"The prophecy says I'm supposed to marry Ben?"

Jim knew, then, that I didn't know a thing. But we were in this far. He lowered his voice. "Back before we come up here, back before even Ben's family came here, when it was just Gabby and Issy and Abraham, Abraham had some kind of dream. Now, I don't know the details, I don't know why this dream was the special one but . . . used to be I absolutely one hundred percent believed it. Mostly because Gabby swore by it." He laughs, rubs the back of his neck. "I'll put my money on Gabby most days. So this dream . . . it's about Home. This was when Home was still run-down. Just three people, broke and crazy. But in the dream Abraham has that night, Home looks pretty much exactly like this." His arms swept the air. "It's buzzing with believers, folks who want to Un-thing, who farm and cook and fix shit. Abraham and Gabby are running the place. Issy's nearly grown."

"This is the prophecy?"

"I'm getting there. Abraham sits down and he writes down the dream, every detail he can remember. He gives it to Gabby and hits the page and says, 'I saw it, Gabby. I saw the future.' She's like 'Dude, this isn't a prophecy, this is a wish list,' 'cause she can smell bullshit a mile away. They strike a deal: if he's right about five things, the first five things in the dream, in the exact order he wrote them down, she'll let him call it a prophecy."

"And he was right about the first five things?"

Jim's hairy thumb popped into the air. "First, a family will come with a firstborn son. They'll be escaping a terrible past." He waits for me to figure it out. "Ephraim, Sarah, Ben."

"They were fleeing a terrible past?"

"You're not getting that story out of me." Jim lifts his pointer to match his thumb. "Second, the mother of that family will nourish everyone she meets, turning bounty and harvest out of what others consider to be garbage."

"Sarah."

"Third, the land, though difficult to till, will come around with love and coaxing, and yield a bounty if we work it with gentle hands—"

"That doesn't sound so much like a prophecy as how farming works."

"I'm not done!" He was smiling, though. He'd forgotten Butterfly. He waved the fourth finger into the air. "A man will come to tend that land, a man with a beard of white, who knows the ways of the earth, and he will teach us how to require it to bear us fruit."

"Amos?"

"Amos. These were the first four things in that dream. And they showed up in exactly that order in real life."

"What was the fifth?"

"The fifth was a wise woman who would keep the Homesteaders in balance. Then Marta showed up."

"But none of those have to do with Ben marrying me."

"I knew you liked him! I'm kidding, chill out. You want to hear me tell it? Yeah? Okay, then. Remember, Gabby had said that if there were five things that came true, then she'd let Abraham call it a prophecy. Don't figure she ever thought they would. Not sure if she was happy or afraid to discover he was right on the money. Anyway, once she let him call it a prophecy, well, I suppose the other things in that dream were suddenly, well, supposed to come true."

He answered my question before I asked it. "Like how a girl would come to Home. A girl from the city. She would have flaxen hair and long limbs. The world would have hurt her. But this girl, she would be fiercer than she looked, fierce like fire. She would, in fact, be built to destroy." His voice had turned grim. "That girl would be the one to save us. She would be brave in the face of our weakness. She would know what to do when no one else did. The firstborn son of the first family would love her. She would love him back. They would marry. They would defend Home, side by side, when the Thinged World turned against it. When the Thinged

World came to hurt us, she would use her talents to destroy what needed destroying."

He knew what it was, for me to hear these words. "To be fair, there was one part of the prophecy that didn't come true. Once the girl came, she was never supposed to leave. But you left. You went back to New York."

"I came back, though."

"After Gabby went and got you. All's I'm saying is take the whole thing with a grain of salt."

It explained Ben's coldness from the moment Sarah introduced me, using the same words Jim had. It explained why he had suddenly become nice to me the very day he learned I was leaving, as though he could let down his guard, and why he had cooled off that day on the lake, when Abraham said I was built to destroy.

"Do you believe that I'm that girl?"

Jim coaxed Dog close. "I think what matters more than anything else is whether you believe it."

73

JimBob's is still there, a spiffy sign its only change—those dark windows, gas pumps, the tire gauge hung under the word "Air." Bushrow Road remains a long, graveled horse trail leading up a hill. Ben's house is in the country, but this is rural, open land, with few eyes on it. Xavier slows the car after the first dip in the road. Then we climb.

The driveway into Home is no longer obscured. Maybe if I didn't know what lies at the end of it, I wouldn't notice the gap in the underbrush. Everything Home once was rears up. I'm convinced we'll be talking to Abraham any second. I'm sure I'm not the only one to have these thoughts because as we turn onto the drive, Cornelia chokes out a cry and Xavier's fingers grip the wheel, and Issy's breath grows quiet.

"It's just some empty land the bank owns." Which one of us says this out loud? Maybe it's inside my mind. Probably it's illegal for us to be on this land now, and yet here we find ourselves, slipping down its throat.

74

"*O*h I once had a horse and his name was Bill . . ."

Abraham returned to us on a sun-spangled July afternoon, his baritone skirting down the driveway. He was flanked by a couple of scrawny boys and a girl with a flannel shirt tied around her waist. The Thinged World would have called them adults, but they were newborns at Home. Dog dashed out the screen door, Nora and Tomas at his heels. Dog leapt at Abraham and the new arrivals. Abraham told him to sit, but getting attention only made the animal more frenzied. He leapt at the new girl, nipping her ponytail. She squealed and laughed, but that was politeness hiding terror; I could see in the way she turned away with her hand over her face. Then Nora and Tomas were swarming Abraham, too. Dog turned at the quickness of Nora's hand. He nipped.

Nora shrieked. Gabby was already there, to grab Nora away and pick up Tomas. "Stop riling him," she said. Nora cried and said she didn't mean to, but Teresa didn't mean the children. It was all done in a moment then, because it wasn't quite a bite, and Nora wasn't really hurt, and Abraham bent to stroke Dog, and calmed him under his hands, and everyone surrounded the new arrivals, and since the song was started, it must be finished.

We whirled and clapped our way around the newcomers. We

pitied them for how much they had to learn. They didn't know that to sing something meaningless is to Unthing the rules you carry inside yourself.

When we were done, Abraham made his way through us, Dog never leaving his side. Jim shook his hand with a wide grin, and Abraham clapped him on the shoulder, before turning to ruffle Xavier's hair, then to say to Issy, "Is it possible you've grown taller?" To Cornelia, he said, "Your voice carried us through," which made her smile, then take a careful glance at Ben. But Ben was busy doing Sarah's bidding, handing out the freshly baked rolls that were meant for dinner. Abraham closed his eyes as he bit into one. Then he and Amos exchanged nods, and so it went with Ephraim, until Ephraim spat on the ground. Philip and Butterfly were late up from the water. Abraham's eyes took stock of their togetherness, then flew back to me. "How's that arm?" He meant the arm that threw the hatchet. I held it up in a show of muscle and everyone whooped.

That night while everyone was at the bonfire, I curled up with a chapter about spring edibles in Marta's copy of *Foraging for the Maine Table*. Dog lolled at my feet. Gabby's voice spilled in the bunk window. She must have been on the strip of land beside the dock, where Philip spent his days. "I am your partner in this experiment. Did you forget? You can't just invite anyone you like, Abraham, not without—"

"But that's the absolute point."

Dog went to the door and whimpered at the sound of Abraham's voice. I called him close. I stroked him.

"Those kids are ready. They're ready for the Unthinged World. I spent days on that island with them. They get it. They belong here."

"Who's paying?"

"We'll work it out. We always—"

"I work it out."

"You need to relax, Gabby. You make yourself unhappy."

"While you were on your little drug vacation, I went down to the bank. They almost wouldn't let me have access to our account, because apparently you told them only Jim could be on it?"

"We agreed it would be better for you. You're going to make yourself sick with—"

"What I discovered was not a surprise, because I've been telling you for months, and because Jim is not, shockingly, an accounting whiz, is that we are about to go into foreclosure. I told you not to give him access to that account. I told you to let me handle things. I've been telling you and telling you, we need to figure out a way to save this place because We. Are. Broke. And no, keep quiet, I don't need inspirational speeches about how you're going to raise the money, about how I need to Unthing myself of worrying, because you, Abraham, you are the one to blame for this. Not even fucking Jim. Your precious Philip"—she lowered her voice here, and I strained above Dog's panting—"Goddess bless him, Philip hasn't given us a tenth of what he pledged. All those other donors you said would be banging down our door? I haven't seen a single one. You said you'd institute a tithe, but I certainly haven't been asked to contribute. And anyway, how will these good people, who've given everything in service of your vision, be able to pay? With real money, I mean, not with bread or hours spent hammering nails into rooftops. We currently have two hundred and sixteen dollars to our name. So maybe instead of waltzing off to do ayahuasca with a bunch of teenagers, you should be here, managing your fucking vision."

The sounds of the darkness: the chipper spring peepers—*Pseudacris crucifer*—and the long wails of the loons—*Gavia immer*. When Gabby spoke again, she was farther down the trail. I climbed to the top bunk and pressed my ear against the screen. "You are the one people listen to. So get them to listen. Get those rich kids with their brand-new Patagonia jackets to pay for their vacation from the real world. Get us some fucking money and you betcha, Abe, I'll be a hell of a lot more relaxed."

75

Xavier cuts the engine in front of the Main Lodge. Abraham's cabin, and Gabby's, and the bathing hut have fallen to pieces. But the lodge is a pile of logs built for the ages. Cornelia brings her hand to her mouth and leans toward the windshield like a tourist who's made it to Stonehenge. Sekou unsnaps the chest strap of his car seat and kicks his feet with an elegant whine. He's too small to release the red button between his legs, but Issy doesn't lean over the seat to press it, not yet. I reach back and take her hand. She squeezes my fingers.

"You going to be all right?" she says. "You want to stay in the car?"

I forgot. For just a moment, I forgot it would be strange to simply step outside after sixteen years of not doing so, and I can't decide if it's a good sign or a bad one that simply being here has invited me to forget, but before I can answer, she squeezes my hand to get me to let go, and in the gesture lies her mother—efficiency, Unthingedness. She says she can't get out of the third seat to help Sekou until I move aside.

I get out. It's too soon to be here but it's also been too long. It's the loamy earth and the stink of the lake buffeting up in drafts; it's the frosted rim-lichen on the granite boulders and the haircap moss on the ground; it's the growl carrying up from a motorboat

speeding southward; it's the red squirrels; it's the skittering eastern chipmunks, and the wind roiling the grand white pines, and
the hum of a hungry horsefly—genus *Tabanidae*; it's the *Populus
tremuloides* quaking in a line behind the Main Lodge, and the spi-
derwebs catching the light, and the *Phalangium opilio* suspended
on its long, spindly legs over my shoe, and the *Poecile atricapillus*
chickadee-dee-dee-deeing from above. It's so much right and so
much together at once, so much of everything to long for and hate
that I might cry or I might scream. But instead we stand still, at
the top of it all.

Xavier puts his arm around Cornelia, who is crying. Issy lets
Sekou out of the car seat but he howls in her arms, bucking, kicking, as she tries to move him to her back, into the carrier. I almost
say to just let him run, but the set of her jaw reminds me it's best
to let the mothers mother.

Xavier's phone rings. It's improbable, this sound, in this place
that never knew phones. We shoot him disapproving looks. He
pulls it out anyway. I glance Billy's name on that shiny little screen.
Cornelia helps Issy strap Sekou in, bribing the boy with a lollipop.
Xavier silences the phone. He pockets it, a show of willpower. I
think to offer solace before I remember I'm not supposed to know
about the adoption gone wrong, and then I want to punish him.
A ribbon of wind moves across the lake.

The screen door of the Main Lodge cuts open. We lift our
heads. A young man stands there. He is skinny and tall, the scar
tissue snarled from just under his right eye, across his cheekbone,
down to his mouth. He wears a faded T-shirt and army fatigue
shorts. Dark black hair covers his forearms and shins, and sticks
out at his neckline. We know who he is because of this hair. We
forgot there was another child who grew up.

"Tomas!" A woman's voice cuts from the inside the lodge. "Was
that a car?" She comes out. It takes a moment for her to see us,

as though we are only just forming before her, but we'd know her anywhere, despite the fact that her rambunctious hair is now gray. Teresa, tall and strong. She throws up her arms. She rushes past her son. She sings "A Horse Named Bill" as she approaches. Her walk is a hobble now; something's wrong with her hip. Sekou squeals and laughs and sings along. Cornelia looks like she might throw up.

Teresa stops, mid-verse. "But where's Ben?" She's been expecting us.

76

*P*ast midnight, the salty smoke of burned sage leaked from under Philip's door. The floorboards creaked and Butterfly muffled a laugh. I couldn't bear the squeal of the floorboards under the thin mattress, not tonight. Xavier snored below me but I managed to get by without waking him, and though Dog lifted his head, he didn't follow me into the front room. A hot darkness filled the cabin, still and sticky, but in the free air, a breeze tussled the tops of the pines. A loon lowed somewhere south. I knew the path so well that I didn't need the moon. I discovered a kerosene glow coming from the window of the Main Lodge.

Gabby and Sarah sat at the kitchen end of the long tables, steaming mugs before them, and a pile of papers and receipts. Sarah was finishing a sketch. Gabby admired it. Then Sarah turned it over and started making a list. Through an open window down the line, I could hear their voices.

Gabby pulled the papers over. "He's probably at that bar in town."

Sarah took a long draught from her mug. "We can only change what is before us."

"I just want to be able to live here. And you, and Ephraim. The children."

"You know I can't leave. So I tell myself, all will be well. What else can I do?"

The screen door yawned open. Both women looked up. Teresa was in the doorway, Tomas tied to her back, his head tipped in slumber.

Sarah patted the bench beside her. Teresa came to sit. Gabby put her hand on Teresa's arm. Then she put pen to paper, and started adding, and Sarah went to put the kettle on.

77

*T*eresa's hair is gray from afar, but looking into the curtain of it as she squeezes me, it's a hundred different colors—cloud and silver and stone and slate. She smells as though she hasn't bathed in centuries. The screen door flaps shut. I look for Tomas when I come up for air, but I can't tell if it's him there in the meshed pane, or a shadow.

78

We had grown used to the slosh of the lake, and to the perpetual midnight moans of the loons, but the rev of a motor, followed by the slamming of a car door, and then of a howl let into the cool August night, had Dog on his feet barking bloody murder.

We pulled on our sweatshirts. We raced up the hill, Dog speeding off, Philip calling to us to wait, but we weren't going to miss the excitement.

We were past the chicken coop when we heard the second howl. High and raw, it carried a loneliness I'd only ever felt deep inside my self. Then I was running again. I stumbled over a rock. Xavier reached back and took my hand. We found our way to the driveway.

Headlights interrogated the Main Lodge. This wasn't just any car; it belonged to the police. Jim was caught in the beams. I understood, as he swayed, that he had been the one to make that unfettered sound. I understood that he had made a problem in the Thinged World.

Abraham shook the hand of a man in uniform, who was compact and handsome, with a white, trimmed mustache and shoes so polished that they shone in the headlights. A metal star glimmered on his chest. The sheriff. I shrunk back even though I felt foolish. But it wasn't foolish to be afraid; Sal the sheriff really could take me. Meanwhile, Homesteaders fumbled up the hill while the eyes of the law wandered the Unthinged World.

"Didn't mean to wake you all." Sal tipped his hat to Sarah in her white cotton nightgown. She folded her arms over her chest as though she knew him.

"Don't get much traffic up here," Abraham said.

Butterfly came out of Abraham's cabin. She was dressed in his linen tunic, a sheet wrapped around her legs, golden hair spread over her shoulders. At the sight of her, Philip turned and descended the hill, back into the darkness.

"Whore," Jim muttered.

Abraham moved to stand between Jim and Butterfly. Ephraim stepped forward, and Amos, too, hands at the ready as though Jim was about to turn into a werewolf.

"Same as I told you," Jim said to the sheriff, the words slurring together, "this place is filled to the brim with liars and whores."

"Best," the sheriff said to Abraham, "to get this man to bed."

"Jim." Teresa had arrived. She deposited the sleepy bundle of Tomas into Sarah's arms. "Come on now, Jim. Come on." She pulled at his arm. He shook himself free. Tomas started to wail.

Butterfly said, "Your wife is here." It sounded like a curse. Jim stepped toward her but she went back into Abraham's cabin and shut the door. Jim noticed his wife beside him. He took her face into his hands as though it was no contradiction to long for one woman and keep another.

The sheriff touched the brim of his hat. "I'll be seeing you."

After his ruby rear lights disappeared past the curve, Abraham went to Jim's side. Teresa had one arm slung around Jim's middle. Abraham put his hand on the man's other shoulder. Our eyes had adjusted. The moon had come out. From the gathered group came whispers and grumbles. But Abraham silenced the lot. "Whom among us," he said, "has not wanted to howl at the moon?" He tipped his face away from the earth. Out of his throat came a thin call: "Owowowwwww." Dog lifted his head to howl, too.

Jim's white teeth glinted. He issued forth a low, mournful sound. Then we were all doing it, every Homesteader gathered there, lifting our voices to the sky, a swirl of salt on black velvet. It was vast, the sound of us, all the way up to the Milky Way. Our cry grew to high harmony.

Abraham's hand wandered from Jim's shoulder to the base of the other man's neck. It reminded me of the jaws of the Rottweiler we'd seen in the city, who plucked a Chihuahua from the sidewalk and shook it to its rag doll death. It's easy to kill a little thing when it makes itself available.

79

"So, what are you and Tomas doing up here?" Xavier keeps the tone light, as though the four of us just happened to run into Teresa on a street corner. "Thought this place was abandoned."

Teresa lets out an earthy belch. "We live here." She scratches at Sekou's foot with her marled nails. "For now." I can feel the lightness of her touch without her touching me, a scrabbling tickle I haven't thought about in years. Sekou pulls his foot back of his own volition. A pair of crows—*Corvus brachyrhynchos*—crosses over us in a noisy gale. Laughter rides Teresa's voice. "You coming in?"

"We want to know what's going on first." Cornelia crosses her arms. Her toned biceps are tight, taut, like they might snap.

"Feel free to explore—see what Home is like Unthinged of us. I guess we shouldn't call it Home anymore." The wind presses my eyeballs as I try to name that smell—strident, sweet, bigger than any words I have. Teresa watches me remember. "Fucking crazy, right?"

"Is Abraham here?"

Teresa tilts her head to the side like Cornelia is an adorable child. I suppose we are all adorable children in her eyes—Issy, rooted like an oak; Cornelia, pushing for answers; Xavier, determined to be good. And me? What does Teresa see?

"Is Abraham alive?" That's Issy.

Teresa divides her hair into three lengths. "What do you think?"

"Come on, Teresa," Xavier says.

"You should have brought Ben."

"You don't think we tried?" Cornelia crosses the driveway to Abraham's cabin. It is dark in there, dusty. She rattles the doorknob. The door does not open. Cornelia aims one foot at the door. We're talking full suburban mom kickboxing shit. The door judders and jiggles, but it does not break. Then Xavier approaches, and holds out his hand for her to stop, and slams his shoulder against it. Cornelia is furious now, to be set aside, to be helped, to be met with a locked door, furious at Xavier for bringing us here in the first place. The wood shudders under Xavier's lurching weight. The flimsy lock gives way and Xavier stumbles in.

The chilly familiarity of the cabin would be like a shawl on my shoulders: the fireplace before me, Abraham's armchair to my left, the woven tapestry on the wall, hung from a driftwood branch. I want to know everything that was left behind. I want to know if you are in there, waiting. But I pretend to be Issy. I keep myself still. They return with empty hands, Xavier rubbing his shoulder.

"There's no one on this land but Tomas and me," Teresa says. "Should have said that, I guess."

"She's lying," Cornelia says.

But Teresa's smile drops. "On my son's life."

Issy draws herself up to her full height. It seems an impossibility that there was room to grow, but there is space above her and she fills it. She towers over Teresa's formidable frame, even her hair electric with power. When she speaks, it's with a practiced calm. "I agree with Cornelia. I think it's best you tell us what the hell is going on."

80

*I*t was dark again when I knocked on the door to Gabby's cabin, uphill from the Main Lodge. Issy slept there, too, but we never called it anything but Gabby's. When she opened the door, I spied her collection of paperbacks balanced on a board above the small woodstove, and Issy sprawled on a cot, arm draped over her eyes.

Gabby came out into the clear night. "Everything all right?"

I took the check from my sweatshirt pocket. "I know about the prophecy," I said. "I know that's why you told me that Ben asked about me, when I was back in New York. Because you wanted me to come back. Because you want the prophecy to be true."

"He did ask about you."

"I'm not going to marry Ben."

Gabby smiled. "I never said you were."

I unfolded the check. I handed it over. "I don't think this place needs a prophecy to be worth fighting for."

"This is a lot of money."

"You all could have a big fight," I said. "Or you could just deposit it, and we could stay." Then I stepped back down onto the path, and made my way toward bed.

81

"Two months ago, we were in Iowa." Teresa lowers herself into the chair at the end of the long table in the dimly lit Main Lodge. She groans as she goes down, like an old dog. She rubs at her hip. "A commune, guess you'd call it."

Tomas steps through a makeshift plywood door that cordons off the kitchen. He's even taller than he looked in the doorway, a head above where Jim measured, in memory. The scar has knuckled ugly. He catches me looking. He raises his chin into the light seeping in from a dusty window, and comes to stand at his mother's right arm, laying out a package of Wonder Bread, an unopened tub of Jif, and a wooden paint stick.

"Tomas, can that really be you?" Issy speaks as she would to Sekou. "You went and grew up without me." I do the math—he's thirty, give or take. It's hard to tell whether the impulse to treat him like a child comes from us or him.

Two sleeping bags lie on the bare benches before the fireplace, where a dirty cooking pot hangs, heavy as a bowling ball. Greasy clothes are piled on a metal folding chair, each dent familiar. There's a hole in the roof, and a bucket underneath it. Grimm is gone. The kitchen is barricaded, Teresa explains, due to an unfortunate incident with a porcupine who'd taken up residence.

I want to ask about this incident—*Erethizon dorsatum* is infamously territorial—but Xavier pushes the conversation forward. "So why'd you leave Iowa?"

Teresa's fingertips whisper across the table. "We should have built Home in Iowa." She waves her hand in the direction of the old garden. "The midwestern soil doesn't fight crops. It embraces them." Xavier turns his face toward the window, and I see, then, that he is as restless as I am to know how the land has changed in the absence of our care; that if it was just us two, we would have already covered it all: the chicken coop, our cabin, the dock, and every step in between. But instead, we endure the hard benches while Teresa chatters on about Iowa, where they lived for fifteen years and farmed with two other families and four cows and a hundred or so chickens. They grew so much produce that they started selling it at the farmer's market. Something happened there that Teresa isn't telling us. Her voice skitters over one of the men's names as though it's a bruise.

"Tomas learned animal husbandry." Pride bursts from between the lines of her browning teeth. Tomas unscrews the peanut butter and twists open the plastic bag of bread, then stabs the paint stick into the slick of oil to mix it. Little Sekou has fallen asleep. Good. He'd want some.

It's too personal to ask where they were before Iowa and after Florida, even now, even when we want to pin Teresa to the wall. It was a humiliation to be scattered from Home. The last time I saw her, she was drenched in a terror and despair I couldn't understand, some of it at my hand. I feel, momentarily, like burying her in another hug.

But Cornelia's patience is gone. "Why'd you come here, Teresa?"

"We got letters."

Cornelia sits upright. She would not make a very good spy.

Xavier leans forward. "Letters?" On the other hand, he sounds convincingly confused. "We don't know what that means."

Teresa is put off balance for a split second. "The letters. Isn't that why you . . . ?" Suddenly, she isn't sure of herself—this is interesting, and almost enough to make me believe that someone set her up. The possibility of Abraham flares. Tomas extracts the peanut butter with a glop and slaps it onto a slice of Wonder Bread. Something about this gesture brings his mother back to her power. She lifts her finger and wags it. "I'm not saying anything. Not until it's all five of you."

"Please, Teresa," Xavier says. "You know Ben. Really shitty stuff happened to his family up here. He's stubborn. But the rest of us came. From New York, Connecticut, North Carolina, Ohio. We all came a long way."

"Really shitty stuff happened to all of us here." Tomas speaks with the reedy voice of a new adolescent, despite his man's body. His peanut butter project has turned into a smearing, stabbing affair.

"What I think Xavier means," Cornelia says, her face a mask of a smile, "is that we are so glad you're here. Both of you. We had no idea what was waiting for us up here, and it's just wonderful to see some friendly faces. Personally, getting those letters was an absolute nightmare, and—"

"Don't tell her about the letters," Issy says, exasperated. It's too much for Cornelia—she bursts into tears again.

"You think I don't know about your letters?" Teresa says. "I sent them."

"Well, they worked," Xavier says. "Here we are. So tell us what you want."

Cornelia stutters down into her hands. "I have a life, you know. I can't let anything ruin it. Please, Teresa. I'm prepared to write a sizable check, on behalf of all of us. We'll be on our way and never bother you again. Unless what you need is a new place to stay. My husband Eric and I have a lovely guest house." She blinks in alarm at her ill-conceived generosity. "Is that what you want? A home? I can give you a home." The thought of what her homeowners' association would make of Teresa and Tomas almost sends me into a fit of giggles.

Teresa extends her hand to her grown son. He stops spreading and lays the limp bread on her palm. She folds it in half. She brings it to her mouth. She takes a massive bite, and chews with her cheeks bulged out. The sight of it, the sound of it, makes me gag. I lift my eyes to the window. I try to remember what we want. Cornelia is right, isn't she? We just want to be on our way.

"The thing of it is," Teresa says, "the letters said all five of you. And I only count four." She waggles her fingers toward Sekou, then purses her lips and makes her voice quiet, so as not to disturb his sleep. "Well, five. But not the right five."

"Teresa—"

"When I brought Sarah up here, she was open. Damn it, I thought you guys would be open. I really don't give a shit about Ben's sob story. He should have come."

"You kidnapped his mother," Xavier says. "Maybe you should have thought that through before requiring his presence."

"Kidnapped!" Teresa takes another bulging bite. "Ben has her locked in an old person jail. She's not even old! We sprung her free." Teresa beams up at her son. "My boy sprung her free."

"Someone found her wandering out on Bushrow Road," says Xavier.

"Isn't that the fucking point of freedom? Getting to be free."

Xavier shoots me a look. Maybe that seventh letter was right, after all. Maybe I can be the one to fix this.

"Ben isn't coming," I say. "We asked him to come and he won't."

"Well, then don't ask him," says Tomas.

He has balanced the paint stick atop the vat of peanut butter. The leftovers drip off the stick's edges, onto the tabletop, and the instinct to clean it is so absorbing that it takes me a moment to see what his hand is holding instead of the stick. It's Cornelia's gasp that makes me look.

A gun is steady in his right hand.

Issy backs toward the door, her son behind her.

Xavier puts his hands up. "Put it down, Tomas."

"Come back when it's all five of you."

Teresa raises her eyebrows as if to say, "What can you do?" Issy is gone by then, and we tumble behind her, away from them, eyes on Tomas, who stays in the dark room at his mother's hand.

It's when I step into the sun that you show yourself.

Well, it's not you, exactly, but it's a sign. There, on the ground, in the path leading from the Main Lodge to Xavier's SUV, is the wing of a bird. More precisely, a wing ripped clean from the body of the bird it once belonged to, although the rest of the bird is gone—no blood, no guts, no flurry of feathers on the ground. Just a wing. It wasn't there when we went inside. It's not the sort of detail one misses.

Small, black, unfurled—the end of it tipped in gold.

You have returned to me, as I have returned to you. A simple truth, something that could only happen in the Unthinged World.

I know this even as Xavier and Issy and Sekou and Cornelia move me away from the gun, out across Home. Xavier has me by the wrist. I lean back as though I might still pluck up that strange and real sign from you, but Xavier's hand tightens, and I scream at him to let me go, but then, we are all doing some version of screaming—Sekou, too, his sleep disturbed.

Before I know it, I'm being pushed into the SUV. If I could, I'd scramble out again, but Xavier slams the door shut and Issy wraps her arms around me while Sekou thrashes on her back. Xavier peels us out of there. "Mama, no," Sekou says, "no, there's pee-pee coming out!" The smell of toddler piss fills the car. Issy curses. Sekou wails. The gravel skates out under our tires. I realize I'm crying only when Issy reaches up to wipe the tears off my face.

"I'm so sorry," she says, "I'm so sorry I made you come outside for this. Oh, you poor thing, oh, you poor baby."

She has no idea it's because I want to stay. She has no idea that I have to go back.

82

Marta drove me across the valley in her brown Rabbit, which smelled of turmeric. We shimmied into the gravel at the side of the road, parking below an incline that rose into a dense deciduous forest. We ate hard-boiled eggs and slices of honeydew in the front seat; the dry-roasted peanuts were for later. Then the sun rose. Then we climbed.

My legs were a good six inches longer than Marta's and she was old enough to possess a black-and-white photograph of herself looking just like Shirley Temple, and yet I could barely keep up. Issy had told me that in the wintertime, Marta used a plastic sled, attached to a rope tied around her waist, to transport her groceries from the Rabbit parked on Bushrow Road, all the way to her cabin.

The day turned muggy. The mosquitos found us. One landed on her eyelid and she spoke to it: "Leave me be." We were on a lightly trodden trail, still green. It wound around the side of the mountain, occasionally switching back the other direction. In this way, we climbed toward the clouds.

We came upon an unexpected break in the trees and hiked across a bald spot, a swath of stone underneath our feet. Marta gulped down her water. She kicked at the stone below us. "They

call these the Ledges." The valley below us was an array of green
and blue. We were much higher than the ridge above Home.

"It's pretty," I said, before remembering how she'd frowned
when Butterfly used that same word.

She zipped her water bottle back into her backpack. "I used to
bring my children here." She made her way diagonally away from
me, up the mountain, as though this wasn't the first time she'd
mentioned she was a mother.

The Ledges was made of many ledges, large slabs of yellow
stone sticking out of the mountain. We made our way up and over
half a dozen of them, then climbed back into the woods toward
an unseen, unspoken peak. My thighs burned but Marta stopped
only when we reached the next rocky spread.

I dared to ask, "What do your kids do?"

We had a different view of the valley this time. We were pointing eastward, toward the distant Atlantic. The sun was in our eyes.
I asked my question as Marta was mid-gulp. I asked in a grown-up
way, about grown-up children, because it could be answered with
"they're lawyers" or "the older one lives in Boston" or "my son
works in Singapore," but I might also learn whether they had both
died in a terrible hatchet accident.

She held out the bottle for me to finish. "Why don't you tell me
about your father first?"

My mouth was dry but I couldn't bear to drink. "His name is
William." This was a funny thing to say, except that William was
your name, too, and it was nice to hear you on the air.

Marta waved her hand. "I know. And I know he's serving a life
sentence for your brother's murder. I want to hear the parts I don't
know."

No one had said our story straight out like that that in a long
time. When they had, the facts were only a chance to smuggle

in meanness: by terrible boys at that school Jane got us into, or the ladies Mother had once called her friends. But instead Marta seemed to be saying, remember who you are.

I took a long swallow. The water slipped, warm, into my hidden insides. The sun was feverish on my eyelids, but I forced them open, staving off a sneeze. "Mother met Daddy at a dinner party. They served shrimp cocktail. She said she was allergic, but really she didn't like shrimp." Was that where to begin, now that I was beginning? "She was very beautiful. So beautiful he couldn't look away." He had always said it like an accusation, but I tried to make it sound light.

"They fell in love, got married, had me. Mother's family has a lot of . . ." What was the way to describe it? It wasn't just money. It felt silly to try to explain in a place so abundant, where what we could eat or drink or grow was the only thing that mattered. It wasn't just status, or a name that could get one reservations at the best restaurants, although Grandmother had that, too. I thought of Abraham standing in the morning light at the edge of the lake, and though it was absurd to imagine Grandmother wading in to stand beside him, they shared a quality I could only now put into words. "Power."

Marta's eyes flashed.

"Then Will was born. I think Mother thought that a baby would make things better, but . . . Daddy was already unhappy. He said Mother was a liar. He said the shrimp cocktail was all he'd ever needed to know about who she really was. They were always fighting by then. You have to understand, Mother could be wonderful, she would do my hair however I asked, and on our birthdays we got to have ice cream for breakfast." I was talking of everyone in the past tense even though you were the only one who'd died. If I thought about Mother and Daddy out there, alive without me, I wouldn't be able to say another word. "When she was happy, she was the best. I think that's why he liked her. He thought she could make him happy, too. But that was the problem—no one can make another person happy." There was so much more to tell, like how Mother smelled of orange blossoms, and how Daddy had a nice hum when he washed the dishes, but I felt exhausted. I held the empty water bottle out but Marta didn't take it. She was looking down, over the valley, her eyes shaded with her small, wrinkled hand. We stood there a long time, until I lowered the water bottle myself.

Finally, she spoke. "Do you know the story of Odysseus and Polyphemus?"

"Yeah."

"Start where the one-eyed shepherd returns to his cave from a day of tending his flock to discover Odysseus and his men drinking his milk."

"I thought you wanted to know about Daddy." I felt silly telling a story she already knew. But she just stood there. "Polyphemus . . . was angry to find Odysseus's men in his cave. He pulled a boulder in front of the mouth of the cave so none of the sailors could escape, grabbed two of them, and popped them into his mouth."

"Real monster stuff," Marta said.

"Yeah, well, Polyphemus was a monster."

Marta finally looked at me. "Then what happened?"

"Odysseus was angry, but he was a warrior; he knew better than to waste his energy on that," I said. "And he was in a tricky spot. Only the cyclops was strong enough to move the boulder from the door of the cave, which meant Odysseus would have to outwit him."

If Daddy got home before bedtime, he'd call me into your room at the top of the stairs. The street traffic rumbled below. The globe that lit up, from when he was a boy, would be turned on. You sucked on your middle fingers and he sat on the end of your bed, and the shadows of his hands cast on the wall while he showed us how Odysseus had sharpened a long stick with his knife, then put it into the fire to harden it into a brutal point. Mother came to stand in the doorway. He said that when Polyphemus returned from grazing his sheep, Odysseus apologized for having gotten off to such a rough start.

"Odysseus was skilled in the art of rhetoric," I said, pleased with Daddy's phrase tripping off my tongue. "He got the monster drunk and introduced himself as Nobody. That way, when Odysseus thrust the pointed stick into the jelly of his eye, and the monster screamed in pain, and his neighbors came to help him, Polyphemus would yell through the sealed door: 'Nobody's killing me!' Of course the neighbors thought he meant nobody."

"You like that part," Marta said.

"I mean, that's pretty clever, you have to admit. Anyway, the next morning, when Polyphemus took his sheep out to pasture, Odysseus and his men were finally able to sneak out. Polyphemus opened up the cave, but since he was blind, he ran his hands over the top of the sheep, to be sure none of the men were escaping. But Odysseus was one step ahead of him—he had his men cling to the bellies of the sheep, and they slipped out of the cave unnoticed. When they were finally back on board the ship, Odysseus called out his real name to Polyphemus, which was a big mistake. Polyphemus was Poseidon's son, and you definitely don't want to piss off the God of the Sea if you're planning to sail home."

"Well done," Marta said. "Although you did leave out one detail, and in doing so, omitted what I believe to be the most important part of the story." My heart sank. Of course she didn't like the way I'd told it; no matter how many plants I knew, there was always one I didn't. "When Odysseus and his men snuck out of the home of someone they'd robbed, tortured, and blinded, they stole his livelihood. They took his sheep with them, onto their ship."

"So?"

"So does that sound like something the good guy does?"

"You're saying Odysseus is the bad guy?"

"I'm saying it's easy for a victor to call someone a monster." Did she think I considered myself the victor in our family's tale? I was trying to formulate my answer when she took a long inhalation, and let a great, deep breath out and said, "Saskia, I lost my children. They snuck out of the cave like Odysseus's men."

"Hidden under sheep?" I wanted to make her smile.

Marta lifted her head toward the rest of the mountaintop, still above us. She looked so sad. I breathed then. I breathed in and out. I looked over the sheer beauty of the valley. How far I'd come from that day with Mother weeping in the drive. Saying your name out loud, on a mountain I was climbing, surrounded by pearley everlasting, which is used as substitute for chewing gum, and tansy, which, when squeezed, is a suitable insect repellent. I didn't know all the names that belonged to that place, not yet, but if I worked hard enough, someday I would know as much as anyone could about the Unthinged World.

Marta zipped up her backpack. "Stories belong to the victors. In the end, that's what everyone's fighting for—the chance to tell the story of what happened, no matter what actually did."

83

*B*ack at the ranch, Ben's ranch, Cornelia prepares a sheet-pan dinner. My mind has stayed with that gold-tipped wing on the ground. The house sours with the others' fear but I'm not afraid of our return.

"Shall I check the dough?" Cornelia calls.

"Leave it alone, I said." Issy frowns at my grumpy tone. Cornelia's wearing a "Kiss The Cook" apron, loading the dishwasher. She checks out the window for Ben's van again. She's mentioned that she's roasting chicken and broccoli and chickpeas together on one pan about fifty times, as though we will find this revelation thrilling.

"You sure you're okay?" Issy leans across the couch so that no one else hears.

"Really. I'm fine." I do my best to keep my excitement hidden. To whoop with joy about that wing up on the land would be to lose her. Then Sekou makes the Playmobil ambulance guys scream. "Aaaaaahhhh," they scream and scream.

"Stop that," Issy says.

"Aaaaaahhhh."

"Sekou . . ."

"It's us," I say, as the kid screams bloody murder.

She doesn't get it.

"He's doing us, leaving Home today."

She plops down on the floor and tries to gather him into a hug but he scrambles out of her grasp. He plunges two figures into her hands. "Okay, Mama, you play that you're asleep and you're a big kid and I'll be the mama and I'm going to scream!" He lets loose again. Issy looks like she might cry.

Xavier is upstairs on the phone with Billy. He's been on the phone with Billy for hours. Sekou tires of his reenactment of the day's trauma and finds a deck of cards and lines them up, one by one, across the floor.

"Want to play Spit?" I ask.

Issy frowns. "I can't remember the rules." Cornelia pours us wine. Xavier descends the stairs, eyes red. Ben does not come home.

It's nearly dark when we sit down. There's no sign of the dogs. Cornelia bows her head and clasps her hands. Her lips mouth a blessing and the rest of us exchange looks. When she lifts her head again, I force some flesh onto my tongue. Proper homage is paid to the dinner, oohs and aahs, it's the best we've ever tasted.

Cornelia says, "I've decided to go back to Ohio."

Xavier sets down his fork. The chicken scratches my throat.

Cornelia's folds and unfolds her napkin. "That was . . . too much. Too much for me. I'm not built like the rest of you. The"— she chances a glance at Sekou—"the G-U-N. The whole . . . way they were. We went all the way up there and didn't even get any answers. I'm not sure they have them. And Ben's not going to change his mind."

"But without you," Xavier says, "we can't go up there again, even if we do get Ben to change his mind. 'All five of you. Or else.'"

Issy shuttles Sekou off her lap and onto the floor. Her hand brushes the top of his head. "Honestly, I've been thinking the same thing. I can't take Sekou up there again, especially after the— the G-U-N. And it just . . . it brought up so much shit. To think

Gabby thought it was okay to raise me there. God, and Tomas is so messed up."

"My family needs me," Cornelia says. "My girls, and Eric, they need—"

"We need you, Cornelia," says Xavier.

Tears bead at the corners of her eyes. "It is a practice to be a mother. To make a home. My practice. It's what keeps me sane." She quivers as she says that word, and I understand that she is more like me than either of us care to admit; ever on the brink. "I'm not strong like the rest of you."

"I'm not strong," Xavier says, as though she's accused him of something.

"Your family's going through a crisis, and you're able to make this a priority. As you should, Xavier; I'm not criticizing. I'm impressed by your ability to do what needs doing. But doesn't some part of you want to go home to Billy? Don't you all think we've done our best? We tried to convince Ben. We tried to convince Teresa and Tomas. We escaped when a deadly weapon was pulled on us. It's time to call it a win. Or a defeat. I'm okay with defeat."

"What happens when Teresa comes through on the 'or else'?" I say. "Did you forget why we came? To stop whoever 'knows what we did.' I don't know about you, but I don't trust that Teresa's just going to let us walk free." Really it's you I'm thinking of, you up there, waiting. I don't care about the 'or else.' But Cornelia does. And Cornelia can't leave. Issy can't leave. I need them back on that land, and Ben and Xavier, too, so that I can find you.

"Didn't you think," Xavier says, "that it was odd how Teresa . . . I don't know. How she didn't seem sure of herself?"

"You know what I think." Cornelia nods at a new thought. "They don't know what we did. They just want money, and they figure everyone who lived at Home must feel guilty about something, and they decided to send random letters to all of us, and we're the idiots who fell for it."

"Or it's Abraham," I say.

"Or someone else who knows," says Xavier.

"You sound excited," says Issy. She means me.

"All I'm saying is Abraham could have set Teresa up to get us here," I explain. "She said she sent the letters, but she didn't say she wrote them."

"Or she did write them," Cornelia replies, "and she and Tomas are playing with us, and they don't know anything about how Home ended."

"Why play with us?"

"Because they're crazy!"

"Well, I'm crazy," I say, "and I'm not blackmailing you over the murder we committed."

Her look of shame buys me time. "Please, Cornelia. For all of our sakes. Please don't run away, not until I've had a chance to—"

"I'm not running away. If anything, I'm running back toward the life I've chosen."

"For Issy's and Xavier's sakes, then." I muster a smile. "Solitary confinement would not be a problem for me."

"Exactly. Why do you care so much?" Issy's frowning.

The dogs return home then, bodies slamming the house. They bark for their human. Issy picks up Sekou. Xavier opens the door with a look of trepidation. The animals thunder in. Probably they are covered in ticks. Remarkably, they ignore our chicken. They're well trained, I'll give Ben that. They tear through the kitchen and into the laundry room, where he feeds them.

"You think they want dinner?" Cornelia asks.

Xavier grimaces, then goes that way. Sekou wants to go, too, but Issy holds him fast.

"I can't believe Ben abandoned those animals," Cornelia says.

"He's coming back," I say. "Give me one more day to convince him."

"You two can't even be in the same room together. After this morning's showdown, I can't imagine how—"

"I'll fix things. I promise. But you have to promise, too. One more day. Midnight to midnight. Please."

They do not want me to convince them. But I always do.

84

On the water, we were just teenagers—too loud, jumping off cliffs, dumb, rowdy, unthinged from Unthinging. The velvet lake was cool over our limbs, turning us into otters: Ben pouncing on Xavier to push his head under; Cornelia holding her breath for a minute at a time; Issy floating on her back. The boys tossed me over the side of the canoe when I said I was cold, but this was a good thing, it was good to shriek and swear to get revenge. The warmth from their hands lingered long after I'd swum away.

On Blueberry Island, Cornelia squeezed the ends of my mop. "Split ends. If we took off a few inches it would be so much lighter around your face."

Issy beat the boys in a swim race. We filled our straw hats with handfuls of late summer blueberries. We lay out on the rock, thigh to thigh to thigh to thigh to thigh, hands scrabbling together for the small purple balls, kissing them into our mouths. But the sky turned from blue to golden to pink to red. We had to go back. When we neared shore, I noticed Jim standing in the shadows. Issy splashed out of the canoe.

"You should have peed in the water!" Ben called after her.

"I'm not disgusting like some people I know!"

"I need to go, too," said Cornelia. Issy helped her out, leaving me rocking side to side as they darted into the forest.

Jim waded in and caught Issy's end of our canoe while Ben and Xavier tied themselves to the dock. Jim pulled me in. We dragged the canoe up onto the pine needles. The long fiberglass boat was as unwieldy on land as it was graceful on the water. By the time we had it flipped, the boys were up the hill. Under the evening trees, cool set into my bones. The scent of sautéing onions wafted down from the Main Lodge.

Jim scratched his belly. "What were y'all up to out there?" His oilcloth coat smelled of bonfire. I didn't know how to explain the pleasure of new air in my face, or the longing that that freedom opened, both an ache and an answer. But then I remembered him on the night of his howl, brought back from the Thinged World, and I realized: he knows.

"You ever get lonely?" His mouth twisted. "You didn't tell your friends what I told you about the"—he lowered his voice—"you know. The prophecy?"

I shook my head.

"Seems like a place with no rules. But there's so many fucking rules. Like Sarah, you know? Always controlling the food."

"Without Sarah, we'd starve."

He waved his arm. I was hit with a wave of whiskey. "Who died and made her queen? Isn't it Unthinging, to get to live without everyone acting better than you all the time? Fuck Amos and fuck Ephraim with all the things we've got to fix. Fuck Teresa and all the fucking things she says I'm doing wrong." He leaned forward. "Fuck. Abraham."

"We should head to dinner."

"They talk about you, you know." He tried to fix me in a steady gaze. "They have all these theories. Abraham thinks you're special. You're going to save us with your superpowers." He took a step closer as my heart hammered on that word. "A sweet little thing like you."

"I'm not special," I said.

He stopped. He cocked his head. "Why do you say it like that?"

"Because I'm not."

"But you said it like you are. You said it like you have something up your sleeve." The hairs on the back of my neck stood up. He saw me, plainly, through every layer.

"There you are." A bark—Dog rocketing down the hill, jittering toward me, tail whipping—and behind him, still halfway up the path, Ben calling impatiently, "Sarah needs you, Saskia."

I was moving up the hill before I made the choice to do so. Dog doubled back to me with a yelp. I tripped on a root but I righted myself. I couldn't bear that Ben had seen Jim lean into me like that. I couldn't bear what Jim had somehow understood. I left Ben in the blackening night, and Jim down at the shore, behind him.

85

*E*veryone sleeps, eventually. The boules crackle and whisper when I set them out to cool. I go upstairs. I lay my body down.

Past midnight comes the rumble of his motor. I knew he would return.

86

"I know they're good. Goddammit, they're the best fucking things I've painted. It's time the world knows, too." Philip paced our short hallway—every step, every syllable, wound with pride and manic frenzy. Wind howled off the lake, a hint of the winter to come.

"Can't you send them to New York?" Xavier gnawed on his knuckle. "I bet the gallery would pay."

"Can't trust anyone." Philip stopped in front of one of the bigger paintings—a patch of murky water, overlaid with the inside of Butterfly's wrist, tendons straining against the skin. The painting was two steps shy of obscene. Butterfly hadn't stayed over in weeks, not since we'd seen her come out of Abraham's cabin. Jim was to be avoided—I knew this now—but whatever had broken in him, I couldn't help blame it on Butterfly, or believe that the longing she called up in men had passed, like a virus from Jim, to Philip, to Abraham. I didn't like how close Philip got to the canvas, nor how he pulled himself away from it, veering toward us. "No, I've got to take them down to the city myself. They're going to make a shit ton of money, you know."

Xavier stood, resigned. "I'll pack my stuff."

"No," Philip shook his head mightily, "no. You, my darlings, will stay put. I'll be back in no time. A few days—tops. I'll swing by and take you both back to the city—in time for school."

I opened my mouth—I wasn't going back to the Thinged World, not while I knew you were still at Home. (Did I know you were at Home? You hadn't shown yourself in so long. Were you the reason I wanted to stay anymore?)

But Xavier's protest won: "You can't just leave us." Philip stopped then, and put his hands on Xavier's shoulders, ready to administer some wisdom. But Xavier feinted left and disappeared out the door.

By the next night, Philip and his canvases were gone, our cabin lightened to a tunnel of wood and wind. Ben knocked on the door. Xavier got out of bed. The boys played rummy on the porch. I sat on the porch steps and watched Dog snuffle in the dirt until Nora and Tomas flew up. They were playing witches, using pine branches as brooms. Dog snapped up Tomas's branch. Nora had taught Tomas to never back away so he grabbed it back, and then Dog came at the boy, snarling. Tomas screamed. Nora screamed. I stood to help but Ben was already down the stairs past me, roaring at Dog. Dog slunk to the water. The children's mothers called them in. It was dark by then. I crept out onto the lakeside where Dog had brought himself to cower and called him to me with an open hand. I calmed him. Together, we moved back through the dark. Ben's eyes wandered over me as I climbed the porch stairs with Dog at my side, but if there was something he wanted to say, he didn't.

87

"You must have gotten hungry, hiding out in your van."

My voice, and the sight of me in my ghost-white nightgown cast in the refrigerator's feeble light, gives Ben a good fright. He manages to swallow his terror in his next gnaw of chicken thigh. The dogs lift their heads, their collars clanging in the moth-riddled light coming in from the window. Of course he came home.

"Can I ask about your mom?"

I could have started, instead, with apologies. But Ben doesn't work that way. I could have started with how Tomas pulled a gun on us because Ben refused to come along. But the trick is diversion.

He pulls down a plate. Well trained by years of marriage, I suppose, or perhaps it's the civilizing force of Jenny. "Ma's losing her marbles."

"Dementia?"

He sits. "I mean, she was messed up from childhood. Home—I mean Home, not the home where she was born—was where she felt safest, which should tell you something. But then Dad left, and Home fell apart." He swallows another mouthful. "It was Nora that did her in. Her heart broke when Dad left, but she couldn't survive losing Nora."

How easily he says Nora's name. How good he is at pretending everything is nothing.

"That starter?" I point across the room at the cooled loaves. "It's from your mom."

"She threw it out."

"I have my ways." That makes him smile. "You didn't know I had it in me to keep a dependent alive, did you?"

If Sarah were the one sitting across the table, she'd reply: "The Mother isn't mine." She would say the Mother belongs to the women who came before us, who fed her day after day, and fed their families from her, generation before generation, back to the log cabin where Sarah's great-great-great-great-great-grandmother first made her with a bit of flour and water and air, in an act of hope and the need to feed her children.

Ben smooths his fingers across the tabletop. They skim toward mine. Then, as if it isn't dangerous, he lifts his eyes. That jolt is all it takes, to be back in the memory:

I was fighting laughter from the bed. Ben was young and fit and buck naked. His hardening cock bobbed enthusiastically as he came down the hall, swiping at his wet hair with the towel. Surely he couldn't be ready to go again, not so soon, and I thought: good on you, Ben. I thought: why didn't we do this sooner? Why did we spend all that time circling each other when we could have been doing this? All the rules had changed—disdain had become lust, or maybe we had finally skipped to love. He climbed back in with me, pulling the crazy quilt over his shoulders. What would Cornelia say? And Issy? And oh, Xavier—if Xavier found out, he'd be so mad. It was Ben! The truth hit me then, for just a moment—Ben had a wife, and little Anna, and another baby on the way. This was not as free and easy as it could have been, if we'd managed to get to it sooner. Maybe it was wrong. But how could it be wrong if we'd been moving toward this since the moment we met, years before he ever laid eyes on poor Shelley-Ann? Then I didn't care anymore about poor Shelley-Ann because Ben was kissing me, really kissing me—my mouth still so raw from the night before that it hurt to be kissed, but a good hurt—and I was kissing back. I wanted him. I wanted Ben! Ben, mine, not someone else's, not his wife's, not Xavier's—mine. Here he was, in my arms, in my bedroom, we were coming off a night of doing it, over and over, again and again, and now here we were, here Ben still was, on top of me, inside of me, his breath, my breath. I couldn't even tell if this felt good anymore, just that it seemed to be the only option we had.

Now Ben glances at the living room, where Cornelia and Xavier are sleeping. He lowers his voice. "You never told anyone?" So that's why he invited me to remember; not for the sweetness of it.

"Never."

He leans back, relieved. Runs a hand down over his face. "I don't do stuff like that. Despite what you think about Jenny."

I could ask why he showed up that night, of all nights, when I'd finally decided it was foolish to want a man with a wife and child.

I could ask what made him finally get up the nerve to drive all the way from Maine down to Brooklyn and brave street parking and say his name over the buzzer and still be standing on the doorstep by the time I got down to the foyer, and lift those gentle eyes as I unlocked the latch, and wear baldly, on his face, his need for me, and grab me and kiss me, right there, in front of the world.

I could ask how he could kiss me like that and then leave me.

Instead, I shimmy the cotton drape off my shoulders. "Can't you tell," I say in a fake boozy voice, "that I'm trying to seduce you?" He cracks up. That's when I put my hand on his arm quick enough to scald him. I tilt my head to the side, as if to say, but seriously, all joking aside, "Couldn't you take me to see Sarah tomorrow, so I can bring her a slice of her bread?"

88

I was on my second folding of the twelve loaves, which was no small feat. My wrists ached. My arms were caked. Beside me, Sarah clapped together black bean burgers from a 117-ounce can, adding in some molding oats and almond flour that Gabby had traded for a hen. Nora played with a corn-husk dolly at our feet.

"Couldn't we make a sauce?" The bean patties would be the consistency of hockey pucks. "Aioli—we could use eggs."

Sarah tut-tutted. "An indulgence."

The screen door yawned open. Abraham's tall form was a dark figure against the outside. His head was low. His shoulders sagged. He loped across the length of the Main Lodge. Sarah had her back turned but my hands stopped at the sight of him and rested on the butcher block. Into the kitchen he came, fumbling for the radio, flipping the dial until there was a fuzzy voice at the other end.

"—reports that the boy was armed but on the family's private land, and only approached the FBI after they shot and killed the family dog. We go to our correspondent on the scene in Ruby Ridge, Idaho, from affiliate station—"

"Ring the dinner bell." Abraham's long finger pointed down to the little girl.

"But it's not dinnertime."

"Now."

Sarah pulled Nora up and patted her out the door. Soon the bell was clanging, on and on, much longer than for any meal. The Homesteaders crushed into the lodge, curious, afraid.

The report was over by then. Abraham held up his hands.

"Yesterday the FBI murdered a boy on his family's land in Idaho. Land like this land. Land where this family had made their homestead." Dog trotted into the Main Lodge at Nora's side. Gabby caught him by the neck to move him back to the door, but Abraham called him with a tap. "Except apparently it wasn't private enough for the FBI. They've been camped out there for weeks. Snipers in the woods." Our eyes followed Abraham's finger as it peppered the trees.

"The family dog found the FBI's hideout. Those monsters didn't think twice about shooting him dead." Beside Abraham, Dog's bubble-gum tongue spattered drool onto the wooden floor. "The boy came down the land to save his dog, and they didn't think twice about killing him either. A little boy. When his mother heard the gunshots, she opened her door. She was holding her baby in her arms. Well, those snipers didn't think twice about killing her either. Shot that mother right out from under her baby." He looked at Teresa, holding Tomas.

"I'll say it again. This was on a family's private land, a land they simply wanted to protect. Land they were legally allowed to be on. Land like ours. Now the rest of the family is holed up in their home. There are more kids up there, in the cabin. You think the FBI has backed off?" Abraham's voice trembled. Butterfly cut through the room then, and wrapped her arms around Abraham, the long flush of her hair slipping over his face as he buried his face into her. He wept. It wasn't hard to believe there were snipers out in our woods, too, lying in wait.

"That family you're defending? They're white supremacists," said a voice in the crowd.

Abraham lifted his eyes, brow furrowed. The Homesteaders parted. It was Marta standing there.

"They're defending their land," said Abraham.

"But there's a reason the FBI is up there. That family has a stockpile of weapons and a history of making threats against non-whites."

Abraham's eyes narrowed. "Why are you here?"

"The bell rang."

"The bell for the Homesteaders."

"I wanted to make sure you were all okay." Marta looked to Gabby then. "Are you okay?"

Gabby lifted her chin. Marta looked back at Abraham, then nodded a goodbye. The screen door screamed shut at her heels.

89

"No, Mama, no, I want to play with you. I want to play you the big baby and I the mommy and I screaming."

I got up before the sun and the Mother and I had our turn together, the private slop of me inside her, her quips, her gulps, her hiccups, before the rest of them roused. Now Issy shuffles down with Sekou, but it's far too early for either of them. She tries to tiptoe him through the living room, where Xavier and Cornelia are still sleeping.

"No, Mama, no! I no take off my diaper!"

"You need to use the potty."

"No, no, Mama, I no use the potty!" Sekou shimmies off of her when they hit the kitchen. His diaper swings low over the linoleum floor. Issy glares at him. I take him into my arms right there on the ground, nostrils filling with salty baby piss smell. Issy shuffles to the bathroom. I sing to him, his favorite verse of "A Horse Named Bill," seven times.

> *She loves to laugh and when she smiles*
> *You just see teeth for miles and miles*
> *And tonsils*
> *And spareribs*
> *And things too fierce to mention*

I press my forehead into his, keep my voice quiet so it won't wake Cornelia. The little boy yawns and leans into me. His breath deepens. But the sound of the bathroom door opening brings him awake and he presses off of me, eyes clicking wide. He races to that precious Playmobil ambulance.

"Go back to sleep," I say to Issy. "I've got him." I appear virtuous, but really, I've burned up more words in the past two days than I usually do in a year. I can feel the world straining outside the house, a press of energetic need, calling to me in a way it hasn't in so long. I'm going to have to go back out, which requires intention and attention so I can't afford extra conversation, not even with Issy.

When she finally goes, he says, "I a doggy, Saski." I spread a slab of sourdough with a thick paste of Nutella and put it on a plate on the floor. The little doggy wags.

90

"*S*ammy Weaver." Abraham lit a piece of paper which held the dead boy's name.

We repeated "Sammy Weaver Sammy Weaver Sammy Weaver" as the paper flashed into ash, then ducked off into the autumn wind. The eleven-day Ruby Ridge siege was over, ended peacefully enough, if you didn't count that poor dog, and little Sammy Weaver, and his mother. We blew into our hands, and thrust them into our jacket pockets.

"What can you learn from that warrior child? He was your age. He used his shotgun to keep his family safe." The wind whipped our hair.

"I know where Gabby keeps the shotgun," Issy said.

Abraham put his hand on the back of her neck. "Your teenage hearts are built for fighting. You know what you love and you don't think twice about defending it. Joan of Arc—she was that kind of warrior. And Sammy Weaver—he died protecting his home."

"Saskia has the hatchet," said Issy. "She's getting good at hitting her marks." On my other side, Xavier mumbled something to Ben, who grunted in assent, but the wind carried off their words.

"I'm glad you're thinking along these lines," said Abraham. "I'll confess I've been growing afraid."

"You have?" Issy said.

"The time has come to make concrete plans to defend ourselves when the Thinged World comes calling. Not if—when. We may have to keep these special plans to ourselves. Some of the others might not understand."

"I can't kill anyone," Cornelia said.

"You're not going to kill anyone," Xavier said. The word "kill" in his mouth was full of nails.

"You can sing, Cornelia," Abraham said. "Goddess knows, if it comes to a standoff, we'll need joy."

Xavier broke away. His footsteps cracked a branch.

"We're not done," said Abraham.

"I'm done," Xavier replied, his long stride spilling onto the trail. Ben looked after him, then back at Abraham, then back into the forest. And then he followed Xavier down the path.

Abraham kept his eyes there long after it was strange to keep still. "Marta?"

Sure enough, Marta stepped out from behind a birch at the edge of the trail, her hands up in surrender. The boys had run right by her.

"Spying on us?"

She clasped her small hands before her. "Out for a walk."

"You're not needed."

"You forget yourself. I'm not one of your devotees." Was that what I was?

"You forget yourself," he replied. "This is not your land."

She kept her eyes on him, as though to say, I know you. As though to say, this is not who you are. Then she cast him aside. "Saskia," she said, "do you want to come foraging?"

"Did you know, children, that Marta has befriended the sheriff?"

"So you're the one spying on me."

"These children," he said, "have seen what the law does. Poor little Sammy Weaver. Guns. Violence. All in the name of believing it can offer children something safer than what we have here." He held up his hands, to gesture to the maple leaves above us, the quickening thrash of squirrel tails, the beetles flying, the pine needles sweeping down to the forest floor.

Later, us girls slurped butternut soup in the empty Main Lodge. Sarah fussed from the kitchen: "Are you sure you didn't see the boys anywhere? They've gone into the Thinged World, I just know it."

"Let them be foolish," Gabby said, at the screen door. "It's the way we learn."

Nora skipped around our table, singsonging: "Foolish, foolish, the boys are being foolish." Dog chased her until Sarah grabbed him by his makeshift collar and turned him out.

After dishes, there was still no sign of Ben or Xavier. Issy and Cornelia and I wandered through the darkness to the flagpole. It wasn't freezing out there, but it was close. Butterfly's tapestries glowed over Abraham's windows. I strained to overhear, but it was quiet in there.

Finally, we made out two forms coming back up the drive. Xavier was ahead by a quarter mile. We stood to greet him but he strode past us and didn't look back, not even when we said his name. We had to wait for Ben. Cornelia went to him, as if he was hers.

"He ran from JimBob's." Ben's breath plumed. "His dad's gone."

"Well, yeah." I didn't like how close he was standing to Cornelia.

"From New York." He was irritated. "No one at the gallery has seen Philip since he dropped his paintings off a week ago. He's not at the loft either."

"What about Xavier's mother?" Cornelia said. "Xavier should call her."

"She's in Bali? I think he said Bali. He wouldn't talk to me after that."

We stayed out at the flagpole. The stars were sparklers. I knew I should go down to Xavier, but no matter what I did, talk to him or not, ask him to tell me what had happened or not, sleep or stay up, he wouldn't like me. And it was nice to feel Ben close in the night, to shiver beside him and pretend I wasn't cold. We told stories, which got us around to him and Nora putting a frog in Sarah's shoe once, and how she'd yelled at them. "She was so angry about it the next day," he said. "Honestly, I didn't think she could get angry. She scolds us all the time. But angry? Like that? It was just a frog."

Abraham came out of his cabin. We lifted our heads, the same way deer come to attention when headlights sweep them. He said: "She's dying."

"Who's dying?" Cornelia said.

"Marta. Isn't that what you were talking about?"

"No," Issy said.

"Death is Unthinging," instructed Abraham. "Death is our greatest teacher in the path to letting go. It is the way. Aren't you very cold out here?"

"I'm not," said Issy. But the wind howled.

91

The first person I see at First Community Village is Sheriff Sal. He's planted just inside the sliding glass doors, his once-broad frame now a stack of bones in the sling of a wheelchair. The doors seal us into the disinfected air. Panic flares. But Ben heads for the old man and offers a hearty handshake.

"You promised you'd bring your dogs," the old man says. He's still got the mustache. His face is wrinkled and thin.

Ben gestures to the nurse. She looks like she hasn't smiled in decades. "You think she'd let dogs in here?"

"Who's this pretty lady?"

Ben doesn't skip a beat. "Old friend."

"Well, Old Friend, we've got cherry pie for dessert tonight, if this fella will let you stay."

Ben slips his hand across my back and sidles me away. The mushroom carpet springs under our steps.

"You couldn't warn me?"

Ben grins. "The expression on your face." His gait has loosened. "He's harmless. Brain is Swiss cheese. He was making life miserable for the nurses until they realized he'd shut up if they wheeled him out in the morning and left him until dinner. He likes to keep track of things."

It's out of a heart-pumping dream, walking freely in the world.

Or maybe I'm pretending I'm a version of myself, the one who didn't let Ben leave, the one who's come with her husband to visit his mother, and has special driving sunglasses and hits up the grocery store for margarita mix and stops at boutiques to try on hats. That's who people see, isn't it? The open doors we pass have hand-calligraphed signs beside them—"Mrs. Dotty Smith," "Mr. Rusty Hoggs"—revealing solitary figures draped in thin blankets. Dotty and Rusty look up between the chirps of their machinery, and the murmur of their morning TV, to see a wife and husband stalking down their hallway, and the wife isn't the least bit afraid.

A young orderly approaches, pushing a metal box that spews tubes and buttons. She's younger than Jenny, blond and pink-lipped, her breasts pressed tightly against her blue scrubs. "Morning."

Ben offers only a raised hand. I find myself pleased at this loyalty to Jenny. "Friend of my daughter," he says, "from cheerleading." She takes another glance as we turn onto a new hallway, but he doesn't notice. How can Anna be old enough to be friends with a nurse? In my mind, she's been four ever since that day Ben showed up on my doorstep.

"So, you like this place?" The sun-strewn *Acer saccharum* seem so far off on the other side of the sealed windows.

"Mom started wandering, okay?" he says. "I have to make a living. It was one thing when Shelley-Ann could keep an eye on her." He moves a half step ahead.

I follow him down another hallway—longer, narrower, with even browner carpet. Windows line one side of the hall and doors the other. It's funny to imagine Teresa and Tomas navigating this place in the middle of the night. But it means they're more capable than they seem. A woman with cotton candy hair waves to Ben as he passes, as does a tall, skinny man in a baseball cap. He must come here often; I find that this, too, pleases me.

Almost to the end of the hall, he turns on me. "How's Xavier's sobriety going?"

I arrange my face. It's not completely out of left field, the notion that Xavier found himself dependent enough on alcohol that he has decided not to drink anymore. He turned down the wine at dinner. And Cornelia apologized. Which means she knew.

My ignorance fuels him. "And Cornelia? She doing okay after losing that baby a couple years back?"

"I didn't know about that."

His mouth forms an ugly knot. "You're so sure you know everyone's business. Meanwhile, you spend your life shut up in your fancy house, pretending your shit doesn't stink like the rest of ours."

I open my mouth to defend myself.

"And don't feed me some bullshit line about how we're going to tie this mess up in a neat bow. You think Tomas isn't going to use that gun if we waltz back up there?" Someone must have told him about the gun when I was getting dressed— my money's on Cornelia. Disgust mars Ben's face. "I used to think you were so smart."

"You can insult me all you want but we still have to fix this."

"I don't have to do anything."

"But you're part of it. Just like I am. Just like Xavier and Issy and fucking Cornelia. You think I want to go back up there? This was never my plan."

He steps close then. His face reddens. "Don't blame this on anyone but yourself."

"You really think I sent those letters?"

I can taste his breath. "You were the one who said we should kill her."

92

A knock on our door. It was light outside, but barely. Rain pattered the roof. I was curled behind Issy, who was, in turn, curled behind Cornelia. We had passed out in Philip's old bed, really just a mattress on the floor, which would never lose that smeared oil paint smell. All night long, Dog had tried to climb into bed with us, but we'd taken turns kicking him onto the floor while the wind whistled through the unseen cracks in the walls. These cabins were not built for the cold, and it wasn't even winter yet.

Cornelia hopped out of bed to greet Nora, who shimmied past her down the hallway to stand over me. "What is wrong with you people? It stinks in here."

Issy groaned, pulling her arm over her face. I sat up, landing my feet onto the frigid floor. The room bucked. The previous evening's adventures throbbed into clarity: after Abraham left us to the news that Marta was dying—had he really said that? It seemed impossible in the light of day—Nora had discovered Ben was back, and made him go to Sarah. Then us girls had raided Butterfly's wine cooler stash, hidden in the sandy patch below the dock. It had seemed like a good idea at the time. Now my forehead pounded, my tongue fuzzy with sugar.

"You're supposed to go to Marta's," Nora said. She scratched Dog's head.

"Says who?"

"Marta, duh."

Nora took Dog with her to the Main Lodge. Issy and Cornelia fell back to sweet sleep. I stepped into the sludgy morning. My heavy-duty slicker kept me dry from the rain, but the damp crept in anyway. I remembered to stop and listen—not for Dog, or Abraham, but for you. There were still bursts of hope; you might find me again, out here in the forest. I should have brought Topsy. Maybe you were right there in that stand of birches, ready to reach out. But no, I was alone in the cold and wind, with a slippery uphill path before me. At least I could use Marta's toilet.

Marta's cabin was sided in red clapboard. Her delicate porch cantilevered over the hillside that, in turn, overlooked the lake—a small but decadent amenity that had not been made a priority in any of Home's post-and-beam cabins.

She was at the door before I lifted my hand to knock. Part of me had hardened with Samuel Weaver's slaughter, but I hadn't realized how far I already felt from her, how quickly my transformation had come, until we were face-to-face. She ushered me in. I took off the slicker. I left the hatchet at the door. The rain-lashed world dissolved. She was so real up close: the white hair she cut herself, her worn fingernails, the smoky scent of her skin.

Unlike the Home cabins, Marta's was on the grid, with a tidy electric stove whose coils burned orange, and low, warm baseboards. This was a home built to survive the Maine winters—double-paned windows, well-insulated walls, and a soapstone stove that burned the wood twice. A closet in the far corner held a ceramic toilet, a welcome counterpoint to the latrines. My piss reeked of decayed alcohol; I put my head in my hands.

The main room was friendly with the smell of popcorn. Bookcases glowed with firelight as a Mozart piano concerto burst, tinny, from the radio. Marta whisked simmering milk on the stovetop and shook another pot to melt butter. Her clock said seven. She set out the food on the coffee table and ladled steaming hot chocolate into two hand-thrown mugs, brown as the earth. She settled into a maroon armchair, just her size.

I thought I didn't care for popcorn, but ten minutes on, I'd already finished it. She knew I never ate that way unless I was with her. She reached across the table. Her hand was thinner than I remembered. I let it stay out there, alone. "If you, or any of the others, are scared, or uncomfortable with what's going on, you should tell me. You must tell me."

She was dying; that's what Abraham had said. She was friends with the sheriff.

"Believe me, I know how convincing Abraham can be. But no one is planning an attack. No one is lurking in the woods. And despite what he's telling you about cops, the sheriff is a good man, Saskia. It makes sense that you would be afraid of law enforcement. I'm so sorry about what happened to your brother. But you can't follow Abraham down his paranoid rabbit hole. The world out there is just the world."

Marta was the one who'd as good as said that poor little Sammy Weaver had deserved what he'd gotten. She had nearly tricked me, like a witch in a fairy tale, lulling me with a warm room and good food, when for all I knew, the FBI was listening in right now, guns at the ready.

"No one's out to get us," she said.

"There is no us." I took up the hatchet. "There's you, and then there's Home."

Tearing into the woods, through the morning storm, I thought of what I'd discovered in the bathroom: a pile of tissues in Marta's waste bin, splashed in shades of scarlet and rust. Too many of them to count. Blood, from somewhere inside Marta's body. Blood that wanted to get out.

93

On the bed in Sarah's room lies a pile of hospital blankets. Then I notice a bit of gnarled flesh beside that pile, like a sparrow stunned by a window. My brain finally locates a word for it: hand.

There's an arm attached to the hand, and that arm, in turn, connects to the rest of her, under the blankets, improbable as it seems. Her mouth gapes. Her eyelids lie sunken over her eyes. Her fingernails are yellowed. Worst of all, her hair is cut close, her naked scalp visible in patches. I fill with fury at Ben for letting them hack off her braids. I make myself step toward her. I make myself take that hand.

Death, so close, reminds me of you, getting back to you, getting Ben to make that happen.

"You can't imagine," I say, "how hard it's been to be away." I expected to startle the sleeping thing in the bed with the scratch of my voice. But not even a finger twitches. "From all of you. I won't make excuses. But I will say that we each have our own way of coping, and I suppose that's mine."

Ben crosses his arms. "What's mine?"

I should bite my tongue. "You bury yourself in your work, your dogs. Sex. To avoid being alone with what you've done."

"Is that what you're doing down there in your Connecticut

mansion? Being alone with what you've done?" The mention of sex has infuriated him.

"You like to pretend I don't know you. It makes you sleep better. But you do know me, Ben. You know what I'm capable of."

He swallows. Good. He's still a little afraid.

"And the others?" He crosses his arms in challenge. "What do you know about them?"

"Issy won't put down roots because even though she thinks she hates Home, it shaped every part of who she is. When Gabby died, she had to make her own Unthinged World, even got herself a child to Unthing with, but she's discovering that being a mother is . . ." I've expected to say that she's finding motherhood lonely and awful, the fact that she can't protect her child from the horrors of the world, but all at once, I think of her collapsing into a fit of giggles on the floor of the living room because Sekou had a crayon hanging out of his nose, and then I think I must be wrong. Ben's waiting for my answer. I lamely add, "Different than she expected."

"Do Cornelia."

"Cornelia strives to be the perfect mother because her mother was supremely imperfect."

"And Xavier?"

"Xavier buys happiness. He has come to discover that money makes things seem okay. Or if not okay, then better, at least."

"You think he's superficial?"

"I think he's made a life that seems safe." I suppose this could be said for all of us.

"So you don't like Billy."

"I think Billy adores Xavier and no one can know what's going on inside a marriage besides the people in it. And before you say I've got judgment for everyone but myself, let me remind you that I haven't gone outside in sixteen years. Not because of guilt, or a broken heart—not only that—but because I'm afraid of what I could do to hurt you all. I love you too much for that."

Our eyes have found each other. I feel it thundering through me. I forgot how something that doesn't make any sense can still be too much.

"What a saint." Bitterness laces his voice. "What a fucking saint you are. Jesus. I forgot how manipulative—"

The fingers beneath mine flutter, the wings of a bird trying to break free. Sarah yawns. Her mouth gapes open, then shut. Open, then shut. Her eyes cast around. She lifts her neck from the pillow. Ben reaches toward me. I think for a moment that he's going to touch me. But he's fiddling with the button to raise the bed up. "Hey, Ma."

94

*T*he first dusting of snow came in October. We knew, by then, that we weren't going back to school. There had been no word from Philip. Xavier finally got through to Jane in Bali, on the Jim-Bob's pay phone. "You want me to say I'm surprised?" she said, son number two babbling on her lap. She had no plans to return to the States, said she'd send money, was glad he was having a good time with friends.

The snow melted off in one day. Then there were weeks of capacious skies, the air fresh and cool. The deciduous leaves on the opposite shore were every shade of gold, rust, crimson. But we didn't have time to leaf-peep. All day, for many days, Issy and Cornelia and I chopped firewood, growing sweaty under our Goodwill sweaters, while the boys put the garden to sleep. As soon as the sun cut behind the ridgeline, night came on. The bell rang for supper.

It was a special treat to put on fresh clothes at the end of those days. I was covered in sap, hands blackened, lips chapped. I padded to the cabin, kicked the pine needles from the soles of my boots, and slipped my filthy clothes off. The smell of my sweat hit me when I lifted my arms. Between the undressing and the dressing—a sound, maybe, but more like a sense—made me realize I wasn't alone.

"Iss?"

A moment passed.

"Knock knock." I jumped at the closeness of Jim's voice. He was already inside.

I put on a smile and squared my shoulders. "I think it's dinnertime." He was in the front area, on the armchair, beside the hatchet. The screen door was just beyond him, and the freedom of the golden light.

He kicked his legs out, blocking my way. He stunk like booze but it was the stench of his need that made me recoil. His hand was a tarantula on my arm. He looked alarmed at the sight of that tufted bit of himself on my bare wrist, but our mutual distress only tightened his grip. "I like you."

"Where's Teresa?"

"I don't give a fuck about Teresa." He looked up at me. I could see into the tunnel of his sorrow. Under my fear, I felt a drop of pity. The last drop. I didn't know what he was going to do next, but I already knew it was going to wring my pity out.

"I think . . ." He swayed a little. Then his eyes popped into focus, and he started to rear up. He stood. His fingers formed a noose around my freedom. "I think I'd like to talk about what happened to your brother."

I was powerful then. More powerful than Jim's hands. I didn't need the hatchet. I only needed my knee, right into the corner of his groin. In the breath of his letting go, I ran.

95

Sarah's sketches line her walls. A few of them I recognize, although they're now framed: a moose; a chickadee; the Home dock. But there are also faces—Amos, Gabby, Abraham—perfectly proportioned as though they walked right onto the page. Marta. I haven't seen any of those faces since I last saw them in the flesh, not even a snapshot. A few of Philip's smaller color studies are interspersed: the summer sky at dusk; the lake on a still morning. I wonder if Ben knows how much they're worth. There's a turquoise wonder by Philip in there, too, eight inches square: little Nora, eyes wide in surprise, mouth mischievous, as though she's just flipped someone off. Framed beside it is a photograph from when I no longer knew her: a teenager, with a nose ring and a lost smile, a hazy look in her eyes. She has her arm slung around Ben. My chest aches.

The being that is supposed to be Sarah lets out a burp.

"Ma," says Ben. "I brought you a friend." It moves me, this word, "friend." I know, I know—but it moves me.

She looks my way.

"Sarah," I say. "It's Saskia." I force tenderness from my tongue. "You taught me how to make bread. At Home." I hold the bag of sourdough up. It waggles, stupidly, side to side.

A smile pulls from one corner of her mouth to the other. I recognize her: steadiness, strength, patience. "You love my son."

Ben knocks over the small, carved loon resting on the windowsill. "Ma, you're talking nonsense."

"And he loves you," she tells me, "body and soul."

He tries to pick the loon up. It falls, again.

"The night before he married that girl, he told me he should be marrying you. And I said, 'See? You should have listened to the prophecy. You could have made each other happy.'"

"She doesn't know what she's talking about." He smashes the loon back onto the window sill.

"I don't think happiness was in the cards." My voice goes gritty.

"Yes, I do." She sounds indignant. "You said you wished you'd never heard that prophecy, and I said, all Abraham ever wanted was to help, and you said—"

"Abraham was the bad guy, remember, Sarah?" A voice from the doorway. A wheelchair blocks our way out. Sal.

96

At the chicken coop, I started yelling. Jim was following me, sure, but drunk enough to stumble. By the time I was at the door to the Main Lodge, tears were striping my face, and my shirt was ripped. It wasn't a lie; it was just a few steps beyond where he'd gotten. With another girl, and less whiskey in his belly, he would have gotten plenty far.

The screen door howled open, into the fug of pea soup. "Help," I screamed. It was funny to use this word, as if I hadn't helped myself. The Homesteaders lifted their heads, one by one. "Help, he attacked me."

I made my way to Sarah, at the back of the kitchen. Her arms wrapped around my body, which was shaking then, really shaking. I could see over the top of her head. The men rushed to the door. They thought it was a stranger, a fisherman, the sheriff. But Jim appeared before them, and I lifted my finger to point.

The room grew still. Then the men spilled out of the lodge, led by Ephraim. They brought Jim, spitting and kicking and cursing, to the ground.

Issy came toward me, and Butterfly. Cornelia. Little Nora slipped her hand into mine. The women made a barricade.

Gabby made her way past the men to Abraham's door. She pounded until it cracked open. Dog bounded out and barked. It was horrible. It was easy.

97

"*H*ey there, Sheriff." Ben rises. "Who's watching the lobby?"
Sal stays in the shadow of the doorway.

"I was wondering," says Sal, "when you'd come back."

Ben's laugh tightens the air in the room. "Now come on, you're
making it sound like I never visit."

I don't have to see the old man's eyes to know he's addressing
me. How funny if this is how we're caught, by an ancient man in
an old folks' home, the police surrounding every exit. Some part
of me is rooting for him. Some part of me believes he deserves this.

Sarah's hand pulls me back, insistent. "I want bread."

In my years alone, I've learned to mold time by focusing on every step of a given task. Open the bag. Unfold a slice of sourdough
from the kitchen towel. Pull out the stainless steel butter knife.
Unscrew the mason jar of butter. Spread the yellow cream along
the top of the bread so it covers every centimeter.

Sarah licks her lips. I hold up the bread: does she want me
to feed her? Her hand flies to catch it. While she chews, I tell a
gentle tale like the kind I'd give Sekou, of the bread's making.
Stir the leaven, let it sit overnight, mix it with flour and water in
the morning, let it rise, pour the saltwater over it, then begin the
kneads, every half hour for two and a half hours—one, two, three,
four, five, six—then split the dough, and let it sit again, and shape

before lifting into the banneton baskets. Then the long rise begins. Sarah knows this story better than I. She leans back on her pillow. She closes her eyes, the movement of her jaw the only sign that she's still of this world.

I keep my eyes on Sarah, but I can feel the men: Sal, behind me; Ben, moving toward him. If the law has truly come, there is no way out.

When she finishes, I turn to meet my fate.

Out in the hallway, Ben's talking up that pretty young nurse. She's got her hands on the back of Sal's wheelchair. He's putting up a commotion, and she's soothing him, and Ben is saying, "I have no idea what got him so worked up."

She replies, "Sal's got a great imagination. Don't you, Sal?"

I turn back to Sarah. The fresh sight of her reminds me why I made Ben bring me here in the first place. You're up on that land, waiting. I can't get back up there without her son.

"Sarah." I hunker over her. "Someone broke you out of here. Tomas—you remember? You knew him when he was a boy. He and Teresa took you up to where Home used to be. And then you said that Abraham is back." My breath sputters out. "Sarah. Is he? Is Abraham back?" My mouth grows dry as I lean over her, wondering why it matters so much if he's come back for us after all. How will knowing change the way I convince Ben? But it will, I know, without knowing how.

She opens her mouth: hope.

She closes it: despair.

When her voice finally comes, it's steady. "When I was a little girl, I knew my daddy was up to something. I couldn't imagine what it was—I was just a little girl, after all. If you'd asked me to explain, I couldn't. It was more of a feeling."

It seems I've come all this way just to share my bread, and see her face, and hear some ancient story about her horrible father.

Surely that should be enough, to be a witness. Why can't that be enough?

She holds up one scrawny finger. "I waited until dark. I pretended to go to sleep. I crept outside, up to the window of my daddy's shed, and I peeked right in." She raises her shoulders up to her ears. She shudders. "It was terrible, what I saw."

"Sorry, Ma." Ben stalks into the room again. He presses his hand on my back. "Saskia would love to stay all day, but we can't have her exhausting you." He puts his lips on her papery forehead. Sarah shuts her eyes like an obedient child.

98

*I*t was warm in the front room of Abraham's cabin, with a mug of one of Sarah's herbal brews in my hand, and Dog's head heavy at my feet. There were books and a typewriter, a Persian rug, two sturdy armchairs upholstered in tapestry. A fire flickered in the wood stove.

Butterfly's voice, muffled, came from outside the door: "He said to leave them alone."

"He asked me to get this for her." Gabby.

Gabby, then, opening the door. The need of Butterfly's face as she peered in, before the door shut her out again. Farther out, the men had Jim. I imagined him pacing, cursing, begging, calling me the worst names there were.

Gabby had the hatchet, but her hands held it close: "You don't need this, you know. We'll keep you safe."

"Why should she believe that?" Abraham said. "We haven't done a good job of keeping her safe." He held out his hand. She looked at the tool carefully before giving it over.

"I also brought this." Gabby pulled Topsy from her pocket and held him out. His little head cocked to the side, as if he was asking a question.

"You don't need that anymore," Abraham said. "It's a Thing." Gabby held the fuzzy being out a little longer, but when I didn't take him, she pocketed him. Abraham lay the hatchet on the couch between us. "I loathe what Jim did to you so. It makes me sick." His eyes closed, as though he had to look deep within himself. "I always knew you were brave, but truly, now I see you're the warrior your father said you were."

"My father?" My insides twisted.

"Maybe I'm getting the story wrong. I heard it from Philip— your father, didn't he used to call you a warrior?"

Did he? I breathed in, and out. I had gotten rid of Jim. I didn't need to worry anymore. I remembered his hand on my arm. The twist of it. Maybe something had happened, after all. Maybe I hadn't made up a story.

"I want him gone," Abraham said.

Gabby bounded to her feet. She was already out the door.

Abraham's hand rested over his heart. "Has Jim tried to hurt you before today?"

I shook my head.

"Were you afraid of him? You could have told me. You can always tell me. I will always protect you." Abraham took my face into his warm hands. His eyes began to spill tears. "Please," he said. "No secrets. Anything you are keeping inside, you can tell me. I am here to keep you safe." He was so close then, his breath, my breath, and I thought—Oh. Maybe it really is as simple as one body meeting another. Maybe it really has been this all along.

"Marta told me to come up to her place," I blurted. "It was morning, before anyone was awake. She didn't want anyone to know. She said I shouldn't believe what you say. She said the sheriff is a good guy. That all I have to do is say so, and he'll come take me."

"He'll never take you. Never. I swear it." Daddy was gone. Mother was gone. Jane was gone. Philip was gone. And Grandmother, and before them all, you. But Abraham was with me.

99

*B*en roars the van to life. An old woman's hair poufs as we pull out of the parking lot.

"Ma's out of her mind." He gains speed on the two-lane road.

"Why did you chop off her hair?"

"That old fucker knew exactly who you are." He slams the wheel. "I never should have brought you."

The speed limit says forty-five. We blast past it.

I decide not to remind Ben of his swagger when we first walked in. How he told me to relax. "It did seem like he's been waiting for me."

"Exactly! Exactly. I told you all to get the fuck out of here but no one ever fucking listens." The van groans as it takes a curve going sixty. A couple hundred yards ahead, a sedan turns in to our lane. More than Sal's suspicions—which scare Ben plenty—I know that what's got him blasting through the countryside is his mother saying he loves me.

We are on a crash course with the sedan, which is going at a country pace. "Can you slow down?"

Moments from ramming into the back of the other car, he pulls us into the approaching lane. The van groans as we gain speed. We'd be at an advantage if the sedan braked, but the driver has taken Ben's acceleration as a challenge. Now we are two cars, side by side, on a two-lane road, rocketing up a hill—toward, I'm sure we'll soon discover, an oncoming car.

"Ben."

He's as focused as his mother was eating the sourdough. He clenches his jaw. He leans forward. What I want to say, if I could put it in words, is that only someone deranged by the truth could act this way.

The sedan starts honking. It's teenagers in there. They whoop. They flip us off. They flash their lights. They're too young to know this is not a cause for celebration.

We're almost up the hill now. Ben shows no signs of slowing. If there was ever a dotted yellow line, it's long run out. I think of repeating his name, but then the crest of the hill is there, and I'm squeezing my eyes closed. My breath, in, then out, takes far longer than most.

There is no crash. There is no car coming toward us over the crest of the hill, nor up from the dip below us. But there's another hill ahead, and a car is coming down that, in our lane. Well, it's their lane.

"Slow down."

"Used to be people drove with sense. Now they all come in for the summer. They get wasted. Kill whatever's in their path." I haven't looked at the teenagers in a while, but their energy is frenzied. By now, the car coming toward us, blue, small, has started honking. But there's nowhere for it to go, except into the bushes, and anyway, this is its path, not ours.

"You've got your business advertised on this van," I say, trying to keep my voice steady as we near our deaths. "Think of your reputation."

If anything, that only makes him go faster. In five seconds, we'll be dead.

"Think of Jenny." What I mean: think of that sweet little thing having to collect your body.

He lets up on the accelerator. We're going downhill and the force of momentum carries us anyway, but then he's pumping the brake, and the sedan peels off ahead, and Ben swerves back into line behind it, and the oncoming car speeds past us with the angry blare of its horn. The sedan sails off over the next hill.

Ben brakes. He pulls us off the road. The car shimmies in the sand, then finally stops. We sit there. He keeps his hands on the wheel. He breathes heavily. I think of getting out, but I'd drop straight to the ground and nothing would get me back on my feet. Another car roars by. The people inside it don't know a thing.

100

After Jim:

Cornelia braided my hair.

Issy let me unwrap the deck of cards we'd bought in New York.

Xavier brought me a loaf of Sarah's bread.

The woods ricocheted with the far-off sound of gunshots; hunting season in the Thinged World. Afternoons went dark. Wind careened. We stuffed the walls with rolled-up newsprint. We played Spit before the gasping fire. Mice scuttled with their families along the floorboards. The hatchet stayed under my pillow.

Ben sat on the floor beside me while I slept.

By the time Ben pulls into the driveway, we've shared twenty minutes of silence. He lets his van idle beside the SUV. "I didn't do that," he says, after a minute.

This makes me laugh.

"Chopping off Ma's hair. Teresa did it." He lets me see his fear.

"Okay," I say. "Okay." The others are watching us from inside the house. The dogs yip at the recognition of his motor. "Have dinner with us tonight." And then: "Bring Jenny."

He takes a deep breath.

"It wouldn't be so bad to be together." He startles. I clarify. "All of us. One last time. Then we're out of your hair."

His eyes pass over the windows, as if it's not his home. "Seven o'clock?"

"Cornelia's going to piss her pants, cooking for you lovebirds."

He slaps the wheel again, to say, all right, get on out of here. So we agree, without agreeing, that I will keep the morning's events a secret, and, in exchange, he will allow Jenny, the girl who saved our lives, to spend more than a minute in my company. It's not lost on me that her name was the Hail Mary that saved him from crashing us into oblivion. I tell myself that all that matters is being one step closer to you.

On Christmas morning, Dog nosed me awake. It was snowy and quiet and the light was thin, and all I wanted was the warmth of bed, but he'd heard someone coming down the path. He licked my face, then whined at the door. Xavier grumbled on the top bunk. I brought Dog out into the front room and poked at the reluctant fire, and peeked out the window.

"Mama, no." Tomas, down at the edge of the water, howling into the tundra of the frozen lake, as Teresa held him by one arm. She leaned to his ear to try to soothe him, but he writhed in her grip. He was nimble. He broke free.

"Tomas!" The ice didn't crack under his small feet. She sank onto a log. She dropped her head into her hands.

Out of the woods came Marta. She moved like a shadow across the snow, until she was beside Teresa. She laid her hand on Teresa's shoulder. The other woman startled at the touch, but Marta didn't speak. She simply stood beside Teresa, and watched the boy run.

Was Marta really dying? At our meager Christmas feast, our heads bowed over curried lentils, the aluminum pot sending up a cruciferous steam, I thought the door might tussle open in a swirl of snow and air, and Marta would be standing there, stalwart as ever, bearing popcorn for us all. Instead, we shivered over our bowls as Abraham read aloud from a manifesto he was drafting. Then we sang "Greensleeves," and "O Tannenbaum," and Butterfly performed a solstice dance at the edges of the firelight.

In my frigid bed, in the drowsy moments before full sleep, Marta's small body rushed into my mind, walking ahead of me on the path; the only sound, our steps. I missed her with a skin-thick longing, missed the blueberries—*Vaccinium myrtilloides*—spilling off an alpine meadow, and thickets of *Asparagus officinalis*. Her small, rough hands turned our bounty over in the sunlight. Did that happen every time, or was it only once?

103

Jenny steps inside with a platter of deviled eggs, Ben behind her, as though this isn't his home. She must have an apartment somewhere, or a house, but I don't let myself think of it, not even when his hand spreads across her lower back. We pull ourselves into formation. Cornelia's suitcase is packed for an early morning flight. I can tell, in her careful basting of the roast, that she believes her dinner will make everything good forever. She beams across the kitchen—at Jenny, folding the cloth napkins, at Sekou, lining up his little guys across the floor, at Xavier and Ben and Issy, drinking Allagash White at the kitchen table. She beams at Ben's dogs when they lope across the kitchen, panting, after a day in the sun.

Then we're in the dining room, and yes, all right, the roast is delicious. The flesh hits my stomach and does not alarm me. Everyone is talking, and Jenny's guttural laugh hints at surprising depths, and Sekou loves the meat so much that Issy has to tell him not to put more than one piece into his mouth at once, and Ben catches my eye and then makes a point of putting his arm around his girlfriend.

"And what about you?" Jenny says to Xavier, slopping mashed potatoes onto her plate. "What do you do?"

"I run an art gallery," he says. "In New York."

"A very successful art gallery," Cornelia interrupts. She's had some wine.

"Thank you," Xavier says. "I suppose we could say it's successful."

"There's family money." That's Issy. "I just mean, let's be plain. I'm sure your gallery is doing great, but the real source of your wealth is your mother. Not to mention that your father is one of the most well-known painters of his generation. Complicated relationships, sure, but money begets money. Privilege begets—"

"Privilege." Xavier smiles thinly. "You're absolutely right." But smuggled in there is irritation, discomfort, embarrassment.

Cornelia puts down her fork. "Issy, you shouldn't have to be the one to point that out."

"No shit. But no one else was saying it."

Cornelia looks stricken. "Gosh, you're right. I'm sorry."

"Oh please, wipe that white feminist pout right off your face. Just notice next time."

"I'll notice, too," says Jenny. "I've done a lot of reading and—"

"I like to read." Sekou is down off his chair, standing right beside Jenny.

"Do you?" She puts her hand on his shoulder, and adopts his solemn stance.

"I tell the stories in my head."

"That's the first step."

"Come finish your green beans," Issy says. The boy clambers back into her lap and takes a bite and smiles at Jenny because she's the prettiest girl in the room.

Ben runs his hand over Jenny's hair.

"And do you have a family?" Jenny asks Xavier, moving the conversation along.

"My husband's name is Billy." Xavier draws his phone out of

his pocket, and finds a cute picture: the two of them in Mets caps, overlooking Citi Field.

"Handsome," croons Jenny.

"We're, uh, we're in the process of adopting."

I play at surprise. He was scared to tell me, but only when he looks at me do I know this. "There've been some bumps along the way, but we're hopeful." Ben and Jenny offer their murmured congratulations—him, with practiced reserve; her, with a gooey sigh that doesn't hide how badly she wants to reproduce.

Sekou has somehow managed to pass out. His hand, still holding a green bean, curls between his chin and his mother's shoulder. Issy says, "I'm happy for you, kid."

"I'm scared as hell." Xavier's eyes are wet. "What the fuck is wrong with me?"

"Nothing is wrong with you," Cornelia mutters.

"There's something wrong with each of us," Issy says. "Think of the people who raised us. Or didn't raise us, as the case may be. No wonder we did what we did. Abraham understood how alone we were. He used it as a weapon against us. He used it to make us into weapons."

Ben shifts in his seat, clears his throat.

"But Abraham was right about a lot," Cornelia counters. "Unthinging is the only way we have a remote chance of slowing climate change—if it's even possible anymore. You still follow his best teachings, Issy. You're Unthinged, and I admire that—I really do."

Issy rolls her eyes.

"Why don't you believe me?"

"Because if you admired me so much, you'd be Unthinged yourself, instead of living in a three thousand square foot new build in a fancy suburb filled with white people."

Cornelia looks down at her hands. "I'm a hypocrite."

"Don't call yourself a hypocrite. Do something. You all have to start doing something. It's not good enough to sit around and say how much you want to change when you don't actually make a change."

Xavier is nodding, tears streaming down his face.

"Why the fuck are you crying?" Issy says.

"Because what the fuck are we going to do? We are so fucked. If they find out what we did, we are all so fucked." He starts to sob.

A freeze has descended over the room, Cornelia, Issy, Ben, and me looking everywhere but Jenny. Surely it has occurred to her by now that there's a pressing reason we've come, beyond a casual visit to rural Maine.

I admire her for saying, "If you don't mind my asking, what did you do?"

Ben clears his throat. Issy stands with Sekou, as if she can protect him from her past actions. Cornelia's face is ashen. Xavier's hand is at his mouth.

"Oh," Jenny says, as she looks at Ben. "It's probably better not to tell me, actually. If you did something illegal. Then I can't testify against you, right? Does it have something to do with that cult you were all a part of?" Ben looks like she just told him his hair is on fire. "I didn't mean to ruin the dinner," she says. "I just believe it's better to get things out in the open."

"I thought you didn't know about Home," Cornelia says.

"Well, he"—she thumbs Ben—"does not have a great poker face. And I ran into his ex at the grocery store a few months back and she said good luck with getting him over what happened up there"—Ben is turning redder as she talks, but here she stops, and leans against him, like a friendly cat, and says—"and then you all show up with your meaningful looks. So I called my mom's best friend yesterday. She lived in town back then, and told me there was all sorts of wacky stuff happening back then up out on

Bushrow Road! Some kind of cult, really Ben, you should have told me! My man's got a wild past!"

She's so bright-eyed that it takes my breath away. And despite the truth she's just torn open, Ben intertwines his fingers with hers. So, then, she is the key.

My stiff fingers curved around the handle of the hatchet, ready to sail it into the air for another round of target practice. Far out, at the middle of the solid lake, the scattering of ice huts trailed smoke into the sky. My breath roiled into a fog. Then I heard it. A snarl. A bark. A knot of rage in the throat of an animal, then a yelp, and the scream of a child in terrible pain.

I ran through the white-draped forest toward the horrifying call. The men, too, sprinted toward the sound, snow crystals catching rainbows in the air as they ran. There was a tussle of limbs beside the frozen lake. From their center came a throaty growl, operatic in scale, rageful, unbound. The child's cry crested as they shouted: "Get it off of him!" Someone came running with the pitchfork. "Kick it!"

A mess, impossible to make sense of through the bodies and the sounds, the arms reaching in, the frantic jabs. I wanted to see and I wanted not to see. I wanted to stand back but my body led me forward.

Marta appeared. I stood there, dumb. She took the hatchet from my hand.

105

"I'm going up to Home," I say, when the cherry pie and ice cream are memories across our plates. "Tonight." I look Ben in his worried eyes. "Do you remember what your mom said about her father? About looking in the window? I'm going to go look in the windows."

They try to talk me out of it. It's too dark out (that's the point). I don't have a car and Xavier won't be driving me (I'll walk). There's a man with a gun up there (I know). If I go alone, he'll shoot me on sight (perhaps). I tell them how to keep the Mother fed. Then they know I'm serious.

I rise from the table. I get all the way outside. Framed by the window, Jenny leans toward Ben, with a look that says help her, and I know that I've got him.

Marta went into the fray. The knot of bodies swallowed her. Then there was a different sound: the squelch of a melon breaking. The screaming kept on, but it was joined with other screaming, shouts and cries as we gathered ever closer just as the worst of it had ended.

I was upon them as Amos picked up the limp, small body from the ground. I couldn't understand why Tomas didn't have a face anymore. Where his filthy cheeks had once been there was now a sea of red. His arm dangled in an unnatural way. Amos ran up the land. He shouted, "Get the keys," and those who had not been nearby looked up as he passed, until they realized something terrible had occurred and scrambled up the hill behind him, screaming toward the kitchen for Teresa. Behind them trailed Nora, eyes frozen wide.

On the ground lay what was left of Dog, the hatchet buried in his skull. Marta was beside him, in the scarlet snow, stroking his blood-soaked pelt, her arms covered in such a gush of red, that I thought for certain he had gotten her, too.

107

*B*en cuts the lights and engine half a mile out on Bushrow Road. There's hardly a moon, which will be to our advantage. We sit in the darkness to let our eyes adjust. The night seems quiet through the muffled windows, but when we're out there it'll be anything but, thanks to *Pseudacris crucifer*, the tiny chorus frogs. Perhaps he is thinking of Jenny. Perhaps he is thinking of the others, who stayed behind.

"Surprised you got back in a car with me behind the wheel." His cocky tone doesn't fool either of us. I know what it is for him to come back here.

"Your mom's sketches are beautiful." Did Ben frame them? Or Shelley-Ann? Those faces I once knew, lined up. All these years, I've only held them in my mind.

"She wanted to go to art school."

"That doesn't surprise me."

"My father said she wasn't strong enough to be an artist. So I said, 'Ma, screw him and go to art school now.' And she said that the part of her that knew how to make art went away when Home fell apart. Made me so mad."

"I think I know what she meant."

He's quiet.

"What she said about us—no, let me say this, please, Ben. That night we had together—"

"I'm sorry."

"I'm not sorry. I've never regretted it. It was . . . it meant a lot to me. You don't have to say anything. I just need you to know that I . . . that it wasn't something I forgot. I know it's foolish to have thought you'd leave your wife, especially with another baby on the way. I guess I was . . ." I decide to be brave. "I guess your mom was right. I guess I loved you and that made me want you even though . . ."

Ben nods in the darkness. I can just barely make it out, but I feel it, the vehemence of it rocking the car.

"Why . . ." Be brave. "Why did you drive all the way to New York to be with me, if you were just going to leave?"

"I'm so sorry."

"Just tell me."

"I didn't know I was going to leave."

"So what made you decide to come, on that day, of all days, when any hope of us getting together was long gone? I mean, you'd been with Shelley-Ann for years by then." I swallow. "What made you want to touch me? On that day, after years of never touching me?"

He blows air through his lips. "I never told you, but. The day before. That was the day Nora had her first suicide attempt. I know it's selfish. I just . . . I needed . . ."

I shouldn't have asked.

"I'm so sorry."

"Not your fault."

"Saskia—"

"Don't pity me."

He stills himself. We sit in that vast darkness.

Then he says, "Sometimes I think about it like we were infected.

Like Home infected us with a virus that meant we couldn't live like normal people. Can't. I think we might have had a chance of recovering if we hadn't killed her. But once we killed her, there was no getting free."

I'm so grateful for the darkness.

"I came to New York," he continues, "because I thought maybe I could, though. Be free. Did you ever trick yourself into thinking you could? Just for a little while? Maybe, I thought, maybe it will be easier than I thought, just drive away from the life I've made and find Saskia"—his voice quavers—"and we could make our own kind of happiness."

I'd offered him breakfast. He'd asked if he could use the phone. I watched the curve of his back when she answered. How it closed itself against me the longer they talked. When he got off, he told me Anna had a fever. But I'd known he was going to leave, the moment he asked to use the phone.

He clears his throat. "It wouldn't have lasted. You know that, right? Even if I'd stayed."

Headlights pierce us from behind, coming up Bushrow Road. It's impossible to see who's approaching. Ben curses and ducks. The vehicle slows. It curves toward us from the center of the road, then pulls up behind us. In the moment before it cuts its lights, even I feel afraid. I have not believed in ghosts—you are not a ghost, my darling—but now, in the midnight smudge, we find each other's hand. Ben's palm is slick. We wait until the lights cut. The vehicle behind us is big, bulking, black.

Issy is out of the front seat first. She lifts a hand over her eyes and bends down to glance in our rear window. Relief floods my body, followed quickly by the impulse to jump out and terrify her. But she would make too much noise. Ben pulls away. "I thought you weren't fucking coming," I whisper through my newly opened door.

They are all out of the car by then. They crunch across the gravel. Issy explains that Sekou is back at the house with Jenny. Cornelia declares that it was smart of us to park out here. Now there are four of them to manage, when I had it down to only one. But, no, it is best to get this over with, to finally answer our call.

Ben closes his glove compartment, and puts whatever heavy thing he has removed from it, wrapped in a dish towel, into the inside pocket of his jacket.

108

*I*t was so cold, our eyeballs hurt. It was so cold, the air crackled in our lungs.

"Tomas was lucky," Sheriff Sal said, addressing those of us gathered in front of the Main Lodge. "Relatively clean tear, as these things go. The doctors in Portland say he'll make a full recovery." Sarah covered her hands with her mouth and turned away to cry.

The sheriff leaned down to Nora, wedged behind Issy. "He got to ride in a helicopter," he said. She eyed him but she didn't flip him off. "I need you to tell me what happened," the sheriff said. He was looking at her, but he was talking to all of us. "No one's in trouble. But we do want to prevent future attacks."

Abraham held his arms wide. "You see any other dogs here, Sheriff?" The sheriff chuckled as if they were in on the same terrific joke. Over Abraham's shoulder, beside the parked cruiser, Ephraim crossed his arms and glowered. A gust hit; there was no way to know when another whip of snow was coming down from the sky or churning up from the ground. Abraham led the sheriff into his cabin. We scurried into the Main Lodge.

Sarah gave us carrots to chop. Ben was so close I could feel the heat coming off him. I was happy to have an excuse to be close to him, until I remembered the reason; then I felt shocked all over by sadness. Nora wept into her mother's shoulder. Cornelia cried, too, and Issy drew her knees up to her chin. Xavier looked at the floor. Surely they were all sad for Tomas. In theory, I was sad for Tomas—his pain, his fear—and for Teresa, too. But what I felt—what I actually felt, as a drenching weight inside my chest—was the loss of that velvet spot behind Dog's ears, and of the haphazard wetness of his licks on the back of my hand, and his warm weight on my feet in the middle of the night. We pressed around the table together, waiting for the young officer, hand resting on his holster, to call our names.

Later, in the dim light of Abraham's cabin, Sal was friendly but serious. Diplomacy, I thought, a word I didn't even know I knew.

"Tell him the truth," said Abraham, hands spread wide. I knew he meant it how Grandmother meant it. So I told of loving Dog and how Tomas did, too, and of the moose jerky Tomas had been carrying around, and how kids can be, how they can tease a dog with something delicious and then take it back, how they can wallop a dog and the dog doesn't know any better but to do what it was born to do, and how terrible we felt for what happened to poor Tomas, and how brave Marta was, how smart, to do exactly what was right when the situation required.

I had gotten Topsy. I held him like you held him. I wept. I wept for the slice of the hatchet into Dog's head. When I imagined Tomas in a white room in the hospital in Portland surrounded by beeping machines, inside me began a crawling horror—but the sheriff didn't need to know that. He saw me crying, with a bunny in my arms. A girl, crying, poor little thing.

The policemen left. Abraham stood in the middle of the driveway, one hand up in a fixed wave, until they were off the land. Then he turned back toward us. It seemed he would say something that might end our sorrow. But instead he walked past us. Everyone listened to the cold slip of the bolt into its lock.

109

*I*t is the closest to dark this part of the world can be, no moon, no clouds; only the speckle of the Milky Way. But my eyes don't need to work out here. It's mostly my ears and memory leading us along the edge of the gravel road that skirts the top of Home. I'm not practiced in overshooting the driveway and taking the other way in. It would be helpful to use a flashlight, but the threat of Tomas's gun makes that unwise.

I listen for the stream. I remember the boulder under my hand. The two steps built from stones, just down from where she used to park her Rabbit. I remember. I remember. I find our way onto Marta's land.

110

*I*ssy and Cornelia and Xavier and Ben and I played Spit before the meager fire, rotating front to back to soak in the heat before our icy beds. The hatchet, newly cleaned, sharpened, and returned to me by Amos, glimmered in the firelight. He'd made me a belt out of rope, with the ends burned so they didn't fray, and a deerskin holster. I hadn't wanted to touch the hatchet, but he'd pressed it into my hand and said, "It's a tool, girl. Just a tool." No trace of blood. But it wasn't only the hatchet that brought back that day: every conversation, every thought, every sound seemed to return that moment to me, and the moments before it, when Dog's nails would tick across the floorboards for a scratch behind the ears.

"How long do you think Tomas and Teresa will be gone?" I asked.

"Don't they have to build him a new face?"

"Issy!" Cornelia said.

Issy didn't look up from tossing her cards. Grief had made her flippant. "I'm just saying, I bet that takes a while."

"He's going to be okay," Xavier said. He looked up at Cornelia, missing the chance to slap the smaller pile. "That's what Teresa said in her letter, right? There's nothing wrong with his brain. He'll have a little scar but he's okay."

"He's not okay." Tears spilled over Cornelia's cheeks. "He's never going to be okay."

In the corner, Ben's face washed with pity.

"It wasn't Dog's fault," I said.

"We should have trained him." Xavier put his hand on Cornelia's back.

After a moment, Ben said, "I overheard something. Something my dad told my mom."

Issy slapped the smaller pile. "Well . . . ?" She gathered up her cards to shuffle them. Xavier let his lie.

Ben cleared his throat. "I wasn't down there, at the water, when Dog attacked Tomas. None of you were, right?"

"We've been over this," Issy said. "A million times." Xavier gestured for her to shut up. She set down her cards with a dramatic sigh. A mouse scuttled along the hallway, a dart of movement into the shadows.

"Butterfly and Abraham were down there, with Dog, before Tomas came by. My dad saw them from the roof where he was working. Dog was with them, sniffing around."

"Being a dog," Cornelia said.

"Then, after the attack, Butterfly took my dad aside and told him that Abraham was . . . he was kind of, like, teasing Dog. Being rough with him. Dog snapped a couple of times and then she saw the kids coming down the hill and told him to calm Dog down, told him to, like, put him on his rope or whatever. But Abraham wouldn't."

"So?" said Issy.

"So then Tomas asks if anyone's seen his mom. And Dog is still all riled up. Tomas is just being, you know, a kid, but Dog goes for him. Lunges."

"Exactly," said Issy, ready with a card. But Xavier's attention was on Ben, who had leaned forward, into the story, his face now lit up in the firelight. I couldn't look away either.

Ben's voice was low and careful: "Butterfly said that when the Dog had Tomas, you know, by the face, before everyone came running, before anyone tried pull Dog off, Abraham . . . laughed."

Issy shuffled and bridged the cards. "I know she's your mother," she said to Cornelia, "but I would not trust how Butterfly tells any story about Abraham."

Ben ignored her. We all did. "That night at the bonfire, Butterfly took my dad aside. She told him the story, I guess, and he said, 'Well, what do you want me to do about it?' and she said something like how Abraham seems one way to all of us, but he's not really that way, not deep down. She said, he's, like, playing a game. She said she chose my dad to tell because he's the only one who could take Abraham on if things got physical." Ben fidgeted with the toe of his mended wool sock. "So then my dad told my mom about it, in the middle of the night. They thought I was sleeping. She said she didn't ever want to hear him talk like that again. My mom, you know, she doesn't usually yell at him. I mean, she wasn't yelling, it was the middle of the night, but there was something in her voice, like—she was more than scared. It was like she knew he was right, that Butterfly was right, but no one else could ever know."

Ben flashed a doubting smile. "It doesn't sound like Abraham, though, right? Laughing while Tomas got attacked? And I mean, we all told the sheriff that Tomas was, I don't know, taunting Dog, and I just don't feel right if—"

"You want your mom to be safe?" We all looked back at Issy then, because of the sharpness in her voice. "Ben, look at me. The Unthinged World is the only place your mother's safe."

Ben turned his face toward the window.

Xavier caught my eye. He frowned. We had no idea what Issy was talking about.

"Your mom did the right thing, telling your dad to shut up. He shouldn't talk about it. None of us should." Issy met each of our eyes, then, one by one. "Okay? No one talks about this anymore." She picked up Xavier's cards and shuffled them, and made him keep playing.

111

The dark of the forest seems impenetrable, but we must go in. It's impossible to read the trees in front of us—even the birches, which should be glowing white. Within a minute, each of us is injured—from a cheek, an arm, a toe.

What's worse is how quickly we fall apart. Marta's trail is difficult to find. I know it's there, but they whisper behind me, far too loud, full of doubt. If I were Tomas, I'd have shot us already. I shush them like children. Perhaps I mention the gun. Anyway, they hush.

There's no helping it, we need a flashlight. Cornelia brings out her phone. It buzzes as she unzips it from her purse, the screen lit up. We hiss at her to turn it off. It lights her in a bluish glow. Longing flushes her face. One of the daughters, calling mommy from the belly of a beautifully appointed family room. Homework help, boy troubles.

Xavier reaches for the phone. She refuses to hand it over. There's a tussle in the dark, a tug-of-war that's ridiculous and louder than ever, despite their whispers, because of them. The phone goes sailing. Xavier pulls out his own phone, then there's a grapple in the dark for Cornelia's, whose greatest concern, it seems, is whether the screen is broken. It is not. She is so happy about this that I must physically restrain myself from kicking her.

The light from Xavier's phone is reddish as he beams it through his T-shirt. He crouches low, waves the light back and forth until he finds the path. As I suspected, it is not overgrown, which means that I am onto something.

112

"Take that thing out of here." Sarah pointed to the hatchet at my hip. Nora cracked a smile for the first time in days—she loved it when anyone who wasn't her got in trouble—but by the time I came back inside, she was kneading the dough, solemn once again. I kept thinking Dog would be in every room I entered, that I had just missed him. The hatchet bobbed on its branch in the whipping wind. We worked in a veil of yeast, until darkness turned to morning. The room filled with the heat of pumpkin muffins.

"Haven't been seeing much of Marta, have you?" Sarah asked.

The plump dough sprang beneath my fingertips. "There's nothing to forage in the winter." I missed Dog in my bones, but I knew it was wrong to blame Marta. If you had to choose between a dog or a child, the dog was the one who should die. I kept thinking of the moment she'd appeared before me and held out her hand. How she knew what to do and had not been afraid to do it. I also kept thinking about how I would never feel Dog's hot breath at my ear, first thing in the morning, ever again.

"That bread's rubber now," Sarah said, her chin gesturing toward my overworked dough.

"Sorry."

The door to the Main Lodge squealed open, as the first arrivals of the morning stomped off the snow and ice against the fireplace. I'd assumed the muffins were one of Sarah's morning surprises, but she pressed the basket into my hands.

"Take Marta some breakfast," she said.

The wind knifed through my wool mittens as I made my way down the main Home path. My eyes watered in the sun reflected off the lake. In front of one of the fishing huts, a man looked my way. I wondered if he thought us as strange as we thought him and his kind; showing up on their snowmobiles before the sun rose, hanging out in their snowsuits all day, drinking beer on the ice until the world got dark again.

I could find the cold beautiful when I let it swallow me. Ice had formed at the tips of the branches, setting the air tinkling. Before, I would have taken that dulcet sound as a sign of you. Was it that Home was enough now, and I didn't need you to be there to make it enough? Just thinking that felt like a betrayal, but where Home had, at first, seemed gilded with the possibility of you, now every brittle trunk, every brown leaf chattering in the icy wind, was enough in and of itself. I pronounced their names easily: *Picea mariana, Betula cordifolia, Amelanchier laevis, Pinus strobus, Acer saccharum.* Maybe their names could be enough. The hatchet banged against my thigh.

"You look like Red Riding Hood."

Abraham was leaning against a birch that lined the path. Warmth flushed from my collarbone down across my chest. He held out his hand. He took the basket. He said, "I suppose this makes me the Big Bad Wolf, and here we are, on our way to Grandmother's house." I Unthinged myself of all my burdensome thoughts. Unthing yourself, Unthing yourself, Unthing yourself. How good it felt to simply follow.

We climbed to Marta's house. Icicles hung from the gutters. I looked at Abraham looking at the tidy building. In the clench of his jaw I saw that he blamed her for something worse than the slaughter of Dog. He took my basket, Sarah's basket, to the door. He should have knocked. But he went right in. So did I, I suppose.

The flush of the hearth was a gift, the smell of coffee a surprise from the Thinged World. But then I got a glance at Abraham, who suddenly looked afraid. I turned to see.

There, on Marta's couch, lay two people, one on top of the other: Marta and the sheriff, naked as the day. Him below, her above, breasts lying against the gray smattering of his chest hair as a Mozart piano concerto tinkled away. Their clothes were spread across the floor. A kiss passed between them. Her eyes were closed. A moan. They did not know we were there, not yet.

113

I let myself believe we are quiet as we pad down Marta's trail. Sure enough, her cabin appears. A yellow glow spills from its windows, which seems almost an obscenity against the black night. We stop to regroup. It will truly be just as Sarah said: we will walk up and look in the window.

There are voices in the cabin. I let myself feel it then, how close we are. On the other side of that wall waits the answer.

Then comes the click of the safety. We wheel around. Tomas's scar is lit up in the scant light. Cornelia's hands clasp her mouth. Ben reaches into his jacket pocket, for whatever he placed there from his van.

"Abraham!" I shout.

The voice inside Marta's cabin switches off. A radio. We turn to look that way, even Tomas. A figure inside makes its way toward us, its shadow harried and jerky and hard to decipher. It could be a stranger, or Teresa. It could be the dead, back to claim us.

The shadow makes way for the body it belongs to. Step, step, step toward the dark. Toward us. The body is thin, far thinner than it should be. But it's tall, and as it places its hands against the window, a bit of light catches its eyes.

He watches as he always did, hardly blinking.

114

"With him? With him?" Abraham's voice was raw and high and unfamiliar.

Marta and Sal lifted their heads. A startled cry, but I couldn't tell who made it. Marta pulled off of Sal's lap. His penis bobbed, purple, in a way that made me feel sorry for it. He tossed Marta the afghan. I backed into the cold while she was still a slip of flesh. I leapt off the porch and ran until the stripped trees swallowed me. The men's voices rose behind me over the ice-crusted snow. I was already back to the land, past the ice, past our cabin—where a slice of Ben's face caught me out the window—pressing up the hill, sweat dripping down my spine and pooling into my long johns, hatchet thudding my leg, fingers frozen—where were my mittens?—up up up and up and up, panting now, legs burning from running through the snow, to the Main Lodge, with a chimney trail pluming into the sky. Inside I met a wall of warm air, and Sarah, and the bread, and the chopping, and the onion salt cabbage curry lentil rice aroma that could be my armor.

"Well?" Sarah lifted her head. "Marta glad to see you?"

The penis hung in my mind's eye, slick and bobbing. I laughed. I covered my mouth. "You might have brought the basket back." But Sarah didn't mind so much once I loaned her my extra set of hands. I kept my eyes on the door. Abraham would come soon.

He would look at me and we would both know what we had seen.
I couldn't imagine what he would say. I couldn't imagine what
I would do. Then I wished I had stayed at Marta's; to have stayed
would be to understand what had happened and what was going
to happen because of it. My hands and mind did their folding folding folding. I couldn't forget Abraham's face, the high pitch of his
pain when he called to her. I couldn't forget how he had reacted like
he owned whatever she did.

I shivered. Sarah switched places with me so I could be closer
to the oven.

The door opened later, much later, when that late afternoon
blue that comes just before a winter's night had settled over the
windowpanes. There was a blast of cold. Butterfly plunged toward
us, face plastered with tears.

"He left us! He left us!"

Sarah folded up her dish towel, corners matching, before she
went Butterfly's way. It was difficult to get off the Home land in
February—the driveway was not plowed, and it was dangerous to
go at night when the temperature plunged. But Abraham had gone
down the darkening lane in his snowshoes, toward roads that led
him elsewhere—"and I tried to stop him, I begged him, Sarah,
he didn't even have a hat but he had his bag, the one he takes
when he's going, oh he's leaving us, he wouldn't even talk to me,
he looked so upset, it is different this time, I swear it is, something
happened, he wouldn't even talk to me, someone should go after
him," on and on. I was thankful for Butterfly's spectacle, because
no one noticed me.

The next morning, my lost mittens were balanced on the doorknob of the cabin. I brought them in, pretending I didn't know
Marta had found them on her floor. The muffin basket was waiting on the table in the Main Lodge. Sarah stirred the porridge.
"That Marta's an odd duck."

I lived in rapturous fear of what would transpire when Marta showed up at my door. But she didn't come around, and neither, for that matter, did Sal. Were they in love? Was it just some weird sex thing? Did old people have weird sex things? It hadn't even occurred to me that old people had sex—and yet, the penis. The penis! Maybe Sal would arrest Abraham for trespassing on Marta's property. Would they make me be a witness? I'd feel that giggle burning whenever I circled back to Sal's penis wagging in the open room.

"What is wrong with you?" Issy said. Nora got off her lap and squatted before me and squinted hard, as if she could read my mind. There were whispers by then, that Marta and Abraham had gotten into a fight. But no one knew what I had seen. Nora stuck out her tongue. We were in the kitchen. We were in the kitchen as much as possible because it was the warmest place. It was evening again, and the room clattered with spoons and slurps and sighs. Snow dovetailed and swirled and sang over icicles the length of oboes hanging from the outside eaves. I kept my secrets.

115

"Abraham." It's Issy who breaks the spell.

He moves from the window.

"Go on now," says Tomas from behind us.

"Put the gun away." Cornelia's voice is motherly. "The five of us came, just like you wanted. No need for a gun."

Tomas complies. Kudos to Cornelia. Once he's stashed the weapon, he's relentless as a border collie, herding us to the front porch. We climb Marta's steps—Xavier first, then Cornelia, Issy, me, and Ben. The porch is covered in moss, rotten in spots, but it's sturdy enough to bear us to the front door.

What stands in that open doorway, waiting, isn't so much Abraham as a slice of him. He holds on to the door, not for power but support. His pajama pants hang off his torso, hiding his legs. What were once his cheeks are now hollow cavities.

Xavier stands aside, then Cornelia, then Issy, until we form a reluctant amphitheater, with Abraham the stage.

"I see you got my letters."

"What the hell do you want?" says Ben.

Abraham's grin grows. The cabin glows behind him. He turns away, leaving the door open. Tomas urges us forward.

We fill the little place with our adult bodies—limbs and hair and faces and knees, the smell of our armpits, our swallows, our sniffs. It's much smaller than I remembered. Nothing is missing; there's the couch, and the little table, the four mugs, the kettle, set onto the small ivory stove. Even Marta's books are still here. Two kerosene lamps—one set on the kitchen table, the other by her favorite chair—do plenty of work to stave off the darkness outside.

Tomas skitters past us to maneuver Abraham into the armchair. Abraham moans as he eases down. We look away, all but Ben, who observes the old man's obvious pain with a small but satisfied smile. "So, where've you been? Canada? Mexico? And who the fuck did you kill to make it look like you were dead?"

"Sit, please," Abraham says from his chair. Tomas backs up and offers a strange butler bow. Abraham catches me smile. To Tomas he says, "Might you pick up where you left off?"

Tomas scurries to the kitchen and returns with a full basin of water, a jar of Epsom salts, and a folded towel. He kneels before Abraham. He folds the other man's pajama bottoms up from ankle to knee, revealing legs so skinny it hurts to look. He unrolls the raglan socks, from Abraham's ankles down to his yellowed, marled toenails. Tomas measures out a cap of the Epsom salts and dumps them into the water, stirring them with his bare hand.

"I'm sorry but the water cooled," he says, as he lifts Abraham's feet into the the basin.

"Jesus Christ," Ben mutters.

"Ah, Benjamin. Are you a Christian now?"

"Just tell us what you want," Ben says. "If you're not going to tell us where you were or take any responsibility for what you did to us, then at least tell us what you want."

"What I did to you?"

"Jesus fucking Christ."

Xavier places a hand on Ben's shoulder. Tomas dips his hands into the water and rubs at Abraham's ankles. Abraham's eyes close involuntarily, like a baby at the breast.

"I'm a Christian," volunteers Cornelia. She touches the bare base of her neck.

"Well, that," says Abraham, "does not surprise me."

"I do my best," Cornelia says, lifting her chin, "to live by the principles of Christ. I'm prepared to help you in whatever way I can."

"Always the gentle heart. Do you still sing?"

"In the church choir."

He nods, closes his eyes. "A gift like yours."

Ben fiddles in his waistband, eyes narrowing. He's managed to move whatever he got from the car from his pocket into the tuck of his pants. We can't have violence, not when we've just arrived.

"You want money?" I say.

"Money?" Incredulity tinges Abraham's voice. He gestures around the small space, and sweeps his hands to include us, to include the young man fervently bathing his feet. "I've got all I need."

"Why did you send us those letters, then?" Xavier is doing his best to hide his fear. I don't know why he bothers; Abraham sees through each of us. "Are you lonely? Did you really need to black-mail us for . . . company?"

That makes Abraham laugh again. But it's a dim performance. He's out of practice.

I sink down to the couch. Dust puffs around me. "We're here now," I say. "We won't leave you." Ben glares at me. "I want to help you. Please. Let me help you."

Abraham's hands form a tent before him, his pointer fingers lifting to his lips. The others watch us watch each other. Tomas works the arches of his feet, limp and pale. "I believed it would be so. I wanted for it to be so." Abraham waves Tomas off and leans back against the chair. His eyes close. "Only I didn't think you'd come in the middle of the night." He yawns.

"You've got to be fucking kidding me," Ben says.

"I am not, in fact, kidding anyone." Abraham's voice grows wan. "Tomas will see you to your cabin. Teresa will give you breakfast in the morning. Then you'll come back and we'll discuss. There is much to discuss." His eyelids shut again. That quickly, yes. Tomas lifts his legs but they are floppy. Tomas struggles with the basin. Water sloshes onto the floor. Tomas enfolds Abraham's feet in the towel. Abraham begins to snore.

"He fucking passed out," Ben says.

"We don't really have to sleep here, do we?" Cornelia asks.

"Shut up," says Tomas.

"Don't tell her to shut up," Issy says.

"Everyone calm down," says Xavier.

All this time, we have been here, in this room, waiting for ourselves to come home.

116

*T*hen, without warning, Abraham came home. It was dinner again, a full three hours earlier than we would have had it in the summer. Snow fell from his hunter's cap as he stomped his boots. Butterfly rushed to him. We pretended not to see when he stepped past her.

"Where you been?" Gabby lifted a brown puddle of lentils to her lips.

Butterfly inched closer but he went to Gabby. "We need locks. Locks on every door."

Sarah dished up soup. "When was your last meal?"

"The gun," he said. "Get the gun. Knives. The pitchfork. Whatever we can use. We should have planned better." Beside me, Cornelia trembled.

"Sit and eat," said Gabby. She reminded of me of Teresa when Tomas was driving her crazy but the only way to win was to pretend she didn't care. Teresa would have known what to do. I missed her then, in a great swell.

"You haven't heard, have you?" His voice was quiet now, too quiet. "Waco? Texas? Anybody?" He slammed his fist on the table, right next to Gabby's bowl. Her soup splashed. "I told you to listen to the fucking radio."

Gabby rose. "And I told you never to swear at me."

He wheeled away from her, arms spread wide. "The feds blew up a compound four days ago. A compound like ours, with people just like you and me. Filled with kids. They murdered six people." He pointed at six of us, then—Issy, Xavier, Ben, Cornelia, himself, and me. "People like little Sammy Weaver. Now they're setting up out there on the edge of those people's land, waiting—the FBI, with guns, and bombs. Lying in wait for those poor little children. You know what's going to happen? They're going to slaughter them. The Thinged World wants to bring us down. Don't forget it, don't forget it for a second."

Butterfly started for him again. "Unthing yourself from me," he said through gritted teeth. She hiccupped, then backed away. She began to cry. Ephraim offered a handkerchief, but when she tried to steady herself on his shoulder, he looked down at the floor with a grimace, and didn't touch her heaving back.

"What happened between you and Marta?" Gabby said in an even tone. "I went to her place and she wouldn't let me in. Said you told her she's not welcome here."

"I found Sal up there with his dick inside her. Saskia saw, too."

The Main Lodge went silent.

There was such ugliness in that way of telling it, like they were animals. But it wasn't a lie.

He pointed to my silence as proof. "Needless to say, Marta is no longer one of us. You see her on our land, you have my permission"—he looked at Amos—"to do whatever you want."

"Oh, come on," Gabby said.

"She is fucking the goddamn enemy, Gabby. And I'll admit, I was weak. I let that discovery send me away. I let my feelings control me. But then I was out there in the Thinged World and I heard what the Sals of that world are doing to good people, people like us, living on their land, minding their business. When Sal comes for us—and believe me, he'll come for us, believe me, Marta's helping him plan it as we speak—we will protect ourselves. We will protect our home." He pointed to the hatchet at my waist. "Saskia knows. She's ready."

117

The wick of the kerosene lamp flickers our old cabin into cobwebs and rodent dung, dust and leaves, rickety furniture piled by the front room's fireplace. Tomas and Teresa must have worked hard on Marta's to make it seem like no time has passed.

"Are there blankets?" Issy asks.

"Latrine's dug." Tomas ignores her. "Well's working, but you'll haul your own water. Breakfast's at seven."

"Let us go back to Ben's for the night," Cornelia says. "Please. We promise to return tomorrow."

Tomas holds out his broad hands. "Phones."

"I need my phone," says Issy. "I need to keep in touch with—"

"I need mine, too," Cornelia says.

Tomas shakes his head. "You'll call the cops." His long fingers wiggle in a "put it here" gesture. He taps the gun in his pocket. "Don't go anywhere."

Cornelia chokes back a frenzy of tears. Issy shakes her head. Ben says, "We're not going to call the fucking cops." Xavier relinquishes his phone. Then Issy. Then Ben. Eventually even Cornelia hands hers over. Tomas looks at me.

"I don't have one," I say. The truth would set him straight— I'm more like you, Tomas, than any of these people; I don't even know how one of those works. But instead I put my arms in the air like a hostage and let him pat me down, front and back. Up close, he smells familiar—his body a ripened version of his child-hood grubbiness. The memory of his small body, so much like yours, tugs at me. I almost put my hand to his cheek. But they are watching.

"What's wrong with Abraham?" Ben asks. "What kind of sick is he?"

Tomas says, "I'm real sorry about Nora."

Ben sucks in surprise. "Yeah, man. I'm sorry, too. I know you guys were . . ."

"Like a sister," Tomas says. His voice has grown meek. He hangs there, at the door, pockets bulging with technology.

"You think she'd want this?" Ben says. He means us, here, the gun.

"She wants you to pay for what you done."

"What's that supposed to mean?"

Tomas grins. "You know exactly what you done. So does she." He points out to the woods. "I hear her out there. Wandering around. Crying."

The others think he's mad. But the longing for you swells: the discovery of the bird wing, the promise that you have been wait-ing, are waiting, right out there. "You sure it's her?"

"Of course it's not her," Ben mutters.

Tomas's eyes push over mine.

But then Ben shuts him out. Tomas's face flushes as the out-side slices shut. We have done this many times before; make him leave so we can be alone. Tomas's footsteps were much smaller and quicker the last time they crossed the porch away from us.

"Well, he turned out fucked up," Ben says.

"No more than the rest of us," Issy says.

"Childhood trauma leaves invisible scars," Cornelia says. "It's

not something to trifle with. Therapy has been immensely helpful for—"

"I'll be sure not to 'trifle' with it, then."

Issy shoots me a look which means fix Ben's mood.

"It's nice what he said about Nora," I say. It's hard to imagine
her getting older than the sprite who blasted through the forest,
fists and swears, but she did grow up, there's that at least. She tasted
enough of life to decide that she didn't want to live it. Ben leans
his palms against the door. The kerosene lamp flickers.

"I don't think Teresa and Tomas know what we did," Xavier
says, after a minute. Cast in the yellow lamplight, he looks a decade younger. "The way Tomas said, 'You know exactly what you
done.' Plus that whole thing about taking our phones."

"What does taking our phones prove?" Issy says.

"He knows we did something. He knows it was bad enough to
bring us back here. But he doesn't know that what we did was bad
enough that we'd never get the police involved. Remember, they
weren't here at the end. They don't know what it was like."

"Abraham could have told them."

Xavier shakes his head. "I just don't think so. I think it feels . . .
intimate to him. Like something he shares with us. Special."

Ben makes a disgusted face.

"What does it matter whether they know though, in the end?
Abraham knows," says Cornelia. She yawns. "What do you think
he wants from us?"

But it's too late in the night to go down that road. Cornelia
and I take the bunk room. Issy and Xavier claim Philip's bed. Ben
takes up a station at the door. If we have any guesses about what
tomorrow holds, we keep them to ourselves.

118

Gabby got the Ford working in the subzero temperatures, no small feat. I watched her out the Main Lodge window, hunched over the carburetor. Then she snowshoed down to JimBob's with a gas can strapped to her back. The chains went on next. There was swift steadiness in her movements, as if there was somewhere pressing to go, but the wind howled on and the snow blew sideways. A drift as tall as Nora blocked the drive. If the feds were watching us, they were pretty cold.

Back in the cabin, Issy beat me at Spit, after trouncing Xavier and Cornelia, who'd promptly gone up to the Main Lodge in search of heat. My fingers could hardly move in the cold air, but at least Nora's head was on my lap, keeping that part of me warm. I scratched behind her ears like I would with Dog. She didn't mind.

Gabby knocked on the cabin door. "Get your boots on. We're going to town."

Nora sprang up. "Can I come?"

"It's not a trip for little kids."

"I'm not a little kid."

Gabby watched me look toward the hatchet. "You don't need that." She went back into the snow.

On the path, Nora slipped her mittened hand into mine. "Please can I come?" Her knees knocked against me. "I won't be any trouble." It was hard not to feel sorry for her, always underfoot, lonely since Tomas had gone.

Gabby shot me a look.

"Sorry, kid."

Nora dropped my hand. I didn't have to see her middle finger in the tent of the mitten to know what she was doing with it.

There was a plow attached to the front of the pickup, but I'd never seen it used; our food stocks and lumber lasted the winter, which made leaving before the melt unusual. But only twenty minutes on, we were skidding down Bushrow Road, which had gotten municipal plowing. Heat blasted our feet and made our eyes teary. Gabby gripped the wheel and leaned toward the windshield. The radio howled about Waco Waco Waco, until we remembered we could turn it off. I pressed my face against the glass as the trees needled by, already missing the sounds of the Main Lodge, wondering what Abraham had thought when he'd seen us plow away.

There were so many questions to ask—where were we going, did Gabby believe the feds were going to kill us, why was Abraham angry with Butterfly, where had Abraham gone, why had seeing Marta and Sal together sent Abraham away, did Marta and Sal really love each other, did old people have weird sex things—but Issy scrunched down to lay her head on Gabby's shoulder and I knew not to say a word.

Town was kids making a snowman on a crusty lawn. Town was men in parkas unloading shopping carts in the Food City parking lot, and women in cloth coats walking groomed dogs. We pulled into a shoveled spot in front of the bank, a pillared stone building, all right angles, at the center of town. A man with a briefcase came down the steps. He grimaced at the roar of our busted motor.

Gabby slammed her door and ran up the steps. The man watched her disappear inside, then moved up the street alone. The heat had already leaked out of the cab. Issy shuffled the deck of cards until her fingers didn't work anymore, then buried her hands in the armpits of her parka. "I saw Butterfly with Ephraim," she whispered. "It . . ." Her breath shuddered in. "It wasn't just talking. She was doing that thing"—she stuck out her tits and batted her eyelashes. "And you know how it works; first she's talking to a man, then she's . . ." and she wanked her hand up and down.

"Not Ephraim."

"He hits Sarah, you know."

I didn't let myself think about it. Sometimes Nora scrambled away when he came into the Main Lodge, and other days, she crawled right into his lap. "Yeah, but he wouldn't dress like that if he didn't love her."

"She's not the one who makes them dress like that."

I'd assumed Sarah liked looking plain, or maybe it was a way to keep her brood close in the midst of everyone else. But something about it being Ephraim's choice made it less charming.

"You know in the cabin?" I said. I couldn't believe it, but I felt nervous. "When you told us we shouldn't mention what Ben told us? You said Sarah can't go back into the Thinged World." I was remembering Sarah on the banks of the lake while Abraham spoke about love, how she had leaned back against the trunk of Ephraim's body, and how he'd closed his eyes in the morning light. "Why?"

Issy wouldn't look at me. "She did something against the law."

"But you don't believe in the law."

Then Gabby was coming down the steps, chin set. She got back behind the wheel.

"Where to?" Issy asked, glad to be out of our conversation.

Gabby's eyes were fixed at the part of the road that dipped downhill.

"Gabby?"

Gabby took a throaty breath. She turned to look at me. "All that money you gave us? It's gone."

"Money?" Issy said. "What money?"

"Where did it go?" A whole year's worth of money—as Grandmother reckoned it—disappeared. A terrible magic trick.

Gabby nodded up the road. A man, bundled in a Goodwill hat and parka and scarf, was making his way toward the truck from the other side of the street. I knew him from his lumbering cadence.

Issy put her hands over my legs. "Keep going, Gabby. It's Jim."

But Gabby rolled down her window.

"Mommy," Issy said. "Mommy, it's Jim."

Gabby waved. Jim waved back. As he approached, Issy turned toward me, putting her arms around my shoulders, gathering me in. She made herself a shield. I could have gotten out, but that seemed worse, to share the open air with him. Now he was almost to the truck.

"Money's gone, right?" Jim's voice was just as I remembered it: friendliness frosting self-disdain.

"I should have seen it coming."

"You still think I took it?" A car honked as it approached. He waved it around. "I'm not the greatest, but shit, I don't steal food from kids' mouths."

"You just try to rape them," Issy said.

"Told you they'd be thrilled to see me," he mumbled.

Gabby turned toward me then. "You trust me?"

"He assaulted her," Issy was shouting now. Meanwhile I had grown quiet, a mouse, my hands still, my feet freezing against the floor.

"Saskia," Gabby said, "when things get desperate, we must listen to whoever tells the truth. Do you trust me? Because I believe this man—whatever he may have done to you, whatever price he must pay for that—I believe he is the only one telling the truth, and I believe we must listen."

Jim didn't dare look at me—at least there was that. "Abraham's not who he says he is. I don't even know if that's his name. Personally I think he's a sociopath—"

"You're a sociopath." Issy's arms tightened around me. In fact, I was finding it hard to breathe.

"I'm a scumbag, maybe. But, Saskia, come on, you and I both know I never—"

"Just say what you've got," Gabby said.

Jim sighed. "The sheriff's a pretty good guy, okay? As sheriffs go. He could have gotten you out of there a hundred different ways, but he lets you all stay. No matter what folks around town say, he says you've got a right to be there. But that land is in foreclosure now. Abraham drained the account that was your last chance to pay what's due. Who knows where your money went? My bet? He lost it all on blackjack. You think someone who believes in Unthinging withdraws money that belongs to some kid, takes it to the nearest casino and loses it on blackjack?

"Look, I know I was stupid, Saskia, and fuck, you're a kid, and I'm sorry, okay, I'm really fucking sorry, I was messed up. Drinking way too much, okay, making bad choices. But at the end of the day, I want you kids to be safe. I don't want you caught up in something stupid. Pretty soon the sheriff's going to have to go up there and get you all off that land. The bank needs you off it, and Abraham's not doing his part to move things along. You just—you listen to me now." His fingers gripped the ledge of the unrolled window. Icy air flowed in. "I know Abraham's got everyone riled up about this Waco stuff, but the sheriff has had plenty of chances to break shit up at Home and he's never gone for it. He doesn't want to hurt anyone."

Jim drew his hands back into his pockets. He stayed where he was, next to the car. Gabby turned on the motor. "Anything else?"

"I don't know what shit went down between Philip and Abraham, but Butterfly got us all messed up pretty good."

"Don't blame this on Butterfly," Issy said.

He ducked his head, but he met my eyes. "I'm sorry to hear Philip hasn't come back."

Tears stung my vision.

"We're a lot alike, him and me. We try to do right but we fuck it up, don't we?" His fingers found his way back to Gabby's window. "Hey, you know how to get ahold of Teresa? Last I heard she took Tomas down to Florida with her sister."

"Teresa and Tomas went to Florida?" Issy said. "I thought they were still at the hospital."

"I just want to talk to my family." Jim's voice broke. But Gabby was pulling the truck forward. "Please, if you talk to her, tell her I'm stuck here. Please, Gabby."

In the rearview mirror, I watched Jim standing in the middle of the road. Then we were up and over the hill, back to the woods.

119

*F*rom Cornelia's perky climb down the ladder, it seems she more than survived a night on the ancient top bunk. Meanwhile, my neck will barely turn, my joints are stiff from a night in jeans, and I have to pee so badly that the trudge up to the latrine will be as unpleasant as using it.

Ben has kept his word; he's still sitting, eyes wide, against the door to the cabin. Xavier and Issy stumble in from Philip's bedroom; from the tousle of their hair, they both dozed at least a little.

Before Ben opens the door, he checks what he's hidden in his waistband. Then the world comes bursting: the flurry of the chickadees, the wind in the trees, clouds like white sheep, the wind roiling the tops of the pines. Tomas said he hears Nora out in these woods. But how does he know it's her? My mind returns to that gold-tipped wing with every step.

In the Main Lodge, Teresa insists on hugging us, one after the other, as if she hasn't sicced her gun-toting son on us. "That baby of yours!" she exclaims to a slack-armed Issy. "He's just adorable!" Tomas shovels in two helpings of his mother's sticky porridge. We sit and eat. I find I am obedient in this strange reality—chew, taste, swallow. Again, again.

"Remember Grimm?" I say. All that's left of the moose head above us is the hook it once hung on.

"Tomas thinks he was stolen by teenagers," Teresa says. "Teenagers like to steal big things, you ever notice that?"

"Construction signs," Tomas offers.

"Mascots," says Xavier.

"There's cow tipping," says Cornelia. "Does that count?"

They keep talking as Teresa settles in beside me. She peers into my emptying bowl. "You like it?"

"Yeah."

"Liar. You only liked what Marta cooked."

"I saw Sarah yesterday."

She nods as if she's not surprised.

I glance up to make sure Ben's not listening. "Why'd you cut her hair?"

"She asked me to." Teresa shakes her head at my shocked expression. "You should have seen how happy she was to get back up here. She said it made her feel free again. Made her want to start drawing. You know, back in the day, she told me this was the only place she ever knew who she was. And then, up here again, out of the blue she said she didn't know why she'd kept her braids all these years. I mean, you know, she was in and out. Half the time she'd kind of drift off. But when I asked her to tell me what she meant, she said the braids were Ephraim's thing." Ben's eyes lift at the sound of his father's name. I soothe him with a smile, and he lets me be while Teresa goes on, oblivious. "He always wanted her to be, you know, that good little wife. I don't know, I just thought I'd give her a little freedom, right? Show her she didn't need to keep her hair the way he liked it, however many years after he left her for that slut. Didn't surprise me at all, actually, when I heard Butterfly had gotten into his—"

"Did Sarah meet with Abraham?"

"Poor thing wandered off before he was available." This sets a fire in my chest. Teresa glances at Tomas, who's laughing at something Xavier just said. "My boy looks up to you all so much. It's good to have you back." As though we're not being kept here against our will.

Then Issy's standing over us. "I need to call my kid." Teresa looks to Tomas. He shakes his head. "His babysitter knows where we are," Issy continues. Ben's eyes flick back to us at the use of the term "babysitter" to describe Jenny. "If I don't call, she's going to send someone up to look for me. That was the plan."

Tomas says: "I'll call."

"You have to let her call her kid," Cornelia says.

Tomas removes the gun from his pocket and places it on the table. "I'll call."

Teresa says, "I bet he's ready for you." She means Abraham.

It's a quick walk up to Marta's. Pine needles scatter over us. Along the water, a mallard—*Anas platyrhynchos*—frantically flaps his wings, and above us, the *Sayornis phoebe* lets out its steady chip. We find Abraham in Marta's bed, like the wolf in a fairy tale. His hair is long but scraggly, his beard unwashed. A bowl sits beside the bed, with a crust of this morning's gruel. Tomas kneels at his bedside. Their whisper is out of a Dutch Master painting, light streaming in.

"Wait outside," says Abraham.

Tomas's shoulders droop, but he lifts the bowl. Abraham's mouth forms a wry smile when it shuts behind him.

Ben crosses his arms. "So, tell us what you want."

A breath from Abraham. And then: "I need you to kill me."

120

*I*t had snowed a powdered sugar dusting in the couple hours we'd been in town. Gabby's boots imprinted dark tracks on the plowed driveway as she went to Abraham's door. She opened it, and left it swinging wide. Out spilled light and the shock of radio voices. I could still feel the press of Issy's hands, bruising with love, as I pulled into the cold air.

Gabby was already yelling. "I'm talking about your xenophobic, self-centered bullshit that allows you to think money that is supposed to feed all of us is yours to spend. Spent in a world, by the way, that you claim is so fucking tainted that none of the rest of us is allowed to go there, or have our own money to spend in it. But you feel free to take ours?"

Abraham was in there, we could hear him, but we couldn't make out what he was saying, not over the radio, a jabber of sound and anger and Waco, always Waco.

"Turn it off," she said into the cabin.

He turned it off.

When Gabby spoke again, she didn't yell. In fact, I wouldn't have heard her if we hadn't crept close. "That was our mortgage, Abraham." When he didn't reply, she turned and pointed at Issy. "Pack your things." Her breath was a cloud.

Abraham appeared in the doorway, shirtless, hair loose over his shoulders. "Do you know your mother didn't want you, Issy?"

"What did you say?"

But he wasn't looking at Gabby. Even though he was barefoot, he moved across the snowy ground toward Issy. "The day we met, she told me you were too much. Those were her words, 'she's too much for me.' She said she was thinking of giving you up."

"That's a lie," Gabby said. "Issy, baby, he's lying to you."

"Oh, poor Iss." He took her face in his hands. "My heart broke. To think of someone not wanting you. Wonderful you. Vibrant you. Electric you. Why do you think I asked Gabby to join me here? It would have been much easier without two extra mouths to feed. I would have welcomed the quiet. But Issy, my heart was filled with love for you. I couldn't bear to let her—"

"You don't believe him, do you?" Gabby said.

Issy's chin quivered.

Right then, a feather drifted down onto the crown of Abraham's head. There was not a bird in the sky. It was a black feather—not touched in gold, not like the one you gave me the day you died. But a feather, nonetheless, and as Abraham felt it land, and pulled it off, and held it in the air, a smile spread over his face as though Gabby wasn't there anymore, and he held it high as the Homesteaders gathered to witness this strange omen—Sarah, Ephraim, Amos, Xavier, Ben, Cornelia, Butterfly, Nora. Hope zinged through me; you had given me another sign. Issy gripped my hand. She pulled me away, down the hill, into the safety of our cabin, away from the person who had given her life, back into the belly of Home, back into the chance of your return.

121

"It's not murder," Abraham says, "if I ask you to do it."

"It's not not murder," Ben says, with a certain amount of relish.

"I'm not killing anyone." Cornelia's eyes dart over each of us. "We are not killing anyone."

Abraham puts up his hands. "Surely you've noticed I'm not at my best. I've been ailing, for some time. I came back here to—"

"Yeah, where the fuck you been, man?" Ben says. "The only good thing about finding out you're still alive is that—"

"Shut up, Ben," Issy says.

"Thank you, Isobel," Abraham says.

"It's Issy, you fuck."

Abraham suppresses a smile, then opens his hands as if to say, shall I continue? No one stops him. "I've been in pain—"

"Good," says Ben. Issy offers a warning growl.

"A lot of pain. I don't want to bore you with the details, but the symptoms will certainly be familiar."

Xavier's fingers comb through his lovely crest. "If Ben was allowed to talk right now, I think he'd say to get to the fucking point."

"Ah, yes," Abraham says. "There are contingencies in place to make sure you consider my request with fair and open minds. You have two days. I assume you're all quite grown-up and moral now and will need a little time to hammer this out among yourselves. So. Two days, then. If you kill me by sundown tomorrow, I'll have Teresa call my lawyer to destroy the letters I've written to your families"—he glances over to me—"in the case of those of you who have families; to your employers; and to the papers in each of your hometowns."

"Oh boy, more mystery letters." But no one tells Ben to shut up now.

"And if we don't kill you?" Xavier asks.

"If you fail to kill me, or you leave without doing so, then, well." Abraham's hands lift toward the ceiling in a trill of surprise. "That little thing you did, that terrible little thing, gets out."

Cornelia crosses her arms. "How do we know you know what it is?"

"I mean the murder," he says, right quick. No mistaking that.

"The murder you promised would mean we could stay here? The murder you orchestrated and then abandoned us to? We were kids, Abraham." Issy's voice swells with emotion. "We'd been told, by the person we trusted most, that we wouldn't be able to survive in the outside world."

"You were old enough to know that murder is bad, weren't you?"

Ben turns to us. "I'm good with killing him. Can I do it right now?"

"Why does it have to be us?" Xavier says. "You could take sleeping pills. You could shoot yourself with Tomas's stupid gun. Heck, I'm sure Tomas would be thrilled to shoot you himself."

"Because you're good at it."

The hairs on the back of my neck stand up. He's looking right at me. They all see.

"Because you knew Saskia wouldn't come if we didn't come, too." That's Ben. "It's about her. It's always about her."

"You mean," Cornelia says, sounding more than a little relieved, "you want Saskia to kill you?"

"It will be all five of you," Abraham says. "You'll plan it and carry it out together. If it's a gun, you all touch the gun. Doesn't matter who pulls the trigger, because it's all five of you deciding together. If it's not all of you in on it, I know you'll turn on one another. To know this tears you apart will hurt me so. Think of this as coming full circle."

"You're a psychopath," Cornelia says, the word carrying both horror and amazement.

"A sociopath, I think? Or at least that's how my mother diagnosed me." He yawns. "Oh goodness, I'm tired. I get tired so quickly these days."

"No," says Ben, "you don't get to go to sleep. Not until we're done talking."

Abraham waves his hand in a vague gesture of dismissal. "I'll call for you again. After some shut-eye."

Ben barrels out of the house. We follow, down into the woods. Tomas is out here somewhere, watching us. We move down to the water. We try to keep our voices down.

"Fuck it," Ben says. "Let's shoot him."

"Shoot him with what?" Cornelia's eyes scan the horizon. "I don't think Tomas would easily—"

"Ben brought a gun," I say.

"You did what?"

Ben touches the spot at his waistband. Xavier and Issy sigh in exasperation. "No," Cornelia says. "We are not shooting anyone."

"I say we sit it out and let him send the letters," Issy says. Ben whips his head toward her. "Maybe paying our due wouldn't be the worst thing. Maybe it would feel good to answer for what we've done."

"What about Sekou?" Cornelia's really asking about her own girls.

"I say we leave." Xavier. "Act like we're considering his proposal. Then one of us sneaks out in the night. Someone fakes an illness or something. Creates a diversion."

"You've watched one too many *Law and Orders*," Cornelia says.

"Get to town, contact the police. Tell them we're being held hostage up here. You think they'd believe that lunatic over the five of us?"

"Then he sends the letters," Cornelia says. "Then Billy finds out. And Eric. And Jenny. My girls. Everyone we know."

"You folks need something?" It's Tomas, coming out from behind one of the great pines. Who knows how long he's been here.

"Have you called my son?" Issy asks.

"I tried the number."

"You leave a message?"

"No."

"That's not acceptable, Tomas. You need to call back."

"I tried."

"I told you, she's going to send the cops. That'll be complicated for you."

"It'll be complicated for you, too." It's clear he's got a chip on his shoulder. An early childhood spent nipping at our heels. He's heard stories about us, even remembers some things. He knows we forgot him.

"Tell you what," Xavier says, "let's go up to the Main Lodge and call Jenny. We just want to make sure Issy's boy is okay, you understand that, right, Tomas?" Xavier looks to Ben. "You'd probably like to know how she's doing, too."

"If it's all right with everyone, I'll stay down here," Cornelia says.

The others look to me. I can't imagine the anxiety of the phone call, Teresa's body pressing toward mine, the smell of pea soup bubbling on the open fire. Out here lies the world Marta taught me to see. Out here, there's the chance to see you flitting.

122

The ghost-white trunks of the *Batula papyrifera* groaned. White crystals whipped into my eyes and my breath clouded the air. In the biting chill, away from the others, I tossed the hatchet, my eye on a knot. It hit its mark without a shred of doubt.

The feather, whatever its specific meaning—why it was raven black, why it had chosen Abraham—meant, at least, that you were still out there in the woods. I thought I might be crying—the cold could mix me up—but I was laughing, really, or laughing as I cried. My heart was buzzing like a hornet, but I would hold still. I would be little Sammy Weaver, lying in wait. You had been testing me. I would not let you down.

My knuckles rapped the prearranged triple knock. There was a thunder of furniture inside the cabin before Ben opened the door. His breath nipped at my cheek as I pushed past him into the small cabin.

"Gabby coming back?" he asked, putting the chairs back into place as a barricade.

That's right; I had told them I was going outside to make sure Gabby wasn't lurking, so that Issy could slip out to pee. Day and night, Gabby had been knocking, then going away, then coming back to beg at the blocked door. Issy had insisted on keeping her locked out.

Now Issy sobbed as she paced, still in her slippers. Xavier shot me a look; Issy was not, by nature, a sobber. Finally, Cornelia got her calm enough to sit before the fire. She stroked her arm. "Why don't you come up to the Main Lodge for supper? I'll sit with you the whole time, and after, we can come back and play Spit."

Issy sniffed hopefully at the mention of cards.

"And maybe it wouldn't the worst thing to at least hear what she has to say, you know? Maybe you could tell her how you—"

"I'm never speaking to my mother again," Issy said.

"But she's sorry," Cornelia said, trying not to cry. "She's so sorry. Can't you forgive her? She's your mother, Iss."

Issy's jaw tightened. She shook her head. "Jim is a monster." She looked to me. She blinked once, twice, like you used to, when you needed me to be in charge. "Right?"

Jim was weak and pathetic and drunk. He was lost, confused, unhappy. To call him a monster was to make things too easy.

"Yeah," I said. Because if Issy forgave Gabby, they would reconcile and leave Home, and I couldn't live at Home without Issy, and I needed to stay, because I needed to see you. Really, Jim was just a man like most men, who want what they want and believe they can take it, and don't we let them? Don't we just.

123

"We could sneak off while they're gone. Call our lawyers."
Cornelia's voice is crisp. Wind fringes the surface of the lake. Off
Blueberry Island, a pair of *Gavia immer*, common loons, dive down
long past the count of fifty, then pop again far off, their black heads
distinctive against the shoreline. Maybe you're out there on that
island, awaiting my next move, or watching from the tip of a pine
high above us. Certainly you're laughing at how incompetently I'm
handling this. I stormed in with my troops and now I'm just . . .
stalled. Maybe this was your lesson. Maybe you showed me the
wing to get me back, only to disappear again so I'm reminded of
all the ways I've let you down.

Cornelia's right; it wouldn't be easy to walk off the land, but
we could manage it. Beat our way through the bush, clamber
over the stone walls that separate one plot from the next. Happen
upon a cabin with a fisherman inside, frying up his bacon. We'd
beg to use his phone. We might call the police, or sure, lawyers,
although I'm not quite sure how that would help us, but Cornelia
does, and she's better equipped for the Thinged World.

But then Abraham would send the letters, and I'm not sure even
lawyers could fix that. Maybe Cornelia knows this. Maybe that's
why she stays where she is, perched on a rock at the lip of the lake,
arms around her legs.

"I keep thinking about how Tomas used to shit everywhere."

A vague memory surfaces: little Tomas lifting up his shirt to squat in the middle of the path. Cornelia wiping him with a maple leaf.

"It was this joke we all had. We used to laugh about it. 'Watch out for mines!' We thought it was so funny." She shakes her head. "Poor kid."

"We were kids, too."

"Does that really make you feel better?"

Point taken.

"And then Gabby. The way we treated her. She was the only one who saw the truth."

"Jim knew the truth, too. To be fair."

"You don't have to be fair to him." She narrows her eyes. "Why do you think he attacked you?"

At the time, I thought I was lying, that he had only grabbed my arm but done nothing more. But now that I am older, I know I wasn't lying, not exactly. "I think he was heartbroken about, you know, Butterfly moving on to Philip."

"Everyone seems to forget she's my mother. Everyone seems to forget she abandoned me. Everyone's like, oh, poor Ben, he lost Ephraim; what a slut that Butterfly was, good riddance. But I lost my whole family the day she walked off the land." She watches the loons.

"I'm sorry."

"You're not sorry."

"I am. I know exactly how that feels."

She looks at me for a moment, then nods. "Jim tried to rape me."

"When?"

"The summer he attacked you. After my mother dumped him. He tried to crawl into my bed." She throws a rock into the lake.

"Why didn't you say something?"

Another rock. "I wasn't going to let anyone call me slutty."

"We wouldn't have called you slutty."

"Really, Saskia? Seems like you're always looking for reasons your friends shouldn't like me." Her mouth forms a wry knot. "Anyway, I fought him off. I wasn't going to be like my mother."

I flush with shame. "You shouldn't have had to bear that alone."

She keeps quiet while the loons dive. "Whenever I'm around you, I hide myself. I'm so afraid of what you'll say. I didn't even let myself pray in front of you until the other night." She reaches up to fiddle with that invisible chain at her neck—a crucifix, must be. "I've spent thousands of dollars in therapy, but it still comes down to that dumb part of me that wants to measure up."

"To what?"

"To you, Saskia. To how Ben looked at you—looks at you. Yes, he does, you know it. To how special Abraham believed you were. You were always the special one." She clears her throat. "You're sure Abraham never touched you? Sexually?"

"No." Why does it feel so important to defend him against that accusation, when what he did to us was terrible in a different way? "Did he touch you?"

"No." She decides to believe me. "But you know it's because of Abraham that there were no rules. And it's because there were no rules that Jim attacked us."

"There were lots of rules."

"You thought there were rules because they were built for you. Built to make you know you were powerful. Important. Special. Rules to teach you to Unthing, so that you'd feel holy while you walked up and down these paths. It's because of those rules that Abraham brought you right where he wanted you, so that when he was ready to use you as the weapon he kept telling you you were, you were at his beck and call."

"That's not fair," I say.

"Isn't it?"

"You were there, too."

"I certainly was." She dusts off her pants as she rises to her feet. "And for that, I'll never forgive myself." She looks off along the bank. "We have to try to fix it, right? Even if there's no way to fix it?"

"Yes."

A gust comes off the water. She narrows her eyes as it tumbles my hair. "If I didn't know, I'd never guess you'd been shut inside your house for sixteen years."

"What does that mean?"

"You're so . . . happy."

"I'm not happy."

Cornelia goes up the path without me. I listen for you, but you're hiding.

124

Come the end of March, the snow thinned. The air, though not yet warm, promised something besides cold. Abraham's radio droned theories about the fed's tactical maneuvers, about what David Koresh must be planning. But that particular morning, a keening cut through the radio's clatter and carried down the hill, sending us running to the driveway to discover who had died—all but Issy, who stuck to the cabin, avoiding Gabby.

Sarah was on her knees before the Main Lodge, tearing at her clothes. I didn't think people actually did that.

Ben skidded toward her. "What is it, Ma?" He turned, frantic, for news from someone, anyone. But the only sign of another adult was Abraham's door, closed, the radio droning from the other side.

Nora darted from behind a tree and pointed to the twinned footprints leading down off the driveway. "Daddy took his tools."

Amos appeared then, and spat on the ground. "Your dad ran off with that whore."

"Butterfly is not a whore!" Nora screamed, as if she'd had to say it a dozen times already. She tore away from us, into the woods.

Ben was back to his mother. "He left? He left with Butterfly?"

Cornelia was backing away now. Xavier lifted his eyes toward her, and then to me, before following Cornelia into the woods, which meant I didn't have to.

"I knew," Sarah said, looking out at the driveway. "I knew he had eyes for that woman but I wouldn't let myself believe it. He's a good man. He's a good man."

Ben tried to gather his mother into his arms, but she pushed him off. Her sound had become a bleating. "He'll come back, Ma." But Ephraim taking his red toolbox off the land made his departure more certain than anything else. I knew he should say something to ease her further, to bring her back to reason. But he was struck dumb.

"Your bread," I said. The first thing that came to mind. "The Mother." I meant, your bread will call them back. I meant, put your hands back into it, expend your sorrow into its making. I meant, feed us.

Sarah lifted her head as though my words had carried past her on the wind. She followed them into the Main Lodge, swiping at her wet cheeks. It wasn't long before we heard the slam of the kitchen door, at the other end of the lodge. From inside, someone shouted: "She took the Mother."

We started down the trail to the latrines, but by the time we reached Sarah, she had already dumped the Mother into the reeking black hole. Ben lifted his arms in surrender and jogged down the hill. I followed him, past the closed chicken coop, and the snow-sleeping garden, and the cluster of cabins. Issy was still in ours, locked away. I thought to tell her what had happened, but Ben was ten yards offshore, standing on the ice.

The smooth sheet crackled under my feet. Every step, a pop. "We shouldn't be out here. It's not frozen over yet." The sun was blinding. White hillocks offered shadows here and there. Blueberry Island was a snowdrift.

"You think she'll start using again?" His question was simple. He thought I knew a secret that I didn't. But without the facts, I knew that he meant Sarah. "She did something really bad, Saskia.

I don't know what, not all the way, but I think she might have killed someone? I know she was selling drugs. Transporting them for her father. I guess my grandpa is some kind of big drug dealer or something? My dad told me he saved her. He said he likes fixing things and he knew he could fix her, too. He heard about this place and he knew she'd be safe, without anything to tempt her. He said we could never leave." Ben shielded his eyes against the endless white. "But maybe I should take Mother and Nora and go." His chin wobbled. "If the sheriff's really going to come up here and shoot us up."

I reached my hand out. I traced the length of his arm. "She's safer here than anywhere else. We all are. Anyway, where would you go? We have nowhere else to go."

"Yeah," he said, after a minute. Then he took my hand.

125

*L*unch is of the old school—lentils and rice. When Sarah cooked the same recipe there was a velvety secret embedded in its flavors, but in Teresa's hands, the meal tastes, at best, like lentils and rice.

Teresa watches me choke it down. Cornelia and Issy are busy in some worried conversation about their children, so I take the chance to ask, "How's Jim?"

"You think I spoke another word to that man? After what he did to you?"

"He was your husband, Teresa."

She shrugs. "Marriage counts a lot less than friendship, far as I'm concerned."

Is that what we are—friends? "So why are you blackmailing us?"

"And just so you know, I didn't lie to you. You asked if Abraham was here, and I said he wasn't on the land. He isn't. He's on Marta's land. I'm not a liar."

"Why are you helping him?"

She sighs. "Tomas talked about coming back ever since we left. He was so little, and the dog attack was awful. You'd think he'd have blocked it all out. But having to leave the way he did only made the place more special to him. He grew up feeling like he missed out on the best time in the world. So when Abraham found us, and offered the chance to return, well, I couldn't say no."

"But it wasn't the best time in the world. Abraham used us. He's using you, Teresa."

"Oh, I know." She's looking at her boy. "But I wanted to give Tomas his time here. He deserves it, after the price he paid." She flashes me a quick smile. "I guess you could say I'm using Abraham back."

If a stranger stumbled upon us, they'd think we were exactly what Teresa called us, friends. Tomas shovels in food. Ben's eyes dart from face to face. Xavier tries to keep up the conversation. Issy's brow sits heavy over her worried eyes. Cornelia's fingers fiddle, near constantly, with the phantom crucifix. And me? I look out the window every chance I get. You, you, you.

126

*T*he sounds of the Texas apocalypse buzzed open our sleep—first one man's voice, then another, frantically recounting: "Two CEVs have been deployed into the Branch Davidian compound. A battering ram has broken a hole ten feet in diameter just to the left of the building's front door. Shots fired! I repeat, shots fired!"

We awoke like soldiers, the battle begun without us. It was light outside, plenty into morning, but the rhythms of Home breakfast just past dawn; days of manual labor—had relaxed now that teenagers made up a significant portion of the population, and Ephraim and Butterfly had left, and Sarah had given up on all kitchen activities. We were becoming so lean. Abraham stuck mostly to his radio, and Gabby to her cabin, where she subsisted on a stockpile of nuts and whatever Nora swiped from the kitchen. Our meals were indistinguishable: pintos, navies, or limas over rice, which Amos stirred to oblivion. Every morning, the previous day's beans slipped from our bodies into the latrine, fast and wet and stinking.

We were surprised to discover Abraham crouched on our porch, hands arced over the tinny, talkative crank radio like it was a source of heat. His shotgun leaned against the railing, in quick reach. Through the filigree of pine branches, the sun offered warmth. "They're going to gas them."

Cornelia opened her mouth, then closed it, then opened it again. "Maybe they're rescuing them."

Gunfire again, peppering the Texas morning, and ours, too. "That sound like rescuing?"

"How do you know about the gas?" Issy looked like she might cry.

"It's what I would do."

Ben met my eye, for just a moment. The touch of his gaze filled me with vain hope, as though it, and the feeling it swelled in me, might be enough to save those strangers' lives. The radio crackled with people turning the destruction before them into a story. Cornelia curled into Issy. Xavier put his hand on my shoulder.

Abraham led us to the water, holding the radio like a beacon. Spring ephemerals poked up between the wet pine needles. The modest blossoms only existed before the leaves came in on the deciduous trees; when bare branches allowed the sun to hit the forest floor. Sweet little trailing arbutus; wood anemone, dancing in the wind; and wild columbine, electric and fuchsia. Marta had trained me to find them, but it had been all study—I'd never seen them with my eyes.

It was hard to imagine a sunbaked Texas morning, but the ice was finally out, after crackling around the edges of the lake for days, loosening from the shore, then breaking up, like congealed grease skimmed from a cooled pot of Sarah's bone broth. The air was still cold enough for shivering.

"The CEV to the right of the building appears to be using a battering ram. One hesitates to speculate, but these appear to be steps toward introducing some kind of weapon, perhaps gas, perhaps tear gas, into the compound." How could a place so far away seem so much closer than town? I closed my eyes and Unthinged myself of my body and let the sounds of that world carry me to the children huddled inside, walls quaking, burning gas filling their lungs. I willed them to look at me, a kind face that could carry them out of their story.

Amos joined us, propping himself on a stump. He whittled a rabbit into a piece of driftwood. Abraham stood to face the expanse of the lake. He spread his arms wide. "Observe the scope of this changing season." His voice carried over the radio's ricocheting gunshots. "Observe the vastness and perfection of our world Unthinging." Abraham ululated his white breath into the bitter blue sky. Sarah joined us, wrapped in a shawl. Before she killed the Mother, she'd have brought rolls. Nora crouched behind a stump, firing pebbles with a makeshift slingshot.

Was that Marta moving above us, along the path? Something about the Branch Davidian children hunkering inside those walls made me long to go back to the era before I even knew her, so that I could be small enough for her to take me into her arms. But no, it was just a chipmunk, out at the first scent of spring.

"Who wants to practice?" Abraham said. He meant the shotgun. The news kept churning. It would be our backdrop all day. "Xavier?"

"Yeah, okay." Xavier shuffled up.

Abraham handed him the weapon. "Treat it like a wild animal." Xavier's fingertips repelled from the machine. He lifted his eyes to Abraham, and all his own vain hope was clear—perhaps the man would praise him.

"Well, maybe less like a wild animal," Abraham said, chuckling, "and more like someone you hope to make your friend." Abraham placed his hands over Xavier's. Ben watched the careful touch. His expression reminded me of my own longing.

"Put down the gun." Gabby's arms were crossed. She was only ten feet up the path. Sarah's gaze darted between Gabby and Abraham as he lifted the shotgun from Xavier's hands. He pointed it, not exactly at Gabby, but in her direction.

"No!" Sarah shouted.

Abraham offered Sarah a smile. He lowered the gun. "Just having fun."

Amos kept whittling.

"The children shouldn't hear this." Gabby pointed to the radio.

Abraham capped his free hand on Xavier. "They're warriors."

"You're children," Gabby said. She was speaking to Issy's turned back. "The people in that compound are brainwashed. The adults are brainwashed. Those poor kids will pay the price for their parents following a child abuser." She turned to Sarah. "The fact that Abraham is siding with David Koresh means he's forgotten every single thing we dreamed of doing up here. You know I'm right. You know it's time to leave."

"So then leave." Abraham's voice flared. "You keep talking about going, Gabby. So why don't you just get the fuck out?"

"This isn't about the goddamn feds." She turned to Amos. "He's telling you it's about upholding ideals and whatever else bullshit, but he stole food from your mouths because he's a gambling addict. Now he's got you gunning for some apocalypse because he's bored. His boredom is going to get you killed."

There was something in that last bit that Sarah agreed with. But Abraham cut her off before she could say so. "You can go now, Gabby. Issy already knows you didn't want her."

"Baby." Gabby shook her head. "That's bullshit."

"Issy doesn't want you either."

"Baby, give me a few minutes—"

"Tell her." Abraham turned toward Issy. "Go on. Tell your mother that I'm not the one who forgot the meaning of this place.

Every day, thanks to you"—he meant us, the five of us, gathered close—"I get closer to understanding what we are capable of here. The bounty of our gifts." He stepped toward Issy. He lifted her chin. "Go on. Tell your mother what you want."

A single tear curved down over Issy's broad cheek.

"Baby." Gabby's voice had gone gentle. "My sweet baby, let's talk. Just you and me. Like it used to be. If you want to stay here after that, we can talk about that, too. Please. Oh please, just a minute. That's all I'm asking. A minute of your time." Gabby held her free hand open. It kept itself steady even though it had intentions, desires, to push through the empty space between them, grab her daughter's shirt into a fist, and pull her close. "It was just you and me."

Something about that statement brought Issy back to herself. She moved across the open bank of wet snow, right toward that outstretched hand. She was more than full head taller than her mother, but when she neared Gabby, she drew herself even higher. "And it wasn't enough."

"It was more than enough."

Issy shook her head. "You said we'd be stronger when it was more than just us. We'd be happier." She ignored her tears. "You said a family shouldn't only be two people. Well." Issy gathered us toward her. "You got one thing right." What she said next came out in a low growl: "Go. Now. And don't come back."

Gabby's breath went shallow. But she didn't plead. She didn't grab her girl. She didn't give us a last, careful look. She simply stood there for a moment, on the cusp between what had been and what would be. Then, with squared shoulders, she went up the path. Sarah stood to follow, but Abraham's narrowed eyes were enough to make her sit back down. Amos was still whittling.

"This is a full-on military assault the likes of which has rarely been seen on American soil," went the excited newscaster, his babble filling up the space Gabby left behind. A chipmunk stuck its head out of the hole right beside Abraham's foot, darting back into the ground with a squeak. Abraham smiled down at the creature, then lifted his eyes and pointed out at the fishing cabins on the opposite shore, still boarded up for winter. "They're lying in wait." He meant the sheriff. He meant the cops and the feds. "They can see we're well defended." We were down to one shotgun and a hatchet, the kitchen knives, Amos's knife, and, somewhere in the forest, Nora's slingshot.

"Remember"—he pointed at the dark windows across the lake—"the law protects them if they take you. Saskia, Cornelia, Xavier, and Issy—you're on your own here, at least in their eyes. You are 'underage'—whatever that's supposed to mean. The Thinged World doesn't recognize that we are family. They're gassing those kids in Texas, right this very second. I want to keep you safe. I'm going to keep you safe, no matter what they try to pull."

It was hard to wait, in fear and anticipation, in readiness, in calm. Abraham watched me until I offered a smile of appreciation. Then he turned around, putting his back to the lake. He lifted his parka. He unbuttoned his pants. He dipped them down over his bare bottom, and mooned the opposite shore.

Cornelia's giggle lifted musically, manically. Nora flitted back from her hiding spot with a darting need: "What? What? What's so funny? Tell me!" At the sight of Abraham's ass, she was laughing, too, and then even Amos put down his knife to chuckle, and Sarah was shaking her head as if Abraham was a naughty boy who amused her, Gabby's departure forgotten.

But Ben didn't laugh. He looked out at the icy spot out on the lake where he had taken my hand. It was a place that would soon disappear, and then never exist again.

"You don't need her." Abraham gathered Issy close. "You don't need a mother."

Ben's eyes lifted to Sarah. Without him looking at our spot, I knew I'd never be able to find it again.

127

We spread out to wait for Abraham's summons—Issy and Cornelia to their motherly concern on the porch of the Main Lodge, Xavier to muse on the steps of our old cabin, Ben to kick at the rotting beds where the garden used to be, no doubt imagining Abraham's head under the tips of his steel-toed boots. Tomas is somewhere lurking. Teresa stands on the steps of the Main Lodge, arms folded, watching us move away.

We should wait until she finds us boring. We should gather when she goes inside. We should whisper. We should plan. I should stick close, so they don't decide without me.

But I am free. The Unthinged World opens itself: the *Tamias striatus*—chipmunks—skittery when I move even an inch their way; the silvery green lichens, gradations of fuzz and scale atop granite rocks and running up the trunks of every tree; the relentless falling patter of the pine needles, slipping from their branches down over the forest floor. Every frond, every pinecone, every wing is fringed with light, and it's dangerous, my footsteps leading me away from the others, into the heart of the bounty. I am giddy now, when I should be grim. I'm girlish and alive and curious. It's inappropriate; that's the word Cornelia would use. I think of how she looked at me when she called me happy. The breeze is a whisper from your lips. You kiss my eyelids when they close in the sunlight.

"What's with you?"

Ben. How he got down to the water before me is a mystery. He glances up the hill. We're alone. He takes a step closer. Every inch of me flushes.

"I figured it out." His voice resonates in my skull, as though it was made to live there. "You, um, you forage something. Right? You know what I mean. You forage something and then we . . ."

Oh, to be back in the moment before. Before this, before the smell of him, before the reminder of the brutality he will always demand of me. He wants Jenny. Jenny, sweet and trusting and fertile.

"Where are you going?" he says. "We need a plan."

You, you, you.

128

*D*awn was drawing its purple line along the horizon when they came. It was blackfly season, that space between Mother's Day and Father's Day, holidays none of us wanted to celebrate. They came without fanfare or guns, and there were only two of them: Sal and a young cop, who'd been told to keep his mouth shut. I didn't see them arrive. I was sound asleep and then next thing I knew Nora was telling us to run, hide, her untied shoelaces scattering along the floor of the hallway, a vision in her nightgown with a snarled braid.

We stumbled into the chilly morning. Issy wore her blanket as a shawl. Cornelia trembled. Xavier's forelock rose like a rooster's comb. Ben's eyes startled wild. Voices carried down from the driveway. I fleeted through the woods, off the land, needles crunching, branches crackling, heart a gallop of terror and, yes, excitement—the cops would be upon me any minute. Gunshots would ring out, surely. There was a twinge of disappointment when it became clear the showdown wasn't delivering as quickly as predicted. But it was good not to be shot in the back, or be incinerated like those children in Waco. And you had to remember: even without firepower, they would take us if given the chance. One could never lose sight of this. I turned back to say as much, but Cornelia and Issy and Xavier and Ben and Nora were gone.

I knew they hadn't vanished, but for a moment, it seemed that way. The forest frittered with life—the squeaks and toots of the red-breasted nuthatches as they gossiped; and up above, far up above, an osprey—bearing the regal name of *Pandion haliaetus*—chirping on its hunt. But without my friends, it seemed that I was the only human left in both the Thinged and Unthinged Worlds.

129

"Saskia. Hey, Saskia. Saskia. I know you can hear me."

I couldn't, actually. Or didn't. Or didn't want to. But now Issy has gotten me to pause, out on that peninsula along the water, where we spoke for the first time when we were still girls.

"What the fuck?" She reaches for my shoulder.

"You need something?"

"I need us to figure out what we're doing so we can get out of here. You know Ben's going to use his gun unless we talk him out of it."

"Have you tried? Talking him out of it, I mean?"

"By 'we' I mean 'you.' He's only going to listen to you." She's up close now, as close as she was that first day. She scrutinizes me as clearly as she did then. "What are you doing out here?"

"Looking." The Unthinged World sparkles, even if we're not supposed to call it that anymore. Blueberry Island is just where we left it, floating on the water. You're here somewhere. It's just a question of being in the right place at the right time.

"Are you all right?" she asks.

"Of course I'm all right."

"You're not telling me something."

If I had a nickel.

But whatever my face does changes her face, too—she's no longer curious. "I felt so bad for you, back in Connecticut. You seemed so scared of everything, and I thought, there's no way she's going to survive this. But you don't even seem . . . cautious here. If I didn't know better, I'd think you're glad. Glad to be back." She's been talking to Cornelia.

"Of course I'm not glad."

She crosses her arms.

"Well, it's not so terrible, is it? I mean, there's a reason we literally . . . killed someone to stay."

"You have got to be fucking kidding me. Three days ago, I wasn't even allowed to say the word 'kill.' Now you're just throwing it around? Justifying it?"

"I'm not justifying it, I'm saying—"

"No. You know what? No. Fuck you. My kid is crying for me in the arms of a stranger because I am being blackmailed for murder, and the only solution is to commit murder again? No. You don't get to sit out here, having googly eyes at the fucking water, full of romantic memories of the worst thing we've ever done." She breathes in, then out. "The worst thing I've ever done, at least." I let that go. She turns around now, toward the forest. "What do you keep looking at?"

"I'm not looking at—"

"You keep looking behind me. Is Abraham back there?"

"I'm just distracted, okay?"

"Distracted? No. No. You don't get to be distracted. We are literally in a life-or-death situation and you're admiring the view. You are so out of touch. You've been out of touch for years. In a castle on a hill with a fucking gate and a moat—"

"I don't have a moat."

"And yeah, I get it. You're crazy. You're sad. Some fucked up things happened to you when you were a little girl. But guess what? Really bad shit happened to me, too. A lot of the bad shit that happened to you happened to me at the exact same time! Only you only see what it meant for you." She turns again, toward the forest. "What. Are. You. Looking. At?"

"It's nothing."

She's not going to let it go.

"Look, it's doesn't make sense."

"Yeah. I know." She steps closer. "Say it."

"Sometimes, I think . . . sometimes, not for a long time, except when we were first up here, right after Tomas pulled the gun on us . . . I saw . . . a sign. Of him."

"Yeah, no shit, he's up there in that cabin twiddling his thumbs as he ruins our lives."

"Not Abraham." Here it comes. I'm actually going to say it. "William."

Issy just stands there. She stands there for a long time. First I think she will say something nice. Then I think she will say something mean. Then I think she won't speak at all, ever again. Then she says, "Even your madness is selfish."

We stand like strangers, across a great distance.

"You really think some ghost of a child is more important than my son? My son—my actual, living, breathing baby—is a few miles away, waiting for me to come home. Your brother's dead. He's been dead since you were a little fucking girl. I don't know what happened the day he died, or if you had something to do with it, yeah, I'm finally saying that out loud because I've been thinking it for years, we all have, and no one has the guts to say it. Honestly, I don't want to know. I don't care. Because it's not relevant to my son, and that's the only thing I care about right now. I would love for this chapter of my life to be over, like, today so that I can be whatever kind of mother I need to be to him. And fuck, yeah,

I need your help for that. So get it together. Say hi to William or whatever the fuck you need to do, invite him along, invite him to help us, sure, but do not opt out. You are not allowed to opt out. I will not allow your selfishness to let you think you're more important than my living, breathing, beautiful boy."

130

Marta's house was squarely in my sights, so I lay on the pine needles and crawled past it on my belly. I'd go up to the ridgeline, check for fiddleheads. My stomach growled and my vision swayed. I realized I hadn't eaten the day before. All those beans ripping through us, the long sleeps, the din of the radio, the waiting—it was hard to keep one day from the last.

But at least there were the others. Issy and Xavier and Cornelia and Ben. At least we were staying together, at Home. At least there were white pines and red squirrels and blueberries—*Pinus strobus*, *Tamiasciurus hudsonicus*, *Vaccinium myrtilloides*. At least summer was coming back, and Abraham hadn't shot anyone and they hadn't shot him. Maybe now we didn't have to be so scared. We could be alone and be left alone and we didn't have to be lonely.

Footsteps crunched down the trail. I was already on the ground. I backtracked, hiding the rustles in the sound of the footfalls, landing parallel to a downed, mossy log on the edge of the path. I couldn't be seen.

Boots. A man. The sound of a motor idling on Bushrow Road. A whiff of cigarette smoke. A knock on Marta's door. I was far back enough that I could lift my head and see through the knotty roots and branches and fallen leaves.

The sheriff.

My stomach flipped. The memory of his thing moving out of her. Why did I hate to think about it and want to think about it? Was he showing up to do it all over again? Would I lie out here and listen?

The door opened. I could see the sheriff's back—I would have to duck whenever he came my way—but Marta's face was obscured by the trunk of a silvering birch. He'd taken off his hat. He turned the brim in his hands. "Meant to bring you some casserole."

"Don't bring me her cooking."

"How you feeling today?"

"How'd it go?"

"Like you said it would. We came in unarmed. It spooked Henry, but I reminded him to treat Abraham just like anyone else. He's heard all sorts of stories. They eat babies, that kind of thing. I told Abraham he's got to get off the land—he's got ten days, far as the bank's concerned. He smiled and slapped me on the back. Played it like he doesn't mind one bit." The hat stopped spinning. "I don't get the sense he's going to get violent."

"He pulled a gun on Gabby."

"Jesus. Really?"

"She left Issy behind—the girl wouldn't come."

"I can get him on that, you know. The kids—"

"Hold off. If you mess with the kids he'll take it to the next lev—" Then she started to cough. The sound was wet. I could see one hand gripping the doorway, and how the sheriff wanted to reach out to bear the weight of her, but clenched a fist instead.

"We should get you in to the doctor," he said, when the rattle had settled.

"Doctor's not going to do anything."

He cleared his throat. "Marta, I wanted to say—"

"She know you're here?"

One step back. "Come down off this cursed hill. We'll find a place for you in town."

"She'd love that."

"She won't know."

"I'd know."

His feet were planted. He was looking right at her, but I couldn't see whether she was looking back. "There's nothing for you up here," he said, after a minute.

"He's here."

He cleared his throat. Lifted his hat to his head. Stepped back, away. I flattened myself on the ground as he came down the four steps. He crunched back up the pathway toward Henry and the waiting patrol car.

I must have missed the sound of Marta's door closing in the sheriff's footsteps. But if I hadn't, and she was still out on the porch, she'd see me. So I counted to a hundred and then to a hundred again. Surely she was back inside. I strained to hear her— Mozart on the radio, the toilet flush. But there was nothing. My leg itched. The more I tried not to think about it, the more it itched, and anyway, I had probably just missed the closing of her door in the sound of his boots crunching away, so I lifted my head.

She was standing above me, in her sweatpants and lumberjack shirt, arms folded, with a frown. "You got a tick on your face." I swiped at my cheek, cursing, but she motioned to me to get up. "I'll pull it out, you little snoop."

131

"Is he going to meet with us or not?" Ben's knee shakes the table.

Teresa shrugs. Tomas keeps chewing. It's spaghetti with peanut sauce for dinner, too salty, too dry.

"Don't tell me he's still sleeping." The utensils rattle. "I know he's in that cabin laughing at us." Ben points his fork toward Tomas. "He's laughing at you, too, you know. You're not above his ridicule, even if you get to hold the gun."

Are we really going to decide tomorrow whether to kill Abraham? If we don't—we aren't, are we? But what if we are?—then is the world actually going to find out what we did? The reality of our situation is absurd and alarming. We are reduced to shoving noodles into our mouths on a table rattling with Ben's rage.

Ben throws the fork into his bowl. He turns on Xavier. "You going to back me up?" Abraham claimed to want to bring us together but of course he has managed to tear us apart. Ben stands. He reaches toward his waistband. The others see it, too, Xavier's eyes shock large, Cornelia gasps—he's going for his gun—so I grab his hand. I pull Ben along, over the smooth floorboards, groaning, familiar under our steps, out into the night thrumming with peepers. The windows of the Main Lodge spill yellow. We blunder down the trail to the lake, only this time we don't need a flashlight, even without the moon; we know this path better than any other, with memory our guide. The water shushes along the edge of the land.

"Give me the gun."

"No."

I reach for his waistband. I can't have him shooting Tomas and getting the rest of us killed. He resists but then, somehow, I have the edge of it—the handle. I pull it out into the moonlight.

"What the fuck is this?"

It's a slingshot.

"You assumed."

To be fair, it's an executive slingshot, made for grown men, out of some kind of titanium bullshit. But the fact remains, it's a slingshot. Next thing I know, I'm doubled over, laughing so hard that I'm gasping for air.

"Ha ha," he says. "Very funny."

It is, though. It is.

"Can you stop? We have to do something."

"What are we going to do?"

Ben laughs then, too, but it's angry. "If even you don't know, we're fucked."

I wipe the tears from my eyes and give him back his weapon of choice.

"It's all I had," he says.

The moon is rising now. I cut my eyes across the white line it draws along the top of the water. We can't really make out each other's features, but it doesn't matter—I know the map of Ben's face, the frown stitching together his brows, the pout of his lower lip, the way he runs his fingers over the ridge in his nose.

"I'm going to talk to him." My heart is hammering at the thought of going to that cabin alone. But now I see that's what today was for: Abraham waiting for me to become bold enough to demand an audience. He's so many steps ahead.

"Can you wait here?" I say. "Just here, by the water, however long it takes. Promise you won't shoot anyone? With pea gravel?"

"Fuck off." Ben's voice is full of laughter.

132

Marta tweezed the deer tick from my jowl, made sure it was squeezed to death, and dabbed on antibiotic ointment. She didn't say a word beyond the task at hand, certainly not about me spying on her and the sheriff.

We walked up to the ridgeline. A light breeze tufted our hair and a red squirrel shrieked from above as it darted back and forth along a branch. Marta didn't notice. I had to slow my steps. The spring morning unfurled—electric greens, chips and chirps and coos and quips—but Marta leaned on her walking stick and didn't look up. She had to stop to cough. A *Sayornis phoebe* darted above us. Eventually we made it closer to the sky.

The fiddleheads were curled in sweet pockets of green, newborn fists nestled together. Marta unzipped her backpack and offered an old Oraweat bag, writing worn off, to gather them. "Only take what you need." As if I didn't know.

That omelet, so long ago. My stomach growled again, a far-off sound, as far off as that memory. She pulled out a chunk of sourdough. She held it in the air between us. My mouth filled with saliva. I didn't think I'd ever hungered for something more, not since that first day at Home, when Issy had offered me sourdough the very first time. I remembered Persephone and those pomegranate seeds. "But Sarah threw out the Mother."

"The gift of the Mother is that she makes herself anew." She offered the bread again. "Sarah gave me some of hers, years ago. I feed it. I make it my own way."

I took a bite. The doughy chew nudged open a hollowness I didn't want to know was there. The bread in my mouth turned to mush as tears filled my eyes. Another person would have looked away, or uttered a phrase of comfort. But instead Marta said, "I felt certain Philip would come back for you."

"People leave. Anyway, I like Home with fewer people." Not quite the truth.

The cough set upon her again. Up close, it was an ugly thing—a monster attacking her from inside, over and over, relentless. She held a handkerchief to her mouth. Scarlet spilled into it. But she didn't name it, just as she hadn't named my tears. She folded the piece of checkered cloth into the smallest bundle it could make and put it in her pocket.

"I've worried for you since the moment we met," she said, as if I was the one who'd just choked up blood. "That day in the forest? When I saw you throwing the hatchet?" Marta's hand flew to her chest in the memory. She shook her head. It was the gesture of an old person, which irked me, honestly. "The prophecy." She leaned forward. "You know about Abraham's prophecy, don't you?"

"I know I'm supposed to marry Ben."

Her seriousness gave way to an unexpected smile. "Yes, I suppose that's the part you'd focus on." She put her hand out onto my arm. "Only I mean, that's the part you should care about. It's normal for a girl your age to care about that."

What a comfort, that word.

There was a dreaminess in her eyes as she looked down over the slope, the miniaturized houses on the lakes below us, the boats finding their way out after lying dormant for so many months on shore. "Of course I dismissed the prophecy as hogwash. Abraham fancies himself a seer, and I've long believed it my job to prove him wrong. For so long I just wanted to prove him wrong. He'd hold up some truth of his and I'd punch it down. I thought that was enough."

She waved her arm as though to say, dismiss what I have said, even though I could see that it went beyond just idle chatter. She blew air from her puffed cheeks and started again. "When I saw that hatchet in your hands, I thought about what he'd said about you being built to destroy. I'll admit, it terrified me. 'The girl will be built to destroy,' and then, there you were, wielding that weapon." She chuckled. "Then I noticed you couldn't throw worth shit. Oh no, I'm sorry, I don't mean to laugh at you. I mean for us to be laughing together. It was a relief to see you weren't as gifted as I feared you'd be. I let my guard down."

Her expression grew grave. "Then you went to get the hatchet from the tree and stopped at that spot and looked down. You'd discovered the destroying angel, without even looking for it. Of all the mushrooms on all this land"—her eyes swept the cloudless sky—"the most dangerous had presented itself to you, right in front of me. I took it personally, to be honest. I felt . . . attacked. Oh no, not by you. Not by you, my dear. By Nature, handing the girl who he'd said would be built to destroy something built to destroy." That cough was worming inside her, eager to reclaim her, but she wasn't letting it, not yet. "You see, I believed I was the one Nature had chosen. I thought all that time I'd put into understanding her would help me understand . . ." Her eyes were sparkling. She wanted to speak, but it wasn't the cough keeping her from speaking.

I'd never seen Marta cry. The others would be worried. If Abraham found me up here, with her . . . he couldn't be allowed to think I had chosen her over him.

She put her small, soft hand onto mine.

"What I mean is, I had to give myself to believe, for the very first time, that he wasn't delusional. That maybe he was right. Because he had said you were built to destroy, he had claimed to prophesy your coming, and then, there you were, happening upon the most poisonous mushroom out here. So I thought, perhaps I don't know everything. Perhaps he is right about some of it."

"I have to go."

Her hand gripped tighter. "You see him sometimes, don't you?" She looked to my waistband, the knot of raised fabric at my hip, like the ground cover over a destroying angel. The wind lifted, in a shiver, over the top of the ridge. She opened her hand and held it out. I knew she would wait all day. I pulled out Topsy and flopped him into her palm. She turned him over in her hands. "I saw you out there, that day. You were talking to someone. Someone no one else can see. Little William. You spoke to him." Her voice had grown gentle. "It's okay. You'll feel better if you don't have to keep it a secret."

I nodded, just once, just a tiny bit.

"Good."

It wasn't. It meant I was crazy—hoping, believing, that you, a dead boy, wandered these woods. That if I did things right, you'd present yourself to me. It felt so strange, to have that truth outside.

"And he's friendly? He doesn't want to hurt you?"

"Of course not." How did she know to ask about him?

"This is good," Marta said. "This is good." She handed Topsy back. "It means you know when you make a mistake. It means you feel remorse."

133

Abraham's waiting in the armchair, wearing his frayed pajamas. There's an expectant lift to his eyebrows. He wasn't sure I'd come alone.

"Ben wants to shoot you."

"He's not doing a very good job of hiding that gun. Tea? Something to eat? Teresa's not much of a cook, I'm afraid."

"We'll be going tomorrow."

"Ah yes, either way." He looks a little sad.

I venture into the living area. Find my place on the couch. "You don't really want us to kill you, do you?"

"You think I'm joking?"

"I mean, why? Why now, beyond your being sick? I think I understand why us—at least, why you believe it has to be us."

"I knew you'd understand."

"I don't think it's okay, that's not what I mean about understanding. You always did go for a power trip."

"A power trip? You think that's why I called you all here?"

"You want to control us. Decades have gone by but you still believe you have the right."

"That's not it at all."

"It's not?"

A flash of a smile. "Well, maybe just a little. But no, wait, no, please. It's a joke. Please, listen. I've had, as you put it, decades to think about this." He stops, gathers his thoughts, his pointer fingers and thumbs forming a triangle. He is relaxed now, not afraid to show his hunger for company like mine. "I ruined your lives. I know it. I believed I was saving them, but I ruined them instead. That's why I left without saying goodbye."

"You left without saying goodbye—that's how you think of it? Funny; we think of it as you having framed us for murder."

A breath. "I didn't frame you. I ran away."

"And killed—who, Amos?—so that it looked like you were dead?"

"You think I had anything to do with that? I swear, that was pure coincidence. Amos was angry at me for leaving. Told me I was a coward, and I agreed, but I couldn't stay to find out if you'd gone through with it. So I ran, and I guess he must have eaten one of the mushrooms he'd foraged. He had a stockpile, you know, in case we were invaded. He was raving at the end there. But they didn't find the body for long enough that the forest had gotten him by then."

"You mean buzzards. You mean they ate him."

"I'm not proud of taking advantage. But look, I was sure the law would come after me, any moment. And then they didn't. Nothing happened. I got some news, here and there, I figured out the foreclosure had gone through. Figured you guys had gotten away with it."

"We killed her because you told us to. And then you left anyway, and so we had to leave, too."

"It was so easy with you. So much easier than with the adults. At a certain point, they stopped believing, one by one. They doubted me. But you never doubted. And I never doubted you. We made a whole world we could believe in—together. I couldn't bear that being taken from us."

"Was there really an inheritance?"

"I thought so. At the time, I thought so. I holed up, Saskia. It wasn't like I went out and lived gloriously. It's been lonely. And I'm sorry about Amos. I am. But when no one came after me, and I saw the papers, and they said it was me up there in that forest, I thought, why not just die with the place? You know? A fresh start."

Now I'm the one laughing. "Easy for you to say." The laugh turns to grit in my throat. "None of us got fresh starts."

"But you did! Don't you see? You were so young. So brilliant and beautiful and alive. Strong, courageous. So many times, Saskia, I was amazed by you. That day when the sheriff came to interrogate us about the dog attack? How you somehow knew to bring Topsy and cry? It worked like a charm."

"I cried because I was sad."

He looks down at his hands. "You want me to say I'm not proud of you?"

"Yes."

"But I am proud of you. I'm not proud of myself. The way I ruined you . . ." Here he looks into my eyes, for the first time, really looks into them, and I have to tell myself to keep my gaze steady, not to falter. I used to think him so beautiful, every fiber of him, every inch, every cell. I used to think that what I felt for him was devotion.

"Why now?" he muses. "Why now? Well, I suppose I wanted to give you the chance to punish me. For a time, I thought staying dead was the way to go. Just to give you the gift of believing I was gone."

"We wanted you to suffer."

"So make me suffer."

"I believe you think you're helping us in your fucked up way, but Abraham, honestly, just go ahead, kill yourself. We'll watch if you want, I can't believe I'm saying that. I bet Ben would love to film it in slow motion and watch your suicide every day for the rest of his life. So just do that instead of this. They don't deserve it."

"And you?"

"And poor Teresa and Tomas. They think they matter."

"I needed someone to get you here. You wouldn't have come without the others. And the others wouldn't have come if they'd known, for sure, it was me."

So it is about me, then. Finally, he has said it, without knowing he's given it away. It's all my fault we're here.

"I know you," he says. "I know you need to punish me. I know it's the only way you'll be done with me. But you won't do it unless I make you."

I shake my head, but my words are gone.

"You deserve to be free, Saskia."

I am already moving into the night.

134

"*R*emorse?" That word meant feeling bad for something you had done. That word meant she knew.

Her eyes danced over my face. "Saskia, what if you told a different story about yourself? To yourself, I mean? I think you think . . ." She stopped. "If you could say one word to describe yourself, what would it be?"

The question called up a feeling—dark, ugly, sickening. Regret. Shame. Tears were coming, hot.

"Tell me."

I shook my head. The word thundered in my chest, trapped, refusing to release itself: "Bad."

Her eyes dazzled with tears. "Honey, why don't you just tell me what really happened to your brother? Let it out."

Before I could, she was coughing again, crouching. The thing inside her was ravenous. She squirmed with it. I almost placed my hand on her back, but then I didn't. Then I watched her cough, grateful for the chance to observe her untamed. She had gotten me to say so much. She wanted me to tell her everything. I almost had. She was in love with the sheriff. She could tell him anything. She would. She was down there on the ground, sick and small, and I was part of the Unthinged World. I could see, now, how dangerous it had been to come up to the ridge with her.

This time, the handkerchief didn't make it out of her pocket. Blood splattered onto the dirt. I peered down at those red splotches as they soaked into the earth. She wiped her mouth with the back of her hand, and looked up at me. She saw my face was closed. She said: "You reminded me of my son for so long that I forgot to notice the ways you're different."

From her pocket, she pulled a feather—small and brown. She tickled it across the palm of her hand.

"Clever. Aware. Always watching other children. Always . . . studying them. I say 'study' because he was like a student. It was as though he didn't exactly know how to act on his own, and he was clever enough to know it shouldn't necessarily be like that, and it scared him. He hid it very well. But a mother knows."

I felt that perhaps if I held quite still, I could both listen to her and pretend I didn't care that she was describing me how Mother would have, if Mother had been kind:

At the Natural History Museum, under the shadow of the big whale, little Xavier had run toward me, a smile on his pudgy face. I picked up the shoe he'd removed and left beside me—a dress shoe, since it was our joint birthday celebration—and threw it as hard as I could at his head. Not because I wanted to hurt him. Not because I didn't know that it would hurt him. But because I wanted to see him react. I wanted to observe the shock, the pain, the chin quiver, the startled hastening away from me, the howling filling that massive hall, the tears cascading down his face, his flushed cheeks, Jane running to sweep him up, Mother coming to scold me, the other mothers who'd seen what I did pulling their children close. So much movement out of one simple act—letting go of a piece of leather at just the right moment.

I didn't want to hurt Xavier.

But if I wanted to see what hurting him would do, I would have to hurt him. So I did.

"He tried to hurt his younger sister," Marta said, startling me out of my memory. "Multiple times, in different ways. Pushing her backwards off the swing. Putting his own hand in boiling water to try to convince her it wasn't a big deal. A hacksaw to her finger—don't worry, I caught him before he did real damage. Would have cut it clean off, though, if I hadn't run across the yard and pulled the saw from his hand. It was as though he didn't hear me when I called to him. Or didn't want to hear me. He was too interested in the cutting to stop himself. And he loved her—that's what the world gets wrong. He loved her so much. But it was as though the loving and the hurting did not exist in conflict to each other."

I was nodding.

"Of course I thought it was my fault. He was my firstborn. I was older. His father was preoccupied with work, and didn't think I should keep the pregnancy, and when I did, was very much of the opinion that the kids were my responsibility. I didn't think I could have kids, frankly, until my son came along, and my daughter, right after. Boom, boom. It seemed wrong to have harbored a secret skill like that—the secret of fertility—and not to take it up on its offer, do you understand? I hadn't much considered what it would be like to be a mother; I had spent so long in laboratories and classrooms. And then, I saw that he was like me—observing, watching, waiting. Well, that's a scientist. Just like me. It took me a while to understand that he lacked . . . perhaps compassion isn't the right word. That he lacked something most humans possess—a sense of grace, you might call it?

"By the time I realized that, I believed it was a maternal lack that had made him that way. I say that like it's in the past, but some part of me still believes it. My daughter certainly does. She left home the moment she was able and hasn't looked back. I can't say that I blame her. But I couldn't reject him. I couldn't be like your mother. I couldn't leave him. How can you leave someone who you know has the potential to hurt someone terribly, but hasn't done it yet? Are you really supposed to abandon them to the world? I knew she would be all right. It was him I worried for." Then her eyes glimmered. "She says I love him better and maybe there's some truth to that. I made him, in my very body, when I didn't know my body could do that. That seemed a miracle. I bound myself to him. I would stay close. I believed I could protect the world from him and protect him from what he wanted to do to the world. I believed I could stop him from being his worst self. I could advise. I could observe. I could pull the hacksaws away before he did real damage."

She was unreachable now, her gaze distant.

"My husband wanted to name him Abraham because he liked the strength in that name. That story in the Old Testament, Abraham on the mountain, ready to slit his son's throat because God commanded it. Resolve. But every day I think, what if we had named him after someone who couldn't manage that? Should we have named him Isaac?" She shook her head. "I see what I was supposed to do, all along. I was wrong, all along. I was supposed to stop him, wasn't I? I'm his mother. All along, I've been gathering those plants, and he considers it a nice little hobby. But he has no idea which ones are poisonous." She turned to me then. "I can stop him, right? Tell me I'm brave enough to stop him."

135

In the Unthinged World, the night isn't silent—*Pseudacris crucifer* peeping away, *Lasiurus borealis* chirping, the far-off, barking call of a *Strix varia*. Ben is where I left him. I sense him there, at the edge of the water, without needing to ask.

"He's not going to let us off the hook."

"You thought he would?"

The water is broad, open, alive. It's our last night with it, no matter what. "I thought I might talk him out of it."

"Yeah." His voice carries a touch of apology, as though he wishes he could protect me from myself.

"Want to go out on the water?"

We find the canoes below the deck of the outermost cabin. They've been waiting like big-bodied mammals for someone to let them out to pasture. The top one flips at our touch.

By now our eyes are adjusted, but that's not why we turn the canoe so easily. We share a knowing, out in the dark we once called ours. I know the smile that jumps to his lips unbidden, when the stern of the canoe smatters back into the lip of the water, splashing his ankles. I am the weathered handle of the varnished oar he pulls from inside the old vessel, priding under his open hand. What lies between us is beyond words, or under them, or away from them, somehow, and we stand on either side of the boat and thrust it away from us, the slide of needles beneath the keel, hands bucking as the canoe jitters from the land until the hull is bolstered by the lifting waters.

He stops. He kicks off his shoes. I know I'm blushing, I can't help it, it's such a silly thought, but he is undressing now, even if it's only his legs: socks off, pants rolled. There's a quickness there, a desperation. I remove mine too, steadying myself on the gunwale, first the left, then right. I imagine what it would be to keep going, to remove everything under the cover of this night. I could go to him, and let my heat bring him surprise, and feel his lips along my collarbone.

He clears his throat. No words, then. I'm grateful. I'm grateful to the others to have left us to this, no matter what they think. Even Tomas and Teresa, and Jenny, sweet Jenny, down toward town, tending to a toddler she barely knows, knowing only that we have done something bad enough to keep us trapped up here, trusting us—trusting Ben, trusting, yes, me—to do what is right, trusting that we know what is right.

So, then, I brace my hands along the bow, feel the thrust of his foot as he steps onto the flooring, then the rocking, tipsy, back and forth as each of his feet carry him away down the keel, over the bow seat, over the thwart, hands searching the vessel's wooden parts, all the way back to the stern seat, where he'll steer. He settles down onto the bench and becomes a slightly darker shadow against the night. He faces me. He waits. Every inch of me recalls the sensation of climbing into bed for a man. (How many times has that happened? Not many. Not many, if I'm being honest, and none of them mattered as much as that night with him, as long as honesty is the measuring stick, but they did happen, those hungry gazes along my body, the twist of lust in my low belly as I neared their touch.)

I put my left foot in. With my right foot, I push. The boat

judders its last gasp along the shore, then finds its way home.
The draft glides through the surface of the lake. Ben's oar parts the
water, dip and dip and dip. I sit down. The canoe obeys. Ben turns
us, around, around, until we are facing the dark lake, and then my
oar joins his, and we pull together, out, efficient, racing into the
span of night.

There are stars, I knew this, but what escaped my notice was
how still the water lies tonight, and how cloudless the sky is, and
what the arithmetic of those two elements means about the reflec-
tion of the sky upon the water. As we make our way to the center
of the lake, away from the cover of the trees, a globe of dotted light
surrounds us; above, below. We find ourselves suspended inside
the sky.

Ben's head tips back in awe, in resignation, and humility.

When he speaks, his voice is much quieter than expected.
Husky with affection. "That fucking prophecy."

He's all around me by then—not his body, but the feeling of
him, his Ben-ness—all that I honor in him, all that I wish I could
touch. This has happened before, hasn't it? His mind inside mine,
even if I haven't earned it, haven't worked for it the way I've had
to work for other loves. Is it even love? It just feels as though it is
supposed to be this way.

Then I know: you.

Sharing this globe of stars with him resembles the bliss of finding you. Even a glimpse, even a touch of you in the air urges
the reminder that you once walked the earth beside me, and it's
enough—knowing you're still somewhere even if you can't be
touched. That you forgive me. The gift of the world can ease the
agony of missing. How did Issy put it? "You really think some
ghost of a child is more important than my son?" They arrive then,
they circle us: Nora and Ephraim; Mother and Father; Cornelia's
matched set of girls; her husband, even (why not throw him in?);

Billy, and the babies—the one who was supposed to join Xavier's family, and the one who someday might; and Philip and Jane; Sarah; Butterfly; Amos; Marta; Gabby; Ben's daughters; his wife; sweet Jenny; and Sekou, held, right now, in Jenny's arms.

All the ones who have been here, either at Home when it was called Home, or when we carried them here, in our minds or bodies.

All the ones we have loved.

All the ones who are gone.

Issy's plaint rings through me: "You really think some ghost of a child is more important than my son?"

I climb through an opening to understanding: what I feel for you, and for Ben, for these friend loves of mine who have their own loves, is that we are not alone, not in this loving, not even if we love our people differently, not even if they are dead or living, or divorced from us, or rivals to each other. Not even when they hurt us. Not even if they hate us. Not even if we will never speak another word to them again.

How is it that, being suspended in the stars sharing a vessel with someone I have loved, and wept over, someone who makes me understand myself and yet who I will never hold again, gives me to understand that my loss of you is not, in fact, the most unusual part of me, but the most mundane?

I find that I am crying. I find I know what must be done.

136

I left Marta up on the ridgeline. She called my name but I became
the wind, tearing down through the *Pinus strobus*, racing back up
past our cabin, where, from the porch, Issy lifted her head, and
Cornelia called out. But I didn't stop. I didn't bother to knock.

Abraham was lying on the couch, feet up on the armrest.

"Marta's your mother?"

He lifted one hand from behind his head. He stroked his scraggly beard. "You saw her?"

"Why didn't you tell us?"

"Why does it matter whose mother she is?"

Because he had turned us against her. Because he had made us
believe that the reason to turn against her was based on philosophy, or principles, when all along, she was his mother. "Because."

"When Marta heard about Home, when I first told her about
it, when it was just Issy and me and Gabby, she said she wanted
to learn about it. She wanted to see it with her own eyes. I hosted
her here for a time, under the condition that she would tell no
one about our biological tie." He smiled his impish smile. "I
wanted her to see my project, like a schoolboy with an award-
winning science experiment. But I didn't want her to take it over.
She kept to the pledge. Gabby knew she was special to me, but if

she suspected Marta was my mother, she never once said as much. We don't look much alike, do we?"

Out the window, a *Cardinalis cardinalis*, red and upright, bragged its chipper melody. A solemn expression had replaced Abraham's smile. "Marta liked it here. She liked Gabby. She loved Issy. She said she wanted to stay, but she cut me off when she saw my look—the look sons give their mothers—and said, no, not here. She would buy land nearby. Well, what could I say? My mother wanted to be near me. This was a compliment. Mothers love their children—even yours, Saskia. But she wasn't telling me something, something it took a long time to understand: the real reason she wanted to stay so close was because she doubted me."

What she had said up on the ridgeline: "I can stop him, right? Tell me I'm brave enough to stop him." How far would she be willing to go?

He frowned. "Have I ever made you feel that I doubt you?"

I was still standing in the open doorway, but now it felt awkward and strange, to expose this conversation to whomever stumbled by. I took a step inside. I closed the door behind me. "No."

He moved his feet from the end of the couch to offer me a spot to sit. It seemed odd, to have spent all that energy flying over here, to have come in ready to fight, to stand over him in a way I never had before, demanding answers, only to find myself now moved to his side, sitting reasonably and hearing him out. He was like his mother in ways I hadn't noticed. They shared an influence that was obvious now that I knew to see it.

"Doubt does terrible things to the mind," he said. "You know that, better than most. When you were out there, in the Thinged World, they doubted you, didn't they? Your mother. Your father." He listed them on his fingers. "Nannies. Teachers. The other kids in school. Your grandmother."

You didn't. You were so small and so smart. You forgave me for my curiosity—more than forgave me. You trusted me.

"You know, I went to see your father," Abraham said. "After Philip took you away, after your first summer here. It required some doing, getting in to see him. But I talked to the right people, who convinced him to agree. Did you ever visit him?" He didn't wait for my response. "I'd never been in a prison, if you can believe it. It was much more . . . mundane . . . than I expected. Clean, orderly. In any case, he wanted to know who I was, and why I cared, and I said I wanted to help you. I said you had come to me, and I wanted to help you, so I needed to know more about who you are."

He watched my hands and torso rattling in the air. I was letting myself remember: the softness at the nape of your neck. Your tiny toes. Finally, someone would say it.

Abraham stood about a foot away, and lifted his hands to my cheeks, and smiled his beautiful smile as his eyes searched mine. He leaned forward and I thought, oh, here we are again, it really is going to be this stupidly simple after all. I wondered, as he approached, how I was going to react, because even though I knew all the reasons not to kiss him, I also knew that I would follow any place he led. But, just as the last time we'd stood this close, he went past my lips. His Adam's apple was a lozenge I could have licked. His voice, low and steady, dropped a plumb line deep inside of me:

"He said I wouldn't believe him if he told me the truth." He lifted his mouth away, but he was still so close. "What do you think he meant by that?"

I could tell him. I could say it all. But Grandmother's voice was somewhere deep inside, keeping my memory locked away. Marta's voice was there, too—did I want to be like Abraham or not? Was it possible to want both?

He frowned, surprised, when I didn't answer right away. For

a moment, I thought I'd just say it, but he went on. "You know we can't go back out there, to the Thinged World. People like us, who've been broken by it? We can't go back where they doubt us. That's why we made our own world here. You want to stay, don't you? You want your friends to be safe here, with me, where I can take care of you?"

Of course that's what I wanted.

"I know how hard you worked to become a warrior. But now I see: we don't have to fight the way Sal and his men want to." I imagined helicopters hovering over the cabin, rattling its windows with their mighty rotors, dropping down onto the roof with machine guns, coming down the ridgeline in camouflage. He was right, of course: we had no defenses. We had no chance. "We can't outsmart them."

"You don't think so? You're very clever, Saskia." He shrugged, then acquiesced. "We might not be able to best them with words, perhaps. What about with sacrifice?"

"Like a fatted calf?" Or did he mean me? "Or a virgin?"

"Marta," he said, "has a sizable inheritance. Did you know that? She's a millionaire, in fact. Many times over. You wouldn't think of it, given how she dresses, or that cabin she calls home. My father left me enough to buy the property, but not enough for taxes. Marta got the lion's share."

"You should ask her for money," I said. "For the bank." Something was ripping around inside me, clawing to get out. Up on the ridgeline, she had said she was going to stop him. What did that mean, stop him?

"You may have noticed," he said, "that she isn't doing particularly well."

The blood on the ground. "The cough."

"Stomach cancer. It's spread to her lungs."

All I could think of was Home. Save Home. "So you'll inherit everything, then—that's great. And you can use the money to keep us here."

He shook his head. "She won't be gone before they repossess. And stomach cancer is . . . well, it's not a pretty death. To be honest, I wouldn't be surprised to learn it's spread to her brain as well. That can happen, you know. I tried to convince her to go to the hospital, to get a nurse to come in, but she insists she wants no help. Only, it breaks my heart so, to think of her suffering. I don't want her to suffer, you know. She's my mother, no matter our differences. What if . . ." he began. The cardinal flew off. "What if you helped her?"

"Helped her?" We were on a path now, leading into a dark wood.

"Helped her leave this world. It would be a kindness. Quick, easy, surrounded with love. The way she's planning to go, it's agonizing. She'll be so alone. But you could make it easy for her. Think of how the money would flow to us then, to keep Home alive." He pushed aside my hair.

"I think," I said, "that she might want to hurt you. She told me that she might hurt you."

His hand stilled. "Well. Now." A quick, wry smile. "All the more reason. She's much cleverer than I am, that's for sure. If she wants to hurt me, then there's a safe bet she'll succeed."

There were tears in my eyes but I hated them. I hated crying, since you'd gone.

"It's funny," he said, watching me. "I got it wrong. All this time, I thought . . ." He shook his head, as if to rid himself of whatever doubt he was holding. "You're ready for this. You're a warrior."

Everything was mixed up.

"Oh my dear, you won't be alone. That's what you're afraid of, isn't it? Loneliness?"

I was shaking in his hands.

"The others will help. You need them, as much as they need you to lead them into battle. Those of us built to destroy need to be lifted out of our destruction. Ben works hard, so he'll see the job is done. Xavier is loyal, so he'll make sure to keep everyone close. Issy will be the one to lift you out of the darkness, after all of this is over. And Cornelia—"

"Will sing?"

Abraham guffawed, quick and mean. I did, too. It was funny, what I'd said. I liked how mean I could feel.

"Well, sure," he said. "But really, honestly, Cornelia will doubt you. That's good, too, Saskia. Doubt firms our resolve. It makes us stronger."

"But how would I convince them? They love Marta so—"

"Why, you use their talents. You know what makes them special. So now you figure out how to use it."

My mind left my body then. I was standing there, with Abraham, but I was also above us, calculating, understanding, imagining. What awaited was unfolding in front of me, as if it was a story that had already been made. "And you'll help, too?"

A sharp intake of breath. "The thing of it is, Marta won't let me near her. I want her ending to be peaceful, but it won't be the least bit peaceful if I'm there. But you, and your friends, oh, Saskia, she'll invite you in the moment you knock."

137

Xavier is waiting on the shore. "Where've you been? You can't fucking disappear like that."

Ben splashes into the water and brings us in. "We took a canoe out."

"Well, you didn't tell anyone." Xavier's looking between us now, sniffing out evidence.

Once Ben has the canoe on shore, I step out. Take the step toward Xavier, let him smell me, let him know I haven't touched that other man, not beyond my mind, at least. "You're going to make a wonderful father," I say. "In spite of Philip, and because of him."

"Where did that come from?"

Ben's breath is loose. He's happy.

"What the fuck are we going to do?" Xavier says. "Don't say shoot him, we can't shoot him."

"Why not?"

"Because we'll be sent to fucking jail. There's some way out of this. Saskia, can't you talk to him? Can't you get rid of him? Why does it have to be murder?"

"What do the ladies say?"

"The ladies went to sleep." Xavier's fingers work through his hair. "Why is no one panicking?"

"Because Ben's going to shoot him." I'm grinning. Ben cracks up.

Xavier sighs in exasperation.

"What time is it?"

"Past midnight, I'd guess." We walk then, the three of us, back to the cabin. "We need a plan."

"We need to rest." Five hours then, give or take. Let them sleep. Let them dream.

138

*I*t was morning. The red squirrels raced up and down the trunks of the trees. A spiderweb sparkled in the window, catching the streaming-in sun. Buffets of golden light, reflected off the lake, roiled and rolled along the ceiling. Marta's eyelids sunk closed in deep sleep. I thought us lucky; she was closer to death than she'd been the day before.

But then, no, she lifted her head from the pillow and rubbed at her eyes and gave us a surprised good morning. Xavier shot me a look. As I came inside, she rose from the bed, so pleased, ever so pleased, to see us. Ben and Xavier and Issy drew inside, behind me. We'd left Cornelia as lookout; she wouldn't stop crying. The hatchet, too, I'd left outside, under Marta's porch, where it would be safe but ready.

"I'm sorry about the other day," I said. "I shouldn't have run off."

Issy took a seat on the couch. "How's your mother?" Marta asked her.

"Gabby left."

"You must miss her."

Issy forced a smile. "Foraged anything good lately?"

"Haven't been out much." Marta's eyes trailed toward the window. She was sick. Outside was too much—and if Marta couldn't go outside, then how could she be happy? We were helping her, that was something to remember.

Ben and I were in the kitchen by then. Xavier, too, but he was supposed to be sitting with Issy and Marta, keeping the conversation steady and safe. Instead, he was hovering. It was too small a space to whisper properly. I lifted my eyebrows and gestured toward Marta. His face was agony, though, just hanging in front of me, his body blocking the counter where I was supposed to be. I pushed past him, opened the bag, took out the folded pieces of cloth, the precious eggs, the new fiddleheads.

"All right if we make breakfast?" Ben asked.

"Oh, what generous hearts."

"This was all Saskia's idea," Issy said flatly.

Marta beamed. "I'm not surprised." She made a show of trying to get up. "Can I help?"

I must have shot Ben a terrible look because he gave me a sure smile as he lifted the skillet onto the stove. "I got it. You all catch up."

"I hope your mother's well," Marta said to Ben.

"Oh yes." How had I never seen how graceful Ben was at lying? "Yeah, she's doing great."

"I heard she threw out the Mother."

"Just wanted a change, I guess."

I nudged Xavier with my foot. Xavier was supposed to charm. Instead, he was frozen like a block of ice in the center of the room. Issy leaned toward Marta. "It's, uh, it's a beautiful day, right?"

"I can't do this." Xavier mumbled. He looked like he might cry. If Xavier cried, we were done.

"Ben."

Ben turned at the sound of my voice. He glanced at Marta, who was only half paying attention. He stepped close to Xavier, turning his back so Marta couldn't see his face, and said in a low voice, "You have anywhere else to go?"

Xavier looked at his shoes.

"You have parents who want you?"

Xavier shook his head.

"This is your home now. You do whatever it takes."

Xavier looked at Ben then, eyes darting back and forth. Ben didn't let him falter. He kept his eyes on Xavier's until Xavier took in a quick breath, and turned to Marta, and plastered on a smile, and strode across the small room. "Read any good books lately?"

Ben melted the butter. I cracked the eggs and whisked them. We found cheddar in the fridge—green with mold, but we cut that off, and grated it. There was just enough to make six omelets. We made our five first, and kept them warm in the oven. Marta's, I made last.

We sat around her tidy living room, even Cornelia, who was calmer when she came inside to eat. Marta didn't have an appetite, but she was polite. I made myself eat as much as she did. Anyway, a couple bites would do it.

"Inky caps?" she asked.

The cheese drew a string between the plate and my mouth. I plunged it in. "Inky caps. Found them up on the ridge."

Then all there was to do was wait.

139

Nausea pangs, but I stand still and stay upright, Marta's cabin in my sights. Maybe he can see me out in the beginning of the day. I can't go to him, not yet, not without a breath.

Five things I can see: a *Populus tremuloides* upslope, leaves rattling silver; the web of an *Argiope aurantia* between branches, dew crystals catching the early light; a sliver of lake, smooth before the wind kicks up; a *Tamias striatus*, cheeks bulging, lifting one paw to regard me; the moon, still risen, in the blue sky.

Four things I can hear: a downy woodpecker—*Dryobates pubescens*—hammering into a dead tree in search of grubs; a mourning dove—*Zenaida macroura*—lowing; the rustle of leaves beneath my feet; the hiss of a motorboat somewhere out of sight.

Three things I can touch: an electric green *Calosoma scrutator* crawling over my thumb; the rough bark of the *Tsuga canadensis* under my hand; a pine needle, landing on my shoulder.

Two things I can smell: my fear, coming off me in waves; but bigger than that, the unnamable scent of Home.

One thing I can taste: what I ate last, bland enough, but already doing its work.

The sun brightens the whole porch as I knock. Another tweak of nausea, but I swallow it down. It takes Abraham a while.

"Let's walk up to the ridge," I say, when he finally appears. "Watch the day begin."

We both know what it will be, for him, in his state, to make it up there. We both know he will say yes despite it. The climb is long and difficult, but I accounted for this, for the gasps of air and his hand on my shoulder, for the times I had to turn aside and not let him see me writhe. For his frail steps and shallow breath, the gasp of air into his weak lungs. But by the time the sun touches all of Home, we are finally at the top.

I suppose I should not be surprised that it came together—the treasure discovered on yesterday's walk. A sign from you. A way to begin to know what must be done.

He stands in the sun, arms outstretched, looking out over the land he named. I stand back, and watch him begin to sing:

> *Oh I once had a horse and his name was Bill*
> *When he ran he couldn't stand still*
> *He ran away*
> *One day*
> *And also I ran with him*

I take Topsy out of my waistband, bury my nose in his head. Set him down beside me. I pick up the hatchet, still mossy on the handle from its years spent under Marta's porch.

> *He ran so fast that he could not stop*
> *He ran into a barber's shop*
> *And fell exhaustionized*
> *With his eye teeth*
> *In the barber's left shoulder*

The blade is sharp, I made sure of that last night. A wincing lurch in the pit of my stomach. My arm shakes. I might not be strong enough.

He hears my hesitation.

He turns. His eyes are sharp and knowing.

I throw the hatchet.

We both watch it sail over the edge of the cliff, three feet off its mark.

"That's it?" Abraham's ending, disappeared into the air. The chance to free the others, lost. He starts to laugh. At me. "That's your brilliant idea? Throw an axe at my head?" His own words make him laugh harder. The sound carries down to the lake and back. They'll hear him. They'll find us. "Did you really think you could kill me with that thing? Oh, poor girl. Look at you. Of course you missed."

No. I can't let him extract his death from the others. It's a terrible tithe they won't survive. They barely survived the first time. This was my chance to rescue them. Quivering inside my fury and disappointment, the secret truth: I was ready to see you.

Abraham laughs at me, he laughs and laughs as he used to, his mouth so mean. It makes me think of Daddy.

I back up, into the forest at the top of the ridge. Into the trees. Into the animals. The flowers. The brambles. The trunks. He's at my tail. He calls my name, as though we are playing a marvelous game from childhood. "I told you how it had to be," he says. "I said all five of you. What part of that was unclear? Did they put you up to this? Oh, poor Saskia. Always alone."

I dodge the evergreens, the maples, the birches, I forget their names in the face of the cramping as it overtakes me once again and I know I won't be able to walk much longer, or keep away from him, or hide myself. All hope of releasing Ben from this—and Issy,

Cornelia, Xavier, little Sekou, all the ones they love—of using my gift to help them, is lost.

"Don't cry," he says. "Don't cry." As if he gets to tell me. As if he gets to know.

Then I remember. That gash in the ground, in the forest. Two hundred feet deep, Marta once warned Butterfly. A place to fall and never be found. It's not so far from where I am, somewhere just within my reach, but I have no idea which direction. It could swallow me. I could disappear inside it forever. Maybe you'd meet me down at the bottom. He's right; I am weak, so much weaker than I thought. I grasp my stomach as it spasms again. Soon there won't be waves of pain; soon I will be pain itself, and he'll stand over me and watch me go.

"Come back," he says. "Saskia, come back. I believe in you. You want to kill me? Give it another shot." He's teasing. He knows I failed. He thinks it's funny. Out of the corner of my eye I see him grasp a cedar trunk to gain his balance. There, wait—he's weaker than he's showing. I scan the forest floor. Rotting leaves, old branches, pine needles, downed limbs. No trail to follow, no hint from Marta about where to go. Just think.

We left the clearing later than we did the day she first told me about the chasm. If I double back, and he follows . . . he's almost caught up, but I stay ahead, I remember he is weak, too, I remember he is dying, too—even if he wants to make us carry out his death, even if he wants us to bear it for him, even if he wants to control us until the end. I walk with my eyes on the ground. I find I'm better able to ignore what's happening inside me now that I have something to focus on. Step. Step. Step.

The same, uninterrupted ground, step after step. Well, I tried.

And then—my foot touches the end of a tree limb. Balanced atop its other end is a pile of pine needles. At my touch, they teeter off the limb's edge and fall down into . . . nothing. They

don't land on the forest floor because there is no floor below
them. Just a mouth in the ground, waiting for anything to swallow. I keep going. I make my way toward it. Don't let him see.
Don't let him know. How lovely, to slip down inside and never
have to think about another thing. Never to have to carry any
hope you might return, or wonder how my life might have been
different if I'd made a different choice. If I'd held on.

"Saskia," Abraham says, "Saskia. Please. You're taking this too
seriously. It is quite funny, you know."

I'm almost there, and then, aha, I see how the mouth of the
chasm gapes wider on one side, but is only a little open on the
other, small enough for someone to step over. I step over it in
one stride, so he doesn't even know I've done so. I don't listen as
it tempts me to sink down into its damp air, cool and musty. Now
the hole is between us, and I step sideways, pretending to look up
at the *Dryobates pubescens* pecking at a maple, so that Abraham
doesn't see that in between him and me now gapes the widest
part of the ground. Ten feet across, I'd say. There's a bush blocking his vision, and leaves, but if he was looking, he'd see it. Of
course, Marta might have told him about it; he might have been
the one to tell Marta it's here. Well, only one way to find out.

I stop and turn and wipe my cheeks.

"I failed you," he says. "I know how it hurt you to set you apart.
I never meant to make you so feel so lonely." He thinks I am crying because of him. He steps toward me. "I thought I had to make
you strong by telling you that you were, so that you'd believe it. I
didn't see how strong you could have been if I'd let you be yourself."

"I was myself."

"A killer?" He laughs. He shakes his head. "You needed the
others to do it for you as much as they needed you to convince
them."

He doesn't know.

"I didn't need them."

He tips his head back and out of his mouth comes the song:

> *She loves to laugh and when she smiles*
> *You just see teeth for miles and miles*
> *And tonsils*
> *And spareribs*
> *And things too fierce to mention.*

He wrinkles his nose in delight. "Such a fierce little thing."

I understand then. I am his Thing. Abraham can never be Unthinged. Neither can I, not as long as he believes he can tell me what to do. He wanted me to kill him and I was going to do it, just like that. He was going to own my story to the end, take what made me special and use it.

"You aren't the one who made me a murderer," I say.

Confusion flares in his eyes.

"I killed long before you met me." Maybe if I finally say it out loud, you can help the others, you and the story of your death.

"I killed my brother."

My truth hits him. His face gapes in curious awe. He can't help himself. He wants to know more. I step back. He steps forward. I step back again as he asks me a question, it doesn't matter what question, the most important part is to keep him talking, keep him going, even as the pain becomes unbearable again. He takes another step, and then another, closer and closer and then—he isn't there anymore.

Then Abraham falls into the earth.

140

I supposed poisoning would be clean, easy. But it was puking and shitting, a terrible stench, moaning, gasps, gags, and pain that wrenched Marta's small body in awful ways. It lasted far too long, into the plunge of night and then back into the thin light of dawn, when the spiderweb was lit up again, in the window, thrashed by wind, bug laden.

It was not friendly.

Marta begged for the doctor. She asked me to go to JimBob's and call Sal. She thrashed. Ben took her by the shoulders and held her down, until she was quiet again. Not dead yet, but quiet.

Xavier paced the room. "How long is this going to take?"

There was no reason to make them stay.

But Ben and Issy stayed, Issy shuffling those cards over and over again so that they became steady as a heartbeat. When Marta grew still—her breath drawing in and out, but her voice gone forever—Issy set down the cards and went outside. When the sun rose, Ben said he needed to check on his mother—Sarah would wonder if no one came by.

Then it was just Marta and me. I thought of her up on that ridge. How she had told me that if I could feel you close to me, and you were kind, that meant I felt remorse. Remorse meant I was not crazy, or bad. Remorse meant I had made a mistake. In my half-delirious state I experienced, for a split second, a selfish overwhelm of joyful relief—until I remembered that the fact that I was currently engaged in the act of murdering the person who'd told me this probably meant that she was wrong.

At any moment, there would be a knock on the door. Sal. The police. Sarah. Gabby. Jim.

But no one came.

Well, that's not the whole truth.

You came. I looked up, across that room, and there you just were, standing near the wall, plain as day, the sweet crop of your white blond hair, your apple cheeks, the sawing rasp of your breath. Your little mouth, puckered. Your eyes, blink blink, watching me. You weren't afraid of who I was. You knew it already. You'd come back when I forgot to look for you anymore. Isn't that always the way?

141

When Abraham falls, I look for you. I grip my stomach. He yelps as he goes, and then there's a sudden, sharp end to that sound. He's hit his head, I think. I wait. Any moment, he'll come out again, climb up, laugh. But he doesn't. No hands. No eyes. I can't even see any trace of him down there. Just darkness. I push that tree limb over the edge and it slips into the darkness, too. There's not so much as a peep from below. No trace.

So then, down the hill. Back to Marta's. Or at least away from here. Sound is growing strange, my feet hardly work. I stop to vomit two or three times. But I keep going. I look for you. I look for you as I make my way back to the clearing, trying to keep upright. I have been patient. I have felt you gathering near. I have imagined this time, this sweetness, the expression on your face as we see each other again, as you choose me once again.

But you do not come.

I can hardly think anymore, the pain becomes like nothing else, and my insides hurt so much that I do truly wish I'd thrown myself in that hole after Abraham, but still I search for you, even as Issy's face appears over mine. She says my name, she holds my face, she says something but I can't hear, my stomach is a hundred thousand lurches, she calls out to the rest of them. I want to speak but I can't find the words to say the feeling of being held in her strong arms, of knowing she and Cornelia and Ben and Xavier and all the ones they love—Sekou, most of all—are free. Free from the story of Abraham, and what he would have us do.

Then I know why you did not return: because I chose the living.

LAST:

*S*even A.M. The kitchen tumbles with light-tossed dust. Outside, *Cardinalis cardinalis* harangues, a bird so proud they named him twice. I sip my Ceylon tea. I check on the Mother. She's ravenous, and I sate and mix her to a tangy slop and shroud her in linen by the window. Next, I marry last night's leaven with a pile of flour and a splash of water. And so the Mother and I begin again what we began yesterday and the day before, and most of the days before that, since the very day seventeen years ago that I made Grandmother's grand, white, shuttered house my own: tomorrow's loaves.

"You overslept." Issy's lying on the floor of the parlor, a London Bridge of Magna-Tiles built over her body as if she is the River Thames herself.

"Did not."

She grins. "You're so easy to piss off."

"Woof woof." Sekou crawls toward me on four legs. "Woof woof."

"Oh, meet my new dog, Macramé."

"Macramé?"

Issy cracks up. "Yup. No idea. Macramé."

"Well, it is a very lovely word."

"Woof woof." He sidles up to me and whispers in my ear. "That means is there any toast. In dog talk."

I nod. "Woof woof." Macramé doesn't need me to translate, because he is a dog.

Later, after they've gotten on their galoshes and raincoats and packed a backpack with toast and cookies and apples because you never know where the day might take you, I find myself alone. They go out across the southern lawn, into the light. He turns and waves madly at the house, looking for me. I know he can't see me but I wave, too, both of us frantic to be seen, until Issy convinces him to come along. It's a good arrangement, this new life we have, my fridge covered in finger painted drawings, the extra boots in the hallway, the pink bedroom no longer pink because the boy adores the color orange and I cannot deny him anything, which drives Issy, in equal parts, to madness and euphoria.

I know she's watching me. I know she promised the others. She has taken up residence after what they refer to as "the attempt." On paper, we say we are helping each other, but I know she believes I need her more than she needs me. I can't tell anyone why I know, for sure, I would never try such a thing again, because I can't tell them that the only reason I ate the destroying angel in the first place was that I was planning to murder Abraham with a hatchet to his head, and I didn't want any of them to pay the price for that. I would kill him and then myself, one two, and they'd be left out of it completely; all blame on me.

But then the earth swallowed Abraham, which none of them saw, and it occurred to me before I passed out they'd never have to know about his end if I didn't want to tell them. Once they found me on the trail it seemed to not matter much since I was so obviously on the path to dying, and it was a full week after that—once the miracles of science had saved me—that they managed to gather into my hospital room, without a doctor or nurse within hearing, and ask me where the hell Abraham was.

"I talked him out of it," I said. "I said he needed to leave, so he left. Did Teresa send the letters?"

They looked at each other. Issy said, "Well, Cornelia's to thank for talking her out of that. Said if he wasn't there to tell her one way or the other whether to send the letters then at least we had to hold off until you got better, so we could ask you."

Cornelia said, "But if you knew Abraham was leaving, why did you take the mushroom? Why did you try to kill yourself?"

This was where things got tricky. I couldn't tell them the real reason, because then they'd know Abraham was lying at the bottom of a cavern and spend the rest of their lives bound up in a new swirl of drama, guilt, self-recrimination. But if I told them the reason that I tried to kill myself was because he'd left, then they'd consider me a fanatic, and steer even farther from me than before. Nor could I whoop with joy and say that despite the hospital bed, despite having lured someone to their death, and having stared death down myself, I felt more alive than ever, not because I was the sociopath I always feared I was, but because I finally knew I had it in me to choose the living, or love, or whatever this grand feeling is called, of wanting to keep my people around me, gather them close, protect their bodies and minds, tend to them, know them.

"Because I'm sorry," I said. "Because it's my fault you killed Marta, which got you into this mess."

No, they said, no. Ben paced and Xavier's chin quivered and Issy took my hand. Cornelia brought me a bouquet of freesias. But we all knew. We all remembered.

The night before we killed Marta, I went down to our cabin, where the others were playing Spit. "Abraham's right," I said. "All along, Marta's been plotting with Sal. They've got a plan to kill Abraham."

They were incredulous, infuriated. Afraid. Cornelia wanted to know how I knew. Abraham was right—she would doubt me, and it would make me stronger.

"Because Marta told me," I said. "Up on the ridge. But don't worry. I have a plan, too." I looked at Ben then, because if he walked out the door in a fit, we'd lose valuable time. "I need your help." I drew open the bag at my waist. Inside, were seven inky cap mushrooms. "I need you to take care of these."

He looked at me like I was crazy. "Why?" I took the destroying angel out of my jacket pocket. "Because we have to keep them apart from this."

"What's your plan?" Cornelia asked, trepidation creeping into her voice.

To Xavier I said: "We don't have anywhere else to go. Your father abandoned us here, and neither of us has a mother anymore. No grown-ups except Abraham give a shit about us. We have to do whatever we can to stay here. You know that, right?"

He said, "You're scaring me." But he didn't disagree.

To Issy I said: "She's sick, Iss. You know it, and so do I. We will have to think of her as if she's not Marta, not all the way. And she's not, not really. She can't go outside anymore. We will have to think of her as someone who has forgotten who she is, and know that we are sending her somewhere she will be happier."

"What does she mean?" Cornelia said.

"She means kill her," Issy said.

"Every single one of us has lost at least a mother or a father. Abraham is all we have. Abraham's our father now. And now she's going to kill him? You think we can figure out how to stay at Home if Abraham is dead?" I looked at Cornelia, finally. "You don't have to figure out the details. I figured it out for us, okay? It'll be quick and easy and once it's done, we'll get to stay."

Cornelia was the first one to agree.

No one living knows that Marta died by our hand. Sheriff Sal suspected us—suspects us still, if he hasn't kicked the bucket yet, but even then he's locked in that old folks' home. As far as locals who even remember Marta know, she was that crazy old forager who accidentally ate a poisoned mushroom. Issy and I have agreed, without agreeing, that we'll put the conversation about all this aside, but I know she knows something is up. She looks at me out of the corner of her eye, trying to untangle it, but then Sekou bounds up and demands our attention, and neither of us can deny him that.

Meanwhile, Jenny updates me via monogrammed stationery, on Ben and the dogs, and the updates on their wedding plans, which I'm going to have to be far too sick to attend, even though Sekou is to be the ring bearer. Cornelia sends our household matching pajamas for every single holiday—even St. Patrick's Day—and plans to bring her family for Thanksgiving. Xavier and Billy text me pictures of the sourdough they've made from the Mother. There is occasional news of Teresa and Tomas; it seems they've joined another commune, this time in upstate New York.

Sekou takes his sweet time across the lawn. He's back down on all fours, so I suppose I should be calling him Macramé again. They're making their way toward the Devil's Ramble, and Grandmother's Japanese maples, and the dense forest beyond. I won't tell Issy it's where I spent the day of your death. I don't want her or Sekou to live on this land as though it is a museum to your slaughter. I want her to raise her son free and unfettered. I think that is what you'd want, too.

The morning you died, it was too hot. You gave me that

folded-up paper and the feather and made me pinky promise for your story, and there was that brightness in the Devil's Ramble. Daddy and Mother were at war. You dropped Topsy onto the roof, I had to go inside for a broom to reach him, a glass broke in the parlor—you know all this, but I keep telling it. One last time, I'll tell it, then. All right? One last time.

I'd hoped Miriam would have forgotten the broom on the third floor, but diligent as ever, she had returned it to its rightful home, so I'd have to risk getting to the broom closet, which lay just off the mudroom. Mother and Daddy were in the parlor. She was making a horrible sound, one I tried not hear as I made my way down through the house, dodging the creakiest stairs. I'd have to sneak past them twice: on the way to get the broom, and then when I had it in my hand.

As I reached the foyer, I could hear the crimson in Mother's throat. I should cut away, back through the dining room and kitchen. They'd never know I was there. But I couldn't help myself. I looked, for just a moment.

Daddy said: "Your children ruined our lives."

Mother said: "They belong to you, too."

Daddy said: "Olivia, I wouldn't give a shit if they died."

He saw me. He became Polyphemus, one-eyed, gigantic, blocking the door. He stepped into the foyer. She lunged onto him from behind. As she pummeled him, I wanted, more than anything, to ruin him. I wanted to end those fights forever, set Mother free, have her to myself. He claimed to hate us, but I wanted to put him in a world when he'd look back on this day and envy the life he'd had.

I didn't know how to destroy him, not yet, not quite, but I knew it had something to do with the widow's walk. I ran up the stairs two stairs at time. I knew he'd shake Mother off him soon enough. On the second flight of stairs, thighs screaming, I heard her cry out as her body thumped the wall, followed by his feet thudding up the stairs. It was a race to the roof then, Mother chasing Daddy; Daddy chasing me.

I burst into the open air. You were perched again, on the banister, feet dangling over the world. You swayed at the sight of me. You caught yourself. You frowned. "Where's the broom, Saski? I want Topsy."

"Come down from there."

"I want Topsy now!"

"Come down or you'll fall." I took your wrist. You began to howl. Daddy burst through the door. He was moving slower then, like a storm, his face gray and determined. He was making a sound, wordless, yet it held a kind of story, like an answer to a question I'd never thought to ask. The wind again. Mother climbing the stairs, calling to me. Daddy and me in the sun, and you crying for your stuffed bunny. Your wrist squirmed in my hand. You had stopped doing the balancing yourself as soon I touched you. You trusted me to keep you steady—expected it, without asking. They all did, as if it was my job. All the while, Daddy moving in, that horrible sound, the meanness on his face.

A startle of truth, as I realized how easy it would be. Obvious, even. Then I wondered what gravity would do with the right story put onto it; those two things together could change everything. I still had you—for a brief moment I had you. Then you squirmed. Then I didn't have you anymore. Then you were sailing down, past Topsy.

I looked toward Mother as she came through the door. I said, "He pushed Will, Mama. Daddy pushed him off the roof."

I ran down through the house. I ran across the lawn to the Devil's Ramble. I ran into the deep woods. I told myself it was out of my hands: you might have caught yourself, or only broken an arm. Daddy might have grabbed you up somehow, and saved you with mouth-to-mouth. I worked my way into the heart of the forest, telling myself that if I didn't look back, I wouldn't have to think about my hand letting go. Whatever was to come would come, but as long as I stayed in the forest, it didn't have to be mine. I could let the story decide.

Acknowledgments

The year 2020 offered extraordinary challenges to finishing a book (this will come as no surprise if you did work of your own in 2020, especially creative work, especially if you live with children). Luckily, I've had the support of many wise, generous smart people whose belief in this project gave me the strength to press on. It's thanks to them that you're holding this book, but any oversights and faults are entirely my own.

Home is a fiction, but I have Astrea and Al Fatica to thank for opening their land and beautiful cabins so that I could imagine a physical setting for the Unthinged World. Dr. Jesse Dubin gave me invaluable mycological instruction local to the Sebago Lake region of Maine. And Kenneth, Phyllis, and Bruce Forman live on in the legacy of their beautiful home, the place where the idea for this book was born.

I have been blessed with a generous literary community, which includes Emily Raboteau (who read the earliest drafts of this book, and told me this was Saskia's story); Jessie Chaffee and Amy Wilkinson, whose Zoom check-ins got my butt in the chair; the phenomenal BFG: Kristi Coulter, Claire Dederer, Tova Mirvis, and Joanna Rakoff, who read my draft in record time and helped me reshape it; Stella Fiore and the rest of the Cut + Paste ARIM group (and Lenka Clayton for inventing an Artist Residency in

Motherhood—if you're a creative who is also a mother, look it up!); Siobhan Adcock; Marcy Dermansky; Rachel Fershleiser; Julia Fierro; Tammy Greenwood; Brian Gresko; Leslie Jamison; Nicole C. Kear; Victor LaValle; Amy Shearn; Robin Wasserman; and countless others who have offered support, guidance, and advice, in person and online.

Special thanks to all those who provided shelter as I wrote, including Madhavi, Hormuz, Zahaan, and Cyrus Batliboi; Amy Ben-Ezra and Farnsworth Lobenstine; and Sophie McNeill and her family. And there's simply no way this book would have been finished without the Chanoffs—Liisa, David, and all the rest—who gave us a haven in magical, seaside Loveladies for three months, at the drop of a hat, at the beginning of a global pandemic.

Anne Hawkins has been an amazing agent for, what is it, almost twenty years? How did that happen? Moses Cardona helped me so much when I had no access to my papers. Since working with Christine Kopprasch on *Bittersweet*, it has been my dream to build a whole book with her. She made the experience as fantastic as I knew it would be. Thank you to the entire Flatiron crew, including (but not limited to): Megan Lynch, Caroline Bleeke, Maxine Charles, Cat Kenney, Bob Miller, John Morrone, Jason Reigal, Nancy Trypuc, and Samantha Zukergood. I appreciate every moment you've given to this book.

Thank you to Steve Koski for teaching me the songs the Homesteaders sing. Thank you to those of you who were raised communally and have shared your tales over the years. Thank you to Rosanna Murray for keeping me safe and sane. Thank you to all the women who kept me aloft through this turbulent time, too many to count, most of them mothers (what would we do without the mothers who save us, day in, day out?). Thank you to my children's many teachers, for all that you do, every single day. And to Maia Davis, who has awed me with her tireless work ethic and compassionate care: I love you.

And finally, to my quaranteam(s)—shelter in the storm; readers and researchers; childcare providers; cheerers-on; cooks; and always the reason to keep showing up: Molly and Annikki Chanoff; Amy March; Elizabeth Beverly and Rob Whittemore; and Kai Beverly-Whittemore and Artemis, Eon and Rubidium Wu. And last but not least, David, Kitsune and Quentin Lobenstine, who are strong, brave, kind, and smart, and who make me laugh every single day.

Sources

Angier, Bradford. *How to Eat in the Woods*. New York: Black Dog & Leventhal Publishers, 2016.

Hoffman, Claire. *Greetings from Utopia Park*. New York: HarperCollins, 2016.

Marrone, Teresa and Walt Sturgeon. *Mushrooms of the Northeast*. Cambridge, MN: Adventure Publications, 2016.

The National Audubon Society Field Guide to North American Birds: Eastern Region. New York: Knopf, 1994.

Penniman, Leah. *Farming While Black*. White River Junction, VT: Chelsea Green Publishing, 2018.

Pritchard, Forrest and Ellen Polishuk. *Start Your Farm*. New York: The Experiment, 2018.

Seymour, Tom. *Wild Plants of Maine*. Topsham, ME: Just Write Books, 2010.

Stout, Martha. *The Sociopath Next Door*. New York: Harmony Books, 2005.

Sundeen, Mark. *The Unsettlers*. New York: Riverhead, 2016.

Fierce Little Thing

DISCUSSION QUESTIONS

1. This story is told from Saskia's point of view, but in the early drafts of this book, the narration was also close to Ben's, Issy's, Cornelia's, and Xavier's viewpoints. How would that story have been different? Why do you think I made the choice to strictly stick close to Saskia instead?

2. Is Saskia a good person? Is Issy? Is Xavier? Is Cornelia? Is Ben?

3. When we meet Saskia, Xavier, Issy, Cornelia, and Ben in the present day, they have all put distance between their lives and the people they were when they lived at Home. But in what ways are they each who they've always been? And in what ways have they changed?

4. How and why do Saskia, Xavier, Issy, Cornelia, and Ben come to rely on one another as children, despite their differences? How does Abraham exploit these connections? Should the adults be forgiven for a crime committed when they were children and believed their safe place, Home, was under threat of attack? Or should they be held accountable?

5. Home is not exactly a luxurious place to live, but the individuals and families who make it their home find peace and happiness there, at least initially. What is it about Home that makes it such a refuge for Teresa, Jim, Sarah, Ephraim, Gabby, Philip, and Amos? How does Abraham exploit the very characteristics that make these characters feel comfortable at Home in order to bind them closer?

6. What really happened on the day Saskia's brother, Will, died holds the key to how Saskia thinks of herself, even in middle age. Is she right in letting this idea of herself affect every aspect of her current existence? Can she—should she—forgive herself? How did her idea of herself make her vulnerable to Abraham's manipulations?

7. Where do Abraham's manipulations come from? Is he bored, sadistic, passionate, curious—or something else entirely? What are his dreams for the Homesteaders? As he becomes increasingly concerned about the threat posed by the outside world, why does he turn against the Homesteaders in his midst?

8. How do women, especially mothers, fit into the world of Abraham's imagining? Is it possible for women to have power in a world conceived of, and controlled by, men (or a man)?

9. How does the pattern of adults leaving children behind—from Saskia's mother, to Jane, to Philip, to Ephraim, to Gabby—counterbalance Marta's decision to stick with Abraham? What are our responsibilities as parents to our children? In what ways do the parents mentioned uphold those responsibilities? In what ways do they let their children down?

10. What is it about the natural landscape and its promise that enlivens Home in Saskia's mind and leads her to believe Will is close at hand? Why does knowledge of Home, especially through Marta's lessons, make Saskia feel more one with it?

11. Why does Marta take Saskia under her wing? What is it about Marta's knowledge of Saskia that makes Saskia decide that she must convince her friends to carry out their crime against her?

12. At the end of the book, Saskia decides not to tell her friends what has really happened to Abraham. Is this a good decision? Was it a good decision to do to him what she did?

13. Does this story have a happy ending? For now, Cornelia's, Issy's, and Ben's children will never know about the crime their parents committed—is that for the best? Do our parents owe us the sins of their pasts? Is telling them something we owe our children?

14. Where will Saskia be in five years? What about Issy and Sekou? What about Xavier and Billy? What about Cornelia and her husband and children? What about Ben and Jenny? What about Teresa and Tomas?